A Raging Heart

A Raging Heart

KAYLIE SMITH

HYPERION
Los Angeles   New York

Copyright © 2025 Kaylie Smith

All rights reserved. Published by Hyperion, an imprint of Buena Vista Books, Inc. No part of this book may be reproduced or transmitted in any form or by any means, electronic or mechanical, including photocopying, recording, or by any information storage and retrieval system, without written permission from the publisher. For information address Hyperion, 7 Hudson Square, New York, New York 10013.

First Edition, July 2025
10 9 8 7 6 5 4 3 2 1
FAC-004510-25135
Printed in the United States of America

This book is set in Minion Pro, 1726 Real Espanola, and Caslon Antique Pro/Fontspring
Designed by Tyler Nevins
Map © 2022 Sveta Dorosheva

Library of Congress Control Number: 2025931985
ISBN 978-1-368-10887-4

Reinforced binding
Visit www.HyperionTeens.com

Logo Applies to Text Stock Only

For my younger self—you did it, Kayls.
Welcome to the finale of your very first book series.
Thank you for dreaming so big. I love you.

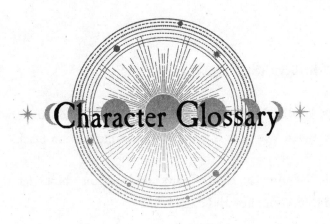

Character Glossary

THE WITCHES

Onyx

Lysandra Black (she/her): The Onyx Queen, mother of Gideon and Ezra.

Gideon Black (he/him): The elder Onyx Prince, son of Lysandra. Gideon is also one of the six fated Blood Warriors and is soul-bonded to Calla Rosewood.

Ezra Black (he/him): The younger Onyx Prince, son of Lysandra.

Caspian "Cass" Ironside (he/him): An Onyx witch and Gideon's best friend. Kestrel's beta in the Onyx Queen's Guild, alongside Gideon.

Kestrel Whitehollow (he/him): Commander in the Onyx Queen's Guild.

Rouge

Myrea (she/her): The Rouge Queen.

Calliope "Calla" Rosewood (she/her): A Blood Siphon and one of the six fated Blood Warriors. She is soul-bonded to Gideon Black.

Hannah Carmine (she/her): Calla's and Delphine's best friend. Trained in necromancy and dark magic.

THE SIRENS

Delphine DeLune (she/her): Calla's and Hannah's best friend. Formerly part of Reniel's Shoal in the Siren's Sea.

Reniel (he/him): Leader of a Shoal in the Siren's Sea.

Celeste (she/her): Member of Reniel's Shoal. Delphine's former roommate and love interest.

Eros (he/him): Member of Reniel's Shoal.

Zephyr (he/him): Member of Reniel's Shoal.

Bellator (he/him): Reniel's brother.

THE VALKYRIES

Ignia (she/her): The Queen of the Valkyries.

Amina (she/her): A once-exiled Valkyrie and Lyra's and Sabine's best friend.

Sabine (she/her): Lyra's and Amina's best friend.

Lyra (they/them): Sabine's and Amina's best friend.

Meli (she/her): Sabine's ex.

OTHERS

The Gods of Fate: Four beings who rule over Illustros.

The Wayfarer: A mysterious magical being who is cursed to roam the planet.

Jack of All Trades (he/him): Calla's former landlord and leader of the largest black-market trading group in Estrella. Human.

Witch Eater (they/them): Ancient immortal being that resides in a cottage within the Neverending Forest and tracks the affairs of the Gods of Fate.

Em (she/they): The Witch Eater's familiar—a soulless shapeshifter bound to do the Witch Eater's bidding until their debt is paid.

Prologue

When the wildfires reached Lysandra's doorstep, her last bit of hope finally burned to ashes. The Wastelands were bone dry, devastated by the endless revelries of the courtless fae bastards that had been cast out of their lands, settling among the once-fruitful territories that she and her mortal sisters had been raised in. Territories shunned by the surrounding immortal lands, deemed too unsightly to risk the endeavor of crossing through or bringing their goods for trade.

Not that the Wastelands had anything to trade anymore. Not when the earth was so parched that even spillage from the faes' goblets—as they danced and raved from dusk until dawn—was unable to quench its thirst. Not when all their cattle and crops had been starved for so long they'd decayed and withered away to dust without a spare glance from the immortals.

A fate humans like herself were on the cusp of facing.

"Althea is back," Myrea noted as she peered through the curtains of their tiny worn-down cottage, their voices like whispered omens in the dark.

Lysandra rushed to the front door and pried it open for Althea to squeeze inside before the candlelight in their dining room attracted any unsavory beings looking for mortals to toy with. As she worked to secure the door, Lysandra reached into an apron pouch for the dried elderberry powder she needed to dust along the doorframe for added protection.

"You look ghastly." Myrea gasped as Althea pulled back the hood of her cloak.

And it was true. Althea was just as thin and pale from hunger as she'd been when she'd left the Wastelands two weeks before, but now she was covered in deep festering scratches that made her pallid complexion shiny with infection. Her golden-brown hair was missing clumps along her crown, and her right eye . . .

"I got it," Althea told them. "Everything on the Witch Eater's list."

"Now all we need to do is spill our blood," Lysandra declared.

"It looks as though you already have," Myrea muttered as she gaped at their sister's empty socket, the dried blood caked down her face. "Did one of the fae—"

Althea shook her head. "It was a dragon-shifter. They caught me after I stole their egg." She revealed the gilded item in question from beneath her cape. "It was a fae who . . . saved me, actually. A man. He was kind, Sandra. And on the other side of the Wastelands, there's food and water and shelter. We can leave—"

"Save it," Lysandra hissed as she stepped forward. "Leave? To trade these immortal devils for different ones? Shall I get you a mirror to show you the state of your appearance? Should I turn you loose outside and call for them to find you and see how they treat you? Should I tell you how many days of food we have left before we *starve*? I do not care if one of them showed you kindness. I do not care if we can get out unscathed and manage to find another place to live. This is *our* land. And we are *taking it back*."

Althea glanced over to Myrea, who nodded in agreement, before returning her gaze to Lysandra and dipping her chin in a nod of deference.

"Blade," Lysandra demanded, and Myrea procured a knife instantly.

Lysandra began to recite the words she'd memorized from the Witch Eater's directions as she spilled all their blood on the pile of objects before them, the magic in the ancient language warming her tongue while the air around them grew heavy. And when the spell was done, every flickering candle snuffed out at once.

A beat of silence.

A flood of golden light.

A taunting cacophony of voices.

What is it that you dare summon us for, little humans? the Gods asked them.

Lysandra grinned as she rolled her shoulders back and lifted her chin. "We want to make a bargain."

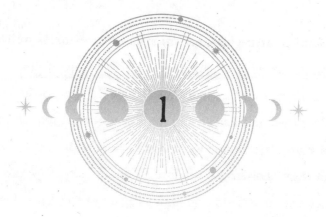

1

Hannah Carmine felt death nearby. She felt death *within*. Crawling beneath her skin, writhing through her veins.

The stars seemed wary tonight, and the dark magic coiled in her core was aching to get out—to call on the corpses it knew were buried beneath the dense earth she was lying against. Since escaping Myrea's palace, Hannah had kept her magic locked away, as deep inside herself as she could, but she knew it was only a matter of time. After lying dormant for so long, it was ready to be unleashed. *She* was ready to be unleashed.

Hannah tried not to let Calla or the others know what was lurking under the surface, didn't want to add to the stress they were all already under, but memories of her mother's bone brothel haunted her every waking moment, and she wasn't sure how much longer she could resist the hymn of darkness calling to her blood. . . .

It had been nearly two weeks since the four of them—and Thorne, the fifth Blood Warrior—had fought their way out of the Rouge Queen's palace. Since they'd begun to brainstorm how they would find and unite the rest of the Blood Warriors as well as locate the Fates' Dice. None of which was particularly easy to plan from the tiny remote village in the Dragonwoods where they'd been hunkering down.

Though the Dragonwoods were a neutral territory, like Estrella, the dragon-shifters weren't necessarily keen on five wild-eyed witches running amok and causing a flurry of rumors—not to mention the giant target they brought to the small town. For people who could turn into massive dragons at will, Hannah found them to be surprisingly skittish beings. But the lukewarm welcome was only one of the reasons she and the rest of the group were ready to leave. The largest reason was that having to share a single room between the five of them would drive them all mad.

Their lodging situation was precisely why Hannah was atop this cliff that overlooked the woods and the quaint village below, where she could pretend she was getting some fresh air instead of suffocating from the feeling of death all around her. She didn't think the others missed her too much anyway; Caspian and Thorne had become quick friends, and the two of them spent most of their time either writing cryptically coded letters to be sent to every conceivable corner of Aetherius in hope that one would reach another of the Blood Warriors, or trying to hustle the other out of all his money. Of which Thorne had none to begin with. Which meant neither endeavor had proven fruitful.

And then there were Calla and Gideon.

Whatever was going on with the two of them, neither had bothered to put a label on it and Hannah hadn't dared ask. She knew it was killing Caspian to act like he didn't notice the way their friends would make sure not to sit *too* close together or linger for too long in the rest of their presences but then sneak outside to have whispered conversations in the middle of the night or squeeze each other's hands in moments they thought no one was watching.

"I promise the climb will be worth it," a deep masculine voice suddenly cut through Hannah's thoughts.

Hannah pushed herself up and peeked around the large boulder a few yards behind her on the cliff. She knew who the voice belonged to before she spotted the witch, of course, but she was still somewhat surprised to see Gideon, the blue of his hair a bright cobalt beneath the moonlight. Sure enough, Calla crested the cliff's horizon right behind the prince, as if Hannah's thoughts had somehow summoned them.

"I don't know why I continue to believe you when you claim something *isn't too far*," Calla huffed as she caught up to Gideon.

Gideon grinned as he threaded his hand through Calla's. Before he could respond, however, Hannah cleared her throat and stepped out from behind the boulder. Calla startled at the sight of her and instantly dropped Gideon's hand.

Gideon's body went rigid with alert until he realized it was Hannah, the black and silver of his irises still swirling as his shoulders relaxed. "Hannah. I didn't realize you came up here."

"It's okay," Hannah said. "I was just . . . getting some fresh air."

"Are you all right?" Calla asked, concern bleeding into her voice.

Hannah simply nodded as she brushed past them. "I was getting tired anyway. I'll leave you both to . . . enjoy the lookout."

"Hannah—" Calla started, but Hannah was already twisting back around and striding away as fast as her feet would carry her without breaking into a run.

She couldn't get away quickly enough; she felt her skin beginning to prick with the too-familiar sensation of death.

A sensation that had been growing stronger and stronger every time she was around Gideon.

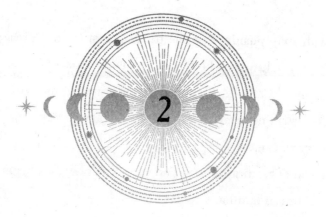

Calla's stomach dropped a bit as she watched Hannah run away from them.

From the moment Caspian had snapped Hannah's neck, things had been strange, to say the least. He'd done it to save her from the Rouge Queen's control, of course, but it had taken them nearly three days to break whatever insidious trance the girl had been stuck in, and though Hannah swore she'd recovered just fine from her broken neck, it wasn't mended bones the rest of them were concerned about.

Calla and Gideon had felt the shift of Hannah's power when she woke up in the carriage. They had *smelled* the unmistakable charred scent of dark magic. And then there was the fact that Hannah's eyes had remained a haunting depthless black—not a trace of pupil or white, only the unmistakable signs of a Rouge witch falling too deep into necromancy. All of this would have been much more harrowing if Hannah hadn't inexplicably pulled herself out of the horrifying unconscious trance of dark magic.

Calla quickly pushed the unsettling memories out of her mind as Gideon ushered her around the large boulder near the edge of the cliff's lookout. They sat on the ground, side by side, and peered out at the clear, starry night hanging above the sprawling Dragonwoods below. The dirt-packed ground was pocked with scars from countless dragon-shifters sinking their talons in for a landing. Trees covered a majority of the land, their twisting branches tall and gnarled and covered in black-and-gray leaves that looked like overlapping dragon scales. These trees produced a few variations of a fruit that reminded Calla of the sweet plums she used to find in Estrella's marketplace, a nostalgia that hit her with full force each time she tasted one.

Gideon shifted next to her, no doubt restless at the onslaught of emotions emanating from Calla's side of their soul-bond. He gently nudged her arm as a reminder that he was right by her side. They were sitting on this precipice together.

Calla was unsure what to expect of their soul-bond, especially now that there was a war brewing. There was an unspoken risk that intensified the closer they became, but Calla found more and more that she no longer cared about that risk. She had stood in front of the Fates and the Witch Queens, despite all her efforts to avoid that very situation. Now she was going to do whatever she pleased, and when she inevitably ended up on a battlefield before them again, she would remind herself that she'd already walked away from their encounter once before.

"What's going on in your head?" Gideon murmured.

"A lot," she admitted as she began to comb her fingers through her hair, unraveling the knots throughout the long tendrils. "I'm worried about Hannah. I hate that I don't know how to help her."

"That's a sentiment I more than understand, but I think giving her some space is the best thing we can do. I'm learning there's no way to solve every problem, despite how much we want to." He sighed, then made a beckoning motion with his hand. "Come here, you're making that worse."

Calla wrinkled her nose but did as he asked, moving over to sit between his legs so he could undo the tangles for her. Her hair had reached a length where no matter what she did she could not keep this from happening, but she couldn't bring herself to cut it. Even Gideon's hair had grown out considerably, except *his* made him look handsomely disheveled instead of like he had just woken up from a night of tossing and turning. She found that to be quite annoying.

During the daylight, they both had to keep up their glamours—just in case anyone might recognize them, despite being miles and miles from anything familiar—and Calla had begun to look forward to dusk, when the two of them could sneak away after dinner and spend time together as themselves.

As Gideon continued untangling her hair, Calla looked down at a compass attached to one of the utility clips on the side of his pants. She reached out, unhooked it, and used the pad of her thumb to push open the lid's clasp with a satisfying *click*. The enchanted arrow spun around aimlessly, refusing to land on any specific direction now that she wasn't using it within the Neverending Forest. And though the compass's enchantment should have ensured it still worked for Gideon *anywhere*, it hadn't been cooperating for him either.

Calla let out a low sound of frustration as she snapped the lid shut. "I'm not sure how much longer we can continue to wait for this damn thing to start working again."

"I know. Until we get it figured out, we might have to find someone who can scry for the Fates' Dice."

Calla clipped the compass to Gideon's pants. "I *can* scry," she said. "It just might take some practice...."

"And a few earthquakes?" Gideon smirked.

He was right. Scrying came with very noticeable side effects unless you were practiced enough to mitigate them, and Calla was definitely not practiced enough.

"I wonder if someone in the village can help with the compass. Or at least point us in the direction of someone who can. I'm sure they'd be more than willing to assist if it meant us leaving," she mused as Gideon continued to sift his fingers through her thick tresses. After another beat, she whispered, "What are we going to do if we can't find the dice?"

Gideon was quiet for a long moment. Suddenly, he gathered Calla's long hair with one hand and gently pulled her flush against his chest with the other, casually draping an arm across her stomach. Calla's eyes fluttered closed at the familiar scent of him—notes of citrus and cedarwood.

"The Fates have been treacherous every step of this journey, but I guarantee they want those dice back in our hands more than anyone," he said, resting his chin on the crown of her head.

Calla flicked her eyes up toward the stars—toward the Gods—and wondered how many moments of peace the two of them had left before everything changed forever.

By the time Calla woke the next morning, it was well after dawn. When she and Gideon had returned to the room the night before, the others had already passed out—Caspian and Thorne snoring in sync on opposite sides of the large couch and Hannah curled into a ball so close to the edge of the bed that Calla was surprised the girl hadn't rolled right off.

It hadn't taken Calla long to drift off while Gideon made himself as comfortable as possible on the makeshift palette of pillows and blankets a few feet away. He and the other men rotated their sleeping arrangements despite both Calla and Hannah insisting they should also take turns on the floor. Their protests had been consistently ignored. And the one time Calla fell asleep on the floor while the others were out, when there could be no protests, she still woke up to find herself tucked into the bed.

Now, as Calla rubbed her eyes and looked around, she saw that she was alone, early afternoon sun streaming in from the window and spilling across the small, tidy room. Small because of their finite funds; tidy because of Gideon's unrelenting cleaning schedule. She stood and stretched before walking over to one of their two dressers, ignoring the way her stomach growled as she dug through the drawers for something to wear. Gideon and Caspian had gone overboard on stocking them up with clothing and supplies after they hawked a few of their knives and some pieces of jewelry. Though Calla did have to admit, the overzealous precautions had been enormously beneficial the day she and Hannah had started their cycles at the exact same time.

Luckily, as Rouge witches, the bleeding part of the whole ordeal was always over in a blink. No, the worst part for them was definitely the full-body cramps that wreaked havoc for four days straight. *Them* referring to Calla, Hannah, and, because of the soul-bond, *Gideon*—something not a single one of them had seen coming. Calla's cycle was such a constant pain she'd had years to acclimate to, she'd completely forgotten to warn Gideon.

Witches and Valkyries were the only beings that had one cycle every season—four total in a year—and that apparently meant they were destined to have cramps ten times as painful as fae or other beings. Calla and Hannah knew to anticipate this, of course, but Gideon . . . Calla would never forget the look on the prince's face when the first cramp hit him. It took Calla and Hannah an hour to convince Gideon the hot springs on the west side of the woods would give him the relief he needed even though it was an excruciating walk.

"Regret keeping the bond yet?" she had asked, smirking as he nearly shattered his jaw clenching his teeth with every painful step.

"I will never complain about a battle wound ever again" had been his only response.

Gideon had been pleased to find that Calla and Hannah were right about the hot springs, and as soon as the whole thing passed, the prince had become noticeably more reverent of the girls. He even left them little gifts he found around the woods—odd-shaped acorns, interesting feathers, dragon scales—as if he were a gracious being of the fae. Calla smiled as a few of those bits he'd collected rolled around at the bottom of the drawer she was riffling through. She yanked out a shirt and a pair of trousers and bumped the drawer shut with her hip.

The clothes they'd collected in the Dragonwoods were almost entirely created from a dragon-shifter invention of special woven fiber. It was stretchy but compressing, and the crew had quickly learned it was fantastic for training and fighting in. Water wicked right off, and it somehow managed to be either cool or warm depending on which need arose.

She peeled off her sleeping clothes and rolled the tight black bodysuit over her voluptuous frame, hopping a bit as she tugged on a matching pair of pants with dragon scales sewn into the knee and shin panels. The last thing she did was strap Heart Reaver's sheath to her hip. Its presence had become a comfort, an anchor to a soul she would always dearly miss. Calla was grateful Gideon remembered to grab it during the chaos with the Witch Queens. She would have been devastated if it had been lost in the fray.

"You're awake," Gideon's voice rang out from behind her.

Calla startled a bit as she turned to find him leaning in the open doorway.

"You let me sleep too long again," she chided.

"Calliope," he began, giving her a *look*. "As long as the world isn't on fire, I'm going to let you sleep in. You're up right on time, though. We discovered something. With the compass. And Caspian just returned with food."

"The compass?" She raised both brows in surprise. "Is it working?"

"You'll see." Gideon beckoned her with wave of his hand.

Calla hurried outside into the golden afternoon sunlight, letting Gideon lead her down the open stretch of clearing in the middle of the two identical rows of cottages. The quaint homes ran along the outer line of the small village, making them just a quick walk to the market square in the town's center. Gideon wasn't leading her into town, however. Instead, they walked all the way down the sunny passage and out into the woods, toward a familiar shallow crater that Caspian and Thorne had turned into their own personal hangout spot—complete with five tree-stump stools and a larger center stump as a makeshift table.

Calla seemed to be the only one who noticed that when she and Gideon approached, Hannah stiffened uncomfortably. Caspian and Thorne waited for Calla to choose between the last two empty chairs. She settled on Thorne's left and gave him a smile, which he readily returned.

Calla still couldn't believe how drastically Thorne's appearance had changed since they'd first met in Myrea's dungeon only a few weeks ago. He'd been little more than skin and bones then, with a paper-white complexion contrasted by long dark hair and an overall unkemptness. Now he was clean-shaven, his skin radiant with a newfound sun-kissed glow, and his hair neatly cropped with a single wayward strand curling down over his forehead. With regular access to food—not to mention Gideon and Caspian's rigorous early morning workouts—Thorne's atrophied muscles had made a full recovery, and every passing day his bright green eyes seemed to grow brighter. Even Caspian had recently commented on how handsome the Terra witch was, and Calla had to agree.

"Good morning," Caspian finally greeted them, tone cheery as he slapped a card he had been mulling over onto the makeshift trunk table. As Thorne shuffled through the cards in his own hand to decide his next move, Cass reached over to grab something out of the leather sack at his feet. "I got breakfast."

Cass tossed Calla one of the familiar green fruits from the Dragonwoods before lobbing a purple one at Gideon. Calla opened her mouth to take a bite, but before she could taste the fruit, Gideon reached over and plucked it from her hand, replacing it with his. She blinked over at him in surprise, but he was already leaning over to snag a peek at Caspian's cards. She *much* preferred the sweet taste of the purple ones to the crisp, sour flavor of the green, though she was certain she had never actually mentioned that aloud.

Thorne played his turn next, and Cass and Gideon bowed their heads together, trading whispered strategies.

"Hey." Thorne jabbed an accusing finger at the other men. "No cheating."

Neither Cass nor Gideon paid him any mind. Cass simply threw down another card, which elicited a small groan from Thorne.

Calla leaned over so she could see Thorne's cards. "Let me take a look...."

Thorne didn't hesitate to fan out the options, and she took a moment to shuffle the order around in his grip before tapping twice on the one she wanted him to play.

Caspian narrowed his eyes at the move and quickly countered. Calla tapped a second card in Thorne's hand, and Cass made an indignant noise as he looked back and forth between the two of them.

"Shark," Caspian accused Calla.

Calla gave him a toothy grin. Out of the corner of her eye, she saw Gideon trying to hide a smile by taking a bite of his breakfast. Cass played his final move, and then Thorne went in for the kill.

"Aha! Finally!" Thorne exclaimed. "I win!"

Cass rolled his eyes and tossed the remainder of his cards onto the stack in defeat. "No, *Calla* won. This is precisely why we don't let her play."

"Don't be a spoilsport," Thorne admonished as he and Calla high-fived in victory.

Caspian sighed deeply before turning to Calla. "Did Gideon tell you about the compass?"

Calla shook her head as Gideon unclasped the object in question from his pants and flicked open its lid. "What's going on with it?"

"Hannah figured it out," Gideon explained. "This morning."

Calla watched curiously as Gideon showed her the compass's faceplate and tapped two little pin-sized holes at the top—easily missed if you weren't looking for them. Her blood began to warm as it recognized his magic suddenly flare up between them, a bit of wind shooting from his fingertips and right into the small holes.

Calla's breath hitched. She leaned forward in disbelief as Gideon's wind magic made the center of the compass flip to reveal a hidden second side.

"I've seen mechanisms like that before," Hannah explained. "My childhood home . . . The fireplace would do something similar between rooms when air was pumped into a little channel with a bellow. The pressure of the wind in the chamber made it spin. So, when I saw the holes . . ."

"Hannah, you're a genius," Calla said as her eyes flicked to Gideon's face. "The other needle didn't work, but this one . . ."

As she spoke, the arrow began to turn leisurely—unlike the frantic way it had been turning on the other side the past few weeks—assessing the direction it wanted to point. When it finally stopped, Calla sucked in a breath.

It pointed due north. Toward the Land of the Valkyries.

"What in the Hells?" Calla wondered. "What's the difference?"

Gideon shook his head. "No clue. But as long as it's working..."

"What are the odds that there are any Blood Warriors *there*, though?" Calla asked.

"Low," Caspian noted. "Though... if we could manage to find our way around the outside borders, we might be able to pinpoint where the compass is trying to lead as well as run into someone from the Guild. It would help if I could make sure everything was going as planned on that front."

Gideon nodded in agreement before taking a deep breath. "Looks like it's time to go."

3

Delphine's skin glittered with the scattered rays of light reflecting off the spinning mirrorball overhead. She was sitting on the lap of some drunk fae, sipping a glass of amber wine as she tracked the movements of her target across the room. It had taken her two weeks to track down the man in Estrella, and another to finesse her way into this underground sin den. But despite the depraved scene before her, she relished every minute she was here and not in the Neverending Forest.

Well, except for the night she had returned, when she sought out Allex to sever whatever remained of their relationship. There had been nothing to relish in breaking the poor witchling's heart, but after disappearing without a word, she figured it was the least she had owed them. A part of Delphine was sad that she might never see the sweet mortal again, but another part of her felt relieved—like she was a snake who'd just shed the old skin of her past, shiny and new with possibilities.

Tonight, she was in her element—sitting in the most exclusive club in all of Illustros, run by the same insidious beings who controlled the black markets. It was so selective, they let in new members as infrequently as once a decade. However, after a few demonstrations of her siren's song, her claws, and the diamond dress she was wearing, she'd conned her way in.

"Want to get out of here, sweetheart?" the fae she was perched atop grunted in her ear, his hot breath making her cringe.

Delphine was careful not to let her disgust show, but before she could respond, something caught her attention—her target was on the move. Delphine hopped off the fae's lap in an instant, straightening her dress as she dodged the drunk man's grabbing hands.

"Why don't you get me a refill? I'll be right back," she purred at the stranger, shoving her half-full glass into his chest before making a beeline for the other side of the room. Her target was quick—he didn't move without purpose. Which meant there was a very small window to catch him alone before he went on to whatever else was on his agenda tonight.

She wove her way through the crowded tables, each of which hosted different games and an array of peculiar gamblers. Her target had slipped through a door in the back that Delphine was almost certain didn't lead to a restroom—or anywhere else so tame—and when she found it unlocked, she had to admit she was surprised. As she reached for the glass knob, her eyes darted around the room, hoping no one was paying attention to her, but of course, most people *were*. Even without the diamond dress, or the fact that she was the only siren, her presence could never be missed.

Delphine flashed her audience a fiendish grin, slipped through the doorway, and stepped into . . . a courtyard. It was narrow and dark, the blistery night air sticky with salt from the nearby coast. An empty shadowy passage stretched all the way to the end of the back half of the building, where another door awaited.

She hurried to the exit and pulled it open, and was immediately filled with the distinct feeling she was walking into a trap.

"Hello, Delphine," a deep voice murmured as the door slammed shut at her back. "It's been too long."

The small room was covered floor to ceiling in plush onyx velvet. There was a long, tufted couch along the far wall and an insidious-looking cage off to the right. Thankfully, the cage was empty.

A faint glow from the impressive overhead crystal chandelier splashed warm light across her former landlord's face.

Delphine's mouth twisted into a feline grin. "Jack."

His expression was carefully blank as he spoke. "I was wondering when you would finally find me."

"If you knew I was looking for you, why didn't *you* find *me*?" She crossed her arms and leaned back against the door. For a moment, there was no answer, only a brief flare of light and the quick hiss of something igniting. A cigarette.

"People come to me," he told her. "Never the other way around."

Delphine tapped her foot impatiently and watched as Jack took a drag, blowing out a lazy ring of lavender smoke. His shrewd gold eyes searched for answers in Delphine's expression, but she knew he wasn't going to find anything useful there. She was too busy raking her own gaze over his impeccable outfit—a crimson suit embroidered with swirling floral patterns and small ruby beads. It was almost nicer than her own ensemble, and a flare of jealousy warmed her skin. Jack's attire was custom-made, while hers had been stolen from a laundering shop.

Jack was the only mortal Delphine had ever met who was able to exude confidence in the presence of beings that could easily kill him. Not even Allex—who's witch half meant they possessed actual magic—was able to hold a candle to Jack's simmering presence.

"Get on with it, then." Another drag of the cigarette. "Tell me what it is you're here for."

"I'm surprised you're a smoker. Aren't you worried the smell will linger on all your nice clothes?" Delphine gave a light sniff. "Is that faery root?"

"Why worry about things I'm only going to wear once?" he responded. "And yes, it's a very rare strain of faery root, in fact. Worth triple what those diamonds in your ears cost. Would you like some? It's good for . . . nerves."

She smirked. "Are you saying I make you nervous?"

Jack pushed himself up from the couch, cigarette hanging between his lips as he strode across the room. He leaned a hand on the door behind her and bent down until their noses were almost touching. They were about the exact same height, but the way he took up space made it feel like he was towering over her. The scent of the burning faery root was thick as wisps of smoke curled into the air between them.

"In about five minutes, this room will be occupied by beings with a few very specific activities in mind that they'd like to enjoy this evening. Activities I don't think you'll stomach, no matter how many layers of bravado you've donned tonight." He made a point to flick his honey eyes up and down her figure. "So either tell me what it is you've spent the last few weeks trying to get me into a room for or take a seat and let's see how long you last before losing your last meal all over the carpet."

"You know"—she reached up and plucked the cigarette from his mouth—"I've never really believed that you, or this empire you've built, are as impenetrable as you try to make it seem. I think you're just so bored and lonely that it's easy to act like you have everything under control. Because you have nothing to really lose if something goes wrong, right? At least that's what I've been told in these last few weeks while I hunted you down. Nothing to live for. Nothing to die for. I imagine that means making risky decisions is an easy thing to do."

Delphine brought the cigarette to her own lips and inhaled deeply, Jack's eyes tracing the movement. She could use the faery root's calming effects for what she was about to do next.

"You said people come to you, never the other way around, but maybe you should rethink your stance on that." She huffed a laugh. "Because when you let an ember linger too long . . . you'll find the fire will roar back to life, stronger than before." She brought the burning end of the cigarette down onto his custom lapel and extinguished it.

"You have no idea who you're toying with," he told her evenly.

"Oh, but that's what I'm trying to tell you, *Jack*." She tapped the point of one of her incisors with the tip of her tongue. "I know *exactly* who I'm toying with. If you knew I was looking for you, you should have given me your audience. Instead, you left me to network with people who just happen to have lots of secrets. Secrets that, don't get me wrong, were often incomplete pieces of larger secrets, bigger pictures—but that's where I come in. Secrets are my specialty."

"What are you here for?" Jack asked, tone more clipped than before.

"I want to know where Hannah and Calla are."

"Is that all?" He huffed a laugh. "Last I heard, they were taken from the Neverending Forest by Myrea's guards and hauled off to the Rouge Realm."

"Are they still there?" she demanded.

"I'm a very busy man, sweetheart. I only keep track of those I need to." He stepped away from her. "We're done here."

"No, we aren't," Delphine shrieked as she reached out with lightning speed and wrapped her hand around his neck, embedding her claws in the soft skin there. She was becoming rather fond of the sensation of ripping out throats. Reniel may have been onto something. "I want to know where Ramor and Boone are."

A dangerous shrewd glint flashed in his golden eyes, and he slowly reached up and extracted her hand from his throat. Delphine didn't know why she let him remove her so easily; maybe it was the odd way his expression hadn't changed, not even a flinch. There was truly no mask he was wearing, nothing to slip away or see beneath.

"Why shouldn't I kill you for coming here?" His tone suggested he was genuinely curious. "For stalking me and making demands you have no right to make?"

"Because if anything ever happens to me by your hands, I've guaranteed that your secret, and all its tricky little pieces, will be for *everyone* to know. Because as much as you think you have nothing to live or die for, we both know if that were *really* true, you wouldn't be bothering with all of *this*." She gestured to the room around them. A very small example of his very large empire. "Hope is infectious, don't you think? Always festering somewhere in the darkness even when you think you've snuffed it all out."

There was a long lingering minute of silence, and though his expression never wavered, his breathing had gotten ever so slightly shallower.

Then he said, "Our five minutes are up. If you're looking for Ramor, you're in luck. He and the albatrosses will arrive any second."

Delphine curled a lip. "Albatrosses?" She knew of them—creatures whose kiss would trap you for six long years at sea, make you unable to step on land a second sooner. She wondered why such beings would be here for Jack.

"Entertainment," Jack answered her unspoken question. "Fun is surprisingly sparse out at sea—"

From across the room, a door Delphine hadn't noticed before burst open, cutting off the rest of Jack's sentence. She watched with morbid curiosity as a slew of unpolished scoundrels came pouring inside—including Ramor himself.

"Welcome, friends." Jack smiled as he addressed the newcomers, not bothering to turn and face them. "Please settle in. We have quite the acts to look forward to tonight."

"Boss?" Ramor asked as he approached where Jack and Delphine stood, trying to peer over Jack's shoulder to get a peek at her. The troll's eyes widened as soon as they landed on her face.

Delphine sidestepped away from Jack, giving Ramor a saccharine smile. "It's so nice to see you again, Ramor. Remember me? Of course you do. My good friend Calla introduced us once or twice."

Ramor shifted on his feet, perhaps a bit nervous at her looming presence, but he didn't back away. He only stared blankly at Jack, perhaps awaiting orders or an explanation for why Delphine was there.

"For tonight's first bit of entertainment," Delphine announced to the very confused crowd hovering at the back of the room, "I'm going to perform a very special trick."

If Delphine thought Jack would attempt to stop her, she was wrong. The man only watched, waiting to see what her next move would be.

"Or should I say, *Ramor* here is going to perform a very special trick," she continued. "He's going to give me his heart."

"How romantic," someone crooned from the shadows as another person muttered, "I thought there was going to be blood."

Ramor opened his mouth to demand someone tell him what was going on, but Delphine was already singing. It was a lovely ballad, one of her favorites, the melody haunting as it rose to a mournful crescendo. Magic laced each note with a heavy dose of influence, and in mere seconds, every being's eyes were glazed with rapt focus. Ramor's left hand began to rise in front of him, and his concentration on her song broke ever so slightly. He looked at his hand in horror as it turned toward his own body without his permission. Delphine kept singing.

Jack straightened up a bit in realization as Ramor's hand involuntarily plunged itself into his chest, right over his heart, his jagged nails ripping at the material of his shirt and the mottled skin underneath until it was a mess of blood, flesh, and linen.

"Wait," the troll managed to wheeze as his mind finally caught on to what was happening. "Wait."

Delphine did no such thing. She simply kept singing and singing and singing until his hand had dug so far into his own chest that it finally clutched around the beating heart within. Only then did she go silent.

The room around her pulsed with anticipation as Ramor's heart pulsed with fear. She slowly leaned down until her eyes were level with the troll's. "This is for what you did to Calla."

"No," Ramor whispered.

A giddy feeling bubbled in her stomach as she demanded, "Hand it over."

Ramor ripped his heart out of his chest and dropped it at Delphine's feet with a sickening *squelch*.

When his body hit the floor, a round of applause broke out, but

Delphine ignored it as she scooped up the troll's odd-shaped heart and tossed it over to Jack. Jack caught it without a word, dark maroon blood splattering over his expensive ensemble and the sharp angles of his face, yet he still didn't blink.

"Another heart for your collection. You're welcome," she told him as she stepped toward the door that led back to the courtyard. "Tell Boone I'll be back for him eventually."

Jack tossed the heart up into the air a couple of times in contemplation. "You were right, you know."

She paused, hand on the doorknob. "About?"

"I don't have anything to live *or* die for. It's why I surround myself with vulnerable people who have plenty to lose. Ramor was particularly useful. Not too bright but always did as he was told. I should make you pay greatly for this."

She laughed. "Oh, but you won't."

"Actually, I will. Just not in the way you might think." He strode over, swatted her hand away from the knob, and yanked the door open himself. "Because there's one thing you were wrong about. There's no hope festering here, sweetheart. I found a way to squash that little bug long ago. Permanently."

Delphine flicked her hair away from her face as she stomped outside, fists balling by her sides.

"Go reunite with your friends," Jack taunted. "And hope that my payback for you will hurt far less than yours did for Ramor." With that, he slammed the door.

Delphine scurried across the courtyard and back to the club, hurrying past belligerent gamblers still playing their games, making their bets, drinking their wine. A slurred voice called out whatever made-up name she'd provided, and she turned to find the man she'd been using earlier—the one she'd flirted with for weeks to get access in here. Without stopping to see what he wanted, Delphine raced for the exit.

Delphine would not let Jack's threats derail her plans. All she'd done was get information on Hannah and Calla's whereabouts. All she'd done was avenge her friend.

I'll deal with the consequences later, she thought.

When she finally made her way out into Estrella's starry night, she had only one thing on her mind: get to the Rouge Realm and rescue Hannah and Calla from wherever Myrea had them imprisoned. It should be a relatively easy task.

After all, she held the key to everything.

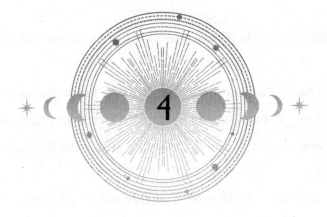

"Do you really think heading closer to the Land of the Valkyries is the best idea?" Calla whispered to Gideon as they watched their friends frantically pack up all their belongings.

Gideon was the first one ready, every garb and weapon he owned meticulously secured in his pack or on his person. Everyone else scrambled to find matches for their socks, frantically stuffing random articles of clothing and knives wherever they could fit them. Caspian was currently digging under the bed for a missing shoe while Thorne sifted through the couch cushions. Meanwhile, Hannah was repacking everything Cass touched.

"Unfortunately, we don't have any other leads at the moment," Gideon said. "I think Cass has the right idea—we see where the compass might be leading and then split up from there. He can go with Hannah to find Delphine, and Thorne can stick with us while we go after the other Blood Warriors and dice. There's a clock ticking over our heads now. We don't have time to ruminate on our next steps any longer."

Calla nodded in agreement just as a loud knock pounded on the cottage door. Hannah cautiously pried it open, and Calla strutted over, Gideon on her heels, all of them crowding the threshold to see who it was.

If it wasn't easy enough to tell from their bulky build or the way their irises flickered like the dancing flames they could breathe, the emerald scales lining their forearms was certainly a dead giveaway that this was a dragon-shifter. Not to mention their uniform was made of the same stretchy compression material Calla had taken a liking to—allowing easy access to the leathery wings folded at their back.

"Can we help you?" Gideon demanded.

The shifter silently stared at Hannah, eventually turning to address Gideon's question. "You all need to evacuate this area immediately."

"We were just—" Calla began to explain, but before she could get her entire sentence out, three large beasts fell from the sky.

Multiple dragon-shifters landed nearby, and the ground shook beneath all of their feet. Before Calla could lose her balance, Gideon had a steadying grip on her elbow. Hannah was as still as a pillar.

The dragon-shifter before them turned to take in the newcomers. "Here we go...."

Gideon was already tugging on his backpack. "Grab whatever you managed to pack and get outside," he snapped at the others. "Now." He tossed Calla her bag and waited for Cass, Hannah, and Thorne to file outside.

All of them watched as the three shifters finished transitioning back into their human forms. Their dragon forms came in vibrant jewel-toned colors: sapphire, ruby, and topaz. It was odd to watch the way their bones twisted and cracked as they transformed, their scaly skin melting away everywhere except the few places it remained for protection in their vulnerable human form.

One of them—the one with sapphire scales—marched up to the group, her pale face contorted with anger. She was almost three inches taller than Gideon, her raven hair shaved on one side and braided on the other. Within the blue eyes that matched her scales, a fire blazed as she roared, "Which one of you is in charge of this coven?"

The group turned their heads toward Gideon and Calla without hesitation.

Calla narrowed her eyes, arms crossing over her chest as she asked, "Why? Who are you?"

"We're members of the Trove," the dragon-shifter replied.

Gideon recognized the name. The Trove was the elected council that ruled the Dragonwoods and, perhaps more importantly, the only beings in Aetherius who knew where the hidden isle of dragons was.

"And you've overstayed your welcome," the sapphire shifter continued.

"What's the rush all of a sudden?" Calla pressed.

"Valkyries," the ruby shifter spat. "Three of them to be exact. Saying they're hunting down a group of troublesome witches. Which means you either leave peacefully or by force. Your rivalry isn't welcome here."

It wasn't much of a threat. The Dragonwoods were a neutral territory, magically spelled to harm anyone who engaged in physical conflict. Even so, Calla was sure dragon-shifters had rather creative ways to make people leave if they truly wanted—something involving dragonfire.

Gideon cursed at the mention of Valkyries, pinching the bridge of his nose.

"Where were the Valkyries last seen?" Caspian asked.

As if worried that sharing this information would be considered an allegiance, the shifter hesitated.

Calla tapped her foot. "The quicker you give us a direction, the quicker we're gone."

"Due north," the ruby shifter grunted. "Now leave."

"Well," Thorne said, looking ruefully at the rest of them, "at least we know for sure the compass is working again."

Everyone turned to Gideon, and he dipped his chin in a sharp nod. Permission to move out. Caspian didn't waste another moment, waving a hand at the group to follow his lead into the woods while Gideon lingered behind, eyes trained on the shifter as they left.

"Is something wrong?" Calla murmured, slowing her steps to keep pace at his side.

"They're burning the cottage down," Gideon noted.

She glanced back at the dragon-shifters to find that the ruby one was scrutinizing Gideon as carefully as Gideon was them. The other shifters had, in fact, disappeared into the cottage. A noise of shock fell from Calla's mouth when she noticed billowing puffs of smoke wafting from the open doorway.

"Do you think they're trying to cover our scents or something?" she asked.

Gideon shook his head. "No. I think they're sending someone a signal."

5

Plumes of gray smoke wafted into the air from the distant clearing in the middle of the Dragonwoods, and the sharp smile on Amina's face turned anticipatory. She flicked her gaze over to where Lyra was hovering in the air on her left.

"Think you can follow them overhead without being spotted?" Amina asked.

Lyra wrinkled their nose in disdain. "Don't insult me."

Amina nodded in satisfaction. "I'll head back to Sabine and make sure she hasn't maimed our prisoner—yet. We have less than forty-eight hours to deliver the Siphon to Ignia. Do whatever it takes to make their feet move quickly. We'll see you at the border."

Lyra gave Amina a smile before they dove down through the air and speared toward the witches in the woods below. Amina gave a powerful beat of her wings and soared higher, breaking through the first line of wispy clouds before shooting herself forward. Flying at this altitude meant it only took about an hour to reach the borderline, where they'd left Sabine and their prisoner, but as she gracefully drifted to a landing in front of her friend, she noted their hostage was nowhere to be found.

"Sabine," Amina greeted the girl with an impatient tap of her foot.

Sabine, calmly sharpening one of her blades, glanced up with a delighted grin. "That didn't take long. I assume Lyra's sources were right? The witches were holed up in the Dragonwoods?"

"Yes," Amina answered, the word clipped as she propped her hands on her hips. "Now, does something look wrong to you here?"

Sabine tilted her head, her jade-green eyes darting around the space between them in confusion. "No?"

"*Sabine,*" Amina growled. "*Where is he?*"

"Who—? *Oh!*" Sabine gave a nonchalant wave of her hand as the realization hit her. "Don't worry, he's just getting me a snack."

Amina sputtered, nearly at a loss for words. "You *let* him out of your sight? He's a prisoner, Sabine!"

"But I was hungry," Sabine complained. "And he wouldn't stop asking questions. I figured it'd be safest for us both if he was preoccupied elsewhere."

"Sabine." Amina sighed in frustration. "Go find him. *Now.*"

Sabine straightened up, rolling her eyes. "Yeah, yeah. I'm on it." Then a wicked look gleamed in her eyes. "Actually, I have an idea."

Amina gave her friend a wary look. "Gods help that man."

But as Sabine prowled into the forest, Amina was sure that not even they could save him from what was coming. Not from Sabine, or the Valkyrie Queen, or the war she could feel looming on the horizon.

6

For the first time since he'd awoken, the forest was silent enough for him to hear his thundering heartbeat as it echoed in his ears.

He could still feel the tremors of shock deep in his bones from the moment he opened his eyes back in the Neverending Forest, the three Valkyries looking down on him with anticipation. It had taken some time to reorient himself in his body, like maybe his soul had forgotten what it was like to be tethered. It didn't take long, however, to realize why he felt so different. So out of sorts.

His being was . . . changed.

It was small differences at first—a faster heart rate, blood that warmed with each shift of his emotions, the way certain things refused to respond to his call. He couldn't shift the wind, and the rain no longer energized him.

Though it wasn't as if he felt empty. Not at all. In fact, it felt like something powerful was prowling beneath the surface of his skin, a beast waiting for permission to be unleashed, though he didn't know how to let it out. Or if he even wanted to.

That beast began to perk up now, unsettled by the lifelessness around him—a lack of birdsong, the absence of any breeze. Or maybe it was just alert to the sudden feeling of being watched, a fact punctuated by the prickling hair on the back of his neck.

A twig snapped.

He sharply spun to his left, holding his breath and narrowing his eyes toward the thicket. Silence.

He crept forward, treading lightly on the balls of his feet. Someone was here. Or maybe something. The same sort of something that was lurking beneath his skin.

A ruffle of leaves.

He bared his teeth and spun for the tree on his left, watching as one of the lower branches bobbed in the air. Empty.

"Come out!" he demanded.

There was a *thud*, this time from directly behind him, and he whirled. He sprinted forward, following the sound of the pounding footsteps, an unfamiliar instinct to become the predator rather than the prey. He dodged trees and ducked beneath branches as a strong gust of wind swirled around him. Up ahead, a figure dashed behind a particularly large trunk, blanketed by shadows. But when he rounded the thick trunk, there was no one.

"What the Hells?" he muttered to himself, slowly turning around and—

—staring straight into a pair of piercing jade eyes.

He didn't even have time to make a sound of surprise as the Valkyrie swept his feet from beneath him and his back slammed onto the ground. She had his shoulder pinned down in seconds, her clawed hand wrapped around his throat as she gave him a toothy grin.

She laughed. *"Ha—"*

Before she could finish whatever else she was about to say, however, something inside him snapped. He wasn't sure if it was from the surprise, or from being pinned down, but the beast had finally decided it was ready to release itself.

Sabine looked cautious now. "Your eyes are doing that strange thing again. The flames."

"Get off me," he warned, his voice not sounding at all like his own.

Sabine scrambled up, green eyes sharp as they roamed his face. "What's happening to you?"

He couldn't answer. Not only because he didn't know, but because a searing ripple of magic suddenly burst out of him, right into the earth.

What's happening? he demanded internally as a roar ripped from his throat, the unfamiliar magic in his veins exploding out of him all at once. *Who are you?*

I am you, the beast answered back.

Who am I? He did not know this version of himself. *Who am I?*

At first there was no answer, just fire and pain.

Then his name began to echo all around him.

Ezra Black. Ezra Black. Ezra Black.

The earth began to shake.

"**H**annah!"

Hannah quickly snapped out of a trance as she felt the first wave of the earthquake. Caspian tugged her to the ground beside him, propping their backs against a large boulder to brace themselves for impact as the earth continued to shake. Her shoulders were sandwiched between his and Thorne's. She watched Gideon and Calla duck behind a large severed tree trunk several yards ahead. They were all fine. Everything was going to be fine.

"You okay, little witch?" Cass questioned, but all she could do was give him a wooden nod.

Thorne said something to her right, but she couldn't make out the words over the roaring of blood in her ears. Earthquakes always brought her back to the bone brothel.

Hannah loved strawberry tartes. Today's tarte was particularly enticing. Mother had taken the extra step of making sugared cream and drizzling it on top in the shape of a flower. As Hannah took a too-large bite, she knew she'd done well this week.

So well, in fact, that her mother said she didn't have to sleep in the drafty back room anymore. Hannah was getting her own bed in one of the cozier rooms at the front of the house, where her mother's other wards slept. A hard-earned prize—one she received because she'd finally unleashed enough of her power to cause an earthquake. Not even her mother's more experienced wards had been able to achieve such a feat.

"Hannah, love," *her mother crooned as she returned to the dining room, petting the top of her daughter's head as she passed.* "What do you think? The cream really finishes it off perfectly, doesn't it?"

Hannah swallowed the bite. "Yes, Mother. It's wonderful."

"Good." *Her mother nodded.* "You earned it. And if you continue to do just as well next week, there will be even more surprises in store for you."

Hannah paused. "Next week? But I'm supposed to have a break until next month. Mrs. Carnation said I shouldn't summon my magic like that too often or it could . . . hurt."

Her mother's smile tightened, and Hannah knew instantly she had said something wrong. Her stomach dropped.

"Yes, well, there is a reason we let Mrs. Carnation go, Hannah," *her mother said in a clipped tone.* "She kept spreading lies, and they were beginning to frighten the other children. But I thought you would be cleverer than to believe such things."

"I am!" Hannah protested. "I . . . I didn't believe her. I'm just surprised I'll get to practice more so soon. I'm . . . excited."

"Yes, you should be." Her mother nodded, satisfied with her answer. "It's an honor to spend time with me. You know how much the others wish they could have the same privileges you do."

"I know," Hannah whispered.

"Good, now finish your tarte and come meet me in the study. We'll discuss your new routine."

With that, her mother disappeared as quickly as Hannah's appetite. She stared down at the half-eaten tarte, the bite she'd taken now churning in her stomach.

Mrs. Carnation had been lying, *she told herself.* Practicing Mother's sort of magic won't hurt me. And if I'm good, I'll get more time with her. Maybe if I'm really good, she'll even let me spend time with her when I'm not practicing my magic.

Hannah pushed her chair back from the table and brought her plate over to the sink. She scraped the rest of her tarte into the compost collection. Then she headed off to the study.

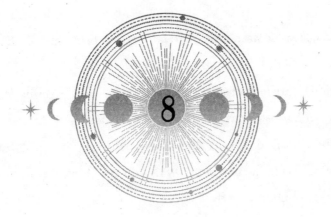

S abine wasn't necessarily an expert on witches, but she was rather positive they weren't supposed to suddenly hemorrhage enough power to cause an *earthquake*. And she was *definitely* certain they weren't supposed to spring *wings* from their backs.

It had taken a moment for her to recover from the shock of seeing Ezra convulse on the ground—his flaming eyes rolling to the back of his head as his spine arched and snapped in a most disturbing way—in order to alert Amina. Luckily, the earthquake had finally stopped, and now she and Amina were left to gape down at Ezra's unconscious form.

Sabine prodded one of the black leathery appendages that had sprouted from the witch's back with the toe of her boot, as if it were a giant insect she'd never seen before. The wings had small shiny scales crawling along the tendons and looked an awful lot like those of a . . .

"Dragon-shifter," Amina hissed. "*Hells*. I knew his eyes were a bad omen."

"How do you suppose—" Sabine began, but the realization dawned on her quickly. "It wasn't his heart we used to bring him back. It was Rovin's."

"I didn't realize such a thing would do . . . *this*," Amina claimed, splaying her hands toward Ezra's unconscious form.

Sabine shrugged. "Well, what's done is done, I suppose. Do you think he's going to be mad at us? Wait—do you think this means we'll have to teach him how to fly?"

Amina only pinched the bridge of her nose.

Sabine tapped Ezra's shoulder with her foot next. "Hey, pal, it's time to wake up now."

Ezra didn't move.

She tapped harder. There was a tiny part of her—a *very* tiny part—that might have even been . . . worried for the witch. Not that she'd know what that sort of thing even felt like. All she knew was that the uneasy warning in her stomach meant he might not be all right. It made her feel very out of sorts. After all, he'd been the one taking care of *her* the past few weeks. As much as she'd hated it.

Amina and Lyra had given the witch about five minutes to acclimate to his resurrection back in the Neverending Forest before explaining that if Ezra wanted to see his brother or friends again, he needed to listen to them. Sabine had been in so much pain she couldn't remember now if he'd put up much of a fight as he climbed out of his coffin to scoop up her writhing form and flee with the others from that forest. Lyra had said carrying Sabine was paying his dues for her sacrifice—and Sabine agreed. Giving up her wings in order to summon his soul from the afterlife was not something she would ever let the witch forget. But if any of them had expected him to argue over the task at some point, they were all sorely mistaken.

At first, Sabine thought the lack of protest was probably out of some sort of pity. A notion she *loathed*. But after a few days, she realized the look in his eyes had never been anything so shameful. It had been more reverent, in fact. And that's when she had known Amina's plan was going to work.

Regardless, during their travel back to the Land of the Valkyries, Amina and Lyra took turns sleeping and keeping watch at the tops of the trees—leaving Sabine and Ezra alone. Those first nights had been the worst for her. She hadn't once cried or complained; she'd have rather died, but her spiked fevers and full-body chills were miserable, and it wasn't lost on her that he'd stayed up and changed the cooling rags on her wounds every few hours when the heat from her skin turned them hot.

She supposed it shouldn't be a complete shock that she might feel a tad... sympathetic for his current predicament.

"Oh, Lyra is going to die when they see this," Amina said dryly, cutting through Sabine's thoughts. "I just know they're going to want every little detail for their research. He'll be lucky if he doesn't get dissected. Again."

Sabine was only half listening to Amina's ramblings as she unsheathed one of her daggers and flipped it into the air by its hilt. "Do you think if I were to—"

Ezra groaned.

"Good timing," Amina murmured as they watched him slowly come to, blinking his obsidian eyes open in confusion.

"What the Hells happened?" he grunted, immediately attempting to push himself up from the ground—only to topple sideways at the unfamiliar weight of the wings. The back of his shirt had been torn to shreds, and now the useless piece of clothing hung off his frame awkwardly, giving Sabine and Amina flashes of the toned muscles of his stomach beneath.

"Funny story," Sabine began as Ezra managed to climb to his feet while gaping over his shoulder in utter shock. "You may or may not be a dragon-shifter now? Don't worry—we're looking into getting a third opinion."

"*What the fuck?*" he yelled.

"Does this mean you don't like them?" Sabine asked at the same time Amina said, "The heart we used in order to bring you back belonged to a dragon-shifter. Clearly there were some side effects."

Ezra looked at them both, aghast, and Sabine found that she thought he was even more handsome when he was upset. Not that she should have been thinking he was handsome at all.

"Why didn't you use *my* heart to bring me back? It isn't like you didn't know where to find it," he accused.

Sabine and Amina exchanged a loaded look. Sabine eventually shrugged, deferring to Amina's judgment on whether or not they should finally divulge more details of the current situation to him. They'd all been pretty tight-lipped up until now. Though not for Ezra's lack of prodding.

"What are the two of you hiding?" He balled his fists. "I know you only brought me back because you're trying to extort a favor out of Calla and Gideon. So what is it? The big secret Sabine refused to tell me even when she was half dead?"

"Wait—did you try to get secrets out of me when I was *half lucid*?" Sabine keened.

Ezra threw her a look that seemed to say *Obviously*, and part of her had the urge to bite him. Another part admired his shameless tactics. Hells, for all she could remember, they might have worked. She'd been in such excruciating pain that she hadn't been able to tell reality from hallucination. If there was information he couldn't pry out of her even in her most vulnerable state, she was impressed with herself.

"We couldn't use your heart because we no longer possess it," Amina finally admitted.

Ezra scowled. "Then who the fuck *does*?"

An eerie low-pitched whistle echoed through the trees around them, and Amina instantly tensed.

"The Valkyrie Queen," Amina answered before turning to Sabine. "And that was Lyra's signal. Stay here while I get an update—and this time don't let him out of your sight, Sabine."

"I have wings now," Ezra said. "How would she be able to stop me?"

Sabine couldn't help it; she laughed. Ezra's scowl deepened.

Amina snorted. "Sure, Prince. Fly away. When I get back, I'll make sure to search the entire five feet of distance you end up traveling."

"I have a name, and it isn't Prince," he snapped.

Amina tilted her nose up at him. "You're already on thin ice with me, Prince. I suggest you adjust your tone."

"Or what?" Ezra asked.

When Amina's fists tightened at her sides, he smiled.

"You need me," he taunted.

"Keep pushing my buttons, *Ezra*, and soon you'll find yourself without a beating heart for the second time," Amina warned. "You're a convenient ploy, not a necessity, and you'd do well to remember that."

With that, Amina launched herself into the sky. Ezra looked to Sabine with disdain.

"Whatever you're planning to do to Calla and Gideon, I'm not going to cooperate," he told her. "I'll take myself out before I let you derail their mission. The Fates' War is coming; I know you can all feel the shift in the air. In the earth. And I won't let you interfere. You all need to mind your own business."

"Unfortunately, the business of your friends is now our business as well. Believe me—this was not my first choice of a vacation." Sabine strode closer to him, waving a hand at his wings, and to his credit he didn't flinch away from her like most beings did. "You need to start conditioning those if you want to even *attempt* flying. I'll be right back."

"Where are you going?"

"Rocks," she said. "You need rocks. You're going to learn how to hold yourself up with the extra weight first. Then, when you're ready, you'll remove them and be able to trust that your shiny new appendages can hold up your body weight with ease."

Ezra crossed his arms over his chest, ripping away what was left of his shirt and tossing it to the side. "Are you saying you're going to train me?"

Sabine gave him a lazy smile, not bothering to hide the fact that she was languidly admiring every inch of his bare torso. "Any individual's weakness—prisoner or otherwise—is a detriment to the entire group. Which means you better be able to learn quick."

"Catching on quick won't be the problem," he bragged.

Sabine smirked, and before he saw her coming, she lunged forward, a thrill coursing through her body at the feeling of her dagger sliding into his abdomen, right between his ribs.

Ezra grunted in pain and clutched his hands around the protruding hilt of the knife. "What. The. Fuck," he gritted out.

"I thought you said you catch on quick?" Sabine grinned at him. "Don't ever let your guard down for *anyone*. If I had chosen to slice through your wings instead, you'd be fucked. Wings take *forever* to heal compared to other body parts—believe me. Now, I'll be back. Keep my blade warm for me, won't you?"

Sabine spun on her heels and left him there, bleeding and muttering about *deranged harpies*. As she strutted away, her smile never faded. Nor did the butterflies in her stomach.

9

The ground was still shaking with aftershocks from the earthquake when Gideon's loosened his hold on Calla. She was sitting across his lap, tucked against his chest with her face pressed into the crook of his neck, and she wished they didn't have to move.

"The worst of it should be over," he murmured, smoothing a hand over her hair.

Calla pulled back to look around them. She couldn't see where the others were; the large tree stump they'd taken cover inside of was at least six feet tall and just as wide. But she didn't hear any signs of distress, and that was comforting enough.

Calla shifted her eyes to Gideon's. "Where in the Hells did that come from?"

"The border between the Dragonwoods and the Land of the Valkyries *is* on a major fault line."

"Did the Onyx Realm get many earthquakes?"

He shook his head. "No. What about Rouge?"

"No. Just the occasional hurricane. We were right on the coast of the Celestial Sea."

Gideon nodded casually, but she noted that his eyes, now swirling with silver, kept darting down at her mouth as she spoke. The corners of her lips curled up, and he smirked back at her, knowing he was caught.

"Sorry," he said. "It's a bit hard to concentrate when you're this close...."

Calla slowly slid her hands up Gideon's chest, making his breathing turn shallow, before reaching around to twirl her fingers in the cobalt tendrils at the nape of his neck. Despite how desperately she'd wanted to, they hadn't kissed since that time in the forest, moments before the Rouge Queen's army had shown up and hauled them all away.

Neither of them had admitted aloud that they were ready to throw caution to the wind and surrender to the disastrous consequences of really being together, but Calla knew all he had to do was make a single move and she'd give in. She was so tired of fighting it; she wanted to sink into him and enjoy every precious moment they had before the world around them went up in flames. And after the dream she'd had in the Rouge Queen's dungeon . . .

The Witch Eater's words had replayed in her mind a thousand times by now.

I can't take a heart that's already been stolen.

Gideon shifted forward, bringing her back to the present as he brushed the tip of his nose along hers, making her breath hitch. He tilted his head until their lips were only a centimeter apart.

"Calla? Gideon?" Cass called, footsteps approaching.

"Gods, I wish we had more time," he groaned, before, much to her disappointment, pulling away and hauling them both up to their feet.

"Where's Hannah?" Gideon turned to ask Caspian as Calla collected herself—reining in the butterflies that had yet to get the memo that Gideon's lips were no longer anywhere near hers.

"She needed a minute," Cass said. "The earthquake sent her into another one of her, uh, death trances? That's what I've been calling them. She snapped out of this one much easier, at least."

The moment he finished explaining, Hannah appeared.

They all watched as she opened her mouth to say something, eyes trained on Gideon—

—and vomited all over the ground at their feet.

⟩⟩⟩●⟨⟨⟨

Hannah was going to have a hard time explaining herself this time. The urge to run away was damn near too excruciating to ignore. It was in her nature, after all, to avoid conflict and pain until she was practically on the edge of death.

She had ran from her mother and the Rouge Realm. From her magic. From admitting her feelings to Delphine . . .

And now she wanted to run from her friends. Except they wouldn't let her.

"What's going on, little witch?" Caspian asked as he helped her clean up away from the others.

Hannah pressed her lips tighter together. Truthfully, she didn't *know* what was going on, which was half the issue. All she knew was that the feeling of death clung to the air around Gideon and that every time she came out of another one of her death trances, the feeling grew stronger. But the fact that this time had made her *physically* sick was alarming.

"I know you've been avoiding Gideon," Cass accused, as if he'd read her mind. "Every time he's near, you flinch. What's going on?"

Hannah swallowed. "Since my ... transformation ... I can feel death."

Caspian waited patiently for her to continue.

"It's everywhere," she explained. "In the earth, in the air. Little echoes of dark energy anywhere someone, or something, has passed on. But that's all it is—echoes, remnants, memories. Signs of things that once existed but no longer do that I may call upon if I wish. Except for ..."

"Except for?" he prompted.

She squeezed her eyes shut tight as she whispered, "Gideon."

Caspian stiffened, his hands freezing on the hem of her shirt where he'd been trying to scrub out the vomit with a damp rag. "What do you mean?"

"It clings to him," Hannah gushed, the words finally tumbling out all at once. "It's like a blanket of putrid darkness all around his being. It's not an echo like the others. It's loud. Blatant. And it makes me sick. At first it was just small headaches. I didn't even realize he was the source of them. But then the headaches turned to migraines. And then nausea. And now..."

Caspian cursed. "We have to tell them, Hannah. We have to get to the bottom of this before..."

She sniffled. "I know. I know. I just didn't want to upset anyone. I can't stand the idea of making Gideon or Calla feel like I can't be around them—"

"They're your friends, Han," Cass interrupted her firmly. "As much as you want to spare them discomfort and hurt, they want to do the same for you. We'll figure it out, okay?"

She sniffed again but nodded.

Cass told her to hold tight, and she watched as he jogged back over to Thorne and whispered something to the man, gesturing in her direction with his head. Next thing she knew, Thorne was ambling over to her, hands casually shoved in his front pockets.

"Caspian said I should distract you for a bit." Thorne leaned against the tree she was propped against. "If you're okay with that?"

Hannah snorted. "A distraction would be nice."

Thorne was quiet for a moment, like he was trying to decide on a sufficient topic for his task. Hannah almost laughed at how serious he seemed to be taking his job, and it warmed something inside of her.

Finally, Thorne said, "The girl we're supposed to start looking for. Delphine, right?"

Hannah's heart began to pound as she nodded.

"Caspian said you and Calla were very close with her."

Hannah nodded again.

"How'd the two of you meet?" he wondered. "Is the story any good?"

A small smile found its way to Hannah's lips. "The first time I laid eyes on Delphine, she was threatening to murder someone. It was in Estrella's marketplace. I'd been alone for so long. I tried to keep to myself, not make too much noise, too many scenes. And there she was, about to rip out a merchant's neck for accusing her of stealing something."

"Was she stealing something?"

"Without a doubt."

Thorne gave a low chuckle. "Did you expose her?"

"No," Hannah said. "I didn't even talk to her. She was the most beautiful being I'd ever seen."

"Ah." Thorne hummed in realization as he scrutinized her face. "You're in love with her."

"Yes" was all she said.

"If you didn't talk to her then, how'd you end up becoming friends?"

"Two weeks went by, and I never saw her," Hannah recalled. "And in those two weeks I found myself more restless in the city than ever. I couldn't sleep, so I'd taken to walking around at night. I was meandering down a road with a popular tavern, thinking maybe I'd try something different that night. The exhaustion had started to get to me. And I heard someone crying in the alleyway."

"Delphine?" he guessed.

Hannah laughed and shook her head. "No, Delphine's victim."

Thorne's brows jutted up.

"A courtless fae that had tried to spike her drink. She'd taken him outside, and by the time I found them, he was missing a tongue and three of his fingers. And maybe there's something wrong with me," Hannah admitted, "but I was enchanted. Before she had even told me what the man did to her, I was ready to make excuses for her predicament. I was ready to defend her." Hannah's chest tightened with reverence at the memory.

"I was in love with someone once," Thorne said, his words cutting through Hannah's thoughts and ushering her back to the present.

Hannah looked over at him. "How did it work out?"

"Like most things that involve the Fates," he whispered. "Tragically."

Hannah's breath caught. She was unsure how to comfort him. It wasn't as if she had any insight into being on his side of a tragic lost love. So she said nothing, and they stood together in the quiet of the forest, reminiscing about the ones who didn't make it here with them.

Calla and Gideon had been staring in shock at Caspian for what felt like an eternity before Gideon finally broke the silence.

"I make Hannah sick?" Gideon reiterated aloud.

Cass nodded and then clarified, "Well, something about your essence does, at least. Not your personality, though, don't worry."

Calla shook her head with exasperation.

"She said it has to do with death," Caspian pressed on. "Apparently, it clings to you."

Gideon looked at a loss.

"Okay, let's look at this logically," Calla suggested. "Hannah said it's only gotten worse since she's been going into death trances, right?"

Caspian nodded. "It's like her magic is slowly taking over every single one of her senses. She's becoming a walking death detector."

"And if the sense of death is getting stronger only around Gideon..." Calla trailed off as she looked to the prince. "Then I'm assuming it doesn't have anything to do with you killing someone before, right? Because that would mean Han is affected by me, too."

A spark of realization began to bleed into Gideon's swirling silver irises. "Are you suggesting—"

"That you've experienced death before?" Calla nodded as she finished his thought.

"Well, until we can get to the bottom of *that* little revelation," Caspian inserted, "we need to get to the bottom of how we make Hannah comfortable around you."

"We're almost to the border of the Land of the Valkyries," Gideon stated. "This might be where we split up. You all go for Delphine while Calla and I go for the Fates' Dice."

Caspian nodded, expression glum. "That's probably the best course of action."

Calla didn't argue. She knew this separation had been coming, but she wasn't ready for it, because she knew that every time they parted, there was a very real possibility they wouldn't come back together.

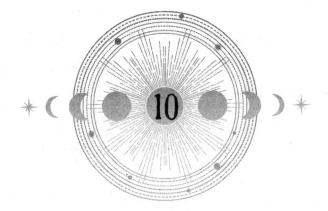

10

Delphine was discovering she had quite the talent for getting captured and dragged away to dungeons. This time, at least, it was intentional.

Sneaking across Estrella and through the Ashwoods into the southernmost corner of the Onyx Realm was relatively easy. She had made sure to change into a less ostentatious outfit than the ones she'd been wearing for the past two weeks—opting for a silver silk slip dress covered by a billowing emerald cape. No one in Estrella had looked at her twice, not even as she trotted through the streets on the fawn-colored mare she'd stolen from outside a random little tavern on her way to the Ashwoods. Once she'd crossed into the forest, she'd found the land all but barren since they were still in their colder season. Only the ice pixies had remained.

It was really the Onyx Realm she'd been worried about. Calla always claimed there were very little pieces of the Witch Realms that weren't teeming with witch covens, so Delphine was more than a little surprised to find the land just as deserted as the Ashwoods—not a single witch in sight. The Fates' War was coming, and it seemed like everyone finally knew it.

When Delphine arrived at the border of the Rouge Realm, it was the same story. Her horse, Apricot, had carried her miles into the heart of the Rouge Realm, to Myrea's palace, before she saw a single witch. The first witches she came across were a line of guards walking a perimeter surrounding the bone palace peeking over the distant horizon. The witches were dressed in crimson uniforms, and there were several makeshift camps littered around them. Delphine tied Apricot to a tree and left a smattering of apples at her feet.

"I won't be too long," she'd promised the mare before slinking out of the woods like a sylph to approach the witches head-on.

At first, there seemed to be a lot of confusion.

"A siren? In the middle of the realm?"

"Should we risk taking her to Myrea? The queen doesn't want anyone leaving their stations. . . ."

The guards ultimately decided the wrath of leaving their stations was better than risking the wrath of letting an intruder walk through the realm without repercussions. And as they patted down the outside of her dress, she was grateful they never thought to check what might be *beneath*. A smile curled on her lips as they determined she had no bulky weapons strapped under the silk gown, leaving the Obsidian Key, which was carefully stuck against her sternum, inches below the garment's neckline, completely unnoticed.

One of the two grunts who'd been assigned her escort regarded her warily, making sure to stay hovering just out of reaching distance of her claws. Smart. The second grunt, however, only seemed to become more dazzled with every passing second. He was clearly young, and Delphine thought it was rather embarrassing that his comrades hadn't been astute enough to give him a reality check. Especially since most of the other guards had stuffed torn shreds of their shirts into their ears to prepare themselves in case she decided to sing.

"She's clean. Myrea's waiting for her in the throne room," the head of the palace guards barked at the two grunts. "Take her in."

"Don't fret too much, gorgeous." The infatuated one gave her a look of pity, but as he let his gaze linger over her figure, the lust beneath unveiled itself as well. "She'll probably just interrogate and throw you into a holding cell for trespassing. Few days later, she'll have us dump you back at the border. And if you're looking for a place to stay . . . I . . ."

As he worked up the courage to finish his offer, she gave him a vicious smile. "Whatever fantasy is playing in your head? You wouldn't survive me, witch." She leaned closer, and his breathing became shallow. "Have you ever even heard a siren's song?"

He swallowed and shook his head.

"First, I'd sing you into a stupor," she explained, holding his gaze. "You'd lose complete and utter control of every single one of your limbs—but your mind? It would remain sharp." She reached out with her hand, letting the back of her sharpened nails trail lightly down his face. "And when I use my claws to shred every inch of your skin from your bones? You will only be able to watch. Happily, even."

When her hand fell to her side, he snapped out of a trance and cringed away. The grunt on her other side snickered at the poor man.

"What's the matter?" Delphine purred. "Is that not what you had in mind?"

His gaze shifted away from her with lightning speed, and he muttered for them to start forward, quickly walking ahead to lead the way across the foyer to a set of glittering red doors. The guards that were stationed in front of the throne room's entrance were already pulling them open for her, and she made an impressed sound in the back of her throat as she admired the room. Ivory columns crafted of bone and carved into trees, marbled floors with splashes of crimson, and the crowning detail of the room decorated with blood and bones: a magnificent throne made of skulls.

A touch dramatic, but Delphine had to admit the Rouge Queen had style.

As the two guards brought her before the dais, Delphine and Myrea measured each other up. The infamous queen was dressed in vermilion, the opulent beaded gown glistening with scatters of rubies and polished bones. A rabbit skull was placed at her hip. Small phalanx bones lined the bodice of the dress for structure. And atop her head was a crown of scarlet jewels dripping down onto her forehead like blood.

"This is a delicious development," the queen purred as she took

Delphine in, but there was something hard, like anger, beneath the mask of her expression.

Delphine tilted her head. "Why is that?"

"You've just missed your friends," Myrea told her. "But don't worry, I'll see to it that they know you're here, and if they want to see you again, alive, they can come get you."

Delphine nearly sighed in relief, but she kept herself composed. They'd gotten away. Thank the Gods.

The queen's eyes narrowed on her. "No biting retort? I thought your kind was supposed to have a way with words."

Delphine shrugged. "There's nothing you can do to me that I haven't already been through. Use me for bait all you want; my friends aren't foolish enough to fall for it."

Myrea's smile turned downright elated, and an alarm went off in Delphine's head. "No? Not even when we send them proof of your distress?"

The queen snapped her fingers, and before Delphine could blink, a guard lurched in from her right. He snatched up her left hand and, with a blade as quick as the strike of a serpent, removed her index finger. The queen laughed as Delphine bit down on her tongue so hard to keep from screaming that blood filled her mouth.

"I'll send them a new part of you every day until there's nothing left," the queen told her. "Pray they return quickly."

Delphine bared her teeth. "Tear me apart all you want. It won't stop your fate—Calla is going to rip you to pieces one day, and your blood will sink into the ground and water my bones."

Myrea gritted her teeth together as she hissed, "Remove her from my sight."

The grunts next to Delphine pulled her away, a trail of navy blood splattering across the floor in their wake. They brought her out to a stone staircase that led below the palace. And so she ended up in another dungeon, missing a body part and bleeding.

Delphine had half a mind to start singing instead of wasting one of the few uses the Obsidian Key had left. But she didn't necessarily trust the queen's claim that all her friends escaped and wanted to see the proof for herself. The grunts led her into an empty gray chamber before spinning a wheel on the wall across from her and lowering the steel bars that would trap her inside. The first guard left without hesitation, but the other man paused. He approached the bars, staring down at the missing digit on her hand.

"Will you heal?" he wondered.

"Yes," she said, tone clipped.

"They escaped about two weeks ago," he informed her.

Delphine narrowed her eyes at the man's face. "Why are you telling me this?"

He was quiet for a long moment, eyes glazing over as he became lost in his own thoughts. Then, "I've always been loyal. Never really questioned the queen. I thought her ruthlessness was to protect the sanctity of the Realms—a peace the Blood Warriors are trying to destroy. But then..." He shook his head. "She would've let that Siphon kill every last guard in this palace just to avoid letting her go. And the ones that girl did kill? Her Majesty didn't even acknowledge their sacrifice. Wanted us to throw them in a mass grave and move on. I started to get the feeling that's the ending we're all going to face if we continue following her with unquestioned loyalty."

"It will be," Delphine confirmed. "Calla doesn't want this to be the way it goes down. She would never *want* people to die."

He nodded. "That was clear the moment she saw what her power had done, and she chose to stop."

With that, he left, and Delphine's heart began to swell with admiration for Calla. If only she had her friend's patience for those who wronged her. But then, people like Reniel and Ramor would still be alive, and she much preferred the weight of the world on her shoulders without them in it.

"Ah, well." Delphine shrugged to herself. "I'll work on killing my enemies less in my next life maybe."

When she was sure she was alone, she reached down into the cleavage of her dress and removed the Obsidian Key from where she'd stuck it to her skin with sap from an Ashwood tree. She turned the key over in her hands, the task made awkward with her missing finger, and counted the marks on each side for what felt like the hundredth time. Fifteen on the completed side, and eight on the other. It only had seven uses left—soon to be six. But she couldn't bring herself to be upset about this one. Not when the key had already given her the entire world and the alternative of not coming would've been possibly leaving her friends in the clutches of the Rouge Queen.

She took a deep breath and stuck the key into one of the iron bars, watching as it sank into the metal before turning it and making the bars evaporate into thin air. The key warmed with magic as another tally of use etched itself into the shaft. She tucked it back into place along her sternum and strutted out of the cell, searching down the dungeon's corridor. She peered into the other dark chambers for any signs of life but found nothing from her cell all the way to the end. As she headed back toward the staircase, only a couple of yards away from the exit, she heard a raspy cough.

She froze in place, slowly turning toward the cell on her right, and a pained voice whispered from the shadows, "Delphine?"

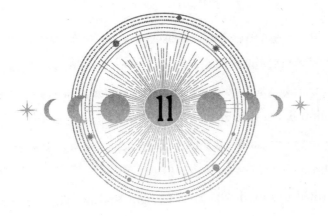

Almost an hour and a half had passed since Sabine returned with three large rocks, each bigger than Ezra's head. He worked on balancing them all in his arms while learning to open and close his wings, over and over and over. Meanwhile, Sabine was sitting atop a boulder a few feet away, grooming herself.

Ezra's task was so grueling that after the first thirty or so minutes, his body had already been begging for him to stop. Fortunately, the beast that had been prowling beneath his skin must have been satisfied with its earlier display because it seemed to be back on its leash deep inside his core. Unfortunately, the side effects from said display seemed to be permanent. His back was so sore that he had half a mind to cut the damn appendages off so he didn't have to worry about them. Instead, he'd pushed through. Deciding to distract himself by making conversation.

"So has Amina always been so uptight?" he started.

Sabine snorted. "Yes. I'm the easygoing one."

"Somehow that doesn't shock me, harpy." Ezra flicked his eyes over to her, lingering a second too long on the angles of her pretty face. The wicked glint in her pale green eyes seemed to shine brighter.

"Are you nervous about seeing your friends again?" she asked.

His brows lifted. "Why would I be nervous?"

She tilted her head. "Because I might find out you're not the hot prince?"

He wrinkled his nose at her, though he could feel the corners of his mouth itching to curl upward. "Never in my life have I suggested I was *hot* in the first place."

"No, that was me," she allowed, flicking her eyes up and down his figure. "Though you need a haircut. I could give you one, if you want."

He glanced down at the dark strands of his hair, which now reached just past his shoulders and *were* becoming a bit unruly. Still, he shot her an indignant look and said, "There is no way I'm letting you near my head with a knife."

"So you *can* catch on quick." She let out a delighted laugh. "All right, what about worrying that your friends will decide to let you die again instead of cooperating with a bunch of Valkyries?"

"I don't worry about that. If that's what they decide, I can't exactly blame them. The three of you surely aren't up to anything *good*, or you would have admitted what the details are by now, aside from using me to get them to *cooperate*."

She shrugged. "Fair."

"And we've all already made our peace with my death anyway."

She tilted her head. "What do you mean you all made peace with it? How would you know how they feel about it?"

He hesitated. It wasn't that revealing Calla and Gideon's trip to the Valley of Souls would necessarily cause any harm, but he wasn't sure he trusted her enough to discuss something as intimate as his last moments with his brother and his . . . whatever Calla was to him.

Ex felt too casual for what they'd been through together—considering she'd crossed multiple planes of existence for him—but it was fitting enough.

Sabine leaned forward eagerly. "Tell me."

He sighed. *What harm could it do?*

"Wait, wait, wait." Her hands paused their combing in her hair when he finished divulging everything that had happened between Amina taking his heart and putting a different one in its place. "The Blood Warrior is your ex-girlfriend? Isn't she soul-bonded to your brother now? Amina told us that's why she had to take your heart instead of his."

"Yep," he confirmed.

Sabine's interest seemed to be especially piqued now. "So when you say you all had made peace with your death . . . does that mean, now that you're back, you don't think you and her will—"

"*No.* We both got our closure. In fact, I'm hoping she and Gideon have stopped being hardheaded and are . . . whatever they've decided to be by now. Especially considering the turn everything is about to take when they get here and have to deal with all of *you*," he answered before finally heaving the rocks in his arms to the ground. "*Hells.* This is not fun. Flying better be worth all of this."

"It is," she said quietly.

A pang shot through his belly at the fleeting look of mourning in her eyes. It had taken a single glance at the mess of her severed wings back in the Neverending Forest for him to know he wouldn't be arguing about carrying her out of that Godsforsaken place. It'd been the least he could do, if he was honest.

Ezra cleared his throat now. "Thank you, by the way. I should've said it before. I know what you did was an enormous sacrifice."

The wicked glint in her eyes quickly returned, and she tilted her nose up at him. "As if I did it for *you*, witch. But, hey, if you want to show me how *thankful* you are, you could let me rip yours off."

He felt the corners of his lips curl up at her indignant dismissal of his gratitude. She was a sharp one. Her tongue was cutting; her edges, rough. And it amused him greatly. She was a challenge—one that he suspected not many survived. A fact that most likely thrilled her. It certainly intrigued him.

Maybe because he'd already met death at the hands of one Valkyrie, but he found himself rather unafraid to do it again. Especially because he suspected in *this* one's hands it'd at least be fun.

"I'll keep that in mind, harpy" was all he returned as he stretched out the soreness in his limbs.

Before Sabine could continue her poking, Amina suddenly landed back in the clearing. Ezra was once again miffed by how the woman could move so quietly. Amina gave him and his wings a once-over, frowning a bit. Then she turned to Sabine.

"Change of plans," Amina announced. "You need to bring him into the Dragonwoods. The witches are planning to split up before they get here."

Sabine straightened up. "But we won't be able to maim them in the Dragonwoods—"

"What a shame," Ezra interrupted with dry amusement.

Sabine bared her teeth at him. "Be careful, Prince, or I'll take it out on *you*."

Ezra smiled back at her. "Do your worst, harpy. I'm not scared of you."

Sabine's expression didn't falter, but the wicked twinkle in her eyes grew.

"Enough," Amina hissed at them both. "*Gods*, directing the two of you together is like herding cats. You're right, Sabine, we won't have the ability to threaten them in the Dragonwoods with pain like we do here, but that's where our previous discussion . . . about your new abilities . . . will come into play."

Sabine flicked her gaze up and down Ezra. "Excellent. No complaints from me, then."

Ezra's eyes narrowed at them both. "I don't know what the two of you have up your sleeves, but have you ever considered the fact that I just won't go?"

"Oh, you'll go," Sabine purred, her tone turning saccharine.

Ezra's skin began to prick with anticipation, something in his core buzzing at the sound of her sickly sweet tone. He wanted to resist the feeling but found that he couldn't. It was oddly disorienting.

Amina huffed a laugh at the change in Ezra's demeanor before quickly sobering and telling Sabine, "You need to get moving *now*. Lyra and I will go ahead, but your feet better move as quickly as possible behind us."

"Yeah, yeah." Sabine waved a hand at her friend in dismissal. "We'll be right behind you."

Amina gave a single sharp nod before taking off once more. Sabine patted herself down to make sure all the weapons hidden on her person were situated and then threw him a look that said *Let's go*. And damn it if he didn't follow her into the forest without a single protest. He told himself that it was because he was eager to be reunited with his friends—despite the inevitable hostage situation he was about to be engaged in—but deep down he knew it was something more. Something worse.

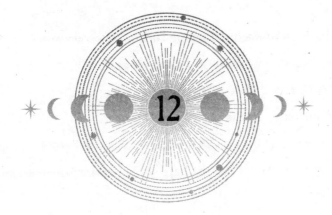

12

The last person in the world Delphine expected to see in Myrea's dungeon was Kestrel Whitehollow. But there the commander was, sitting against the far wall of the wide-open cell, drenched in darkness. His hair had been chopped off, making the angles of his face even more severe than before. His clothing was dirty and torn; his eyes, haunted as they stared back at her. She strutted toward him, crossing her arms over her chest as she paused a foot away from his outstretched limbs.

"What in the Hells are you doing in here?" she questioned. "Did you finally piss off the others so bad they decided to leave you here?"

He gave a single sharp laugh. "Long fucking story. What are *you* doing here?"

"I escaped the Siren's Sea and was told Hannah and Calla had been brought to Myrea. I came to rescue them."

"Well, no need for rescuing. They all made it out," he told her.

"Lysandra is undoubtedly tracking Gideon down as we speak, though. Only a matter of time until she finds him again."

Delphine raised a brow. "Lysandra was here, too?"

"You missed quite the showdown."

"Why wouldn't the Onyx Queen take you with her?" Delphine narrowed her eyes. "Aren't you in charge of her entire army or something like that?"

"Something like that," he murmured, eyes becoming glassy. "She ordered me to stay here until she gave word for me to leave. She didn't want me to go back to the Onyx Realm and find a way to cause discord or suspicion among the Guild. This way, she can pretend I'm still giving the orders while I'm away in hopes they won't notice anything is off."

Delphine gave a low whistle. "A lot has changed."

"The understatement of the century."

"If she ordered you to stay, and you're obeying"—Delphine glanced to the unobstructed opening of the cell—"your Rolls of Fate—"

He wrenched back the left sleeve of his shirt to show her his numbers. "Completed."

Delphine cursed. She didn't understand the full scope of the witches' situation, or the Fates' War, but she knew Kestrel's completed set of rolls meant that he was now on the opposing side. Along with Hannah. But unlike Hannah, Kestrel was highly trained for destruction and leading legions of witches. He was not an enemy anyone wanted to have.

"Whatever you're thinking," he answered her unspoken thoughts, "it's so much worse than that. You need to go find them. Tell them I'm going to do everything I can not to end up across from them on that battlefield, but if I do—they need to kill me the first chance they get."

Delphine was silent for a long minute as she looked down at the commander. She wasn't sure what had transpired since she'd been absent, but something about him was different. A sadness had replaced the anger that used to simmer beneath the surface. She almost felt pity for him. Almost.

"Do you know where they went?" she finally asked.

Kestrel shrugged. "If Gideon and Caspian learned anything from me, they went somewhere neutral—the Dragonwoods, most likely. They're close enough, and the queens wouldn't be able to outright attack them there. But they were still pretty set on going to find you, so you might want to hurry before you miss them again."

She gave him a nod and turned on her heel to leave.

"Siren?"

She glanced back over her shoulder.

"Promise me you'll tell them to kill me," he demanded. "Promise you'll do it yourself if you have to."

She gave him a solemn smile. "Don't worry. I will."

His desperate stare followed her all the way out of the dungeon, until she slinked up the steps and slipped out on the main floor of the palace. As she made her way out of the castle, leaving trails of blood where necessary, she felt the weight of her vow settle in her core like a rock. Because it was true—if she had to take Kestrel out herself, she absolutely would. But for the first time, she was facing the realization that he was not the only one who might ask her to perform that act.

And while she would eradicate Kestrel without a second thought, she was afraid it wouldn't even matter at the end of the day. Because she'd burn the rest of the world down before she'd let anyone harm Hannah. No matter what side that would place her on.

Calla and Hannah spent their last meal together yards away from the others, barely able to talk. The *meal* aspect was nearly as nonexistent as their words, considering both of them could hardly stomach to eat at a time like this.

"I hate this," Hannah eventually whispered.

"Me too," Calla agreed, shifting forward to grab the other girl's hands between hers. "It's going to be okay. We're going to be okay. You're going to find Delphine, and then the two of you will head off into the sunset, as far away from the Witch Realms as physically possible. Another continent if you can."

Hannah's eyes widened. "Delphine and I are not going to leave you to fight alone, Calla."

"You can't be near Myrea, Han. She could make you do heinous things—"

"We're going to figure it out," Hannah inserted, voice surprisingly firm. "But I will not cower away while you fight for the future of our people and the Realms."

Calla wanted to argue, but she didn't think she should. Hannah could make her own choices, and Calla was hardly one to talk about putting herself in unnecessarily dangerous situations.

"I'm sorry I didn't mention anything before, about my aversion to Gideon. It all got out of hand so quickly," Hannah said after a beat of silence.

Calla gave her friend a smile. "I know. I promise no one is holding it against you. I've just been so worried. You kept avoiding us, and I thought maybe... you were disappointed in me."

Hannah's eyes widened, their depthless black turning glassy. "Calla, what in the world could I ever be disappointed in you for?"

"Moving on too quickly? Falling in love during such a treacherous time while our friend is out there somewhere, possibly hurt?" Calla recited absentmindedly.

"What did you just say?" Hannah asked, a shocked giggle falling from her lips.

Calla's eyes widened. "I—I—"

Hannah's smile softened. "Calla, I would never ever be disappointed in you for being happy. And at least one of us shouldn't have a tragic love story."

"Yours won't be tragic," Calla swore. "You're going to get Delphine back. And you're going to tell her how you feel. Finally."

"Are you going to tell Gideon?" Hannah wondered.

Calla took a deep breath. "I don't know. It's hard for the timing to exactly feel right with everything going on."

"Screw perfect timing," Hannah said, surprisingly firm. "You should tell him. Before it's too late. Don't make the same mistakes I have."

"It feels too soon, too selfish," Calla whispered. "I don't want to say it until I know we're both going to make it out of this."

Before Hannah could respond, they caught Caspian cautiously approaching.

"Sorry," he told them. "But we should get going before the sun starts going down. And it looks like it might rain."

The girls nodded in sync before turning to wrap each other up in a tight embrace.

"I love you," Calla whispered in Hannah's ear.

Hannah sniffed. "I love you, too."

When they finally pulled apart, Cass and Thorne were up and ready, Gideon still standing back to give Hannah some distance.

"All right, Thorne thinks we should go all the way south and see if we can find a ship to take us to Estrella through the Celestial Sea instead of going through the Realms. And I have to agree—"

A sudden gust of wind rolled through the tops of the trees, cutting off Caspian's words. The five of them shielded their eyes from the falling debris as they looked toward the sky to see two winged beings dropping like angels out of the heavens. But the moment they landed, it was clear they were no angels.

"We aren't interrupting, are we?" the Valkyrie asked with a pleased smile.

Amina, Calla recalled her name. The woman looked just as sharp and lovely as Calla remembered, but this time there seemed to be less prowess in her eyes and more . . . regard? Especially when she turned her eyes on Cass.

"Did you miss me, witch?" Amina teased. "I've heard quite the tales about you since we last met. You've been busy, haven't you?"

"What are you doing here, Valkyrie?" Caspian asked, his expression guarded, his stance ready for a fight. In fact, every single one of them was braced for a fight—except for Thorne. Who looked as casual and unperturbed as always.

"Caspian Ironside," Amina purred as she turned to face him fully. "The stories I've heard about you have been very intriguing."

Caspian lifted a silvery brow. "You've been asking about me? Cute. I suppose I made quite the impression. Though I always do."

Amina's expression soured at his hubris, but before she could offer a retort, her companion lost their patience.

"Amina," the golden-eyed Valkyrie carped.

Amina glanced back at the other Valkyrie, and they all watched as the two exchanged a wordless conversation. The new Valkyrie was dressed like a midnight sky. An impeccably tailored silk coatdress in a stunning navy color embellished with diamonds that covered their lithe, muscled frame. Their auburn hair had a fawn undertone that complimented their deep complexion perfectly, and Calla was beginning to wonder if being lethally stunning was a trait all Valkyries shared.

Amina turned back to the group. "Lyra and I have come with an ultimatum."

Calla couldn't help it, she laughed. Out of the corner of her eye, she saw Gideon's jaw clench as he glared at the Valkyries' audacity.

"In what world would we ever take an ultimatum from you?" he demanded. "You stole Ezra from us, and we're tired of letting others play with our lives. Leave us the fuck alone."

"Is it really my fault that *you* were foolish enough to offer your heart up in the first place?" Amina quipped.

That made Calla's blood boil, but before she could counter, a pair of viselike arms wrapped around her waist and pulled her back. Caspian.

"Don't let her rile you up," he said soothingly. "That's what she wants."

Amina gave him a taunting smile. "Actually, what I want is for you stubborn fools to *listen* to me for once."

"That might be easier if you stopped insulting us," Calla suggested.

Lyra snorted, then shrugged. "That seems fair enough. Amina?"

Amina rolled her eyes before flicking them back to Calla's face, searching it for something. "You've changed."

Calla's nose wrinkled. "Constantly fighting for your life and losing everyone you love will do that to a person. Now, could you just tell us what in the Hells you want so we can all go our separate ways?"

"Without anyone losing a heart this time," Caspian added.

"All right, I'm starting to get the feeling you all know each other," Thorne commented.

"Oh, Thorne," Hannah pitied.

Amina ignored them as she told Calla, "This is really your business, girl. Are you sure you want to do this in front of everyone? I have a feeling there will be a lot of conflicting opinions."

Calla glanced over at Gideon.

"It's your decision. If you want to speak with them alone, we'll give you the space," he told her, though his lips were so tight she was surprised he got the words out.

Calla looked back to Amina and shook her head. "Spit it out."

Amina picked at her nails. "Fine then. We need you to come with us to see our queen. Within the next twenty-four hours. That part is nonnegotiable."

Calla felt Gideon's blood pressure spike through their bond and instantly knew she should've taken the Valkyrie up on speaking privately.

"You're not taking her anywhere," Gideon snarled, his tone shifting into *that* voice. The one that left no room for arguing.

Amina's amber eyes became strangely cloudy for a moment at Gideon's refusal, but she quickly recovered and said, "It's not really up to you, Prince."

"Why would you need Calla to go to your queen?" Hannah questioned.

"As it turns out, you're not the only ones the Fates' War is going to devastate," Amina answered. "And we currently have a bit of a situation on our hands. Our queen has requested we bring her the final Blood

Warrior by tomorrow—or else innocent people will begin to die."

Caspian scoffed. "Ironic, since it didn't seem like you were too concerned about innocent people dying when you killed our friend."

"See, we thought you might bring that up"—Amina nodded—"but I implore you to remember I only kept up my end of his bargain." She jabbed a finger in Gideon's direction.

Lyra and Thorne were watching the entire back-and-forth in rapt silence. Trying to put all the missing pieces together in their minds. Every now and then, Thorne would lean down to whisper a question to Hannah, who would provide him with a quiet explanation, and Calla noticed now that Lyra had been inching closer and closer to the pair in order to overhear the hushed conversations. Where Amina was bright and bold, like lightning, Lyra seemed to be as stealthy as a shadow. Which meant the latter was undoubtedly the one to keep an eye on.

"What exactly does the Valkyrie Queen want with me?" Calla asked.

Amina tilted her head, her voluminous curls bouncing with the movement. "That I don't know. But if I had to venture a guess? She wants to use you as a bargaining chip with either the Fates or the Witch Queens."

"The Fates?" Calla blanched. "What does she have to do with the Fates?"

"That's where the story gets *really* interesting," Lyra inserted. "Your queens aren't the only ones with a Godly contract. Or with everything to lose in the coming war."

The group exchanged loaded looks. Every day this war became

more complicated. There were too many players. Too many sides. And too little time to untangle the threads in order to decide exactly where they all needed to be standing the day it began.

"Sorry," Calla finally said. "But I will not walk right into a trap. Good luck with whatever part you're playing in this war, but we have enough on our plates."

Amina didn't look put out in the slightest. "And this is where our ultimatum comes in."

"Even if Calla went to your queen, it wouldn't stop anything," Gideon argued. "This war is coming whether any of us like it or not."

"We realize," Lyra agreed. "All you have to do to complete our request is be brought to Ignia. After that, you're free to do whatever you'd like. Honestly, if you knew the full scope of the situation, you may find that we may be able to help each other."

Amina started a bit at her friend's last suggestion, but Calla could see she would not challenge them. Not in front of the group, at least.

"Well, unless you're threatening to kill us—which we all know you can't on this land—it looks like we've reached an impasse," Gideon stated dryly.

Lyra met his eyes. "Death is not always the worst thing, Prince."

As those words hung between all of them, something that sounded like footsteps began to approach through the trees.

"What now?" Caspian murmured.

Amina grinned. "Our ultimatum has arrived."

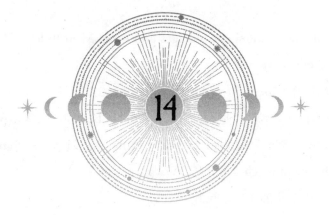

14

Apricot was approaching the end of her rope, and so was Delphine. Her inner thighs were screaming in pain from riding the past two days, and she was tired of seeing nothing but trees and having no one to talk to.

All Delphine wanted to do was complain about how badly her body was aching and how terrible she was at foraging for. In fact, she was so tired of having no one to talk to that she actually *missed* the time she was traveling with Ezra and Kestrel—but there was only so much conversation someone could have with a horse. Most of all, she was desperately tired of missing Hannah and Calla.

"They went north," the dragon-shifter told her, shaking her out of her thoughts.

"How long ago?" she pressed.

"Half a day, maybe?" he said, his ruby eyes tracing up the bare skin of her exposed leg beneath the split of her dress. "They were causing too much chaos among the villages and were asked to leave. You just missed them."

"Shocking," she muttered beneath her breath.

The shifter's eyes traveled up the rest of her body now, his expression appreciative. "Wouldn't expect a pretty thing like you to be wrapped up in the drama of witches and Valkyries."

Valkyries? Shit, she thought.

"But if *you* need a place to rest for the night, I'd be happy to show you my bed," he offered.

Ignoring the offer, she tapped her foot against Apricot's side and directed the mare onward. If this had been any other territory—particularly one where she could use her claws—this outcome would look much different. But perhaps this was the universe trying to tell her there had been enough blood on her hands lately. She'd have to find a way to return to her more civil self, and less of the monster the Siren's Sea had made her, if she wanted to find her place with her girls again.

Less death, she swore to herself. *Hannah wouldn't like it.*

15

As Ezra kept up on Sabine's heels, he couldn't help but rake his eyes over her back, where he now saw new wings had begun to sprout. Brown tufts of down were sticking out in every direction, and he found himself thinking it was . . . cute. Something she would surely gut him for if he said aloud.

So instead he said, "How long do you think it will take for me to get airborne? And do you think this new magic means I'm truly a dragon-shifter? Or am I some sort of strange undead witch-shifter hybrid?"

She didn't answer.

He made a sound of annoyance. "You know, the least you could do if you're luring me into some sort of trap is not leave me alone with my own thoughts. I had enough of that in the Valley of Souls. Do you have any idea how lonely it is in the afterlife? Just an eternity of walking as you relive memory after memory. And then you all bring me back and cannot even keep decent company?"

More silence.

Ezra narrowed his eyes and upped his pace, sliding up next to her and checking her shoulder with his own. "Are you even listening, harpy?"

Sabine's gaze snapped over to him, as if he'd startled her. "When did you start talking?"

"I swear to the Gods," he started, but the sound of voices ahead made him pause.

"Oh good," Sabine said with relief. "We're just in time."

"Just in time for *wh*—"

Sabine shoved him forward, and with the new weight hanging at his back, he nearly fell as he stumbled through the trees. As he straightened, spinning around to tear into that damned harpy, a cacophony of gasps resounded through the clearing behind him. Sabine raised a golden brow and smirked.

"*Ezra?*" someone gasped. Someone familiar. Someone whose voice he'd recognized even in death.

Ezra turned to face her, a smile unfurling on his face. "Hello, Calla. Brother. Good thing you both didn't sacrifice anything to get me back from the afterlife, huh?"

Ezra saw Lyra and Amina looking smug over Calla's and Gideon's shoulders while Caspian and a very unrecognizable Hannah gaped at him in disbelief. They all stared at one another like that for such a long time that Sabine began to shift on her feet with impatience.

"Did any of you even like each other?" Sabine huffed. "This is the most boring reunion ever."

At that, Calla broke away from the others and ran toward him. It was always Calla meeting him halfway. And as he opened his arms to fold her into his own embrace, he felt a deep sense of peace.

"I can't believe you're here," she whispered.

"Me either," he murmured as he pulled back.

Calla's eyes widened. "Are those *wings*? What in the Hells?"

"Yeah, we're going to need a point-by-point explanation of what the fuck is going on," Caspian said as he approached next. "But first..."

Calla stepped aside so Cass could lift Ezra in his own hug. Ezra grunted at the tightness of the man's grip but didn't complain.

"It's so fucking nice to see you again, Ez," Cass said.

Ezra smirked. "I think that might be the first time anyone has ever said that to me."

Sabine snorted behind them, and he shot her a playful glare.

As his brother stepped forward, Ezra knew things would be different this time around. And everything he'd been through was worth it, a million times over, to have the relationship he'd always longed for with his brother.

Gideon reached out to give Ezra's shoulders an affectionate squeeze. "I'd thank the fucking Gods to have you back, but I'm pretty sure for once they had nothing to do with it."

"That is correct, Prince," Sabine inserted as she stepped up on Ezra's left, right across from Calla, whom she was eyeing with a dangerous sort of curiosity. "But if you want to show *me* your gratefulness, I have a few ideas in mind...."

Gideon's brows rose at Ezra in question.

Ezra sighed. "She sacrificed her wings in order to summon my soul back. I suspect that will be held over our heads until the end of time."

"Correct," Sabine confirmed with a pleased grin.

Ezra tensed as Calla gave Sabine a once-over. Until this moment, he hadn't truly allowed himself to believe this reunion would come. Had mostly expected the Valkyries were playing some sort of sadistic game with him. But now that they were all here together, he was forced to face how oddly comfortable he'd gotten around Sabine and the others, and how uncomfortable their two worlds colliding could easily become.

"So you're the Blood Warrior?" Sabine asked Calla.

"Yes" was all Calla said.

"Ezra said the two of you used to be together," Sabine continued.

Gideon and Ezra both shifted awkwardly, a detail that did not go unnoticed by the Valkyrie, but it was Calla's reaction they were all waiting on.

Calla raised her brows, cautious of where this was going. "Yes."

"How in the Hells did you manage to tolerate his mouth?" Sabine huffed. "He always has something to say."

Calla stifled a laugh. "Tell me about it."

"Where's Delphine? She'll be so disappointed to have missed this," Ezra muttered.

"*More* ex-girlfriends?" Sabine questioned.

Ezra nearly choked. "Delphine is not my ex. In fact, I think she'd have threatened to rip your tongue out for saying that."

"She most definitely would have," a soft voice agreed.

Ezra looked past the group to Hannah, who was standing next to a tall man he'd never seen before. Her new pitch-black eyes were unsettling enough to make his skin pebble, and when he took a step closer to her, raising his hand in greeting, she flinched.

Ezra's brows furrowed as he took another step closer. "What's wrong?"

Hannah nearly doubled over now, the man next to her having to wrap an arm around her waist to keep her upright.

"Oh no," Calla said as she ran over to the girl. "Ezra's making it worse, isn't he?"

Hannah moaned as she nodded.

"Well, that confirms things. Take her away from here, Thorne," Calla ordered. "Once we get things situated, Caspian will let you know."

Thorne nodded, bending down to scoop the little witch up into his arms to whisk her away from the clearing as fast as possible.

"What's going on?" Ezra asked. "What's wrong with Hannah?"

"You mean that wasn't a normal reaction to your presence?" Sabine asked.

"Settle down, harpy," Ezra shot back. "Don't forget who spent days carrying you across the continent when you could barely walk."

Sabine's cheeks heated, pink flushing all the way to the tips of her ears, and she snapped her teeth at him as her hands twitched to grab the hilt of the dagger at her hips. It was always her first instinct to attack, but she couldn't cause anyone physical harm here. A fact she clearly remembered, as she dropped her hands and stomped over to stand between Lyra and Amina, glaring holes through his body.

A slight pang of guilt went through his stomach as he watched her disappear. He hadn't meant to embarrass her, knew she had only been teasing, but even with how little time they'd spent together, he knew she was a prideful being.

"Oh, for Hells sake, we're wasting too much time," Amina declared as she broke into the center of the group. "Listen up, we don't have time for an entire history lesson, so let's get all the facts straight now."

Gideon crossed his arms over his chest. "All right, Valkyrie. Say your piece."

"We resurrected Ezra using the heart of a dragon-shifter, which had a few side effects, as I'm sure you can see. If you want his actual heart back, it's in our queen's castle—which will be returned if you choose to follow us home. In exchange for the Blood Warrior, you get Ezra. No strings attached. As soon as the Siphon is brought to Ignia, our task is fulfilled, and you are free to do whatever you want afterward. Kill the bitch, even. In fact, if you're inclined to do so, we'll assist."

"But we already have Ezra," Calla stated.

"Do you?" Amina asked. "Sabine? Would you like to demonstrate?"

Sabine's smile turned vicious as she lifted her hand and curled a finger at him. "Come here, Ezra."

Ezra gave her an indignant look, ready to tell her that he could not be beckoned like a dog, but something strange was happening in his body that made the words dissolve on his tongue. There was an ominous vibration in his body, spreading through him like fire, and the next thing he knew, he was walking toward her.

"*Ezra,*" Gideon said, a demand in his tone. "*Don't.*"

Despite the potency of Sabine's call, the trance nearly broke at his brother's order. But when the Valkyrie crooned at him to continue toward her, he found that there was no resisting.

Calla's expression hovered between shock and fury as Ezra reached Sabine's side. "What the fuck is happening?"

"To summon a soul from the Valley of Souls using Valkyrie feathers, one would need an entire wingspan's worth," Amina explained, summoning her wings and plucking out one of the large brown feathers to hold before them. "Not an easy feat to gather that many. It's why beings like our dear friend the Witch Eater take them as payment and hoard them for decades, centuries, in hopes to gain enough to perform such a ritual. When a Valkyrie sacrifices their own wings to summon a soul, however"—Amina reached over to tuck her feather behind Sabine's ear in an affectionate gesture—"their reward is influence over the resurrected soul. Not even *your* influence could break Sabine's hold, Prince."

The way she spoke about Gideon's influence made it seem as though it was something more than brotherly loyalty, but if anyone knew exactly what that meant, no one said anything. Ezra was trying to fight through the strange buzzing in his veins, but truthfully, he was exhausted. Whatever power Sabine wielded over him was definitely as strong as Amina claimed. Ezra shifted his gaze to Sabine's face, and she smiled, unapologetic.

"Nicely played, harpy," Ezra whispered to her. "And just when I was starting to think I genuinely enjoyed your company. At least this makes more sense."

An emotion he couldn't quite name flitted through her jade eyes, but she said nothing as she turned her attention back to Amina, jaw clenched.

"So Calla will come with us. Or you can say goodbye to the young Onyx Prince for the second time," Amina offered.

Calla, Gideon, and Cass exchanged loaded looks.

Ezra already knew what their decision would be, so he said, "Let them kill me. Death doesn't scare me anymore anyway."

"As I've said before, death is not the worst thing," Lyra told him. "We would not kill you, but you definitely will wish we had by the end of it."

"If I go with you, you said I only have to meet the queen, correct?" Calla questioned. "After that we are free to go and you'll leave us, and Ezra, alone forevermore?"

"Well, there are no promises of *that*," Amina said. "Not with the way things seem to be going with this war. You might find that you need our help."

"And you would help us?" Caspian scoffed at her.

Amina looked slightly perturbed at the implication that she was not honorable enough to do so. "If helping meant we found an audience with the Fates to break our queen's contract with them—yes."

"And what does the Valkyrie Queen's contract consist of?" Cass pressed.

Before the Valkyries could give him an answer, however, the ground beneath their feet began to rumble.

"Don't tell me this is another Godsdamned earthquake?" Calla exclaimed as they all braced themselves.

Then Thorne came bursting through the trees, chest heaving with effort as beads of sweat slid down his temples.

"Hannah," he gasped at them. "She . . . she . . ."

"Spit it out, witch," Amina demanded.

"Her magic erupted," he finally said. "She's about to summon every dead creature in this forest."

16

Long before Delphine felt the first tremors beneath her, Apricot had become apprehensive the farther north they traveled. At first, Delphine thought the mare was wary of the dragon-shifters she likely sensed around them. Something to do with being spooked by the presence of larger predators. But when the air around them began to smell like char and the ground started to shake, Delphine realized something was very wrong.

As the rumbling grew, Apricot whinnied in fear and tried to turn around, ripping her reins out of Delphine's hands with the effort. Delphine scrambled to grab a fistful of the horse's mane as she cooed to the beast, trying to settle her, but Apricot refused to go forward a step more. And when tendrils of inky-black fog began to swirl around them, the horse reared onto her hind legs and bucked Delphine clean off.

Delphine hit the ground with a heavy *thud*, groaning as Apricot bolted away. Small black spots peppered her vision as she pushed herself up, her nose burning as the scent of dark magic grew stronger. There was a shout in the distance, but she couldn't quite make out what it was saying.

Delphine heaved herself back to her feet and started forward—toward the danger. She knew she should have been as spooked as the horse by the clear display of treacherous power bleeding through the forest around her, but something urged her to get a closer look.

Then she heard another shout. And this time the word was loud and clear. A single name.

Hannah.

Before she knew what was happening, Delphine was flying toward the shouting—toward Hannah. Hannah. *Hannah.* She ran until her lungs burned, until she could barely see from the writhing, shadowlike tendrils of magic clogging up the air.

"Hannah! You have to stop!"

It was Calla's voice. A sob nearly cracked open Delphine's chest as she pushed herself even faster.

I'm coming. Please don't move. I'm almost home.

17

A biting chill clung all around Hannah. The witch hanging by his wrists to her right was long dead, having passed hours ago, when the dark magic had melted his flesh from his bones and he had been too exhausted to regenerate. The witch to her left was still holding on, but barely, which meant it was up to her to complete this ritual. The full moon glared at her from above, as if admonishing her for participating in this insidious evening.

But she had no choice. Her mother was resolute in tonight's cause. Reanimating someone who would fetch them a "small fortune" from a high-profile trader who wanted to refuse a soul with the body. She'd failed during the previous month's ritual, and if she failed this time, she didn't think she'd survive it—by her mother's hands or the magic.

Tears slipped down her face as she pulled at the dark power weaving in her core. Chalked runes on the ground and the witch-hazel concoction still dripping over her skin supplied her with the energy she needed to transform her Rouge magic into necromancy magic. Her skin pulled taut with the effort, and her bones stretched and popped until she thought she might pass out. But when she had created and gathered enough of the magic, she unleashed it once again. An inky substance leaked from every one of her pores, sending snaking wisps of charred power through the air and toward the half-assembled pile of bones on the ground beneath her.

The earth began to shake. And Hannah began to scream.

A hoarse guttural sound from deep in her chest as her skin tore apart and stitched itself back together, the magic passing through her corroding body. But the earthquake only grew stronger, and that meant it was working. Finally.

"Yes, Hannah," her mother's voice encouraged from somewhere in the distance. "Push harder!"

"I can't," Hannah choked. "Mother, it will kill me—"

"Push harder," her mother hissed, a monstrous warning beneath the words.

Blood began to run down Hannah's arms, and she blinked up at where her wrists were bound together, the rope cutting so deep that her flesh had been rubbed raw. She saw the spiderweb of black veins that stretched from her fingertips to her elbows, and she knew if she didn't stop soon, her transformation into a full necromancer would be complete and there would be no going back.

"I can't," she cried. "I can't. I can't."

The ground continued to shake; the witch to her left groaned in agony, but Hannah didn't even have enough energy to turn her head and check if they were okay.

"*Yes! It's close, so close,*" her mother growled. "*Keep going!*"

I revoke this magic, Hannah thought. This is not what I want.

Then make a choice, a voice whispered in her mind.

Hannah startled, her eyes wildly searching around her for who might have spoken to her. But there was no one there other than her mother and the witch.

Who's there? she thought.

If you continue on this way, you will die, they spoke again.

"I know," she whispered aloud.

But if you choose to, you can lock this magic away and deny her access, the voice said.

"How?" she questioned, too exhausted to determine whether this hallucination was real or not.

Deep breath.

She obeyed.

Recall all your power into your core, shape it all into a tight, neat little ball.

So she did. Sucking back in the shadowy tendrils of dark magic, knotting it into a tangle of power inside of her.

"What's happening?" her mother demanded. "What are you doing?"

Hannah ignored the woman. Focusing only on gathering every last speck of magic inside of her.

What about my Rouge magic? she thought. I cannot separate it.

That's because there's not much of it left. The dark magic is eating it away.

Hannah sucked in a shaky breath. No. Her magic was everything to her.

It's already nearly gone. Lock it all away now and one day reconcile that the magic you have access to is not necessarily what you want but it's what you've got. Or lose everything now.

Hannah mustered up every last ounce of energy she had, and she made a choice.

The shaking earth beneath her was silenced a moment later, but her mother's screams of fury seemed to continue for hours.

18

Delphine burst through the trees into an actual nightmare.

Hannah was lying on the ground, black veins spiderwebbing across her ivory skin. Her hands clutched the earth, her wide eyes a depthless, unseeing abyss as they stared at the maelstrom of dark magic swirling above her. The loud, crackling roar of power that consumed her ears was almost painful and easily drowned out the sounds of the forest.

Worst of all, hundreds of decaying hands were clawing their way out of the ground.

Despite the fear threatening to seize her, Delphine didn't hesitate to plunge herself into the darkness.

"Hannah!" she called out, but she could barely hear her own voice.

Skeletal hands swiped at her ankles, ripping into her flesh as they tried to use her to pull themselves out of the ground. They tore at the hem of her skirt, nearly tripping her in stride, but she gritted her teeth and kept going. Bile rose in her throat as the dark magic around her became suffocating—almost as if it were thick electrified smoke.

When Delphine finally reached Hannah, her friend's torso had been torn open by the insidious raw magic. Decaying hands were grabbing at her sides, trying to drag her beneath the dirt. Delphine dropped to her knees, hands hovering over the open cavity of Hannah's chest, as if she could somehow protect Hannah's exposed heart. Except there was nothing to protect. Not when the ink-like power seemed to be coming from the organ itself.

Delphine began to yank the undead hands, tossing aside the macabre appendages as they broke away. When her fingers brushed against Hannah's skin, Hannah's hand shot out at lightning speed, grasping on to Delphine's wrist in a painful grip.

"Hannah," Delphine coughed out. "Hannah, it's me!"

Hannah's hold only tightened, and Delphine swore she felt one of her tendons snap.

"*Hannah*," Delphine pleaded. "It's me, Delphine." Delphine cupped her free hand against Hannah's cheek. "Hannah, baby, it's me."

Hannah's unblinking eyes focused on Delphine's face, but the siren worried that even if she'd gotten through to Hannah, the long travel had made Delphine too unrecognizable for it to matter.

In a voice that was not her own, Hannah rasped, "Delphine?"

Delphine nearly sobbed. "Yes. Yes, I'm here."

Hannah opened her mouth to say something else, but a rageful scream tore out of her instead. Her back arched off the ground, the hand she still had clutched into the dirt digging in even further, and then she commanded the magic around them to return to her. Delphine watched in awe as the shadows began to dissipate and the bodies clawing their way free began to sink once more into the ground. The charcoal veins crawling beneath Hannah's skin pulsed with effort as the magic obeyed its orders.

When the storm was over, Hannah's chest began to mend itself as well. The skin over her heart wove itself back together as she shakily pushed herself up off the ground, until her face was inches from Delphine's.

"Delphine," she breathed, pleaded, invoked.

"Hannah." Delphine sighed, brushing a strand of hair off her friend's forehead and tucking it behind her ear. "I'm so grateful that I've found you."

The second those words left her lips, Hannah leaned forward and kissed her. Wildly, passionately, all-consumingly. Delphine was too shocked to move.

Which was just as well, because the moment Hannah broke the kiss, she lost consciousness.

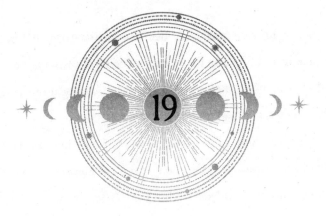

19

Calla couldn't believe her eyes. *"Delphine?"* As the tempest of dark magic dissipated, she'd expected to find Hannah and maybe an undead creature or two. Never in a million years did she think she'd find Delphine.

Delphine stood, careful not to disturb Hannah's unconscious form, and turned toward Calla. She could only imagine that the relief on Delph's face mirrored her own as they ran to each other and collided in an earth-shattering embrace.

Hot tears rolled down Calla's cheeks as she squished her friend as close as she could. "You're here."

"I'm here," Delphine confirmed with a sniffle. "I'm home."

Calla pulled back so she could see her friend's face fully. "How—"

Delphine shook her head. "We have a lot to discuss. First, we need to help Hannah."

Calla nodded and stepped out of her arms to search for Gideon.

"I'm here," he murmured as he approached from behind. Calla spun to face him, and something about seeing him made her pent-up emotions bubble to the surface all at once. A sob caught in her throat as he gently brushed the tears from her cheeks.

"Delphine . . . Hannah . . ." Calla started, but her throat was too tight to get anything out. She wasn't even sure exactly what she was trying to say. But with Gideon it didn't matter anyway.

"It's all right," he told her. "We need to get away from these bodies before—"

Delphine suddenly screeched a few feet away, cutting off the rest of his words as one of the undead hands clasped around her ankle. Gideon unsheathed a dagger from his belt and sliced it down in a quick, precise arc. The blade severed through the rotten sinew and bone, leaving Delphine to rip it up and toss it to the side with a disgusted expression.

"How are we going to stop all of this?" Calla shouted. "There's way too many for just us!"

Gideon poised himself to attack, but the decaying appendages began to shake, before going entirely limp, dead once more. It was clear that whatever magic had reanimated the bodies was slowly slipping away with Hannah's consciousness.

"A delay in the magic," Gideon spoke his suspicions aloud. He crouched down at Hannah's side and scooped her friend's limp body up into his arms. "We'll have to discuss this whole raising-the-dead-thing when Hannah is able, but for now we still have to deal with the Valkyries."

"Valkyries?" Delphine exclaimed, looking to Calla as the two of them fell into step at Gideon's side.

Calla nodded. "One of the many current complications we're dealing with. Thank the damned Gods that you're here, safe, and we can cross one more thing off our list. It's genuinely become unmanageable."

"Someone remind Ezra of that when he inevitably has something to say about me being high maintenance," Delphine quipped. "I took care of my own side quest—you're all very welcome."

Calla and Gideon exchanged a loaded look. Calla wondered if Delphine might become more amiable toward the prince when she heard about Ezra's own little detour through the afterlife.

Calla reached over and squeezed Delphine's hand. "I need you to know we never stopped thinking about you. I swear. Things have just gotten so complicated—"

"I know." Delphine squeezed her hand back. "It was better this way. I needed to sever my ties to the Siren's Sea myself to regain my freedom. And I did."

Calla slowed her steps, looking at Delphine with wide eyes. "You mean—"

Delphine twisted around, brushing her hair off her neck to show Calla her unmarked skin.

"Oh, Delphine." Calla smiled, her eyes pricking with tears, only this time they were tears of pure joy.

As they approached the others, Calla spotted Caspian pacing back and forth, the others braced for whatever might be about to come out of the woods. Calla saw there were more decaying body parts littered around her friends' feet, though most of them were noticeably smashed to pieces.

"Please tell me there isn't going to be an entire undead army about to come out of there," Thorne commented.

"Good thing we have wings," Amina muttered to Lyra.

"The magic has cleared some. Calla and Gideon must have managed to stop—" Caspian began to say before Calla and the others stepped into view, making Cass do a gasping double take.

"Hey, handsome," Delphine greeted Cass. "Glad to see *you* made it." Then she noticed Ezra and sighed. "I suppose I should say I'm glad to see you're unscathed, too, Black."

"Don't you have impeccable timing," Ezra retorted. "Actually, I've only recently returned from the Hells, though I wouldn't say unscathed."

Delphine crossed her arms over her chest with indignance. "What are you going on about?"

"Yeah, so . . ." Calla cringed. "Ezra sort of . . . died. In fact, he just found us again himself."

"Yes, way to overshadow my moment," Ezra mused.

"Wait, wait, wait"—Delphine looked around in disbelief—"there was a time I lived in a world without Ezra Black and I didn't even get to properly enjoy it?"

Ezra rolled his eyes to the sky before looking at Sabine over his shoulder. "What did I tell you?"

"Oh, don't be a baby. I'm only kidding," Delphine said. "I admit it's a little hard to take your death very seriously when you're standing right here, annoying as ever, and— Wait. Do you have *wings*?"

Delphine swung her gaze to Calla in question, but Calla could only shrug. "Something about how he was resurrected. There hasn't been much time to get into that bit."

"Speaking of time"—Amina stepped forward—"you're all wasting it. We need to go."

"Hannah shouldn't be going anywhere," Delphine argued, eyeing the Valkyrie. "She needs to rest. That magic almost shredded her to pieces."

Amina looked at Delphine, unmoved. "Good thing I wasn't talking about her. She can stay wherever the Hells you want. The only people we need to take are the Blood Warrior and Ezra. Though the latter is just collateral."

"No arguments about Ezra," Delphine said. "But no way is Calla going anywhere I'm not."

"It's okay, Delphine," Calla inserted, placing a comforting hand on her friend's shoulder. To the Valkyries she asked, "How long does it take to get to your queen's palace?"

Amina, Lyra, and Sabine exchanged glances. Then Lyra answered, "On foot—about six or seven hours."

"Can you spare an hour for all of us to regroup?" Calla prompted. "I swear I'll cooperate if you could manage to as well."

The Valkyries once again exchanged a silent conversation. And when Amina huffed out a deep sigh, Calla knew what their answer would be.

"Fine," Amina allowed. "But this is not some sort of social hour. Spit out whatever you need so we can get going."

"Before we get started," Ezra inserted, stepping forward, "does anyone have a shirt I can borrow?"

☽ ☽ ☽ ● ☾ ☾ ☾

Much to Amina's impatience, it looked like it was going to take more than just an hour for each person to recount the events of the past several weeks in turn. They had formed a circle on the ground in a way that reminded Calla of her childhood, when the kids in her coven would form similar formations for their lessons or to play games. The Valkyries sat on one side, along with Ezra, who noticeably chose a seat not too far away from Sabine. Calla wasn't sure if it was because of the strange hold the Valkyrie had over him or something else.

Delphine was wrapping up her tales from the Siren's Sea now, ending with the revelation that she'd seen Kestrel—*alive*—on her way through the Rouge Realm to get back to them. Calla placed a comforting hand on Gideon's as he took in the information. Kestrel sitting in Myrea's dungeon wasn't exactly good news, but at least he was alive.

"Speaking of the Guild..." Amina changed course at the mention of the commander. "We heard something quite interesting about your little... project with the Onyx Queen's army."

Caspian narrowed his eyes at the Valkyrie. "Is that how you learned my name?"

Amina gave him a taunting smile. "You've been very busy, treasonous little witches."

"If you spoke to anyone about our plans, we're all fucked," Caspian snapped. "We've spent *years* setting everything up—"

"Don't have a tantrum." Sabine snorted. "We had to threaten that information out of someone. No one's running around telling your business unprompted."

Caspian and Gideon both sighed in relief.

"I think your efforts are rather . . . valiant," Amina admitted.

Cass smirked at her. "Oh yeah?"

"Don't look too pleased with yourself," Amina threw at him. "I'm sure there were plenty of others clever enough to come up with such an idea; you just happened to have the right connections to do so, am I correct?"

"Actually," Gideon inserted, "Caspian is the sole reason this project has worked. Do you really think anyone was inclined to trust the Onyx Queen's son with such a treasonous idea? In fact, his work has likely tripled from having to convince everyone in the Guild I wouldn't sell them out to my mother. I've only ever been his support."

"That's all right, Gideon." Caspian laughed. "All I heard her say was that she thinks I'm clever."

Amina scowled, indignant, while Lyra and Sabine carefully hid their grins.

Delphine cleared her throat. "All right, so what's next? Myrea and the Fates' Dice?"

Thorne and Caspian decided this would be a good time for a restroom break, since they had experienced this part of the story firsthand. Calla broke down the entire interaction with the queens for her friend, how Their Highnesses had tried to force her and Gideon to sever the soul-bond and taken the Fates' Dice to stop them from being used.

"Our turn to take a break," Amina muttered when Calla was through, Lyra and Sabine jumping up to follow after her. Gideon and Ezra ambled off as well, to find Caspian and Thorne, heads tucked together in hushed conversation as they went. Leaving just Delph, Calla, and a still-sleeping Hannah.

"I cannot tell you how much I missed you," Calla said. "Or how proud I am of you."

Delphine's silver eyes brightened just before she squeezed them shut in relief. "And I cannot tell you how incredible that feels to hear." She blinked her eyes back open. "I'm proud of you, too, you know. You've come a long way, Calla. With your magic, your purpose, your . . . love life?"

Calla's cheeks heated. "That last one hasn't gone too far yet."

"Yet." Delphine giggled. "Oh, I cannot wait for the day you and Gideon finally—"

Calla elbowed Delphine in the side. "Behave. Besides, if you hadn't noticed, we're in a pretty dire situation, surrounded by people, and haven't once gotten a chance to really discuss if we want to take the risk of . . . us."

"I can tell you right now that man is undoubtedly ready to take that *risk*." Delphine smirked. "And as for the being-surrounded-by-people part . . . you'd be surprised what men can do with five minutes and a well-placed hiding spot."

Calla nearly choked. Delphine tilted her head back and laughed, and warmth spread through Calla at the sound. How she'd missed that sound and just *them*. Together.

"Any other salacious details I've missed from the past few weeks?" Delph prodded.

Calla was about to shake her head, when she remembered something. "Oh. You will never believe who my mother was once in love with."

"Which mother?" Delphine automatically asked. "Indra, Agnes, or your birth mother?"

"Indra," Calla replied just as she felt Gideon approaching. She looked over her shoulder as he lowered himself to reclaim his spot beside her. Ezra hadn't returned with him.

"He's with Cass and Thorne," Gideon answered her unspoken question. Then, "Your birth mother wasn't Indra?"

Calla shook her head. "No. My mothers couldn't decide which one of them would get to carry me, so they compromised and used a surrogate. The mother that I . . ."

"Ah," he realized before she had to rehash the painful details of how her Siphon's curse had taken the woman during her birth. "I see."

"Obviously no one expected the Siphon curse," Calla went on. "The only reason I know anything about her is because the three of them wrote me a letter every single day during the pregnancy. Telling me about the things they were doing, bits and pieces of who they were before me. Obviously, no one deigned to warn me about Myrea."

"Did you have to leave the letters behind when you left?" he wondered.

"Actually, those disappeared with Agnes," she said. "I suspect now that Myrea's jealousy also had a hand in taking them away from me in that way as well."

"Wait"—Delph sucked in a breath—"are you implying Myrea and—"

"Yep," Calla confirmed with a shudder. "I still haven't truly wrapped my head around it."

They were all silent for a long minute. Contemplating all the strange and twisted ways their stories had played out to lead them to this exact point in time. How convoluted the Fates' plans must be.

"So," Delphine finally broke the silence, "what's going on with Caspian and the only woman I've ever been jealous of?"

"No idea," Calla admitted. "But whatever it is, it's been there since the moment they met. Although, she's surprisingly less aloof now. I don't know how to explain it."

Gideon hummed his agreement. "It's as if the first time we met her she was putting on a performance."

"Yes!" Calla exclaimed. "And then the second time, of course, was a rather unfortunate circumstance. If you'd have seen her take Ezra's heart . . . never in a million years would I have thought she'd be the one *returning* him."

But now . . . as much as Calla wanted to hate the Valkyrie for what she did to Ezra, hate *them* for giving her this ultimatum, she couldn't help but feel a deep sense of understanding. They were all just doing what they had to in order to survive—an unbridled truth that she felt all the way down in her bones.

20

Sabine leaned back against one of the enormous Dragonwood trees, careful with her newly sprouting wings, as she watched Amina and Lyra exchange hushed opinions on everything they'd just heard. She was surprisingly enjoying herself, and the gossip, despite Amina's clear anxiousness to get going. But with everything that'd happened recently, Sabine thought it was nice to just idle somewhere for once.

Not to mention the way the witches were with each other. . . . It reminded her of how the slayers used to be. Once upon a time, when Lyra's brother, Lark, would hang around with them, back when Meli was a part of Sabine's life as well.

Her stomach turned with guilt at the thought of Meli now, the idea that the poor girl was still in Ignia's clutches.

Damn it, Amina is correct. We need to get going.

"Hey," a deep voice murmured from her right.

Sabine turned her head to give Ezra a withering look as he walked toward her.

"Can we talk?" he asked.

Sabine ignored him, sliding her attention back toward Amina and Lyra as she unsheathed one of her knives and began sharpening her nails.

"If I embarrassed you earlier, I didn't mean to," he lamented.

Sabine whipped her head to look at him, baring her teeth. "You're so fucking lucky I'm not able to inflict physical harm on you here."

She pushed herself off the tree and rushed away from him before she could make that very mistake. Given the choice, Sabine would have gutted Ezra Black the moment he'd suggested she was weak in front everyone.

"C'mon, harpy, I was only giving back what you give to me," he reasoned as he chased her heels. "No one here would ever judge you for needing—"

She spun on him. "How *dare* you. I don't *need* anything from you. I have disemboweled men for less than what you suggested back there—in front of an audience no less. Do you have any idea who I am?"

"Not really," he admitted. "But I want to."

She reared back, her brow furrowing. "What?"

"I want to get to know you," he repeated, making a gesture with his hand that seemed to say *Keep up*.

"No, you don't." She wrinkled her nose at him in disgust. "That's just the result of whatever morbid link we have through your resurrection. And I know Amina would likely kill me for telling you this, but given the circumstances, I must inform you—that will fade with time."

"Sabine."

She hated the way he said her name. The way he looked at her. With that unconcealed reverence. She felt her hand, the one holding the knife, twitch. She wanted to plunge it into his flesh so badly.

"Do you know how many difficult women I've dealt with in my life? I was *born* from one. You're not going to deter me," he told her. "And the last one I liked—*loved*—I did not tell her how I felt until it was much too late. So I'm telling you. I've gotten a second chance because of you, and I won't be making the same mistakes this time around."

She gave a mocking scoff. "Meaning what?"

He shrugged. "You'll see."

With that, he walked away. Leaving her to gape after him and his audacity.

"If we help the witches in this war, there's a good possibility of it leading us directly to the Fates," Amina told Lyra. "Whatever the cost, we need to get more information on how to end the tithe and unite our people against our queen."

"It seems like the witches are pretty amicable," Lyra pointed out. "And aside from the tithe, if we can recruit enough of our people to help in the war . . . maybe it will help with the animosity on both sides."

Amina had to agree. As much as listening to the witches drawl on and on about their problems made for the most tedious afternoon she'd ever had, the intel was admittedly priceless. The only pieces of the puzzle they were missing was whatever connection linked the Valkyrie Queen's contract to the Witch Queens. Amina didn't believe for a second that the two were independent of each other. Not with the letter Lysandra wrote to Ignia sitting deep inside her pocket as heavy as lead. Or how the Fates liked to operate—as dramatically as possible.

"What's our next move?" Amina asked.

She and Lyra had been working in tandem, finding their new groove more smoothly than she'd been willing to hope for. Lyra was excellent at finding resources they needed and coordinating plans, while Amina managed to deal with all of the characters in play. She didn't know if the others would say she was *good* at dealing with them, but again, herding cats.

"We take the Blood Warrior to Ignia, rescue Meli, and then convene with Sydni to see how she's responded to our warning," Lyra said. "If we are actually going to help in this war, we need to rally our people. Show them the price of fighting isn't just for the benefit of the Witch Realms, but for us as well."

Amina concurred and excused herself to the restroom while Lyra went to see where Sabine had run off to with the prince. Something Amina couldn't help but feel was a foreboding omen. She wasn't sure what it was about Onyx witches and the ability for them to get under one's skin, but it was proving to be an egregious nuisance.

As she made her way back toward the reconvening group, she saw his silhouette waiting among the shadows of the trees.

"We need to talk," he told her, arms crossed as he stepped into her path.

Think of the Godsdamned devil.

Amina fixed a sensual smile on her face as she crooned, "About what, handsome?"

"Stop with the facade," he said. "If you were as ruthless as you wanted people to believe, you would've taken off with Calla without any sort of ultimatum hours ago. She might have obliterated you all into bloody chunks—because she can do that now, by the way—but the point remains."

Amina loathed that he was right. But still she lied, "Don't mistake my willingness to compromise for a lack of ruthlessness. If I had to, I would kill that prince again and not even think twice about it."

"I'm sure you would," Caspian murmured as he took a step closer to her, tilting his head down, ever so slightly, to put himself eye level with her. "But that's because you have just as much love for your people as I do for mine. So I'll say this once—whatever you would do for your friends and family, I would do tenfold for mine. If you decide to join our side of the war, do not think you'll get away with double-crossing us. I love Ezra, but if that's all the leverage you have, he's already made it explicitly clear to me he's willing to go back six feet under before he allows himself to be used to harm any of our other friends. And I'm willing to take him up on that offer."

A reluctant inkling of respect flooded through Amina at his threat. But all she said was "I thought you were the fun one."

His smile returned easily at that. "I have many facets. Maybe if you behave long enough, you'll get to see them all someday."

With a casual wink, he ambled off. She gave a frustrated huff and trailed after him, eventually crossing paths with an equally miffed Sabine.

"Witches," Sabine grumbled to Amina as they fell into step next to each other.

"Tell me about it," Amina agreed.

When they returned to the circle, the witches looked as if they were finally ready to go.

"All right, Valkyrie," Gideon leveled at her. "If you want Calla, you'll have to take all of us."

"Because sneaking an entire entourage of witches into the Land of the Valkyries is the safest idea?" Amina mocked.

"Hey, if you truly want to assassinate your queen, the more of us the merrier, right?" Ezra added.

"If those who are loyal to Ignia find out a bunch of witches killed her, it could ruin any chance we have of recruiting them," Lyra pointed out.

"Then we'll have to be quiet about it." Ezra shrugged.

Everyone looked expectantly at Amina for the verdict.

She scowled. "Fine. What's your plan to get everyone to Ignia's palace, *quietly*, then?"

A delighted grin stretched over Caspian's face at her question. "Luckily for all of us, I know just where we can find a horse and carriage."

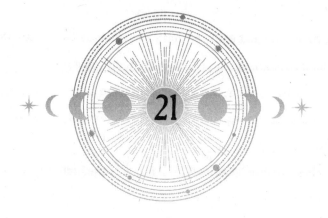

21

This is not going to go well, Calla thought.

As if he'd heard her unspoken words, Gideon hummed next to her.

She was squished between him and Thorne on one side of the carriage; Delphine, Cass, and a still-unconscious Hannah crowded on the other. Ezra and Sabine had decided it'd be best for them to drive. Well, Ezra decided he should drive—since he couldn't really fit in the cab with his new wings—and Sabine threatened to make him suffer a hundred different ways if he didn't hand over the reins. One thing Sabine seemed to be very good at was making one's life flash before their eyes.

One thing Sabine wasn't good at? Driving.

"I'm going to be sick," Thorne moaned before bending forward and tucking his head between his knees.

Caspian let his eyes flutter shut. "If I wasn't so worried about Hannah, I might envy her right now," he agreed.

Neither Calla nor Gideon was very bothered by the bumpy ride, and Delphine was so busy grooming herself that Calla didn't think her friend had even noticed the egregious bouncing and swiveling of the vehicle. Truth be told, none of them had any right to complain, considering the alternative would have been more walking. Amina and Lyra had made a quick trip of flying to the dragon-shifter farm Caspian had sold the carriage to after the group had arrived from the Rouge Realm. They'd needed the money at the time—to rent out the cottage. And though Calla felt slightly terrible taking it back from under the shifter's nose, the Valkyries hadn't seemed to have any moral reservations at all. And Calla was of the opinion that Delphine had always been right—Valkyries were great company to keep if they were on your side.

"Speaking of Hannah," Delphine started, "any guesses on what the Hells that was back there? Or if we should be very concerned for when she wakes up again?"

"Caspian calls them her death trances," Gideon said. "Every time she goes into one, her connection to her necromancy magic grows stronger."

"And so does her aversion to anyone with a past death experience, apparently," Caspian added, his eyes opening once more. Thorne, however, stayed down.

Delphine raised her silvery brows. "Past death experience?"

"It was a working theory"—Calla nodded—"but now I think that must be what helped it break free because that last episode was triggered just after Ezra showed up. And he had *definitely* been dead before."

Gideon nodded. "It's like all of her magic finally erupted from whatever deep well it'd been locked in inside of her. Which is why we should let her sleep as long as possible. Unleashing that much power at once nearly destroyed her and raised another undead army. It'll probably take a while for her energy to replenish."

Delphine looked down at Hannah's pale face in her lap, letting her fingers gently trace the black veins that were still spiderwebbed across her forehead and temples.

"Speaking of working theories," Caspian said, quickly moving on when Delphine didn't add anything else, "have you tried your compass again, Gid? Because it clearly knew where you needed to go when it picked north."

Calla straightened up a bit in surprise. "Wait. That's true. . . ."

"Interesting," Gideon murmured as he dug into his pants pocket and procured the enchanted box. "If it determined what I *needed* was to find the Valkyries . . . and therefore Ezra . . . then maybe before . . ."

"It was showing what you *wanted*, right?" Calla finished. "Maybe that's why it wouldn't work. You didn't know what exactly you wanted?"

"Or I want too many things at once," he countered, eyes flicking over her face.

Delphine leaned forward to inspect the compass closer. Calla watched as a strange expression came over Delph's face, her eyes shrewdly studying the jeweled artifact in Gideon's hand.

"Delph?" Calla prodded.

"Hmm?" Delphine said absentmindedly but never removed her eyes from the compass.

"Is something wrong?" Calla asked.

Delphine finally peeled her gaze away from the artifact to look at Calla. "No. . . . It's just, I don't remember that compass looking so familiar before. It reminds me of something—"

Before Delphine could elaborate further, the carriage suddenly lurched forward, nearly sending Thorne flying into Caspian's lap and making Gideon brace an arm around Calla's torso. Before anyone could poke their head out to ask what was going on, Sabine's face popped up in front of the carriage door's window, making Caspian jump with a curse. Gideon laughed.

"There's a checkpoint up ahead," Sabine explained as she cracked the door open for them to hear her clearly. "Ezra said the hot prince knows how to use glamour?"

Calla pressed her lips together to keep from laughing at Gideon's reaction to being called the hot prince.

"Yes, I can use glamour," Gideon confirmed. "What were you thinking?"

☽ ☽ ☽ ● ☾ ☾ ☾

"All set?" Ezra asked as Sabine settled back in on the carriage bench.

She nodded in confirmation before making grabbing hands for the reins. Ezra pulled them away from her reach and shook his head.

"You're banned from driving, harpy," he told her. "Unless you don't mind me vomiting all over your lap?"

She scowled at him. "You're *such* a baby."

Ezra snorted as he snapped the reins and started the horses forward. He could see the Valkyrie checkpoint just a couple miles in the distance, marking the end of the Dragonwoods territory—as well as the end of his safety from Sabine's knife. And death must have changed a lot more about him than just his magic because the idea of her not being able to hold anything back anymore thrilled him. He'd told her the truth when he said he wanted to know who she was. That he liked her. And whether it was because of her influence over him or not, it felt real enough that he didn't care. As happy as he was that it seemed Calla and Gideon had found their stride with each other, it still pained him the way he'd muddled everything up with her.

The carriage rumbled along as the trees around them grew thinner and thinner, and the grassy earth beneath the wheels turned into a rockier terrain. Ezra glanced over at Sabine, studying her profile. She was gazing straight ahead, arms crossed over her chest, her expression distant. Lost in her own thoughts.

He couldn't help admiring her sharp features. The severe slope of her nose and the way it tipped up ever so slightly at the end. Her prominent jawline, like she was carved out of marble by the hands of a loving artist. Her hair was as golden as the dawn, and she was such a stark contrast sitting next to him that he wondered if they looked like the night and the day found a way to meet at the same time.

"Stop staring at me," she demanded, sliding her green eyes over to his face as her mouth contorted into a frown.

The corners of his own lips curled up at her annoyance as he slid his gaze back to the road ahead. "Tell me something about yourself no one else knows."

Her frown deepened farther, and he could feel her eyes tracing over his face as if she were searching for signs that he'd lost his mind. "Why in the Hells would I do that?"

"Because sitting another fifteen minutes in complete silence will drive me nuts," he replied simply. "And, in case you've forgotten, I want to get to know you."

She rolled her eyes. "That seems pointless. Do you know the likelihood of either of us, let alone *both* of us, surviving this war? Especially considering your new wings and lack of ability to use them and the fact that mine probably won't grow in for another month or two?"

"Then you'll definitely have to keep your promise of teaching me to fly," he reasoned. "That way I'll be able to make up for your lack of flying ability if the time ever comes."

Sabine sighed deeply, leaning her head back against the carriage wall and closing her eyes as if she were in pain. "I should've just let Amina give up her wings. She would never have tolerated all your yapping."

"Tell me one thing and I'll stop *yapping*," he vowed.

"Not going to happen," she maintained. "Besides, there isn't a single thing in the world Amina or Lyra don't already know about me."

"The three of you sound like Calla, Delphine, and Hannah," he muttered.

"Is that jealousy I detect?" she taunted.

Ezra was quiet for a long beat. "Yes," he answered truthfully. "It is."

Sabine raised an eyebrow. "Don't your friends in there know you just as well?"

"Let's see." Ezra tilted his head with mock thoughtfulness. "Gideon is my brother—but we were barely raised together because of the wedge my mother wanted to make sure remained forever between us. Caspian is his best friend, though; don't get me wrong, we get along just fine. But that has more to do with the fact that Cass gets along with *everyone* just fine and less to do with him knowing me all that well. I have no idea who the Terra witch is. He's new. Delphine barely tolerates me, and Hannah is pretty quiet even when she isn't unconscious." He took a deep breath. "Truth be told, out of everyone, Calla is probably the closest person I'd call a friend. She certainly knows me the best. And while I hope we'll get to a place where we can talk to each other like we used to, I think she and my brother deserve a little space from me, especially while they're on the precipice of starting an entire war."

Sabine didn't respond, and Ezra didn't bother to fill the silence further. He urged the horses to trot faster with a flick of his hands, and the features of the faceless Valkyries waiting for them on the horizon became clearer as they approached.

Sabine turned to him and said, "I love marshmallows. I *love* them. So much, that when Lyra had a chocolate-covered-marshmallow swan sculpture commissioned to celebrate her birthday once—a decade ago—I'd eaten the swan's entire head before it even made it to the party.

I let someone else take the blame, of course. But I've had to pretend that marshmallows are too sweet and make me sick ever since."

Ezra gawked at her as if she'd grown a second head. They were only a few yards from reaching the checkpoint now, and when her story was done, she leaned in closer to him, her hands fumbling for something at her thigh.

"Don't scream," she ordered him.

And then the Godsdamned harpy stuck a dagger into him for the second time.

22

Hannah was lost in the darkness. She was afraid she was too deep to dig herself out. She could feel it everywhere now. Not just within but crawling over every inch of her skin. She was changed. A necromancer. No more stamping the darkness down. It had broken free, and it was not going to be locked away again.

And one day it would destroy her. Because that's what dark magic did. It took and took from its host until there was no more host to take from. It used you until it couldn't anymore, destroying itself in the process. It turned you selfish and cruel. It was not used for good. It squandered good.

She'd learned that lesson early on.

The first time Hannah had to take the witch-hazel bath, she broke out in hives.

"Mother, it stings!" she cried as she treaded water in the basin, sloshing a good bit of the bath over the side in her panic as the red welts began to spread over her skin.

"You'll get used to it," her mother told her dryly. "You can climb out now."

Hannah didn't hesitate; she clambered for the side of the tub and pulled herself up, her hands shaking from the hot flashes of pain climbing over her skin. When she was completely out, her mother jutted her chin toward the chalked circle she'd prepared a few yards away.

"Take your place," her mother directed. "The moon will be at its highest point any minute now."

Hannah shivered in the chill night air as she padded her way over to the summoning circle. This was her first real demonstration, and her mother's expectations were high. She raised her arms above her head, and her mother tied each of her wrists with the ends of a rope before the ends of both to the beam, shoulder's width apart. Hannah watched in silence as her mother walked over to the wooden lever just outside of the circle and cranked it back and forth until the beam overhead lifted her off the ground. Her shoulders popped painfully, and panic rose within her once again, making her tug against her bindings and rub the skin at her wrists raw.

She'd seen her mother's other wards go through this, of course, but nothing could have prepared her for the feeling of experiencing it herself. How exposed she felt beneath the moonlight. How vulnerable. She wished to be back on the ground instantly. But if she wasn't strung up into the air, her magic would funnel itself directly into the ground and reanimate whatever rested below instead of the intended corpse her mother was now dragging into the center of the circle beneath her.

Her subject was a half-decomposed stag. The stench of rotting death hit Hannah's nose, and she gagged.

"Keep it together," her mother hissed. "Remember to focus your magic only on the stag."

Hannah choked on a sob as sparks of anxiousness filled her core and shot up her arms. She didn't want to do this anymore. It was too real now. She wanted her mother to tell her it was all right, that she didn't have to if it hurt her, made her feel uncomfortable. But her mother didn't say any of that.

Instead, she said, "Begin."

Hannah's memory of that first time was fuzzy. Only flashes of snapping bones, salty tears running down her face and over her tongue, shooting pain as patches of her skin slowly tore apart. By the time she was being hauled down from the beam, she'd felt it—the darkness had stayed. Decided it would stick around to test if she'd be a viable hose. Burrowed itself into her very core and waited for her to feed it so it could grow.

And her mother still said she had not given enough.

23

"He's been stabbed with a poisonous dagger." Sabine rushed to the Valkyries as they came crashing through the checkpoint, her green eyes wide with faux tears. "We were ambushed in the forest by a group of courtless fae heathens. The queen was expecting him for an appointment two hours ago, and we need to get to a healer as soon as possible!"

Ezra would've been impressed by Sabine's act if his entire body wasn't still radiating with pain from being stabbed. The Valkyries gave his doubled-over form a once-over, their eyes lingering on the spot he was clutching at his side, blood flowing profusely from the wound since he couldn't remove the knife until their charade was over.

One of the Valkyries looked at Sabine empathetically. "We're on strict orders to check through any goods or beings coming through—"

"There's nothing in the cab," Sabine promised. "We stole this from our assailants because he couldn't fly or carry me with his injury. Take a quick look."

Emphasis on the *quick*, Ezra thought as the second Valkyrie walked around to the door. Gideon's glamour skills were good, but making an illusion strong enough to hide six people was not an easy feat.

"Between us," Sabine gushed to the Valkyries conspiratorially, hoping to distract them from any inconsistent details they might find as they poked their head inside the can, "he and the queen are . . . an item. She's going to be furious that he's been held up."

The Valkyrie pulled back in an instant, shifting their gaze over to Ezra.

"Oh shit," the one holding the door open said as the other wrinkled their nose and noted, "He needs a haircut."

"An entire royal makeover is desperately required," Sabine agreed a bit too enthusiastically. "But we all know how Her Majesty loves a dragon-shifter."

The other Valkyries exchanged a loaded look as Ezra shot Sabine a glare.

"All right, everything looks fine." The Valkyrie nodded as they went to shut the door. "You're good to—"

Someone sneezed. The Valkyries' eyes narrowed at the sound, and Sabine looked ready to commit murder.

Fuck, Ezra thought.

Before the Valkyries could look back in the cab, however, something shot down from the sky. No, some*one*. Lyra.

"What is going on here?" Lyra demanded as they gave the situation a once-over.

"Who are you?" one of the Valkyries asked.

"I'm a rare artifact collector," Lyra answered. "I was *supposed* to be arranging a deal for Queen Ignia today, but my cohort here never showed up with the precious cargo. Her Majesty is *not* pleased."

"Please—we have to get him to a healer first," Sabine implored. "He's been stabbed with basilisk venom. I was trying to come as fast as we could, but these fools are holding us up."

Lyra surveyed each of the checkpoint guards as they held their hands up in innocence. "I'll be sure to add every detail contributing to his late arrival to my report when we get to the palace."

"Wait," one of the Valkyries pleaded. "We were only doing our damned jobs—"

"And I'll only be doing mine." Lyra shrugged before beckoning to Sabine with a wave. "Let's go. We'll have to get him healed up and presentable before we take him to Ignia."

Sabine nodded, dashing back to the carriage bench and snapping the reins before the Valkyries could protest. The horses whinnied and huffed as they shot off after Lyra, who stayed closer to the ground now as they led the carriage into the Land of the Valkyries. Ezra gritted his teeth as he finally removed the dagger in his side, letting it clatter on the bench between him and Sabine.

Sabine glanced down at the knife and bit her lip. "How are you feeling?"

"Like I've been stabbed," he deadpanned.

"You don't feel feverish? No muscle cramps? Hot or cold flashes?" she pressed.

He gave her a confused look. "No?"

And just as the word fell from his lips, the next wave of pain slammed through him.

☽ ☾ ☽ ● ☾ ☽ ☾

It took about two and a half hours to reach Valor from the border and make their way to Lyra's house. Two and half hours of Ezra slowly descending into a corpse-like state as the basilisk venom wreaked havoc on his body. His skin had turned an unnatural shade of gray, his disheveled black hair soaking through with sweat. Sabine almost felt bad for putting him through this.

The moment she pulled the carriage to a halt in front of Lyra's manor, Sabine was moving with purpose. She brushed the back of her hand delicately over Ezra's cheek, stirring him awake.

"Still with me, Prince?" she asked as his glassy obsidian eyes blinked open at her.

"I hate you," he swore.

"The most unoriginal experience you've ever had, I assure you," she told him. Then she hopped down from the carriage to bound up the marble steps and head for the front entrance. Behind her, the witches began to spill out of the carriage, looking a bit shaken up. The moment the Terra witch stepped out, he lunged for one of the nearby shrubs and threw up his guts.

Sabine snickered before slipping through the front door and

bounding for Lyra's room. When she reached it, she found Amina standing over Lyra as they searched through a chest of colorful glass bottles for Ezra's antidote.

"How much longer does he have left?" Amina asked.

"Ten minutes, give or take?" Sabine answered just as Lyra pulled a small, sphere-shaped vessel out of the collection.

"Here it is," Lyra said as they handed the bottle over to Sabine. "No more than two drops, got it?"

Sabine saluted her friend before racing out of the room and back to the entrance. When she reached the front door, the witches already had Ezra inside, lying on the floor as they hovered over him in concern.

Gideon shot a dirty look at Sabine when he spotted her coming.

"What in the Hells did you *do*, Valkyrie?" he snarled.

Sabine didn't answer as she dropped to her knees by Ezra's side and uncorked the vial of antidote. She brought the bottle to his lips and carefully spilled exactly two drops on his tongue.

They all held their breath as they waited to see if it'd work.

"Anyone else getting déjà vu?" Caspian whispered.

Calla elbowed him in the side.

Then, finally, thankfully, the color began to return to Ezra's face. His breathing deepened, his eyes grew clearer, and after a moment he was able to sit up with a groan.

"What happened?" Gideon demanded again.

Ezra ignored his brother as he jabbed a finger toward Sabine. "Was it really necessary to actually stab me with a poisonous dagger?"

Everyone gasped and turned to Sabine, but she only threw her hands in the air.

"I needed it to be realistic, and I didn't have faith in your acting ability. What's the big deal?" she asked, annoyed. "You're fine now."

"Oh, I am going to make you pay for this one, Valkyrie," Ezra growled.

Sabine bit her tongue before she made the situation worse.

"All right, a letter has been sent to Ignia," Lyra announced as they walked up to the group, Amina and one of the butlers on their heels. "Elvin here will show you all to the guest rooms so you can clean yourselves up before it's time to go to the palace. Then we need to break down everyone's tasks so we can be in and out as quickly as possible. An acquaintance of ours is preparing her spare home for us in the Miroir Mountains in case things go south. We won't be able to return here if that's the case."

Elvin beckoned for the witch crew to follow him, and Sabine offered a hand to Ezra as he climbed to his feet. He didn't take it. He also didn't bother to look back at her as he followed his friends down the hallway. Ah well.

Sabine turned to Lyra. "Sydni responded to you, then?"

Lyra nodded in confirmation. "She received the proof we sent her about Ignia. She and Baden said we can have their cabin as long as we need."

"What are you going to do about your collection?" Sabine asked. "If Ignia marks us as fugitives, this will be the first place she raids."

"I'm having it packed up as we speak. The staff will stow it all away in our vault until I can get ahold of Lark and my parents to retrieve everything."

Sabine's eyebrows lifted in surprise. "None of them have answered you yet?"

Lyra sighed in frustration. "I knew my parents would be hard to track down right now—they're somewhere on the third continent with no plans to return for the next six months. Lark, however, is just being his usual unreliable self."

Sabine and Amina both nodded in understanding. During all the years the three of them had known each other, Lyra's twin tended to be aloof at the worst possible times.

Lyra waved off Sabine's look of concern. "I'll leave directions for him with the staff who decides to remain in case he shows up. But for now it looks like we'll have to rely on Sydni the most."

"We should go through your collection and see what might be useful to keep on us for the time being," Amina suggested to Lyra. "Might as well do something to pass the time until Ignia's summons goes through. We can strategize how best to use the witches as far as rescuing Meli goes as well. That little blond one is definitely staying back."

Lyra nodded in agreement before throwing an unspoken question in Sabine's direction.

"I'll be right there," Sabine answered. "There's something I need to do first."

Amina and Lyra exchanged a knowing look but didn't say anything else as they went their separate ways.

24

Calla and Gideon were sharing a room. Alone.

When the Valkyrie's butler had shown them the available rooms, Cass and Thorne had taken the only one with two beds after helping Delphine settle Hannah into the room next door. Ezra immediately claimed his own, his foul mood obvious—and justified—as he slammed the door behind him. That left Calla and Gideon, finally, to themselves.

Gideon hadn't even hesitated, opening the door across the hallway from the others and waving for her to step in first. Now she was locked in the bathroom, grooming herself thoroughly in the first mirror she'd seen in what felt like an eternity as the steam from her shower slowly dissipated. And all she could think about was how exhausted she looked.

Tired is not sexy, she thought as she combed through her hair and then watched blush bloom across her cheeks.

Not that she was trying to be sexy. Because that should be the very last thing on her mind right before she had to have an audience with the Valkyrie Queen.

"Calliope?" Gideon murmured at the door now, likely alerted to the wave of adrenaline that had just shot through her body. "Are you all right?"

"I'm fine!" she said too quickly.

Get it together, she pleaded with herself.

This was not the first time they'd shared a room, of course. Estrella's infamous bed shortage had been quite the ordeal for Calla when they'd been on their way to try and get Ezra back from the Valley of Souls. But things were much different now.

Calla took a deep breath, dressed, and returned to the bedroom. She'd allowed Gideon to shower first, since she'd figured it would take her much more time to feel normal again. Now his hair was freshly washed and combed back, the blue tendrils long enough to curl around his ears and the nape of his neck. The grime and sweat of their trek had been scrubbed away, and he'd pulled on a new pair of black leather pants—ones that sat low enough on his hips that they exposed a sliver of his toned stomach. His shirt was so tight, the chiseled muscles of his abdomen were on clear display, and not a single detail of his chest was left to the imagination. Even the outline of the silver bar that ran through his pierced nipple was starkly evident beneath the charcoal material. She swallowed.

"Feel better?" he asked.

Calla padded out of the bathroom, refusing to make eye contact, and began stuffing her dirty clothes into the backpack sitting at the foot of the king-sized bed. "Yes," she squeaked.

"Are you all right?" he asked, partially amused.

"I'm fine," she assured him, still not looking in his direction.

"Calliope."

"Yes?"

"If you're nervous about seeing the Valkyrie Queen, you do know I won't be leaving your side for even a second, right?"

"Of course." She looked over at him. "I'm actually more than ready to get that meeting over with. I'm curious to find out why she wants to see me so we can finally start looking for the Fates' Dice."

He lifted a brow. "If you're not worried about the Valkyrie Queen, then why are your nerves going haywire?"

She blushed, and his eyes narrowed in on her face. A moment later, one side of his mouth lifted in a slow, knowing smirk. He took a step forward.

"Is something else making you nervous?" he asked, tone full of innocence despite the hint of wickedness in his swirling silver eyes.

"No," she lied.

He took another step closer, and her stomach flipped. His smile grew wider. She sucked in a breath as he reached out and placed a finger beneath her chin, tilting her face up to his.

"Are you sure?" he murmured. "Your heartbeat feels as if it's going to burst out of your chest."

She flicked her eyes down to his mouth, and that seemed to be all the push he needed to close the distance between them. This kiss was slow, sweet, and she couldn't help but fall deeply into it.

His hands tangled in her hair as she let her own explore the planes of his chest, eliciting a small groan from his throat when she brushed her fingers over his piercing. He deepened the kiss before leaning down to lift her up into his arms, and she quickly wrapped her legs around his waist. He walked them both toward the wall, pressing her back against it as he continued to make her head spin with his tongue.

The feeling of both their heightened emotions joined through the bond was all-consuming, and Calla knew if he asked her to forget the rest of world and all their responsibilities right now, she'd say yes. Unfortunately, just as his hands began to trail along the side of her body, heading to unknown places, someone else decided that they would not be forgetting their responsibilities anytime soon.

A knock banged on the door.

Gideon broke the kiss with a curse. "I swear to the Gods I'm about to commit murder."

"Calla?" The voice was Delphine's.

Calla gave him an apologetic smile as he set her down on her feet so she could answer the door. When she pulled it open, she found her friend standing out in the hallway, looking stressed and just as unkempt as before. Delphine not taking an opportunity to groom herself was definitely a worrisome sign.

"I'm sorry if I interrupted anything," Delphine said, throwing a sympathetic look over Calla's shoulder to Gideon.

The second Gideon saw what state the siren was in, however, his expression turned to one of equal concern. "Are you all right?" he asked as he came up behind Calla.

Delphine bit her lip. "They want Hannah and I to leave for their contingency house in the Miroir Mountains right now. They've arranged horses for us."

Calla's brows rose in surprise, but Gideon nodded.

"I hate to say it, but that makes sense. Get a head start so Hannah can have somewhere safe while she's ... out," he told them. "The only question is if we trust them or not."

"I don't trust anyone but the two of you, Hannah, and Caspian," Delphine said automatically. "But if you believe their intentions really are to help with the war ... I'll go. Thorne volunteered to come with us as well so I don't have to protect Hannah alone."

"Probably best that we don't have another Blood Warrior right under the Valkyrie Queen's nose anyway," Gideon agreed. "And for the record, despite the blond one almost murdering my brother and the fact that we still don't know what Ignia wants with Calla or that Amina *did* murder my brother—we all have the same goal. To be rid of all these power-hungry queens."

Delphine took a deep breath. "Okay. Then this is goodbye again—for now. They said after you get out of the Valkyrie Queen's palace, you're all going to head straight to us before we decide what the next moves are."

Calla pulled her friend to her as tight as she could. "We'll be right behind you this time. I swear."

When they eventually pulled back, Delphine gave Gideon a nod. "You better take care of her."

"Always," he vowed.

"Take care of Hannah," Calla told Delphine.

"Always," Delphine echoed.

Then there was nothing to do but let Delphine go again. This time, however, Calla felt more than sure they'd be reunited again soon. And if they weren't, at least Delphine would be with Hannah this time around. Where she belonged.

"We're not making a mistake, are we?" Calla whispered to Gideon as they retreated into the room.

"It's hard to say," Gideon told her honestly. "But I don't have the same feeling of despair with the Valkyries as I did back in the Neverending Forest, so I'm trying to take it as a good sign."

Calla nodded. "They seem to hate Ignia as much as we hate Myrea and Lysandra."

"Always a good starting point." He snorted. "Also with your Blood Siphon abilities, I imagine we'd be pretty evenly matched against them if we needed to be. Though I think we should keep that particular trick up our sleeves unless it's absolutely dire to demonstrate it."

"Like killing the Valkyrie Queen?" Calla wondered.

"Precisely," he said, then stepped away to gather their things. "We should probably go find the Valkyries and see what else they're planning. We'll finish that kiss later."

"Later?" She breathed.

His eyes flashed silver with desire. "Yes, later. When I have more time to do all the things I want to do without any interruptions or possible doom."

A flurry of butterflies erupted in her stomach at that promise, and she swore all the blood in her body rushed to her head. "All the things you want to do?"

His smirk was the most sinful she'd ever seen it. "I love our friends, but Gods, staying in a room all together these past few weeks has been damn near torture."

Calla's eyes widened. She thought the reason they'd taken it so slow was perhaps because he might still need space after everything and . . . Ezra. Despite Ezra giving them both his blessing, Gideon's entire being was built on integrity and honor, and she thought he might still not be ready. It's why she made sure not to be too affectionate in front of the others. She didn't want to push his boundaries.

When she said as much aloud, he looked at her like she'd lost her mind.

"What?" she asked, tone defensive.

"Calliope."

She only stared at him, puzzled.

He shoved a hand through his hair. "I don't know how else to tell you, to show you, that I have wanted you since before we even met. Before I even knew your name. And I sure as Hells am not waiting to declare that we're together to the entire world because *I'm* not ready."

"If choosing not to sever our bond wasn't telling enough for you, Gideon Black, I don't know what would be," she quipped.

He narrowed his eyes. "We're on the same page, then?"

"Yes." She looked up into his face, so open and hopeful, and couldn't help the smile that overtook her own. "We're on the same page."

He kissed her again, wrapping his arms around her waist and lifting her off the ground, spinning her in a circle.

A throat cleared.

Gideon placed her back on her feet, and they broke apart to see Thorne and Caspian standing before the open doorway. Thorne with a surprised look on his face and Caspian with a grin so bright it could've outshone the sun.

"*Finally,*" Cass exclaimed, throwing his hands in the air.

"How long have you been standing there?" Calla groaned.

Cass shrugged. "Long enough to start planning my speech for—"

Before he could even finish the sentence, Calla made a squeak of protest, but Gideon only sighed and admonished, "*Way* too much, Cass."

"Whatever." Caspian waved off their concern before gesturing for Thorne to follow after him. "C'mon, you gotta get going."

As the two men strode away, Calla heard Thorne ask, "Who was going to tell me the two of them were *together* together?"

"Don't tell me you've never noticed Gideon's longing stares every time Calla enters a room," Caspian laughed.

"I just thought he looked like that," Thorne countered.

Gideon grumbled all the way down the hall, and Calla couldn't keep the ridiculous smile off her face.

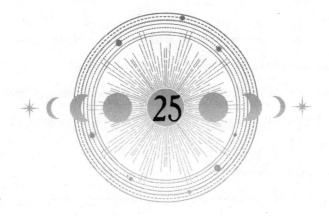

25

When Ezra refused to answer the first three knocks, Sabine decided to stop caring about politeness. By the time she kicked in the door, Ezra had already cleaned up and changed—thanks to Caspian lending him some supplies—and was patiently waiting for her to pry her way inside. He was leaning against the far wall, wings carefully tucked against his back, arms crossed over his chest.

When she spotted him looking at her expectantly, she bared her teeth. "You really couldn't have just answered the door?"

"You really couldn't have not almost killed me with a poisoned blade?" he retorted.

"I see you had that one loaded up and ready to go," she griped. "I told you, I needed to make it as convincing as possible. Do you know what would have happened to your friends if those Valkyries had found them? They have orders to reap any witch they see. Any *being* they see."

"You could have stabbed me with a *regular* blade," he argued. "I know you must have a hundred on you at all times."

"That... didn't occur to me at the time," she admitted. "And besides, I was still pissed at you for making me look weak in front of our peers."

"How the tables have turned," he stated.

She gave him a vicious sneer. "This is *precisely* why I didn't want to indulge your ridiculous little game of getting to know me. Because you can't handle me. Your asinine, romantic delusions are not my problem. Blame whatever is in the magic we used in order to bring you back, but you don't get to look at me as if I disappointed you in some way when you don't even *know* me!"

Ezra didn't respond. He only stared. Waiting for her to get it all out. Her fists balled at her sides, and he could tell she wasn't used to not being able to elicit a reaction.

"I don't need you to like me. In fact, I'd prefer if you didn't. The last person who liked me hates me now. And worse? She's being held by Ignia for ransom and tortured because I used her for information and made her take a blood oath to keep it to herself." She jabbed a sharpened talon at him. "You cannot tame me. I attempted to murder you a few times? Consider yourself lucky. I don't usually *attempt*."

With that, she tried to storm away, but he wasn't even close to being done with her. In two strides, he was behind her, grasping on to her left forearm and spinning her back around to face him.

"The girl you said is being held for ransom by Ignia—was she the one?" he asked.

She wrinkled her nose at him. "What do you mean?"

"The one who fucked you up so bad I'm having to pay for it now?" he clarified.

That really did it. She raised the arm he wasn't holding, and to no one's surprise, there was a knife in her hand. He blocked her from going for her usual spot—his abdomen—and the knife ended up embedded in his shoulder instead. She managed to rip herself out of his arms, and this time he let her leave.

He stood there for a long while, staring after her, not bothering to remove the knife. Until Calla and Gideon came down the hall and Calla did a double take through the doorway.

"Ezra?" she asked.

He finally pulled the dagger from his shoulder as he muttered, "Hey."

"What happened?" she asked as she stepped toward him.

He shook his head. "Oh, the usual. Being a glutton for punishment."

She opened her mouth to press further, but something in his expression must have made her think otherwise because she pressed her lips back together a second later. Then, "Oh, I forgot. . . . I have something for you."

He tilted his head in curiosity as she twisted around to dig into the backpack hanging from her shoulders.

"I'm going to go find Cass," Gideon declared while Calla continued her search, and they both gave him a nod in acknowledgment.

"How is everything between the two of you?" Ezra asked as casually as possible.

Calla's mismatched gaze flickered over to him in surprise.

"What? Did I forget that we all took a vow not to talk about it or something?" he joked.

"No, I just . . . I was trying to avoid anything that might make things terribly awkward," she admitted.

He shrugged. "No more awkward than pretending it's not happening."

"That's true," she allowed.

"I think it's probably better to talk about," he said. "The more open it is, the less strange it will feel over time. And you and I . . . we always talked. I miss that part of what we had, and I don't think I can pretend that I don't. Above all else, Calla, I never want to lose you as my friend."

You were always *my destiny*, he'd said to her when he knew he was dying.

He hadn't been lying. She was always his destiny—for that first life. He was grateful to her for so many things. Teaching him how to be loved, that he had his own light for one. In this second life, his destiny might be different, but he still wanted her to be part of his world. Needed her to be.

She gave him a brilliant smile. "We'll always be friends, Ezra." Then her smile slowly began to fade. "You have no idea how much it gutted me to leave you in the Valley of Souls. I need you to know how glad I am that you're here. Truly."

He nodded. He knew. She sighed in relief and continued her search.

"Gideon and I are good, by the way. Finding our footing together in the midst of an impending war with the Gods isn't necessarily easy, of course." She sighed. "And the soul-bond... it makes things oddly intense—"

"Well, we don't have to be *that* open," he murmured, cutting off the rest of her sentence.

She turned bright red and threw a scowl at him. "*That's not what I meant.*" She huffed in exasperation. "Goodness, you and Delphine—anyway. I *meant* that having a magic link like that makes it hard to tell which emotions are real and what is heightened and exaggerated. I think both of us only just got to a place where we realized what we feel is real and strong enough to risk the Heartbreak curse. But that was only after a lot of bleeding, getting stabbed in the heart by your mother, and nearly having the bond severed entirely. When the thought of losing it forever felt like torture, that's when I knew that what I felt was real. Which brings me to— Aha!"

Of all the things he expected her to pull from her bag, Heart Reaver was not even close to being on that list. His chest tightened at the sight of it. He pocketed Sabine's dagger and took Heart Reaver from her, letting the familiar weight of it balance in his palms for a moment.

"I can't believe you got it back from the sylph," he told her.

"Well, actually, the nymphs got it back," she explained, and when he threw her a confused look, she waved her hand and said, "Never mind. Long story. One day we might all catch up on everything we've been through, but for now, I'm glad to reunite you with Heart Reaver."

He ran his fingertips over the hilt, waiting for the heart-shaped jewel to glow at his touch. But it never came. The telltale warmth of its magic remained dormant.

"I don't think it's for me anymore," he said.

"But—"

Before she could finish, he passed the dagger back to her and watched as the stone instantly came to life after being returned to its rightful owner. Ezra smiled.

"It's yours now," he declared.

"Are you sure?" she asked.

He nodded, pulling Sabine's dagger back out of his pocket. "I've found a new blade to fight with."

And he didn't mean the one in his hand.

26

One thing the Valkyries knew how to do was plan.

In fact, even if they were scheming to somehow double-cross Calla and her crew, Calla thought they'd have earned it. To start, Lyra's collection of enchanted objects was rotund. A locket that stowed away memories until it was reopened, a ring that turned hot and cold around beings with certain ill intentions, a mask that allowed the wearer to speak any dialect they wished. The trove must have taken a century—and an ungodly amount of money—to collect, and Calla was vastly impressed.

Lyra also had a detailed map of the Valkyrie Queen's palace, and to Calla that was the most valuable piece of all. Not going into something aimlessly for once felt much more reassuring than any of their other quests. Not to mention how thrilled it seemed to make Gideon and Caspian to be back in their element, strategizing.

While Lyra, Amina, Gideon, and Cass spoke animatedly about how they should break up their tasks—someone had to rescue the Valkyrie that Ignia was using as a hostage, and then, of course, there was the matter of Ezra's heart—Calla and Ezra stood together, off to the side, and let them scheme.

"Too many cooks in the kitchen," Ezra murmured as Amina and Caspian argued about whether or not jumping out of a window was a plausible escape route.

"You have wings," Cass huffed. "What in the Hells would we do?"

"Hope for the best," Amina offered with a dismissive wave of her hand.

Calla let their voices fade to the back of her mind as she took in the details of the room they were in. Possibly the most opulent place she'd ever been aside from Myrea's palace. But this was a different sort of glamourous compared to the Rouge Queen's style. Plush tapestries adorned the walls with intricate depictions of scenes from ancient battles and lavish feasts, their rich colors adding a depth of grandeur to their subjects.

The ceiling soared overhead, embellished with elaborate molding and intricate frescoes depicting celestial scenes bathed in gold. A chandelier hung from the center rose, each facet of its sparkling crystals catching and refracting the light, scattering a soft golden glow throughout the room. The seating area, where the others were huddled together studying the map of the palace, was decorated with a plush velvet chaise and matching armchairs around a low marble table that probably cost more than all the spéctrals she would have fetched that time Ramor and Boone tried to auction her off at the Starlight Inn. Even the air was redolent with the scent of opulence from the expensive oils that sat atop the many vanities and smelled of jasmine and roses.

"Unbelievable, isn't it?" Ezra commented as he, too, observed the details around them.

"To think that I've been connected to *two* princes, and yet I still will never know luxury like this," she teased.

He snorted.

"Where is Sabine?" she wondered, suddenly noticing the girl was nowhere to be found.

"Probably somewhere deciding how to maim me next," he muttered.

Calla glanced over at his face, and what she found confirmed all her suspicions. Ezra was infatuated. It was somewhat ironic that he'd once looked at her that way but she'd been so set on the idea that her Siphon half made her so monstrous by nature that she was undeserving of love, to the point where she made herself believe she was deciphering that look on his face incorrectly. Now, however, it was so obvious to her that he might as well shout that he was enamored with the Valkyrie.

Calla couldn't help it; she laughed. "Oh, Ezra."

"What?" he said defensively.

"If you were ever wondering what your type was"—she smirked—"it can be summed up as *bad for your physical health.*"

"A little dramatic," he said. "You weren't bad for my health."

"You literally *died*," Calla reasoned.

"Yes, but that wasn't *your* fault."

"Semantics," she said with a wave of her hand. "Regardless, I hope you know—that Valkyrie is not going to soften for you. And she shouldn't have to."

"Don't worry. She told me just as much."

"Then can I give you a piece of advice?" she offered.

Ezra raised a brow at her in curiosity.

Calla shrugged. "Learn to dodge her blades faster."

A surprise laugh fell from his lips, but before he could say anything else, someone called her name.

"I think we're all set," Gideon said as he waved her over. She went to him, and he wrapped a protective arm around her waist as he leaned down to murmur their plans into her ear, tracing his finger over the map of the palace as he spoke.

"Lyra, Sabine, and Ezra will be going after Ezra's heart through here," Gideon said. "And after Amina takes you and me to Ignia, she and Caspian will be responsible for getting back—Meli, was it?"

Lyra and Amina nodded in confirmation. Then Lyra said, "I have something for each group to take. But it comes with a warning—if any of them gets broken, I will gut you all."

Everyone waited with bated breath as they watched the Valkyrie walk over to their vanity and pop open the lid of a large mahogany box. Inside, nestled in a crimson velvet cushion, were three identical rectangles that reminded Calla of gilded cigarette cases. The outside of the cases were fluted and polished to perfection, and as Lyra scooped one of them out and flipped open the lid, Calla saw it was not a cigarette case at all but what could only be described as a metal notepad. Both the top and bottom of the device had smooth black surfaces, but at the bottom there was a small cylinder that hid some sort of stylus.

"This will help us communicate with one another. The pen is enchanted," Lyra explained, clicking the stylus out of its hiding spot and holding it out for them to see. "Whatever message you write with it on the bottom will appear at the top of the other devices. Here."

They handed the first gilded device over to Caspian and then the second to Calla before picking up the third and giving them a demonstration. Calla and the others watched in awe as Lyra scrawled out the word *hello* on their pad and seconds later the writing faded into view on the top surfaces of theirs as well.

"Incredible," Gideon murmured in approval.

Lyra looked pleased at the response. "Now, if everyone is in agreement that you will be guarding them with your lives, I think we're ready to go. Where in the Hells is Sabine?"

Just as the girl's name was said, she walked through the bedroom door, waving a folded piece of parchment for all to see in one hand as she pocketed something shiny and golden into the back of her pants with the other.

"I was getting the mail," Sabine announced. "And great news—the queen's correspondence says Amina may arrive as soon as possible with the Blood Warrior. It *does* say for them to arrive alone"—a wicked grin began to spread across her face now—"but I think we can all agree that if she thinks that's going to happen, she deserves the storm we're about to unleash on her."

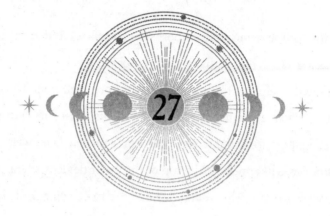

27

The Valkyrie Queen's palace was a vision of white marble and gold—not so unlike the style that Lyra's manor had been. With pillars lining the hallways and impossibly high ceilings that were painted with murals the color of a golden sunset. Calla and Gideon were following Amina's lead through the front foyer and down an expansive hallway, and while Calla's body was being racked by nerves and pumping adrenaline, the Valkyrie strutted through the place as if she owned it.

Calla shoved her hand into the front pocket of her pants for at least the hundredth time since they'd left Lyra's house, fidgeting with the communication device as if she needed to make sure it was still there and hadn't somehow disappeared. The last time she was in some bitch queen's palace, she was put in a dungeon and stabbed through the heart. Not to mention they'd had to leave someone behind. She was determined the outcome would be different this time.

Amina, and the guard she'd been ignoring, finally came to a pause in front of an enormous wooden door. Before the guard could reach out and knock, Amina wrapped her knuckles on the solid wood three times in succession and didn't bother waiting for an answer before yanking the door open. As the three of them piled inside the room, Calla quickly saw that the space was a small library. There were wall-to-wall wooden shelves stuffed with books in every nook and cranny. In the middle of the far wall was an unlit fireplace, two armchairs framing the hearth. The strangest detail of all? A kelpie head mounted above the mantel. Calla wrinkled her nose at it in disgust.

"Do my eyes deceive me," a sultry feminine voice rang out as the fireplace suddenly ignited, the flames warming up the small space in seconds, "or is that Lysandra's beloved eldest son?"

When Calla's eyes finally adjusted to the dim light of the study, she found the woman standing at the back of room and almost gasped. The Valkyrie Queen's reddish-brown hair was pulled up into a pile of ringlets, several gilded feathers pinning it in place. Her gown was made of the same golden feathers, the bodice cut so close to her body Calla wondered how she could breathe. As the woman wedged the book in her hands back into its place on the shelf, she scrutinized the three of them shrewdly. Lingering uncomfortably on Gideon's face.

"Amina, darling, you've been too generous," Ignia said as she glided closer to them. "Delivering both the final Blood Warrior and Lysandra's favorite welp."

Amina lifted her chin. "I completed the task you assigned me by the deadline we agreed upon. Where is Meli?"

"She'll be released," Ignia assured her. "Whenever I'm sure I won't require your assistance any further. Now, if you'll excuse me, I'd like to have a word alone with the witches."

Before Calla realized what the queen was doing, the metallic ringing of a bell filled the space around them and three guards were at the door, dragging Amina from the room. Calla made a move toward the woman, but despite Amina's string of curses and swipes of her shredding claws, she shot Calla a look that was very clear. *Stick to the plan.*

"Take her underground. The other two shouldn't be too far. When you find them, throw them in separate rooms. I don't want them to know which one breaks first."

Calla and Gideon stood their ground, shoulder to shoulder, without a single glance more in Amina's direction. Once the guards had closed the door behind them, Ignia stepped forward, her golden gown swishing with the movement. She scrutinized each of them in turn, running her eyes over every inch of their faces and all the way down to their feet.

"An interesting pair the two of you must make," she said, a condescending smile on her face. "The crown prince of the Onyx Realm and the final Blood Warrior. Lysandra must be thrilled."

Gideon's jaw clenched, but he said nothing. If the Valkyrie Queen wasn't already aware of their soul-bond, there certainly was no reason to make her aware.

"I heard our dear Amina ripped your little brother's heart out," the queen continued with mock sympathy. "I'm sure Lysandra *is* ecstatic about that one. Gods knows she worked so hard to try and kill him that first time."

Another thing they didn't need to reveal—that Ezra was back.

Gideon sucked in a sharp breath, his eyes flashing silver. "What are you talking about?"

Delight sparked in Ignia's eyes as she read the sincere shock on Gideon's face. "Oh, you didn't know? Tell me, Prince, why do *you* think your mother had a second son just to stow him away from the outside world?"

"I must admit I've never tried to understand my mother's twisted ways," Gideon stated.

"Would like me to tell you, then?" she taunted.

"I didn't realize you had any connection to my mother," he said, his expression darkening.

"Oh, your mother and I go way back," Ignia claimed. "I even knew your father at one point. Though I don't believe he's been around in some time."

Gideon reached up to tug at one of the metal hoops in his ear. "You know who our father is?"

"Of course," Ignia purred. "Are you saying she never told you?"

Gideon was silent, and Ignia tilted her head back with a mocking laugh.

"Leaving her own son in the dark about where he came from." Ignia clucked her tongue. "Secrets have always followed Lysandra like shadows. I assume your brother never learned his own history before his untimely end."

"Either reveal what you know or get on with why we've been brought here," Calla seethed at the woman, tired of the cruel way she kept dangling such sensitive information over Gideon's head like a carrot on a string.

"You shouldn't deny a scorned queen her pleasures, girl," the queen said with a languid smile. "But, yes, let me be the one to have the pleasure of revealing that your brother was only born so he could take the Heartbreak Prince curse away from you."

"*What?*" Gideon and Calla exclaimed in sync.

"When you were born, I received a letter from your mother," Ignia explained. "It was mostly just a rageful piece about how she'd burn my land to the ground for creating the Heartbreak curse now that her firstborn was inflicted with it."

"*You* created the Heartbreak curse?" Calla gaped. "*Why?*"

"Not my finest hour," she admitted, her face contorting into a mask of bitterness. "But you can hardly blame me—I was a mere mortal at the time. In love with a ruthless immortal prince. So I did what many foolish mortals have done in times past. I made a deal with the Gods and was not careful enough with my words."

"Let me guess," Gideon inserted. "They decided not to curse only *your* immortal prince, but every prince thereafter?"

The queen shrugged. "At least only one at a time. One dies, another is reborn. Enter you."

Something about where this conversation was headed gave Calla a bad feeling, and from what she could sense on Gideon's end of the bond, she knew he felt the same dread.

"You were born with the Heartbreak curse, and your mother damn near lost her mind. I think she must have searched every inch of Aetherius for a way to rid you of it, but not a single being had the answer—not even the Fates were willing to make an additional bargain with her over you. They said your role in their game of destiny was too important. So she became desperate."

Gideon paled, his eyes squeezing shut as if he were in pain. Calla's mind was racing trying to put the pieces together. Surely, she couldn't be implying that—

"Your brother was conceived, and nine months later, when your mother went into labor, poison went into your bottle. All you needed to do was die just long enough for the next immortal prince to be born and take on the curse. Then they'd give you the antidote and bring you back."

"But Gideon is still the Heartbreak Prince," Calla blurted.

Ignia gave her a vicious smile. "The Fates aren't very fond of cheating. Your mother paid the price for that little trick. The only man she ever loved."

"How do you know all of this?" Gideon demanded.

Ignia laughed. "Pillow talk."

Gideon's mouth twisted with disgust. "You mean with—"

"I've always enjoyed taking things that belonged to Lysandra, and your father was one of my favorites. Bellator was quite the catch back when he enjoyed the political game as much as the rest of us. Before he became an utter, morally sound *bore*."

"Bellator," Gideon repeated. "That's our father's name."

"*Your* father's name," the queen corrected. "I never learned the name of your brother's father."

Gideon reared back a step.

Calla blinked in confusion. *Gideon and Ezra are only half brothers?*

Before either Calla or Gideon could process everything they'd just learned, the queen shifted gears. The amusement in her eyes dissolved in a matter of seconds, the air in the room around them growing colder, and Calla pressed herself closer to Gideon's side as she braced for whatever was about to come.

"Now that our fun is over, I have business to pick with you, girl." Ignia's eyes burned into Calla. "I want the Fates' Dice."

Calla barely resisted the urge to laugh in the woman's face. Even if she still had the Fates' Dice, Calla would not have handed them over to anyone except Gideon.

"Or what?" Calla taunted.

The queen tilted her head. "Would the name Kai happen to mean anything to you?"

28

Amina hated this fucking place. Even more, she hated that she had to allow herself to be dragged to this dungeon instead of shredding those guards into bloody ribbons. It took every ounce of self-control she'd had to watch them close the door to the windowless stone cell without putting up a fight. But above all, she hated, *hated*, that all she could do now was pace and wait for Caspian Ironside to show up and rescue her.

One minute went by. Then two. Then ten.

"I'm going to murder that witch," she seethed to herself aloud. "The next time I see him, I'm going to—"

A loud *thud* sounded right outside of the cell before the door flew wide open.

"The next time you see me you're going to what?" Caspian asked with an amused grin. "Thank me for saving you? Tell me how handsome you think I am?"

Amina bared her teeth at him as she smoothed back one of her curls from her face and pushed past him out the doorway. "I'd rather chew my own arm off, witch."

"You know what I think?" he taunted as he followed too closely on her heels. "I think you secretly enjoy me. I think you haven't been able to stop thinking about me since the first time we met. Don't worry, you're one of many."

"*I* think you should shut the Hells up and focus on our mission," she bit out. "Does this really seem like a decent time for *flirting* to you?"

"Near-death experiences are always a decent time for flirting," he retorted. "They're heart-racing by nature."

As soon as he said the words *near-death*, Amina stumbled across the first body. The Valkyrie, a man with long blond hair, was lying face up on his back, his entire face a macabre shade of purple.

"Asphyxia only knocks them out for a few minutes," Caspian informed her. "So we better figure out where your friend is, quick."

"How many of them did you have to knock out?"

"Eleven or so. Lyra was right—none of you are prepared to handle an unexpected witch infiltrating your midst. I'm pretty sure half of them are going to wake up still confused on what the Hells knocked them out."

Amina refused to act impressed when the element of surprise had done most of the heavy lifting there. So instead she said, "All right, we have to start searching every room down here for Meli."

"Oh, no need," Caspian said as he stepped past her and made a gesture with his chin for her to follow. "There aren't any other prisoners being held in the palace aside from Meli, and she's supposedly detained on one of the upper floors in the east wing. I already squeezed those little details out of one of the guards. Figured if we had the opportunity to wreak havoc by setting a bunch of people free it might be a good use of our time."

"Why would Meli be in the east wing? That side of the palace doesn't have any dungeons," Amina reasoned. "They were probably lying to you."

"Or they weren't lying and the queen is keeping her in a place that you wouldn't have thought to look first," he countered.

Amina's pace slowed as she grew skeptical.

Caspian looked back at her over his shoulder, pausing when he noticed she'd stopped. "What's wrong?"

"I'm trying to decide if you make good bets or not," she answered.

"Do I *make* good bets?" He shrugged. "Not always. But I think anyone who knows me knows that I *am* a good bet." He started forward again. "Stay or follow, Valkyrie. Either way, I'm getting out of here."

Amina followed.

29

"Could you possibly move any slower?"

Ezra glared in Sabine's direction, ignoring her impatient tapping foot, and brushed away yet another cobweb off the tops of his wings. The appendages had become torturous for him, and truth be told, he wanted them gone. Hopefully, getting his heart back from wherever it was stashed in this palace would be the first step in that direction. Every time the wings bumped into something, he had the urge to rip them off himself.

"Do you think if I could control these damned things better I wouldn't?" he shot at her.

"If the two of you don't shut up, I'm going to rip out your tongues," Lyra scolded them both. "Do you think the staff here doesn't have ears or something?"

Ezra pressed his lips together at the admonishment, not wanting to test the limits of Lyra's patience since they were the only one who had actually memorized the way through this dusty nightmare. Sabine, however, took the criticism and stuck her tongue out at him instead.

Gods, she was an infuriating, impatient, bratty little monster.

But damn it if he didn't almost laugh.

"Only two more doors ahead," Lyra informed them. "Move."

The three of them prowled along the narrow passageway until they came to the door Lyra had determined would lead them to the correct part of the palace.

"Sabine?" Lyra prompted, waving their hand toward the door's iron keyhole.

That smile Sabine got every time she had a dagger in her hand made its way onto her face as she stepped forward and inserted the tip of one of her blades—one that was abnormally long and thin—into the keyhole and shimmied it around until there was a resounding *click*.

Lyra let the door fall open naturally, making a gesture with their hand for Ezra and Sabine to wait. A moment later, footsteps approached on the other side of the door. A hand appeared first, wrapping around the door's edge so its owner could pry it open further and peek inside. They never got that far, however, because the moment Sabine spotted flesh, her knife was speared through it, securing the person's hand to the wood. Before the unfortunate soul could even suck in a breath to scream, Lyra lurched forward and gripped the door in order to slam it into the person's body so hard, it knocked them out. Ezra had to look away as the weight of their body slumping to the floor made the knife in their impaled hand slice clean through the bone until it was no longer holding the appendage in place.

Sabine pushed the door wider, shoving the body out of their way and allowing Lyra to slip out before her, Ezra filing out last. He looked down at the poor Valkyrie with pity as Lyra and Sabine assessed what direction to go next, neither one of them giving the passed-out figure a second glance. From what he could tell, they were in a small alcove off a main hallway, each of the other walls around them embedded with their own mysterious doors. He could hear faint voices talking from somewhere beyond the alcove's opening but couldn't make out exactly what they were saying.

"The queen's bedroom door is at the very end, to the right. There are usually at least four guards in this hallway—two at her bedroom's entrance itself and two roaming up and down the corridor. We just took one out, which means the others need to drop quickly and quietly before they can alert anyone else."

"Leave that to me," Sabine said as she procured three more daggers off her person.

How many knives can one woman hold? Ezra wondered, watching her in awe as she shifted two of the knives to her left hand and palmed the third in her right.

"Get ready," Sabine warned.

Ezra and Lyra braced themselves as she dashed out of the little alcove and into the open corridor, assessing her surroundings and launching all three of her blades in less than two blinks. There was a brief sound of surprise from somewhere beyond the walls Ezra could see, followed by a distressed gargling. When Sabine gave them the signal it was all clear, Ezra and Lyra raced after her. As soon as he stepped out of their hiding place, he noticed the blood. Considering everything else around them was white and gold, the pools of crimson beneath the guards and in their open throats was stark.

"That won't keep them down for very long, will it?" Ezra grunted at the Valkyries. Valkyries were just as immortal as witches. He couldn't imagine their rapid healing abilities operated much different.

"They will sense my blades were full of poison," Sabine answered, flashing him a self-satisfied grin.

When they reached the door, Lyra was surprisingly able to shove it right open.

"I guess when you have incompetent guards you don't need a lock," Lyra muttered before turning to Sabine and ordering, "Hide the bodies somewhere, then stand guard inside."

Sabine gave Lyra a thumbs-up before bending down and grabbing one of the two guards by their legs.

"Let's go, Prince," Lyra demanded to him, and something about the calm air of authority Lyra exuded made him compelled to follow their instructions implicitly.

As they moved through the bedroom, he couldn't help but scoff at the ridiculous decor. Wallpaper made of scarlet velvet and a canopy bed so egregiously large it almost made him blush. Lyra, however, had razor-sharp focus. Ezra watched as they found a trapdoor he never would have been able to spot in a million years. They pried the door all the way open to reveal a set of stone steps and yet another underground passageway.

"You've got to be kidding me," he complained. "Can't you just finish this last bit without me so I don't have to drag these wings down yet another of the world's smallest secret tunnels?"

Lyra opened their mouth argue but instantly seemed to think better of it. "You know, I do work infinitely better alone. If you want to put your literal heart in my hands, I have no problem leaving you behind."

"Well, when you put it that way—" he began, but a muffled shout from the hallways cut him off as both he and Lyra whipped their heads in the direction of the open bedroom door.

"Just stay with Sabine and make sure she doesn't get in trouble," Lyra demanded before diving through the trapdoor.

"Keep Sabine out of trouble. Sure," he mumbled as he watched the Valkyrie disappear.

⟩⟩⟩●⟨⟨⟨

Lyra made quick work of navigating the second tunnel system, retracing their steps from memory of the last time they'd been through here with their other slayers. Of course, everything was quick work when you didn't have to deal with two fussy children every step of the way. The migraine pounding at their temples was a clear indication they absolutely did their best work alone.

A few minutes later, they found the door they were looking for and shouldered it open, the weight of it much heavier than they remembered. The familiar room was massive and cluttered, bookshelves and desk still littered with stacks of papers and scrolls, as if no one had touched anything since they'd been through here.

Lyra immediately started searching the floorboards with their feet, bouncing on each one until there was a telltale creak. They knelt down and pried up the wooden slats to reveal the dial beneath.

"Zero, two, one, six," they recited quietly as they spun the knob to each corresponding notch.

When the scraping noise in the stone behind them echoed through the room, a smile of satisfaction curled up on their lips. They hurried to replace the floorboards before rushing over to the stone brick now jutting out of the room's only bare wall. The moment they pulled the brick all the way out, however, a sharp, piercing sound cut through the room like a blade.

An alarm.

Without a second thought, Lyra tossed the brick aside and thrusted their arm into the exposed hole in the wall, yanking out the familiar wooden box that sat inside. Then they darted out the door and back into the shadows of the tunnels.

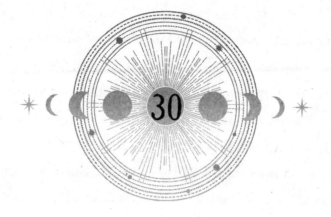

30

Amina and Caspian managed to sneak halfway to the east wing without adding anyone else to their body count. But when the alarm went off, Amina knew their luck was over.

"What in the Hells is that?" Caspian asked as the keening alert made him cringe.

"Trouble," Amina answered as a fleet of guards poured out of a pair of double doors at the end of the corridor.

Most of the guards immediately rushed for the main palace, but three of them lingered, stomping closer and closer in Amina and Caspian's direction, pausing only to throw open every door they came across to check for anything suspicious.

"You're sure Meli is in one of these rooms?" she asked him as she kept her eyes trained on the guards, bracing herself for the moment they spotted the two of them pressed into the shadows against the wall.

"That's what the guard said," he confirmed. "And though they could have been lying, I find people tend to tell the truth more often than not when they're being strangled."

"All right." Amina nodded. "Then you better be ready to get your hands dirty."

Caspian gave her a lazy smile. "Oh, don't worry—I won't need to use my hands. They call me the Valkyrie whisperer, you know."

Amina looked at him as if he'd lost his mind. "I don't even know what to say to that."

"Just watch," he told her.

And before she could protest, the damned witch walked out into the middle of the corridor and strutted right up to the trio of guards. Amina cursed him silently as she waited to see what happened from her vantage point, straining to hear the words he was saying over the still-keening sound of the alarm.

"I think I'm lost," Cass greeted them. "Do you suppose you could point me in the right direction?"

"Don't move," one of the guards snarled after doing a double take. Utterly taken aback at finding an Onyx witch out and about in the Valkyrie Queen's palace.

"Who the Hells are you?" another of the guards asked as they readied daggers in Caspian's direction.

Cass shoved his hands into the pockets of his leather trousers, nonchalant about having three men staring him down with weapons. Men that wouldn't hesitate to reap his soul.

Arrogant fool.

"Don't mind me, I'm just looking for someone," he told them, advancing another step forward. "A Valkyrie the queen is keeping prisoner in this wing? Sound familiar?"

"Secure him and bring him to Ignia," the first guard barked at the others. "I'll continue searching the wing."

As the guards stepped toward Caspian, he laughed. "Oh, c'mon, guys. Can't we work this out without involving the queen?"

Both guards lunged in sync. Caspian lithely dove between them, rolling on the ground and back onto his feet in a single fluid motion.

"I supposed I'll take that as a no," he taunted as he spun to face them once more.

The two Valkyries unsheathed throwing knives from their belts and launched them at the witch's head, but as promised, Cass didn't lift a hand. Amina watched as the knives froze inches away from Caspian's skin, a sudden draft kicking up around her as his wind magic flared to life. With a concentrated look on his face and a slight flick of his chin, the knives spun in place, in midair, until their points were facing toward their owners instead. Then, another gust of wind later, they were embedded right through each of the guards' right eyes.

Blood squirted from the wounds as the leader shouted in outrage and called for more guards to assist. At that, Cass did finally lift a hand, but it was not to physically strike anyone. Instead, he made a circular motion in the air, and Amina watched in awe as the trio clutched at their throats, knees slowly lowering to the ground as they fought to breathe. She had never really seen a witch use their magic up close like this before. And certainly never one with such precise skill. Most Onyx witches she'd come in contact with were a part of the Guild, but their attacks were broad and used blunt force. Caspian knew how to manipulate every single molecule of air around him as sharp and clean as Amina and her slayers knew how to use their wit and claws.

Caspian spun toward Amina and gave her a rueful wink, opening his mouth to begin boasting, she assumed, but before he could get out a single word, or she a warning, a figure closed in from behind him. The lead guard was a sickly shade of blue, eyes bulging out of his face as he fought against Caspian's grip on his lungs, but with the last of his strength, he'd managed to haul himself up from the ground and plunged a glowing hand right into Caspian's chest.

"*No*," Amina shouted, her voice drowned out by the alarm still blaring around them.

She pushed away from her hiding spot and out of the shadows, descending on the man trying to reap Caspian's soul from the witch's body like she was a wraith escaping the Hells. Caspian was frozen in place, eyes glossing over as the hazy blue glow of his soul slowly seeped out of his body. Amina didn't hesitate; she swiped her claws so deep through the guard's neck that she nearly decapitated him, sending a spray of blood across her face. The guard dropped like a stone to the ground.

Amina spun to face Caspian, channeling her magic as she reached out and grasped the wisps of his soul hovering between them in the air. Her fingertips warmed as she worked to fuse it into his body. When it faded back into the vessel of his body without a fight, she damn near let out a cry of relief.

A moment later, life awoke in his eyes once more, but the frame of his body instantly sagged with exhaustion.

"What the Hells?" he gasped as he clumsily stumbled a step away from her. "What just happened?"

"What just happened was that your arrogance almost cost you your soul," she condemned, fury bleeding into her tone. "Your skills with magic might be well practiced, but that doesn't help against a being who can rip away your *soul*."

"I guess that means we make a good team, right, Valkyrie?" he joked, though his words were still a bit breathless.

Amina wanted to scold him some more, but she swore she could hear the pounding sound of footsteps approaching in the distance, and they didn't have any more time to waste. "Start searching rooms for Meli," she snapped before stepping away and beelining for the first closed door in her line of sight.

Amina threw the door open and found only an empty bedroom. She quickly moved on to the next. From what she could tell, there were about twenty rooms down this corridor alone. Their luck would be finding Meli in the very last one they checked. As they continued to move down the hall, searching every single room one by one, Amina spared a moment to glance back at Caspian. Despite the chaos unfolding around them, and the fact that his soul had almost just been reaped, his expression remained calm and confident. But his eyes reflected the same determination she felt burning within her.

☽ ☽ ☽ ● ☾ ☾ ☾

Twenty-six doors, two hallways, and three more bodies later, they finally found Meli. Amina had nearly missed the girl sleeping atop the luxurious down comforter in one of the pristinely decorated guest rooms. And as she and Caspian approached, they both knew instantly something was very wrong.

Meli was as stiff as a corpse. Amina rushed to check the girl's pulse, and though it was faint, it was still there.

"Why would the queen leave her here instead of in a dungeon somewhere?" Caspian wondered. "I don't get it."

"Because, like me, anyone coming for her would never think to check one of the queen's personal guest rooms. Not to mention the fact that she's clearly not moving any time soon." To demonstrate her point, Amina lifted the girl's arm and then let it go, watching as it fell limply back to her side. "Let's go." Amina scooped up the girl's lanky frame and fixed her over her shoulder with a grunt. Cass still looked like there wasn't an ounce of energy left in his body after the almost reaping, and she was plenty capable of carrying the girl herself anyway.

They made their way out into the east wing's inner corridor, their equally long strides carrying them back to the main hall in a flash.

When they arrived, however, they realized their situation had gotten so much worse. Fifteen guards, at least, were waiting for them at the end of the hall—the only exit.

"Feel like just strutting up to them now?" she suggested as Caspian's face turned ashen.

"Retrieve them," the guard at the helm of the unit ordered.

Amina looked around frantically, going over every route Lyra had gone over with them. Unfortunately, their original escape plan was not intended for this part of the palace and the only possible out she saw here was . . . the window.

"Break the window," she told Caspian.

"What?" he called over the escalating noise.

"Shatter the window!" she yelled as she summoned her wings.

A look of understanding dawned on him, and a moment later, his wind magic was swirling all around them, slowly building into a monstrous tornado. When he unleashed the storm toward the enormous pane of glass that stretched on the east wing's outer palace wall, Amina shielded her face against Meli's body. Glass scattered into the air all around them, leaving knicks and cuts across any exposed skin it touched.

Shouts of frustration and surprise rang out from the guards, but Amina was already moving, launching herself through the open window with a powerful pump of her wings, the muscles in her back groaning at Meli's added weight, but she did not buckle.

"Hold them off!" she commanded Caspian. "I'll be right back!"

Before he could respond, she was already diving toward the ground, eyes searching for a safe spot to leave Meli. Just past the front terrace of the palace, she spotted the flat roof of a nearby manor.

That's going to have to do, she told herself as she zipped through the air toward the rooftop, scanning the outside of the palace for any signs of her friends or the witches. But it didn't seem as if the citizens of Valor had caught on to the ordeal inside the Valkyrie Queen's estate quite yet.

She landed atop the manor's roof as gently as she could, sliding Meli off her shoulder and dropping the girl down a little less gently than she probably should've. But the Valkyrie still had yet to stir, so she figured no harm, no foul.

Launching back into the sky, she shot toward the shattered window of the east wing like an arrow, piercing through the air straight and true. When she touched down to perch on the sill, she let her wings spread out to their full span, shaking them out as she reached out a taloned hand in offering to Caspian. Caspian, who was currently holding off fifteen Valkyrie guards through sheer will alone. His muscles were taut from strain, beads of sweat dripping down his face as he held his magic against the guards, but the moment he saw her outstretched hand, he let go.

Leaping toward her with reckless trust.

31

The blare of the alarm came seconds after Kai's name left the Valkyrie Queen's lips. Calla was so stunned hearing her childhood friend's name that she barely registered the sound of the screeching noise in the distance until Ignia said something.

"Ah... it seems like someone has come back for your brother's heart," the queen told them. "You'll have to excuse me while I go deal with them. You wouldn't mind waiting in my dungeon, would you?" A haughty smile. "Maybe being reunited with your friend will inspire your decision to hand over the Fates' Dice, hmm?"

The queen reached for her bell, alerting her guards that she was ready to have Calla and Gideon dragged away like they had Amina, but Calla had reached her limit. She was exhausted, overstimulated, and, most of all, *raging*. Her emotions had been yanked in too many different directions over the past two months, but the one she seemed to be able to settle into most was her fury. Fury that this woman had pried into her and Gideon's past in order to extort something out of them.

Fury that her and her friends couldn't get a moment of peace to celebrate the fact that some of them were even *alive*.

Gideon's eyes never left her face as the guards burst into the room. He was watching to see what move she would make, waiting to support her accordingly. She took a deep breath.

"Be careful not to touch her skin," the queen ordered her men. "She's a Siphon."

Gideon held Calla's gaze as the guards made their way over to grab them. He dipped his chin in a nod.

Do it.

Calla reached for her inner Siphon and pulled, seizing on to every being in the room except for Gideon. "Stop."

The queen's eyes widened as she felt Calla's power pulse through her veins. Calla tightened her grip on all of them, just enough that the veins in their foreheads, biceps, and necks began to bulge.

"Here's what's going to happen," Calla told the queen. "You are going to let us walk away, right now, or I am going to paint every wall in this room with your subjects' blood."

A furious glint sparked in the queen's eyes. "You would kill innocent people? You would let your friend die? Because if you walk away, that's what will happen."

Calla steeled her nerves. The mention of Kai nearly made her give in. Drop her hold and let herself be dragged away. But then she would be a prisoner.

"Any guard that serves *you* isn't innocent," Calla spat. "And Kai . . . if you truly have him here, his death would be on your hands. Not mine. And it doesn't really matter anyway because we do not have the Fates' Dice. Lysandra and Myrea made certain of that."

The queen let out a hiss. "Are you a fool, girl? Giving those sadistic bitches—"

"If I were you," Gideon cut in, spearing Ignia with cold look, "I'd reconsider such an ironic cliché as calling the Witch Queens sadistic bitches when you're clearly cut from the same cloth."

"Now, give me one good reason to not take you out of this fight?" Calla prompted.

Ignia swallowed. "If you kill me, and my deal with the Fates is not fulfilled, all of my people will lose their magic."

"And what is it that you must fulfill?" Gideon pressed.

"Five hundred thousand more souls," the queen gritted out. "I'm sure your new friends can spell it all out for you. They stole the contract after all."

Gideon rubbed a hand over his mouth in horrified disbelief. "Is that . . . is that why you reap so many witches?"

The queen smiled. "And I'll keep doing it."

Calla gave her magic a squeeze, and the woman let out a pealing scream.

"I could do it," Calla told her. "I could take everything away."

Ignia's chest heaved with the effort of her breaths in Calla's vise.

"The reason I won't isn't for you. Remember that."

Calla gave a flick of her hands and slammed the guards right into the queen, leaving her and Gideon plenty of space to slip out of the study and into the fray going on in the corridor. Guards were bustling in all directions; the noise in the palace seemed to be reaching a crescendo. Calla heard Ignia snarling at her guards to *find them*, and she and Gideon picked up their paces.

They dashed down the hallway and back toward the front foyer, sending waves of power crashing into any Valkyrie that dared look in their direction. Only one of the guards managed to land a hit, a throwing knife that sliced through the top of Calla's cheekbone. She only knew because she watched the same cut appear on the side of Gideon's face, blood spilling over his jawline.

As they reached the front door and made their way out into the evening air, Calla bounded down the marble steps outside and asked, "Where do we go? Should we have tried to help the others? Should we have gone search for Kai? Do you think she really has him?"

Gideon opened his mouth to answer, but then his focus suddenly shifted to something in the sky behind her. She twisted around just in time to see Amina jetting through the open air with Caspian in her arms. Calla went to take a step to head in the same direction, but Gideon grabbed her hand and yanked her over to him. Reaching up to cup both her cheeks in his hands.

"I'm so proud of you," he affirmed. "If Kai is someone important to you, I'll go back in there right now."

Calla's chest tightened. She knew he would. But she shook her head.

"I know it might make me a monster," she whispered. "But Kai turned his back on me once. And though I've never held that against him, if I have to choose between checking on the friends who have never wavered from my side or risk leaving Kai behind... I have to leave him behind."

Gideon nodded. "What you said to Ignia was correct—if anything happens to him, it's because *she* did it."

Calla squeezed her eyes shut and pressed her forehead to his chest, just for a moment. "I know there will have to be sacrifices and death in this war. But I *hate* it. I'm so angry. And I don't want to be. I don't want to let them make me like this."

"I know," he murmured as he ran a soothing hand over her hair. "We're going to get through this. One step at a time."

"Together?" she whispered.

Gideon held her tighter. "Together."

32

Another minute of the incessant alarm and Ezra was going to go mad. Lyra hadn't made it back yet, and now there was a blaring alarm and a flood of guards pouring into the corridor outside the queen's room. He and Sabine had barricaded the doors with as much furniture as they could manage to move—which wasn't much considering how heavy everything in this damn room seemed to be—but the guards were only seconds away from busting through.

"How the Hells are we supposed to get out of here?" Ezra asked her.

Sabine jutted a thumb over her shoulder, toward a window. "You better start flapping your wings, dragon boy."

He gave her an incredulous look. "There is no way in the Hells—"

"Sabine! Open the window! *Now!*"

It was Lyra's voice, echoing out of the trapdoor as they came rushing up the steps and bursting into the room. There was something in their hands, which they promptly shoved into Ezra's chest.

"Whatever you do, don't drop that," Lyra told him before taking him by the shoulders and spinning him toward the window Sabine had just pried open. "There are guards coming through the tunnels as well. You need to jump *now*."

"There's no way my wings are fitting through that tiny opening," Ezra told them both. Sabine immediately fixed that by reaching up to the molding at the top of the stacked window panes and pulling herself up until her chin was above her hands so she could place both of her feet against the glass and slam her boots into it until the entire window popped out of the frame and fell into the darkness below.

When she dropped back to her feet and turned to throw Ezra a smug look, he was suddenly overwhelmed by how sexy the entire demonstration had been.

Not the time or place, he scolded himself.

"Stop drooling and *move*," Lyra growled at him.

He stepped up onto the windowsill, looking out into the night sky. They were at least a few stories up. There was no way he was going to be able to jump. He said as much aloud.

And then the guards busted through the bedroom door, sending splinters of wood scattering through the air.

"Time's up, Prince," Sabine chirped.

Ezra looked down at her over his shoulder, ready to tell her they were going to just have to risk the fight, but instead, Sabine threw her full weight into his back and pushed him out the damned window.

A surprised grunt fell from his mouth as he awkwardly somersaulted through the air, clutching the wooden box in his arms like his life depended on it. He tried to gather his bearings, enough to open his wings and—fly. One pump and he evened out, hovering in the air. Another and he rose. Higher and higher. Adrenaline flooded his system as he got closer and closer to the stars. Ezra looked back down to the palace, searching the dark for the Valkyries.

Lyra was launching themself, Sabine cradled in their arms, off the palace's turret. He concentrated on holding himself in place, a feat that was much more difficult that it seemed, and waited as they swiftly made their way toward him.

"Head down before you fall!" Lyra shouted at him.

Ezra did as they said, angling his body as best as he could toward the earth. He couldn't see if Lyra was following him, or if they'd zipped ahead, but he was too focused to look back and check. That is, until Sabine screamed his name in a way that made his heart nearly stop. At the sound, he dropped too quick, plummeting nearly ten feet before he caught himself and was able to roll over in midair to see what was happening.

Sabine was falling.

He didn't have time to look for what happened to Lyra, didn't have time to think twice about what he was about to do. He just dropped the box in his hands and dove.

Ezra tucked his wings in as close as he could to his back. Urging himself in her direction, reaching out with his arms toward her as she tumbled through the air. With every inch he got closer to reaching her, they both got two inches closer to the ground. He kept pushing. Closer and closer and closer. And when he was finally able to grasp her and pull her into his body, they were yards away from crashing.

Ezra unfurled his wings from his back, spreading them out as far as he could, Sabine clutching him so tightly he almost wasn't able to breathe. He could feel her body shaking as they continued their turbulent fall, his wings acting as a parachute with what little space they had left. And just as they were about to hit the earth, he rolled himself over to take the brunt of the impact.

"*Fuck*," he groaned as every inch of his body screamed in agony. Sabine was still clutched against his chest, but he didn't unwrap his arms from around her. Not yet.

He could already feel his magic starting to focus its healing properties on the small tendons that had snapped in his wings from landing on them so hard. But other than that, it didn't feel like anything was broken. He'd managed to slow their fall just enough to avoid that, at least.

"Sabine?" He rubbed a hand down her spine. "Are you all right?"

That's when he felt it. Tears. Sliding over his skin where her face was pressed into the crook of his neck.

"It's okay, baby," Ezra soothed, his voice oddly gruff. "I got you. You're okay."

She stayed there, tucked against him for a long silent minute before finally pushing herself away and climbing to her feet. He slowly followed, gritting his teeth against the aching in his body as he straightened himself up. When he looked at her face, he saw that her tears had already been wiped away, though the stains on her cheeks and his skin remained.

"If you tell anyone I cried," she threatened, though her words didn't have the same bite as usual, "I'll send you right back to the Valley of Souls."

That pissed him off.

"For Hells' sake, harpy"—he shook his head at her—"is having a single vulnerable moment so bad?"

She looked away from him. "We need to find Lyra. The guards—they shot an arrow through their wing. It took them by surprise, and they dropped me."

Ezra took a deep, disappointed breath. It was clear she wasn't going to give him anything more than that, and he was much too exhausted to fight her on it. One step forward, three steps back.

"Sabine!"

Ezra and Sabine both looked up to see Lyra making their way down to them. When they touched down on the ground, the first thing Ezra noticed was the bloody patch of feathers in the top of their left wing. The second was the wooden box he'd dropped when he went to catch Sabine. Somehow it wasn't smashed into pieces.

"Lyra," Sabine sighed in relief, throwing her arms around the other Valkyrie.

"I'm so sorry," Lyra choked out. "I'm so sorry, I didn't mean—"

"I'm fine, it's okay," Sabine cooed back.

Ezra stood to the side, silent, a pang of jealousy spearing through him as he watched the interaction. When Lyra caught his haze over Sabine's shoulder, however, they threw him a deeply appreciative look, and for a moment at least, he knew he'd earned their approval.

Ezra dipped his chin in an acknowledging nod.

When the two of them finally pulled apart, Lyra said, "I have bad news."

They presented the box to them both, pushing in a hidden button to make the lid pop open and reveal . . . a note.

Missing something?
—Ignia

"Please tell me that wasn't supposed to be my heart," Ezra griped.

"She's been onto us," Lyra confirmed. "I triggered the alarm when I retrieved this. An alarm that most definitely wasn't there the last time."

"Well, let's hope your friend made it out safely so we don't have to deem that whole mission as a bust," Ezra muttered, and Lyra nodded in agreement.

"I spied Amina and Caspian just two streets over," they said. "Let's go."

With a mixture of relief and solemness, they continued into the night. But amid the quietness, there was a glimmer of hope, a shared understanding that they had been stronger together.

Hannah awoke covered in sweat, in an unfamiliar bed, in an unfamiliar room. Her body began to panic, her chest heaving in fear as she thrashed beneath the covers tucked in around her.

"Hannah, it's okay. You're safe," a musical voice said from somewhere in the dark.

Hannah's breath hitched as she recognized that voice, her eyes searching the shadows frantically for its owner. A lamp clicked on, and she blinked rapidly, waiting for her eyes to adjust. And then there she was.

Delphine.

"You've been asleep for a while," Delphine told her. "Do you need some water?"

Hannah swallowed, wincing against the dryness of her throat, and nodded.

"I'll be right back," Delph swore.

Hannah watched as she got up and left. Taking in her surroundings, she noted that she was folded into white satin sheets, the mattress beneath her so soft that it dipped even with the weight of her slight frame. There was a wooden dresser across from the bed, but other than that the only furniture in the room was the wooden chair Delphine had been sitting in and a small side table for the lamp. Something about the space rattled a memory loose in her brain, but just as she tried to grasp it, Delphine came back in, glass of water in hand.

Delphine sat down on the edge of the bed as she handed the water to Hannah and motioned for her to drink. While Hannah greedily gulped the entire glass down, she felt her stomach rumble with hunger.

"Thorne is going to make you some food." Delphine smiled. "I would, except I think we both know it probably wouldn't be edible."

Hannah reached over and placed the glass on the little side table. "Where are we?"

She cringed at the sound of her own voice. So unused, it was as rough as sand.

"Some sort of safe house," Delphine explained. "I have a lot to catch you up on. But first . . ." She bit her lip.

Hannah held her breath in anticipation.

"Do you . . . do you remember what happened?" Delphine asked.

Hannah looked down at her hands. "Sort of."

"You terrified me," Delphine admitted. "I've never seen so much dark magic before. There were bodies digging themselves out of the ground."

Hannah squeezed her eyes shut. "I know, I know. I've been trying to keep it in. And then Ezra showed up and he smelled so much of *death* and I just... erupted."

"Maybe that's the problem," Delphine murmured.

"What do you mean?"

Delphine sighed. "Locking away something that is so integral to your very being, like your magic... It's only a matter of time until it forces its way out. Believe me."

"I heard you calling, you know," Hannah whispered. "You're the only reason I came back to myself."

Hannah hesitated for a moment before reaching out and grasping Delphine's hand. Delphine squeezed back.

"I'm sorry I wasn't able to keep my promise. That I couldn't get to the Siren's Sea."

Delphine waved a hand in dismissal. "I'm glad you didn't come. That's not a place I ever wished for you or Calla to see. And I needed to finish things there myself anyway. I was just too much of a coward before." A beat. "I can leave you to clean up in the bathroom while I check on Thorne."

"Where are the others?" Hannah wondered.

"That is a story for over dinner." Delph snorted. "But they will hopefully arrive soon enough."

Hannah nodded, and Delphine hopped up from the bed, plucking the empty drinking glass off the side table to take it back to wherever she'd found it. When she reached the bedroom door, however, she paused and turned back around.

"Hannah?"

"Yes?" Hannah whispered.

"Do you . . . do you remember what happened after I found you in the woods? Before you fainted?"

Hannah's entire body vibrated with adrenaline now. She worried she had imagined it, her kiss with Delphine. The one sliver of light amid a sea of darkness.

Hannah swallowed and admitted, "Yes."

Delphine's expression immediately softened, and Hannah's hope soared. Now was her chance to finally tell Delphine that she was in love with—

"I want you to know it's okay," Delphine assured. "I know it didn't mean anything."

And with those six words, Hannah's hope crashed and burned.

"I just didn't want you to worry about it," Delphine said with a smile.

Hannah only stared as her friend slipped out of the room and shut the door behind her.

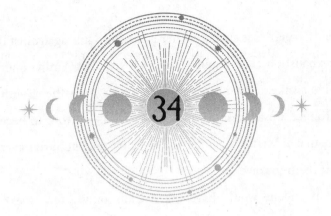

Thanks to Lyra's connections, leaving Valor didn't require much fanfare. By the time the city had realized something was happening at the palace, the group had found one another—in their various disheveled states—and Lyra was quick to fetch and shepherd the witches into the very carriage they'd arrived in. Stealing the vehicle was turning out to be their best investment yet. Though the horses might not have agreed considering how nervous Calla's presence made them.

Lyra and Ezra decided to take the driver spots out front, and the rest of them piled, somewhat uncomfortably, into the cab. Uncomfortable not because of space, but because of the clear tension buzzing in the air and the odd way Sabine was regarding the unconscious Valkyrie Amina and Caspian had rescued—Meli, Calla recalled her name. In fact, after Calla scribbled a quick note inside the enchanted communication device to inform Delphine they were all heading her way, she found herself very cozy as she slowly drifted off against Gideon's shoulder. Caspian was sitting on her right, head lulling against the wall as the exhaustion took ahold of him as well. But Amina and Sabine were wide awake, sitting on the bench across from them, with Meli's body propped up against Amina's side. It was starting to become an odd joke that at least one person had to be passed out in this carriage in order for them to travel.

And if anyone would have asked Calla only a few weeks ago if she'd ever be sitting, amicably, across from the woman who ripped out Ezra's heart, she'd have probably told them only when the Hells had frozen over.

"Here," Gideon whispered to her, and she lifted her head to look at him in question, eyelids heavy. He lifted his arm so she could slide closer into him, wrapping it around her back as she nestled her face into the crook of his neck. When he rested his chin atop her head, she had to resist the urge to hum in contentment, conscious of her audience.

They rode in silence for hours, and Calla found herself sliding in and out of a deep sleep. Light snores sounded through the cab from Caspian—even Ezra and Sabine had both dosed off at some point. By the time they exited the Land of the Valkyries and made it all the way up the middle pass of the Miroir Mountains, Calla was ready to give up the world in exchange for a bed.

The carriage rolled to a slow stop, and everyone began groggily stretching out their limbs before piling out of the cab. When Calla stepped outside, onto a snow-covered ground, the scene she found before her was enough to take her breath away. She'd never been this far north, had only ever heard of the celestial-like wonder that were the Miroir Mountains. But no description she'd ever been told could have possibly done it justice.

Crystal peaks jutted into a diamond-encrusted night sky as far as the eye could see. Their sheer faces reflected the surrounding world like mirrors. But the way they reflected the stars? It made everything before her look like an otherworldly dreamscape, the celestial tapestry above a dazzling muse.

A shiver ran down her spine at both the beauty and the crisp chill that clung to the air here. She knew there were plenty of different types of beings who made the passages between the mountains, and even the peaks, their home. But she couldn't imagine living in a place that was so cold for most of the year. Estrella would have been starting to defrost right about now, but the mountains before her looked as if they had not remembered spring was supposed to be coming.

Something heavy dropped over her shoulders then. Gideon's cloak.

She looked over at him and smiled in thanks. "You won't be too cold?"

"Maybe." A smirk. "Fortunately, I look good in blue."

She snorted.

"The house is a mile off the trail," Lyra announced to all of them. "We can take the horses, but we'll have to wrap their legs for the snow. The carriage's wheels won't make it through, though."

All three men immediately got to work on the horses, unhitching them from the carriage and using the spare clothing they had to tightly wrap each of the stallions' legs. When they were done, they began their trek, sloshing through the powdery ice, teeth clattering together. When the charming stone cottage finally came into view, Calla thought she might weep, and everyone's paces instantly picked up.

The cottage's quaint exterior was adorned with an intricate wooden lattice that stretched along the front facade, icicles as long as her forearm drooping to the ground instead of the vines Calla suspected grew there during the warmer months. A single chimney protruded from the home's roof, emitting clouds of smoke that danced lazily into the clear night sky. Large windows sat on either side of the doorway, but their wooden shutters had been latched closed, likely to keep as much heat inside as possible. Lyra and Sabine led the horses down the footpath toward the back of the house, where Calla could see a stable. The rest of them knocked on the front entrance and waited impatiently for someone to answer.

When Delphine pulled the door open, they stampeded past her—right to the fireplace.

"Thank the Gods," Delphine said as Calla and the rest of them began pulling off their wet socks and shoes to begin thawing themselves out. "Thorne is already passed out for the night. Did you know he could cook? You all missed out on a spectacular meal. Though there are some leftovers in the kitchen if anyone is hungry."

Caspian and Ezra threw glances at each other before breaking into a full-speed run out of the cozy little den and toward an archway that looked like it led to the kitchen.

There was a sound of something clattering to the ground, a grunt of pain, and then Caspian's declarative: "Too slow, Ez!"

"Hope no one else wanted any," Delphine commented.

Sabine made a face and stomped toward the staircase on the far wall without a word.

"Are you hungry?" Gideon asked Calla, scrubbing a hand through his hair to dislodge any flurries that'd gotten caught in his cobalt tresses.

"Yes," she admitted. "But—"

He shook his head as he started for the kitchen himself. "I'll take care of it. You get settled in."

When he'd disappeared with the rest of them, Delphine gave Calla a smirk. "You've got that man wrapped entirely around your finger."

Calla blushed, and Delphine threw an arm around her shoulders, guiding her over to the stairs.

"How did it go?" Delph asked as they made their way up the steps.

"It went . . . interestingly," Calla said. "I'll tell you everything while I change—how are the bedrooms?"

"There are six of them," Delphine informed her. "All only have a single bed, but they're plenty big for two people each if needed. Thorne is already passed out, like I said. I'm staying with Hannah. And I figured you and Gideon would . . . share. That leaves three bedrooms for Ezra, Cass, and the Valkyries to fight over."

Calla shrugged. "Works for me. How's Hannah?"

"Oh!" Delphine exclaimed as she led Calla into the first available bedroom once they reached the second floor. "She's awake."

Calla started. "*What?* I want to see—"

"Well, she's not awake right now," Delph clarified. "But she woke up. Earlier. That's why Thorne cooked. We figured she'd need a square meal to get her energy back."

Calla bobbed her head in agreement. "Okay, I'll fill you both in tomorrow morning, then. I think the plan is for everyone to get a good night's sleep for once before we decide the next steps."

Delphine nodded and squeezed Calla's shoulders one last time before disentangling herself to head back to her own room. "Sweet dreams!"

Calla unloaded her backpack onto the floor the second the door clicked shut and let out a satisfying groan of relief. She didn't hesitate to begin peeling her clothes off her body, folding them into a neat pile next to the bag. The balmy air of the cottage felt wonderful against her bare skin compared to the damp garments. She spotted a little matchbook on a table next to the bed and struck one of the wooden sticks to light the gas lamp that sat next to them. A warm glow illuminated the space, and she quickly grabbed one of the only changes of clothes she had left and padded to the attached en suite bathroom.

There was a single vanity sink, two gas sconces bookending the large mirror that sat above it. She lit those lamps as well and then turned her attention to the giant porcelain tub sitting in the middle of the room. The back edge of the tub had different vials of soaps and oils lined across it, and as she drew a bath, she poured a pinkish-colored one into the scalding water, watching as the running stream churned out clouds and clouds of bubbles.

Calla had just sunk down to her shoulders, sloshing suds over the lip of the tub and onto the floor, when the knock sounded in the bedroom.

"Calliope?" Gideon's deep voice called as he walked into the other room.

"I'll be out soon!" she called.

A few minutes later and she felt shiny and new, her long hair brushed out and plaited into two braids that reached down to her navel. She pulled on a pair of soft cotton pants and a knit top that would hopefully keep her warm if the house became drafty during the night. When she opened the bathroom door and peeked into the room, she found Gideon stretched out on the bed, leaning back against the headboard with his arms folded behind his head. His eyes were closed, and she took the opportunity to just . . . admire him.

Sometimes, when she thought about the girl she was the night they met all those weeks ago, she couldn't believe how far they'd come. How badly she'd wanted him to suffer when she was standing on that stage, being auctioned off by those insidious bastards. And now . . . it felt like he was her whole world. Like if he wasn't tethered to her, if their souls weren't intertwined, she might have let the queens win. Not the war, never that. But let them turn her into the monster she could so easily become. The one the Fates had tried to mold her into her entire life.

One that would have killed every single Rouge witch back in Myrea's palace just to get to the woman herself. One that would have drowned that study in the Valkyrie Queen's blood despite the fact that the queen told her all of her people would lose their magic as a result.

But Gideon's selflessness, his tenacity for always putting others before himself, reminded her that strength was the ability to stay good, and empathetic, despite who the people that raised you wanted you to be. That just because one *could* wield power didn't mean one should. And if one did, to only wield it protecting those who didn't have it themselves.

That's where the queens had gone so wrong.

They swore that they made their bargains with the Fates in order to bring power and health back to their land, but they did not distribute that power equally. Because they didn't care about anyone aside from themselves having real power—they only wanted their subjects to have a semblance of power, enough magic that could be funneled directly back to their rulers.

And the reason she loved Gideon most? He had never once mentioned that he'd want to inherit his mother's throne if—no, *when*—they won this war. He had no interest in playing into his mother's favoritism. No interest in being worshipped as a king.

"I can feel you staring at me," he murmured, slowly blinking his eyes open. "What are you thinking about?"

"After the war, when the queens are destroyed and the Realms are without rulers, what are you going to do?"

He raised a brow. "What am *I* going to do?"

She nodded. "If your mother is gone, you're the crown prince. We've only ever had the Witch Queens, and you'd be the only technical heir...."

He was already shaking his head, and she let her words trail off.

"I will not be ruling anything. Birth is not a good enough reason to be a ruler. So, to answer your question, I am going to go wherever you go."

Her heart began to pound at his words, and she whispered, "Anywhere I go?"

"Everywhere," he confirmed before swinging his legs over the side of the bed and standing. "I'm going to clean up while you eat. I left a plate of eggs and fruit for you down in the kitchen."

Calla gave him a bright smile. "Thank you."

He bent down and pressed a kiss to her temple before slipping into the bathroom to wash up. She headed downstairs to eat and found that everyone else had seemingly already gone to their rooms. Calla wolfed down the eggs Gideon had fried for her and the slices of apple and sourdough bread, heading back to their room when she finished. She could hear the water still running in the bathroom, so she left the lamp lit and tucked herself beneath the plush comforter.

Sometime later, as she drifted in and out of sleep, she felt him return. He snuffed out the light and then crawled into bed behind her, wrapping his arms around her and dragging her body back into his. And she swore she heard him start to whisper something, but she was already slipping under.

35

Sabine couldn't sleep. She couldn't eat. She couldn't stop pacing in her room. Sabine was alone because she couldn't deal with any more suspicious looks from Lyra or Amina.

That damned prince was driving her *mad*.

It's okay, baby. I got you. You're okay.

How dare he affect her like this? How dare she *let* him?

Was she the one? The one that fucked you up so bad I'm having to pay for it now?

Meli wasn't the one to blame. It was herself. Because no matter who she was with, she would not bend. Would not compromise. The price of which, she always knew, was that every relationship would eventually come to a blazing end. It was a fate she'd given herself and was more than happy to bear. She didn't need anyone or anything. She only needed to be herself. Her True Name from the Veritas Tree.

The day she broke up with Meli, she swore she would never commit to anyone ever again. That once she'd gotten her True Name she would never let anyone have the ability to break her heart. Afraid if she did, she'd loathe herself after everything she went through to become this person she was always meant to be. Falling for a man who she barely knew, who she had a magic influence over, was not an option.

She shoved her hands into her pockets in frustration and felt her left hand brush against something cold. She stopped her pacing as she fished out the object and held it out in front of her. It was the brooch she'd found stashed in her room back at Lyra's when she was going through the things she wanted to take with her before they went to Ignia's palace. Truthfully, she'd forgotten she even had it. It was just some random bauble she'd stolen only a few weeks ago from a lover whose name she couldn't even remember. She hadn't known what compelled her to take it then, but now, as she rubbed the pad of her thumb over its surface, a knot formed in her stomach.

Before she knew what she was doing, she was flying out of her room and down the hall.

)·)·)·●·(·(·(

Ezra was wide awake. And still starving. Lying atop his bed, alone, staring at the ceiling.

That damned Valkyrie was driving him mad.

He was starting to worry Sabine had been right, that his fascination with her was only because a part of her was used to bring him back. Or, at least, because of some sick sense of debt that he felt he owed her. But none of that explained why he couldn't get all the little moments they'd spent together out of his head.

How when he'd watched after her, that first week when she was in so much pain, she'd thank him over and over and over again when he brought her damp rags to cool her fever. So out of it that she probably hadn't even realized what she was saying. How she'd ask him to tell her stories to take her mind off the agony. How the second she began to feel better, she showed him how funny she was. How she'd suggest little games on their hike and ask him questions that were much too personal and much too inappropriate much too soon. How a wicked gleam entered her eye any time there was an opportunity for bloodshed. How she looked at her friends like they were her entire world.

And Godsdammit if he didn't think she was the most stunning being he'd ever seen.

A single knock on the door cut through all his thoughts, and he pushed himself up onto his elbows. "Come in."

For a moment, nothing happened, and he wondered if he'd imagined the knock. But then the door slowly creaked open and there she was. He sat up in shock as she stepped all the way inside and leaned back against the door until it shut.

For a while, they only stared at each other. Saying nothing.

It was Ezra who finally broke the silence.

"Can I help you?" he prompted, tone dry.

She lifted her hand, and for a split second, he didn't understand, until he saw there was something in it. He lifted a brow as he stood from the bed, walking over to take the object on her palm.

It was a pin. The piece was in the shape of a dragon's head, two onyx jewels for eyes. He looked up at her, puzzled.

"What is this?"

"A sign," she muttered.

"A sign for what?"

She swallowed. "I want to tell you something."

He waited. She said nothing.

"Okay?" he urged.

"My name wasn't always Sabine," she said.

He tilted his head with curiosity. He wasn't sure what that meant, but whatever it was, he could tell that it was deeply important for her, and he didn't want to interrupt.

"A couple years ago, I made the journey to the Isle of the Veritas Tree. And I received my True Name."

Ah. Ezra knew about the isle from the atlas in his mother's palace. A tiny island between the continents of Aetherius where those who needed to transition into their true forms journeyed.

"I . . ." She trailed off.

"You don't have to tell me this if you don't want to," he assured her.

"I want to," she said, determined. "It's just, now that I get to live as my true self, sharing myself with anyone else isn't easy. I don't like being told what to do, or who to be, or where to go. If I'm honest, I wouldn't even be here if Amina and Lyra weren't so passionate about it. I don't think I'm what you'd refer to as a morally sound person."

He snorted. He had enough memories of her daggers in his flesh to know that already.

She glared at him. "I'm afraid you and your friends are the pure-of-heart types. Wanting to save the world and all that nonsense. Your ex is a *literal* Godsend."

"I can assure you neither Calla nor Gideon wanted anything to do with saving the world, and in fact, half the reason we're in this mess is because they tried to get themselves out of it. Also, there was a reason Calla and I didn't work."

"Because you always have something smart to say?" she quipped.

"Among other things," he said dryly.

"Well, if we'd met before I received my True Name," she pressed on, "I wouldn't even be someone you'd . . ."

He waited for her to finish, but it didn't seem that she could.

"I guess it's a good thing we didn't meet before, then," he stated. "Especially because your name on my tongue sounds so right."

Her breath caught at his words, but before he could say anything else, Sabine blurted, "I stole this pin from some guy I slept with weeks ago. I was sneaking out of his place, and I saw it on his dresser, and something came over me. I just took it."

He furrowed his brow in confusion. "And?"

"I don't believe in coincidences," she said. "Do you?"

He thought about that for a moment before he answered. "Not

anymore. Especially considering the man I was before death is not someone who I think would have been able to take you on. He would have been too much of a coward. Still too caught up on someone not meant for him all because he couldn't handle not being wanted."

"And what if I told you I didn't want you? That no matter how many times you try and take care of me, get to know me, catch me from falling, that I do not want you?"

"Is it that you don't want me? Or is it that you don't *want* to want me?" he accused.

Her jaw clenched.

He smirked and shrugged. "Either way. Perhaps we can table this conversation for when I figure out a way to get an exorbitant amount of marshmallows."

A surprised laugh burst from her lips, and she immediately clapped a hand over her mouth.

He was silent as he watched a flutter of emotions cross her face, and though he wasn't expecting her to say anything more, a moment later she whispered, "The second one."

He took a step toward her, leaning down until their eyes were level.

"I guess we're in the same damned boat, then, harpy," he told her. "Believe me, no one is more surprised than me that I've come to enjoy your company. I mean, you have tried to kill me several times. And I'm sure you're regretting bringing me back from the dead about now, right?"

She was silent for a beat.

Then, "You know, a Valkyrie can only sacrifice their wings to summon a soul a single time. Our wings come back, but our ability to use our feathers for that particular task doesn't."

Something in Ezra's soul sang at her words. Such a rare, precious gift for her to only be able to give a single time—and it'd gone to him.

"Sabine?"

"Yes?" she breathed.

"Please don't stab me for doing this," he said. And then he pulled her into a searing kiss.

36

When Calla woke the next morning, Gideon was already gone, a note left in his place.

Going with Cass and Thorne to get some supplies.
—Gideon
P.S. You look lovely when you're dreaming.

Calla smiled, butterflies fluttering in her stomach at the last line. She stretched and climbed out of bed to get ready to start the day. It'd been so long since she'd done anything that resembled *normal* that she'd nearly forgotten what it was like to wake up in a comfortable bed with access to a sink and mirror. By the time she walked out of her room, she heard others talking downstairs. Notably, Delphine, whose voice Calla would recognize anywhere.

"Oh, Calla! Guess what Thorne made this morning?" Delphine exclaimed when Calla walked into the kitchen.

Delphine was sitting at the small, round dining table that was tucked away in the back corner of the kitchen, Amina and Lyra sitting in the chairs opposite her. By the three octaves Delphine's voice had gone up in that single sentence, Calla was pretty sure she could guess the answer to her friend's question, but even if she couldn't, the smell of cinnamon and yeast confirmed her suspicion. Sticky buns.

Calla turned to see the two pans of pastries sitting atop the stove. One already entirely picked over. Most likely by Delphine alone.

"Who knew Thorne was such a good cook?" Calla wondered as she pried apart one of the sweet rolls for herself.

"He was also a painter, apparently," Delphine added. "You know, before he spent a decade in Myrea's dungeon. And he lived in Noctum for a while. Isn't that wild?"

"You both had quite the conversation, I see," Calla mused as Delphine polished off the last of her sticky bun.

"It was a long trip. And Hannah wasn't available to talk to," Delphine pointed out. "But he's sweet. And hot."

"Who's hot?" a quiet, raspy voice asked.

They all turned their heads to find Hannah lingering in the kitchen doorway.

"Oh, Han," Calla said, a huge wave of relief washing over her at seeing her friend. "I'm so glad you're finally awake. There's sticky buns if you'd like breakfast."

Hannah nodded politely at the sticky buns but didn't make any move toward them. Lyra and Amina were watching her curiously as they finished their own breakfasts.

"Calla? Can I talk to you?" Hannah asked.

Calla nodded and followed Hannah out of the room. As they walked away, she could hear Delphine asking the Valkyries, "So what exactly happened last night?"

Hannah led Calla back up the stairs, to the room she was presumably staying in with Delphine. Calla made herself comfortable at the foot of the bed while Hannah closed the door.

"How are you feeling?" Calla asked, noting that Hannah's already-fair complexion looked paler than usual.

"I kissed Delphine," Hannah blurted out.

Calla's jaw dropped open. That was not at all what she was expecting Hannah to want to talk about.

"You— How— *When?*" Calla finally settled on.

"In the Dragonwoods. She found me," Hannah explained. "I was in a bad place, and she called me back to myself. I thought I was going to sink into the earth and rot there for the rest of eternity, but she called me back." Hannah took a deep breath, and tears sprung to her eyes. "And I don't know what happened. I just—I needed her. I kissed her, and then I passed out. And at first, I didn't know if that part was real. I thought I had imagined her entirely, actually, but then I woke up and she was there, and I *knew*. And then she brought it up last night."

Calla sucked in a breath of anticipation. But by the way tears began to roll down Hannah's face, she knew that conversation must not have gone in the direction they both hoped.

"She said, and I quote, *I know it didn't mean anything.*"

Calla winced. *Ouch.* "Did you tell her that it meant something to *you*?"

A sniffle. "No."

"Hannah." Calla sighed. "She doesn't realize the stakes. She thinks you probably kissed her because it was a strange situation, and you weren't entirely yourself and . . . she doesn't know how you feel about her. I'm sure she only said that to make sure you weren't embarrassed. You need to talk to her. *Really* talk to her."

"And what if she can't ever think of me that way? Where would that conversation leave us? Besides, she's already talking about how hot she thinks Thorne is," Hannah whispered.

"Delphine saying Thorne is hot is like us saying Caspian is charming and Ezra is stubborn. It's a given," Calla pointed out.

Before Hannah could counter, the doorknob wiggled, but with Hannah's weight leaning back against the door, whoever was on the other side couldn't push it open. Or, at least, they were polite not to.

"Hannah?" Delphine called. "Calla? Let me in!"

Hannah took a deep breath as she slowly stepped away from the door.

"It's going to be okay," Calla assured before telling Delphine, "Come in!"

Delphine's head popped inside first. "Everything all right?"

"Yep," Calla said casually as Delphine slipped inside and shut the door.

"Lyra and Amina were filling me in about everything at the palace.

They said their friend Meli still isn't awake. They're worried she's been poisoned."

Calla's brows lifted. "What are they going to do?"

Delphine shrugged. "The people this house belongs to are apparently supposed to show up some time in the next couple of days, and they're hopefully going to be able to help. Cass and the others should be back soon, though. Which means the Valkyries want us downstairs to begin strategizing. They're not really the rest-and-relax type."

"Well, I am," Calla muttered. "If I hadn't slept so soundly last night, I don't think— *What?*"

A wicked grin had begun to spread across Delphine's face at the mention of good sleep, and Calla already knew exactly where this was going.

"Spill," Delphine demanded, pulling Calla up and spinning them both to guide them toward the bed. They climbed up and made themselves comfortable, Delph patting a space between them to demand Hannah join.

Hannah did, silently, and though Delphine didn't recognize any tension in the room and Calla was all too aware of the precarious situation about to unfold between her friends, she still couldn't help but enjoy this moment. All of them together again. Sitting in bed gossiping like they used to in their apartment. Only this time the gossip wasn't about Calla and Ezra but . . .

"Gideon and I didn't do anything scandalous, Delph." Calla fixed her friend with an exasperated look. "Sorry to disappoint."

"*Ugh.*" Delphine scoffed in mock disappointment. "C'mon, Calla, you're sharing a bed with a hot prince, and you're telling me you both just *slept*. How am I supposed to live vicariously through you if this is all you'll give me?"

"I don't think having sex for the first time on the day that my ex was resurrected from the dead would have been the most romantic scenario," Calla joked.

"Fair enough," Delphine allowed. "Speaking of your resurrected ex, though—where the Hells is Ezra this morning? No one has seen him. Or Sabine."

Calla's eyes widened, and even Hannah seemed suddenly piqued by the information.

"What?" Delphine asked.

Calla nearly choked. "No way . . ."

"*What?*" Delphine repeated, and Calla explained, "Pretty sure Ezra has a thing for Sabine."

"Oh my Gods." Delphine's eyes widened. "*How* does Ezra Black keep getting with the hottest women in the world?"

Calla had to keep from laughing. "All I know is that I've seen that *look* he gets around Sabine in his eyes before. The one he gets when he wants to find trouble." She snorted. "And then there's the influence she wields over him because it was her feathers that were used to bring him back. He's enamored."

"You think her influence is the only reason he likes her?" Hannah wondered.

Calla shook her head. "Not at all. I mean, I'm sure it has *some* effect, but I've only been around them both for a day, so it's hard to say for sure. Honestly, though, I think he likes her because when he dishes it out, she takes it in stride and then turns around and gives it right back. He needs someone who will match his attitude when he's in a mood. As opposed to wanting to throttle him or getting lost in the whiplash, like I always did." Calla sighed. "One night we'd be gambling and laughing and running around Estrella. The next he'd be fussing at me for showing up to a place he *invited* me to. It was exhausting."

The three of them were silent for a moment as they thought about Calla's words, reminiscing on the chaos of that time in their lives. And though Calla meant what she said—that her relationship with Ezra had been exhausting, even when she hadn't realized it—she was still thankful for that time she got to have. What she learned about herself from it. What it led her to.

Calla flicked her eyes between her two friends. Wondering if they felt like all this peril was worth finding themselves as well. She asked as much aloud.

"Yes," Delphine said without hesitation. "Having my freedom . . . I'd go through those weeks of Reniel's torture a hundred more times if I had to. And I made it back to both of you. That makes it hard to be upset about anything that's happened."

Hannah wasn't as sure. Looking down at her hands, she said, "I'm not sure I've gotten there quite yet with my own past."

Delphine instantly pulled the girl into a hug, and Calla watched as

Hannah tensed up for a moment before letting herself sink into it fully. Calla leaned forward to join their embrace.

"You'll get there, Hannah. We love you how you are. You know that, don't you?" Calla asked.

Hannah sniffed. "Death magic and all?"

Calla pulled back with a grim smile. "I *could* do without the summonings of undead armies from the ground—but not if it meant we wouldn't have you. We'll learn to deal."

"Plus, the dark, spooky look kind of does it for you, babe," Delphine quipped as she reached over to lightly trace her fingertips over the dark veins still adorning Hannah's temples. "Makes you look like you'd rip out someone's heart and eat it in front of them."

Hannah and Calla both wrinkled their noses at the description.

"What?" Delphine questioned innocently. "I think that's a sexy quality!"

Hannah's face flushed intensely at the word *sexy* coming from Delphine's lips in reference to her, and Calla threw her a subtle look that said *See?*

"Oh! That reminds me—guess whose heart *I* ripped out of their chest?" Delphine told them. "Ramor's."

Calla gawked at those words. "*What?*"

"When I was trying to track you both down, I went to the one source I knew without a doubt would have information—Jack."

Calla's head spun, and it took her a moment to shake off her shock before she demanded, "All right, start from the beginning."

37

The three of them sat like that for nearly an hour, divulging as many details of their time apart as they possibly could, until Calla suddenly felt Gideon's magic return. Delphine stopped her detailed description of the four-way brawl she'd gotten into back in the Siren's Sea the moment she noticed the excited look on Calla's face.

"He's returned, hasn't he?"

Calla smiled as they all clambered off the bed. "I hope they brought back snacks."

"I hope they brought—" Delphine started as they filed out of the room, but her thought was abruptly cut off when they saw who was exiting the room across from them at the exact same time. Two someones to be exact.

The trio watched as Sabine strutted out of the bedroom, throwing them all a wink, and made her way to the stairs without a word. Next came Ezra. Who froze the moment he realized there was an audience.

The four of them stared at one another in silence for what felt like an eternity before Ezra finally cleared his throat and said, "Sabine gave me a haircut."

Calla's eyes flicked up to his hair and realized that it had, in fact, been cut. No longer past his shoulders, his raven tresses could barely curl around his ears now. It made him look older, more handsome instead of pretty. It also made him resemble Gideon even closer. Despite the fact that she knew they were only half brothers. A piece of information she'd forgotten until this very moment and made her grip on to Delphine's arm before she could stop the reaction.

Delph cut her eyes to Calla, giving a look that asked *Are you okay?*

Ezra must have thought Calla's odd response was due to the fact that they'd all just witnessed Sabine leaving his room, and what that implied, because he immediately became defensive. "It's no one's business who I—"

"Bite your tongue before you say something ridiculous, Black," Calla interrupted him, rolling her eyes before dragging Delphine and Hannah to the stairs. "No one cares who you're spending time with."

"Where's the fire?" Delph asked as the three of them left Ezra to stare after them in confusion.

"There's something I forgot to tell you both that the Valkyrie Queen revealed to Gideon and me. About the Heartbreak Prince curse. I wasn't sure if I should mention it until Gideon told Ezra about their fathers first."

"Fathers? As in plural?" Hannah asked.

When the three of them made it to the first floor, she saw the others had begun to congregate in the den, Cass and Thorne showing off the things they'd gotten at whatever trading post they managed to find in these mountains. Gideon was leaning back against the far wall, arms crossed, face stoic as he watched the others start to decide what was most important to take with them. When he spotted her, however, his obsidian eyes flashed silver, and the corners of his mouth curled up in a smile.

"Good afternoon," he greeted the three of them as they walked over, before turning to Calla to say, "I got you something."

He reached down and unclasped something from his belt. A canteen. Calla took it, twisting off the cap as she gave him a questioning look.

"It's blackberry lemonade," he told her. "They had a barrel of it down at the trading post. There was also a tavern next door, which means I had to talk Cass out of filling all the canteens with lager instead."

Delphine smiled. "Ah, but that is why Caspian is our favorite."

Calla took a sip of the lemonade, nearly moaning at the bright, tart taste of it on her tongue. She hadn't had anything that good in so long. Delphine lifted her hand in request, and Calla passed the canteen over.

"Thanks for not giving in to Cass with the beer," she told Gideon.

He nodded, then asked, "Did all of you get to catch up this morning?"

"Yep, though your arrival cut our conversation before a particularly juicy bit of information, apparently," Delphine said, lifting the canteen to her own lips to take a large gulp and missing Calla's dirty look.

Gideon lifted his pierced brow at Calla in curiosity.

"I was telling them about the Heartbreak Prince curse and

accidentally brought up the bit about your and Ezra's fathers," she admitted in a low whisper. "I'm sorry, it's your business to tell. I shouldn't have mentioned anything."

"It's all right," he assured her. "I'm going to have to talk to Ezra about it eventually. I just hate that I have to be the one to hurt him."

"Why would it hurt him?" Hannah asked quietly.

"My mother tried to do something extraordinarily cruel to him in order to save me from the curse," Gideon divulged. "Incidentally, Ignia's story led Calla and me to figure out why you sense death on me. Which, by the way, is that still an issue?"

Hannah paused. "Oh. I didn't even realize . . . The sickness *is* gone."

Gideon look relieved. "Maybe now that your magic is fully unleashed, less of it is stored inside you and making you sick?"

Hannah's brows rose. "Maybe so. I'll have to figure that out, I suppose. But back to your story—that's much more interesting."

Calla narrowed her eyes at Hannah, noting the way she was trying to deflect the conversation from her magic and storing it away to confront her about later.

"Did Ignia know who both your fathers were, then? Are they both alive?" Delphine chimed, taking another gulp of lemonade before passing it over to Hannah next.

"She didn't know Ezra's," Gideon answered. "But she gave me the name of mine. Bellator."

As soon as the name was out of Gideon's mouth, Delphine choked on the lemonade. Calla patted her friend's back as she began coughing relentlessly. Everyone on the other side of the den paused their conversations to make sure she was okay. She gave them a shaky thumbs-up.

When Delphine finally regained her bearings, she herded them all over into the kitchen, regarding Gideon as if she were speaking to a ghost. "Your father—you're sure his name was Bellator?"

"That's what Ignia said," Gideon confirmed, lifting his pierced brow, "and I'm getting the distinct feeling you know something."

"Bellator is Reniel's brother," Delphine said.

"That *siren* that helped you escape?" Calla gasped.

"Yes," Delphine confirmed before flicking her eyes back to Gideon with newfound regard. "That means *you're* the one he gave me the message for. I mentioned once that I knew the Onyx Princes. He never told me he had a connection to you, though!"

"Gideon is part *siren*?" a voice from the entryway exclaimed.

They all spun around to see Caspian standing there in disbelief.

"Oops," Delphine apologized.

Calla bit her lip as she noticed how still Gideon had become. But before she could tell everyone to give him some space, Caspian threw his hands in the air.

"Gods, everything finally makes sense! How you do that strange commanding thing with your voice, the way everyone is so naturally lured to you, *all those times you won our bets of who could hold their breath the longest under water?*" Caspian jabbed a finger in Gideon's direction. "You owe me money! You cheated!"

"Cass," Calla admonished lightly. "Maybe we should let him process this for a second before—"

"I need to talk to Ezra," Gideon said gruffly, striding briskly from the room.

)))•(((

Ezra wasn't sure anything could ruin the day he was having until he saw his brother's face when he asked him to talk outside. And now that his brother, his *half* brother, was finished talking, he wasn't sure anything could fix the newest crack in his heart.

"You're still my brother," Gideon told him, voice gruff. "This doesn't change anything between us."

Ezra quickly stepped back away from Gideon, his boots making a crunching sound in the snow with the movement. "I knew she hated me, but . . . Gods. What the fuck, Gideon? *What the fuck?*"

Gideon closed his eyes. "I know."

They stood there in the blistering cold until Ezra felt like he could take deep breaths again.

"I hate her," Ezra declared. "I want her to be *destroyed*."

"If you want the killing blow," Gideon stated, "it's yours."

And Ezra didn't know which of them moved first, but he held on to his brother as tight as he could until Gideon's embrace melded the fissure in his heart back together.

The rest of the day was spent in the den discussing logistics for everyone's next steps. Hannah was silent the entire time, having little input aside from the fact that she refused to leave Delphine or Calla. Luckily, everyone agreed.

Caspian, Amina, and Thorne were going to infiltrate the Onyx Realm and see if they could get any information on what was going on with the Guild and Caspian's special project. Sabine, Lyra, and Ezra were going to hang back at the house and wait for the owners to show up, a couple named Sydni and Baden who were supposed to help them begin recruiting Valkyries to join the war. Lyra and Amina were hoping if the Valkyries joined and helped the Fates win, the Gods might be benevolent enough to hear them out about abolishing the sadistic tithe their queen had bestowed upon their people.

It was Hannah, Delphine, Calla, and Gideon who would have the most unpredictable next steps. Gideon's compass was still pointing north, and they were all hoping it was trying to lead them to the first Fates' Dice. Or even another Blood Warrior. Either way, the four of them were now packing up their things to take a carriage to the end of the mountain pass, where they would find a port that could take them to another continent. The only issue? There was no way in the Hells the Witch Queens didn't have spies at every port in Illustros. Which meant things were about to get very dangerous again.

The single night of peace they'd gotten had been good while it lasted, Hannah supposed. Or, at least, it would've been if she hadn't been such a coward with Delphine.

Now she was watching off to the side as Gideon and Calla were saying their goodbyes to Ezra, trying desperately to ignore the way Delphine was lingering next to Thorne, twirling her hair as he spoke and laughed a little too loud. Thorne, for his part, wasn't leaning into it, and Hannah had sworn he'd even glanced in her direction quite a few times, but Hannah's gut was still in a knot.

"Hey, little witch," Caspian murmured.

Hannah turned to him, and the sad smile on his face immediately brought tears to her eyes.

"Don't cry," Caspian pleaded. "It'll kill me. And this isn't goodbye."

Hannah sniffed. "You don't know that."

He shook his head and pulled her into a hug. "We'll see each other again, Han. I promise." He pulled back. "Take care of yourself, all right?"

"Caspian?" she whispered. "Thank you. For being my friend. I'm going to miss you."

Caspian's answering smile was almost too bright to look at. "I'll miss you, too."

As soon as he walked away, she realized just how big of a piece of her he was taking with him. Calla and Delphine had been her only family for so long, but it was nice to see that families could always grow. That you could find solace in the most unlikely circumstances.

"Ready to go, Han?" a singsong voice asked from behind. "Done saying goodbyes?"

Hannah didn't know what possessed her, but all of the sadness she was feeling about having to say goodbye and the pent-up anger she'd been harboring toward herself bubbled to the surface.

"Done flirting with Thorne?" she snapped as she turned to Delphine.

Delphine stopped short. "Whoa . . ."

"Gods. I'm sorry." Hannah closed her eyes as she took a deep breath. "I'm just upset."

"With me?" Delphine asked cautiously.

Hannah blinked her eyes back open, ready to lie, but instead she answered, "Yes."

Delphine's brows shot up. "About what?"

Hannah didn't have time to answer before Gideon and Calla were calling them over. The goal was to make it to the port before dawn—which meant they needed to get going as soon as possible.

"Later," Hannah muttered.

☾ ☾ ☽ ● ☾ ☽ ☽

Calla had so many layers on she could barely move her arms, but she was determined not to leave Gideon to suffer alone in the freezing cold as he drove the carriage. They sat in comfortable silence for the first part of the drive until Calla couldn't take it anymore.

"Are you all right?" she finally asked. "I don't mean to pry about your talk with Ezra, but—"

"You're my partner, Calliope," he said. "You're never prying."

You're my partner.

If they were still in the Neverending Forest, the number of sparks that would be lighting up around them would have set the forest on fire.

"I'm all right. I'm just trying not to drown in guilt at the fact that I had to tell my brother such heinous news only to leave him behind. Again."

"I know," Calla whispered. Gideon's guilt was so palpable through their bond that *she* was trying not to drown in it. "But also are *you* okay? What she had planned for Ezra was insidious, but she actually *did* let you die, Gideon. I know you have a thing about not thinking of yourself first, but I can't help it. I . . ."

I love you, she wanted to tell him. To comfort him. To get it out of the way before they were once again in peril and she found herself having to say those words out of fear.

"Don't," he said.

She stiffened. Could he feel what she had been wanting to say? Did the bond betray her? And if it had... why didn't he want her to say it? Because he didn't feel the same way?

"No, I don't think I'm okay," he said before her inner thoughts really got out of control. "I just found out that I'm part *siren*. That means all this time I may have been influencing those around me to do things they didn't necessarily want to do. Maybe even influencing my friends to care about me when they wouldn't have otherwise. And I can't stomach that idea that I'd possibly done anything to make you—"

"Stop that right now," she ordered, knowing exactly where his line of thought was going, her words coming out in thick puffs. "Gideon, your friends have not been forced to care about you. And *I* certainly have not been forced to care about you. You should talk more to Delphine about it when you get the chance. Learn how it all works. But I can assure you it is not some sort of ongoing trance."

He was silent for a while after that, and it took everything in her not to press him any further. Because despite her magical insight to his emotions, he was so good at keeping it together on the surface that she worried he'd fool her one day and she wouldn't be there for him when he really needed her to be.

Gideon's gaze remained fixed ahead, his grip steady on the reins despite the bitter cold she knew was numbing his fingers because she could feel it in her own. She bit her lip, the weight of those three little unsaid words hanging heavy on her shoulders, but for now she would have to leave them unspoken.

Instead she said, "Let me know if you need me to take over, okay?"

"Okay," he told her before lifting his arm and letting her tuck herself against his side, but she knew if she fell asleep now that he wouldn't wake her.

As long as the world isn't on fire.

By the time the city came into view, down in the valley ahead, the sun had just begun to break over the horizon. The port was perfectly nestled at the mouth of the mountain pass, the reflective peaks around them illuminating the colorful buildings in the distance with a glittering luminescence that left Calla completely speechless. And just beyond the cityscape, she could make out an entire fleet of the most enormous ships she'd ever seen.

Gideon pulled them off the main road before they began their descent down and were spotted by any of the city's early risers. He knocked on the carriage door to alert Delphine and Hannah it was time to wake up.

"I've never been on a boat before," Calla told Gideon as they stretched and drank water, noting the unmistakable smell of seawater and salt that came with being so close to the coast.

"I've only been on one, a seventeenth-birthday voyage my mother arranged on the Celestial Sea," Gideon revealed. "But that ship wasn't nearly as big as any of these ships."

"What was there to do on the Celestial Sea?" she wondered. She couldn't have imagined anything more boring than sitting on a boat with nothing to do besides catch fish.

He laughed. "Cass and I mostly just drank for three days straight with a bunch of—"

He cut himself off abruptly with a soft curse, as if chastising himself. Which gave her a very good idea of where his story had been headed.

She laughed. "That scandalous?"

Though there was a slight pang of jealousy in her core, it went away quickly. Anything that happened in his past was exactly that—in his past. Hells, she'd already survived *Kestrel*. She couldn't imagine anything more intense than the commander's gaze burning a hole through the back of her head or being turned over to the Witch Queens. Really, she was less worried about Gideon's seasoned experience and more worried about her lack of it.

"I was a bit more uninhibited back then," he admitted. "But nothing all that scandalous, I can assure you."

"I can't wait to ask Cass about that trip and get the salacious details of what uninhibited Prince Gideon is like," she quipped.

"Mmm," he hummed, his eyes darkening as he took a step toward her, backing her up until she was pressed against the side of the carriage. "Why ask for details from someone else when I can show you myself?"

Calla's lips parted with surprise, and despite the lingering chill in her bones from the long drive, she suddenly felt very warm. Her body was screaming for his touch, but he seemed in no such hurry. He tucked a strand of her hair behind her left ear, lightly trailing the tips of his fingers down the side of her face before sliding them beneath her chin to angle her mouth up toward his. He placed his other hand against the carriage above her head to hold his weight as he leaned down to press a trail of kisses along the underside of her jaw.

She closed her eyes, savoring the sensation of his lips against her skin, the way the bond reacted any time he touched her, like a shock of electricity right to her soul. She found herself melting into him, her hands finding their way to his chest, pulling him closer by the material of his shirt. The hand that he wasn't using to hold himself up now moved around to her back and pressed the length of her body into his further. His touch was gentle yet commanding, and it thrilled her. He knew exactly how to set her ablaze without consuming her completely.

Just as his lips were finally about to meet hers, the door of the carriage swung wide open, causing them to spring apart with a start. Calla made a sound of frustration, and Gideon's expression shifted from desire to amusement as he glanced over to where Delphine and Hannah were now groggily emerging from the vehicle.

"Caught again," he murmured, adjusting his shirt where she'd been gripping it tight enough to make it wrinkle terribly.

"Whoa," Delphine gasped when she saw the view ahead of them.

"I know," Calla agreed as she stepped away from Gideon as nonchalantly as possible. "Now, let's hope we can catch one of those ships."

"Why do I feel like this is going to take a lot of effort?" Delphine sighed.

"Time for glamour," Gideon declared.

Calla didn't waste any time with her transformation. She'd practiced enough by now that making her Rouge magic mold into the illusion she wished to appear was damn near second nature at this point. Her friends watched with curiosity as she shortened her hair to a color almost identical to Hannah's, switched her eyes to a pale green reminiscent of jade, and most important of all, elongated her ears and facial structure like a fae's. Gideon switched on his own glamour, his eyes turning dark brown, his hair becoming an icy shade of white—the same color as the snow on the ground. When he focused on Hannah next, he turned her flaxen hair pink and matched her complexion to it as closely as possible.

"Pink?" Hannah wondered.

Gideon shrugged. "Thought it might be fun."

Hannah smiled. They all turned to Delphine next, but the siren was already holding up a hand and shaking her head.

"I'm all right," she stated. "If we end up needing to persuade anyone, I'm going to need my natural essence."

"If the queens have put out your description, you could be recognized," Calla reasoned.

"Fine," Delphine allowed. "But only my hair color, Prince. Don't mess with my face, it's already a masterpiece."

Gideon smiled in amusement as he focused his magic on Delphine's hair and turned it a deep navy color. Delphine wrinkled her nose as she fingered the strands but didn't put up any more of a fight.

"All right, the plan is to sell the horses to get enough money for our tickets and then head out," Gideon directed. "The Valkyries said the first voyage should leave about an hour and a half after dawn, so that gives us a little over an hour. We have to lie low."

He pulled his compass out then, making sure that the arrow still, in fact, worked and was leading them in the right direction. Calla leaned in as she watched the spinning needle confirm what they already knew: they needed to head north. When he used his wind magic to flip to its other face, they found that the arrow remained aimless.

Gideon sighed in frustration. "I don't get it."

Calla gave him a sympathetic look before stepping back and walking over to her backpack on the driver's bench to get a drink of water. "What do you think you want most right now?"

"For this war to be over," Gideon answered.

"Maybe because that's a concept and not a physical thing or person, it's refusing to work?" Delphine suggested.

Gideon nodded.

"At least one side is working, right?" Hannah said quietly.

"Yet I'd only ever used the other side before, and it led us perfectly fine to everything we needed—through the Neverending Forest, to the Witch Eater." Gideon shook his head. "It doesn't make sense."

Calla winced. "Well, actually, we really didn't need to be in the Neverending Forest. Or see the Witch Eater. We just wanted, desperately, to do those things. To avoid our fates. And now maybe we're realizing what we want and what we need aren't really the same thing."

Gideon tilted his head, thoughtful. "That... is a very interesting idea."

Delphine clapped her hands together. "More on the mysterious compass later. I want to do some shopping before we have to get on a boring old boat for Gods know how long."

☽·☽·☽·●·☾·☾·☾

Hannah was a bit surprised at how easy it was to sell two horses and a carriage when they reached the city. So easy that it left them with some time to kill and little to do considering that almost everything was still closed. Including the place where they were supposed to buy their tickets for the next ship out. A ship that was heading straight north—to Noctum. A place often referred to as the continent of nightmares, something Hannah was less than thrilled about. Her mind was nightmarish enough these days, and she could hardly sleep without seeing her mother's face. And those nightmares were starting to bleed into her waking hours as well.

Her repulsion to Gideon's presence may have faded, but now she picked up traces of death *everywhere*. In everything she brushed against, every inch of ground she walked, there were echoes of that darkness. It was driving her mad. And her friends were beginning to notice.

Even if she hadn't unfairly snapped at Delphine about Thorne, Delph would've known something was very wrong from the fact that Hannah could barely seem to speak. A problem she had never had before, not even those times Delphine would bring Allex around and Hannah thought she might die of jealousy. The darkness in her was twisting her into something unrecognizable, and she was afraid.

"Han?"

Gideon's voice brought her back to the present, and she blinked up at him. "I'm sorry, what did you say?"

"I asked if you knew where Delphine got off to. Calliope and I are about to go down to the port to get the tickets."

"Oh, yes." Hannah flicked her eyes over to the clothing shop on their left. "She managed to convince the shop owner to open up early for her."

Gideon laughed. "I should've expected that. If you can pry her out of there, meet us down at the docks in ten, okay?"

As he ambled off, Hannah turned for the shop Delphine had disappeared into, ignoring the CLOSED sign that was still hanging on the door as she pushed her way inside. There was no bell to announce her entrance, and the store was so packed with racks of clothes that she couldn't see anything past the entryway. She could hear them, however. Delphine's unmistakable lilting voice mixed with the deep, smooth drawl of a stranger's.

Hannah began to follow the sound of their conversation through the rows and rows of garments.

"Oh, c'mon, you're telling me you've never met a pirate before?" the drawling voice flirted. "I bet you had sailors throwing themselves overboard in hopes to be drowned by you."

Delphine laughed. "Not where I'm from, handsome. We didn't spend much time at the surface. Just in the deep dark depths."

"That why you're looking to get out of Illustros?" he asked. "Explore more of the open ocean?"

"Absolutely," Delphine lied. "My friends and I want to see something new."

"Friends? Are they as pretty as you?" he wondered.

"Yes. Why? Are you looking for more people to give free clothes to?" Delphine teased.

"If they look as good as you do in that dress, absolutely."

Hannah was nearly at the back of the store now, and she peeked around the last rack of clothes to see who Delphine was talking to. Flirting with.

She spotted Delph wearing a dress made entirely of pearls. A dress that looked like it was crafted exclusively for Delphine, and Hannah was barely able to pry away her gaze to study the man. He was only an inch or two taller than Delphine, wearing brown leather pants that laced up in the front and a billowing burgundy shirt neatly tucked in to show off the three different belts he had slung around his hips. His hair was a mess of unruly brown curls, and his smile was crooked in a way that promised trouble.

Hannah hated the way he was looking at Delphine.

When he opened his mouth to deliver another nauseatingly cliché line, Hannah stepped out from behind the clothing rack and cleared her throat. The man's eyes snapped to her immediately, and even from several yards away, she could see their unusual shade of scarlet. He didn't seem to be a fae and was definitely not a witch, but he was *something*. Undoubtedly immortal.

Delphine smiled when she turned to spot Hannah. "Hannah, come see my new dress."

Delphine twirled as Hannah strode closer, the pearls of the dress catching the light in a way that made Hannah realize they weren't actually white pearls, but a very faint shade of lavender.

"It's pretty." Hannah nodded. "But I'm not sure we can afford—"

"It's on the house," the man interrupted. "I couldn't possibly let anyone else have it after seeing it on the person it belongs. It would be blasphemous."

Delphine's grin grew wider, and she threw a wink in Hannah's direction in triumph.

Hannah cleared her throat, ignoring the man as she told Delphine, "We have to meet the others at the dock. Now."

"What's the rush, shortcake?" the man mused. "I was just telling Delphine that what y'all should really do is let my crew take you to Noctum. Our boat is smaller, but it's definitely more fun. We have dancing and wine. Not to mention the most enthralling stories about encounters with the most thrilling sea creatures you never even knew existed."

Delphine was enraptured. "What sort of creatures?"

"Sea dragons, krakens, vespers—you name it, doll, we got a story," he claimed.

"Sea dragons and krakens are nothing new," Delphine said. "But I've never heard of vespers."

"Probably for the best," he revealed. "Heinous creatures. They also go by the name of sea ghosts. They're sort of like sylphs—except they'll change their forms into those you love and lure you into the water to drown you."

"Enticing," Hannah deadpanned.

"And the wine?" Delphine moved on. "How much wine are we talking—"

"Delphine," Hannah chastised as sternly as she could. "We have to go."

Delphine slid her gaze back to Hannah, ready to argue, but whatever was on Hannah's face must have sobered her up because she sighed and said, "My friend's right. We should get going."

When Delphine started toward Hannah, he shrugged. "Your choice. But if you change your mind, we're on the boat with the red sails. The *Sea Pearl*. We're leaving right after the first passenger ship sets off."

"Don't you have to run your store?" Hannah grumbled.

The man smiled. "I have people for that, shortcake. I just come back from time to time between voyages to check in."

Delphine hooked her arm through Hannah's and threw one last smile over her shoulder at the man as they left. "It was lovely to meet you, Isaac."

Isaac smirked. "You too, doll."

40

Ezra was avoiding her.

Which would have thrilled Sabine only two days ago, but not after the night they spent together. Not because of the kiss, which she was still thinking about, but because of everything *after* the kiss. Staying awake until nearly dawn, talking about things she'd only ever talked about with Amina and Lyra. Him allowing her to give him a haircut despite his previous refusal to let her near his head with a knife.

And now the bastard was ignoring her?

She made her way up the stairs to his bedroom. Amina had already left with Thorne and Cass for the Onyx Realm and Lyra was watching over Meli while they waited for Sydni and Baden to show up. So that left Sabine plenty of time to make Ezra's life miserable without any interruptions.

She stopped in front of his door, pounding on it twice.

No answer.

"Are we going to do this again?" she called to him. "I'll kick the door in right—"

The door swung open, and there he was. The first thing she noted was how tired he looked. The flames in his coal eyes not burning with their usual intensity. The second thing she noticed was that he was shirtless.

Godsdammit, he's hot, she thought.

Without a doubt the hotter prince in her opinion, though she would never admit it to him. Gideon was just too . . . nice for her taste.

"Can I help you?" Ezra asked, his tone tired.

"Get dressed," she demanded. "We're going to work on your flying. It's atrocious."

He leaned against the doorframe, crossing his arms. "I wonder if that has anything to do with the fact that the only time I ever tried using my wings it was right after I was shoved out of a window?"

Sabine shrugged. "I suppose we'll never know. Get dressed."

He shook his head. "I'm not in the mood today, Sabine."

Sabine. Not harpy.

She hated how such a small detail made her stomach clench. Gods, what the fuck was he doing to her?

"I don't recall asking if you were in the mood," she quipped.

He stared at her for a long moment, silent. She stared back.

Then, finally, he sighed. "Fine."

Sabine smiled in triumph. "I'll be out front. Wear something warm."

The last thing Ezra felt like doing was training. He'd much rather continue wallowing in his room over finding out that the only reason he existed was because his own mother wanted to curse him. But the look on Sabine's face when he'd opened the door had made him feel like an asshole. She'd hid it pretty well, as she did with all her most vulnerable emotions, but he'd studied her face enough these past few weeks to know that she'd clearly been upset he was avoiding her. Well, not *her*. Everyone.

But he went. He threw on one of the sweaters Lyra had modified for his wings, trekked downstairs, and met her out front, where he found her making a pile of little snowballs. Which she launched directly at his head the moment she heard his boots crunch on the icy ground.

He swiped snow out of his eyes just in time to be pelted with the next one.

"Oh, it's on, harpy," he growled as he dodged a third.

He scooped up a handful of snow and launched it in her direction, hitting her square in the face. She hissed, countering his attack with two more hits. Ten minutes later they were both freezing, covered in snow, and out of breath.

One last shot, he told himself just as she turned her back to him. Big mistake.

He launched his last ball of ice, and it arced perfectly through the air and went spraying across her back.

"*Ah!*" she cried, stumbling to the ground.

Ezra immediately froze as he watched her hunch over like she was in agony, grasping behind herself as she tried to dust the cold off her still-incoming wings.

"You hurt me," she sobbed.

Ezra cleared the yards between them in three strides, dropping to his knees next to her in the snow. "Gods, I'm sorry. I'm so sorry, I—"

Before he could blink, Sabine was tackling him back onto the ground, his weight landing painfully on his wings as she moved atop him to pin him down by his shoulders.

"You are such a *sucker*," she teased with a vicious grin.

Ezra scowled up at her. "You are so *violent*."

"Is that a problem?" She lifted a brow.

"Maybe, if it wasn't so sexy," he muttered.

Her smile stretched even wider, but then she was up on her feet, releasing him from her hold and declaring, "All right. On to the next part of our training today."

"That was supposed to be you training me?" he asked with a skeptical tone.

"You were running around and dodging my blows without tripping over your wings, weren't you? Well, for the most part. Learning how to move with your wings on the ground is just as important as learning how to navigate them airborne."

He was actually mildly impressed with her technique. Not to mention he really needed some levity today.

"All right, harpy," he allowed. "Show me what's next."

As soon as Hannah and Delphine put some distance between themselves and the shop, Hannah asked, "What was *that*?"

Delphine's nonchalant humor dropped from her expression as she answered, "That was a contingency plan just in case anything falls through. I've made sure there's another ship we'll definitely have no problem making it onto. A pirate isn't necessarily my first choice—considering they're egotistical charmers by trade." A pause. Then in an odd, more reverent tone she added, "But contingency plans are necessary evils sometimes."

All Hannah could say was "Oh."

Delphine stopped walking, turning to face Hannah fully, a hand propped on her hip. "I saw your face in there. You looked furious with me. What did you think I was doing?"

"Flirting," Hannah admitted.

"And if I was?" Delphine asked. "You snapped at me over Thorne, too. And then didn't speak to me the entire ride here. What in the Hells is going on?"

This was not how Hannah imagined she would tell Delphine about her feelings for her. In the middle of a random street, in a random town they didn't know.

But before she could stop herself, she was blurting out, "You said our kiss didn't mean anything."

Delphine's brows knitted together in utter confusion. "What are you—"

Delph cut off as a loud commotion caught both of their eyes in the direction of the docks. Hannah suddenly realized there were now people buzzing around the streets, beginning their days. And for some reason a crowd was starting to form up ahead.

Hannah and Delphine exchanged a loaded look and then took off running.

☽ ☽ ☽ ● ☾ ☾ ☾

If Calla had a hundred spéctrals for every time someone had put a bounty on her head, she'd be rich. This was, however, the first time that there were *posters*. The queens weren't sparing any expenses.

Gideon had spotted them first, never one to miss a detail. Calla was appalled to see her face plastered on every possible surface next to the loading dock, the words *extremely dangerous* and *possibly disguised* written above the—flatteringly accurate—illustration. Below were details of her *possible companions*, though none of them were named and Gideon's description was omitted altogether. She wondered aloud why that was.

"My mother saving herself from embarrassment," Gideon answered dryly. "Besides, she knows that if she gets you, she gets me."

"What are we going to do?" Calla whispered as people began to form a crowd to get a better look at the generous offer the Witch Queens were making for turning her in.

"C'mon," Gideon instructed as he placed a comforting hand at the small of her back. "Don't pay it any attention. The ticket booth just opened."

They made their way toward the ticket line, getting behind a tired-looking group of fae and a troll couple holding a small crying child. Calla kept her head down, pulling Gideon's cape tighter around her body, praying to the Gods that they slip through unnoticed.

If you want us to start this war, she directed at the Fates in her mind. *You'll let us find these Dice without being captured by any more queens.*

When they reached the head of the line, Gideon quickly purchased four tickets, scribbling in their false names with a steady hand despite the tension in the air. Calla kept watch, her heart pounding in her chest, half expecting the crowd to swoop in at any moment, eager to collect such a wealthy bounty for turning her in. Gideon felt her pulse raise, of course, and reached down with his free hand to grab hers, giving her a squeeze of reassurance.

Thankfully, when he was done filling out their information, they managed to collect their tickets without incident, stepping out of line and blending back in with the other travelers now waiting patiently on the dock to board. But Calla didn't allow herself a single second of relief, not until they were safely on board and tucked away in a private room.

Gideon's gaze relentlessly scanned the area around them for any signs of trouble, and Calla kept a lookout for Delphine and Hannah—though she kept forgetting she wasn't *actually* looking for Delphine and Hannah, but the versions of them wearing Gideon's glamours.

"There," Gideon murmured suddenly, and Calla snapped her head in the direction of his stare.

Sure enough, Delphine and Hannah were hurrying down the road toward the gossiping crowds still gathered around Calla's Wanted posters.

"I got them," Gideon told Calla. "Don't move."

She didn't plan on it. She just kept her head down and watched as he navigated his way through the crowd toward her friends, collecting them and guiding them toward her.

"Silver lining is that you look good," Delphine whispered when the three of them approached. "Can you believe they're doing this?"

"Yes," Calla muttered. "There's not a single place in Illustros not seeing my face right now. Jack is probably getting a kick out of it."

Gideon's expression grew dark when she mentioned her former landlord's name. He cursed. "That bastard probably has people scouring every inch of this continent for you himself."

"Which means we can't trust anyone." Delphine shrugged.

"You just gave your real name to a pirate," Hannah pointed out in a tone Calla had never heard her friend direct at Delphine before.

Delphine looked annoyed. "I used my song to persuade him to only remember my name when I'm physically in front of him. Again underestimating me."

Hannah didn't respond, and Calla and Gideon exchanged confused looks.

"Pirate?" Gideon asked.

Delphine sighed and said, "Backup plan."

As if that were a proper explanation. But it didn't matter. The steam-riddled sound of a horn whisked through the air as the large vessel that had been readying itself at the end of the dock announced it was time to board. Gideon handed out everyone's tickets, and they shifted into the quickly forming line, conscious of keeping Calla in the middle. Most beings wouldn't be able to tell they were wearing glamours, but a fae absolutely could.

"Reason for traveling to Noctum—family vacation?" Delphine read in a hushed voice. "Who goes to the continent of nightmares for a family vacation?"

Gideon threw a look over his shoulder that said *Just go with it*, but Delphine looked like she was certainly going to be bringing this up again when they were somewhere private. Calla couldn't help but laugh.

"Next," someone ordered ahead of them.

The person evaluating the tickets at the front of the dock was, of course, a fae. Carefully reading each passenger's ticket before giving them a full-body scan, the fae looked tired and bored, and Calla hoped that was enough for them to be lazy about the details.

"Let me go first," Delphine said as she stepped to the front of their group, and none of them protested. She was both the most charming and the one wearing the least amount of glamour.

When they stepped up to the fae, a man with bright red hair and a dead look in his eyes, Delphine gave him a relaxed smile.

She handed her ticket over and said, "We're all together."

The man glanced at her ticket, then at her, then handed the paper back before beckoning for the others to step forward and present their tickets. Calla was holding her breath so tightly she thought her face must be turning blue, but the fae didn't say a word as he was checking their paperwork. When he was finished, he waved them through. Just like that.

They all hurried toward the boat in silent relief. Two crew members were waiting inside to record their names for their room assignments and told them to head to the upper deck and wait until someone collected them to show them to their quarters. None of them really spoke as they followed their directions, not until they reached the open air of the ship's deck, making their way to the starboard side of the boat to look out into the open ocean. Calla was stunned by how infinite the blue water seemed to be.

"All right, step one complete," Delphine reassured everyone. "Lets take a deep breath. Calla, you look like you're going to pass out."

Calla resisted the urge to stick her tongue out at her friend as Gideon said, "Enjoy the open air now, because we won't be leaving our room much until we get to Noctum."

"How long is the trip supposed to be?" Hannah asked, looking like she was thinking the same exact thing as Calla—the idea of sitting in a room for days felt suffocating.

"Noctum is about three days away according to the times they had at the ticket booth," he said. "But there's a stop scheduled at a small isle between here and the second continent, so I'd guess add a day or two to that estimate."

All three of them groaned at his words.

The deck slowly filled with other passengers as they waited for their room assignments, and Calla was becoming more antsy as the space around them got smaller and smaller. And when those around them began to whisper about the extremely dangerous witch wanted for treason, she was grateful when Gideon leaned against the side of the boat and gathered her toward him so she could hide her face in his chest.

Another ship's horn blew in the distance, and Delphine perked up.

"That's Isaac's ship," Delphine pointed out to them.

They all leaned over the side to watch the smaller ship pass, its red sails billowing in the wind, a stark contrast against the clear blue of the ocean. Isaac's ship wasn't crowded at all, and the few sailors that Calla could see looked to be drinking or sitting around crates made into card tables.

Maybe Delphine had been onto something, Calla thought. *That looks much more appealing.*

As if she were thinking the same thing, Delphine sighed mournfully, then pointed toward the helm of the ship. "That's him."

Calla had to squint in order to make out any real discernable feature of the man until the boat crawled closer, slowly making its way parallel to them. As the ship passed, Calla noticed that Isaac's sharp eyes were scanning the length of the crowd leaning over the top deck, and for a moment, his eyes seemed to linger in Delphine's direction but quickly moved on.

Delphine clucked her tongue. "A shame. I've heard that pirates are fun."

As if Isaac could hear that she had spoken, his eyes snapped back to Delphine's face. Calla watched as the pirate's expression shifted from curiosity to recognition. His lips curved into a knowing smile.

"Delphine!" he called, and they all went absolutely rigid. "When you get to Noctum, make sure to look me up!"

The buzz of the deck behind them hushed, but Isaac only gave a farewell salute and turned back to navigating his ship.

"Delphine?" someone murmured nearby. "Wasn't that one of the names on the posters?"

The four of them slowly turned to face the other passengers, Calla's stomach dropping when she realized all eyes were on them. The whispers began to get louder and louder as the rumors spread like wildfire in real time, people jostling one another to get a better look at their group for themselves.

"The others are fae," someone pointed out skeptically. "Do you really think witches are that good with glamour?"

Gideon, Calla, and Hannah all turned to Delphine in accusation.

"Okay, in hindsight maybe I shouldn't have given him my name," Delphine admitted. "Before we get into that, though, can I make a suggestion?"

Someone shouted something in the back, and Calla swore the entire crowd tensed at the exact same time. As if they were serpents poised to strike.

"What suggestion?" Calla breathed.

"Jump before Isaac's ship gets away?" Delphine proposed.

A single beat hung in the air as the words registered. And then all four of them were plunging into the freezing water below.

42

Looking down from one of the ledges of the mountain's shoulders, Ezra realized that maybe he didn't didn't care much for flying. Sabine had taken him up much higher than the window she'd pushed him out of, and that fall had been more than enough of a taste for him. Unfortunately, it did not seem that Sabine was going to let this go. Ezra knew stubbornness when he looked it in the face.

How do I always end up surrounded by hardheaded women who want to kill me?

Still, he tried to reason. "This feels like a fifth-or-sixth-training-session sort of thing."

"Don't be a baby," she snapped. "Do you know what I'd do to have my wings back right now? This is torture! And yet you've received the gift of them and don't want to use them? It's selfish."

"I'm sorry, did I forget the conversation in which I asked you to bring me back from the dead?" he countered.

"You're lucky it was me and not Amina. You would not be having such a good time then."

"What makes you think I'm having a good time *now*?" he muttered as he toed a crystal-like pebble off the cliffside and watched it plummet indefinitely to the ground.

She began to pick at her nails. "Do you always kiss people you aren't having a good time with like that?"

Ezra's brows rose. After he'd kissed her, she'd been adamant about not bringing up the subject ever again. They'd stayed up until dawn talking about anything and everything *but* that kiss, and he'd gotten the feeling that she was hoping if she ignored it long enough she could pretend it hadn't happened.

But since she wanted to bring it up now . . .

"Kiss you like *what*?" he murmured as he stepped toward her, until her back was against the mirrorlike face of the mountain.

Something flashed in her jade eyes, something like anticipation, but the corners of her mouth tilted down. "Don't make me push you off another ledge."

"C'mon, harpy, you brought it up. What did I kiss you like?" he taunted.

She opened her mouth to respond, but before she could get a word out, she gasped at something over his shoulder. He was about to accuse her of faking a distraction because she couldn't come up with anything clever in response, but something in the glassy reflection above her head made him pause. Something flying. Right toward them.

Ezra twisted around just in time to see the Valkyrie land. A man, nearly a foot taller than himself, with long reddish-brown hair and a face that looked an awful lot like Lyra's.

"Lark!" Sabine squealed before shoving her way past Ezra and jumping into the other man's arms.

"Hey, trouble," Lark greeted her, leaning down to press a kiss on her forehead.

Ezra hated him instantly.

"Murder anyone lately?" Lark asked.

"She's more into reviving people these days," Ezra inserted.

Lark flicked his gaze to Ezra, sizing him up with a look of distaste, before lifting a brow at Sabine in question. Sabine waved off the claim.

"Don't listen to him, he's only optimistic because I haven't broken his spirit yet," she chirped.

"I'm Lark. Lyra's brother," Lark introduced himself, offering out a begrudging hand.

Ezra shook it. Hard. "Ezra Black."

Sabine observed the interaction intently before turning to Lark. "Lyra didn't mention you were coming."

"Lyra doesn't know I'm here," Lark explained, reaching up to ruffle a hand through his hair as he spoke, his biceps flexing subtly as he did. Ezra nearly rolled his eyes. "Sydni and Baden were gaining some traction with the Reapers and decided it was best if they stayed to make sure your slayers' plight caught fire enough that it'd continue to stoke itself in their absence. But don't worry, trouble, they sent me with some things to help Meli."

Sabine sighed in relief at that last bit. "Lyra's back at the house with Meli now. Go ahead, we'll be right behind you."

Lark nodded and took off just as quickly as he'd arrived.

Sabine looked back at Ezra expectantly. "All right, let's get a move on it, dragon boy. I want to be there when Meli wakes up."

"Were the two of you ever together?" Ezra blurted out, and then immediately cringed at himself.

Sabine's expression turned wickedly amused as she propped a hand on her hip. "Together how? Did we grow up together? Yes. Did he and I share bunks together during our Reaper training days? Yes. Was he the first person I ever kissed? Yes. Was he also the first person I ever set on fire—"

"Dear Gods," Ezra muttered, cutting her off. "Forget I asked."

Sabine slowly approached him then, coming closer and closer until their chests were nearly touching. "Are you jealous, Prince?"

"No," he gritted out, but he sounded like a liar even to his own ears.

"Don't worry, whatever youthful, hormone-riddled thing Lark and I had decades ago burned up with our adolescence," she told him. "There are much bigger things for you to worry your pretty little head about."

He saw it then, the mischievous sparkle in her eyes. And he knew what she was about to do before she even moved.

He took a deep breath as she shoved him off the cliff. The wind whistled past his ears as he plummeted downward, the ground rushing up to meet him with alarming speed. This time, however, he didn't let the panic seize him; he simply focused on spreading his wings wide, feeling the rush of air beneath them as he slowed his descent. It was a skill he was still getting used to, opening his wings with efficiency, but the forced urgency did help. Though he'd never admit it. Sabine was too willing to keep pushing him off things as it was.

As he leveled himself out, he glanced back up at Sabine, who was leaning over the cliff's precipice, watching him with a mixture of amusement and pride.

"Not bad," she called down to him, her voice carrying on the wind.

Ezra couldn't help but grin at her words, the rush of adrenaline still coursing through his veins. Despite his intrinsic reluctance, there was something undeniably exhilarating about flying, and the freedom it offered him. As he circled back toward Sabine, there was a certain gratefulness he felt for her being bold enough to push him out of his comfort zone. Quite literally.

Ezra's landing was a bit clunky when he returned to her side, but she still gave him a nod of approval. "Now, let's get back to the house. We'll pick this up again later."

))) ● (((

When they finally made it back, there were two things that stood out to Ezra upon entering the cottage. The first was the sharp, intense scent of mint. The second was that something was very wrong.

"Lyra? Lark?" Sabine called, her alarm equally as piqued as Ezra's.

A moment later, Lyra came rushing down the stairs. One look at the expression on their face and Ezra knew whatever Lark had brought to heal their friend hadn't worked.

"What's wrong? Is she still asleep?" Sabine demanded.

"She woke up," Lyra explained, tone solemn. "But . . ."

"But *what*?" Sabine snapped, and Ezra tried to place a comforting hand on her shoulder. She shook it off.

"The Valkyrie Queen poisoned her," Lyra said.

Sabine didn't say anything. Only stared.

"Poisoned with what, exactly?" Ezra inserted.

"Bloodroot," Lyra whispered.

The gravity of the situation hung heavy in the air. Ezra wasn't sure Sabine was breathing. Bloodroot was deadly, a toxin that ravaged the mind before the body, leaving its victims hollow shells long before claiming their lives. His mind raced with possibilities, searching for any solution, any way to save Meli from such a cruel fate.

"How far along is it?" Ezra asked.

Lyra's mouth tightened.

"No," Sabine said. "*No.* Ignia was only supposed to use her for leverage. Even if we hadn't stolen her back, Her Highness promised to return her to us once Amina brought the Siphon—"

"Return her to us, yes," Lyra said softly. "But clearly she never specified in what state."

If Ezra had thought Sabine would break down, or cry, or set the world on fire, he would've been wrong. She did nothing of the sort.

Instead, she lifted her chin and ordered, "Have Lark take her back to her family so they can decide how to proceed. Then tell him I want every Reaper we know to be here within two days—or I'll reap them myself before our queen even has the chance."

Lyra was already nodding. "Done. We're going to need some more supplies to host everyone. I'll talk logistics with Lark if you want to handle that—"

"Done," Sabine cut them off, already turning for the door.

Ezra caught her elbow. "I'll go with you. But don't you want to say goodbye to Meli first?"

Sabine shook him off once again. "I said my goodbyes to Meli a long time ago. She doesn't need me to disrupt her peace anymore. And I don't need you to come with me."

Ezra silently watched as she left, sighing when she slammed the door behind her. He looked back at Lyra, who raised a brow at him.

"This is the part where you run after her, Prince," Lyra pointed out.

Ezra took a deep steadying breath. If he went after her, she was absolutely going to light him on fire.

He went after her.

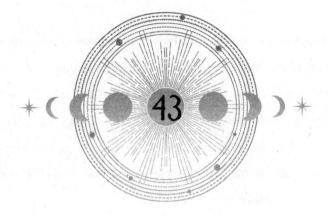

43

As Delphine dropped into the cool ocean salt water, her gills opening with a brief stretch of pain, she was elated to feel an electric thrill slithering through her. When she had been dragged back to the Siren's Sea, she never thought she'd be thrilled to swim again. But this was her element. A place where her soul could sing—pun very much intended—and without the weight of the Siren's oath, it was a place she felt free again.

As she righted herself in the water, gathering her bearings among the sizzling bubbles that indicated where her friends had landed, she felt the Obsidian Key start to unstick from where she kept it hidden against her sternum. The water was eroding the makeshift glue, and she quickly reached through the top of her dress to grasp the key for dear life before it was lost to the depths.

She caught a thrashing movement out of her peripherals. Hannah, her glamour completely gone, was flailing for the surface, panic written all over her face. Delphine wasted no time slinking through the water, wrapping an arm around Hannah's waist, and pulling her up. When their heads broke the surface, Hannah coughed and spluttered while Delphine glanced around for the others. It didn't take long to spot Calla's and Gideon's heads bobbing above the choppy water. Delphine easily swam over to hand Hannah off to Gideon as the roar of the excited crowd above them almost overpowered the sound of waves hitting the side of the boat in her ears.

"We have to catch up to Isaac's ship," Delphine shouted.

"You're the only one who can swim fast enough for that!" Calla yelled back just as someone else on the deck screamed, "Jump in after them!"

I really fucked up, Delphine thought as she frantically spun around to see how far Isaac's ship had already managed to travel. Meanwhile, someone else plunged into the water next to them.

"They're going to try and drag us out of here," Hannah said through clattering teeth. She clung to Gideon, not experienced enough to tread water on her own.

"Start heading toward Isaac's ship as fast as you can," Delphine ordered. "I'll take care of the rest."

Before anyone could argue, she was diving back beneath the water, eyes searching for the fool who thought it was a good idea to go after them.

I can still fix this, she swore to herself.

A few feet away, a man spun in the water as he tried to determine where his target was. By the point of his ears she knew he was a fae, his pearlescent hair a beacon for her in the dark, roiling blue. She grinned as she zipped toward him like an arrow, grasping his throat and pushing him through the waves until his back slammed against the hull of the boat. He let out all of his air in shock as his eyes settled on her face.

He tried to scream something, but only an incoherent muffled sound and a stream of bubbles came out.

"You have two options," she told him, her voice unmistakably clear. "I rip out your throat and let you sink to the bottom of the ocean to be eaten by fish, or I send you back up and make an example out of you."

He frantically made a pointing motion with his hand toward the surface.

"Good choice," she crooned before gathering her magic and wrapping a tendril of water around his waist. A single blast of her power and he was rising out of the ocean and back onto the ship's deck.

She didn't waste a second more. She moved through the water, past her friends, faster than she ever had before. Her abdominal muscles screamed as she tore toward Isaac's ship. Ropes from the mast hung down and swayed against the hull, making her task easier as she used her magic to shoot out of the water and latch on to one of them, wrapping it around her fist. She gritted her teeth and groaned as she pulled herself up the side of the boat—not an easy feat with the Obsidian Key still clutched in one of her hands—before clawing herself up and over the wooden railing and spilling onto the deck like a gasping fish.

"What in the Hells?" someone asked.

Delphine pushed herself to her feet and glanced around the deck at a ship of pirates, their faces filled with curiosity but not malice. A good sign.

A woman with a necklace made of shark teeth gasped. "A *siren*?"

"A siren on board is good luck," another noted with glee. This one was not nearly as attractive as the rest of his peers. He had yellowing teeth and dirt crusted under every single one of his fingernails.

"Delphine?"

That was the voice she wanted to hear. She pushed through the crowd and ran to Isaac, letting him catch her against his chest like a fawning damsel. An act that had always made men fold faster than a house of cards and miss the knife that was almost never far behind.

"My friends and I need your help," she gushed at him. "*Please.* They're still in the water. I need you to slow down the ship!"

His scarlet eyes were instantly pitying, and he smoothed a hand down her spine as he said, "Of course, doll." Then to his crew he barked, "Reef and luff the sails! Deploy the drag anchor!"

The crew didn't argue; they simply followed orders, and as he ushered her to the stern of the ship, she could feel that their efforts were already making it slow. When they reached the narrow edge of the deck, she pointed to where Hannah, Calla, and Gideon were moving through the water in the distance, no bigger than ants. Then he pointed to where a crowd of people were causing an uproar on the deck.

"We need to get them out before they get swarmed. Do you think you could use your magic to pull them closer? I'll lower the lifeboat for them on the side."

Delphine nodded and took a deep breath as he left to do as he promised. She reached out with her hands and began to unfurl her magic into the ocean, the feeling of connecting to the water both familiar yet unpracticed. She hadn't used this much of her power since . . . fighting Zephyr.

She slowly wrapped her magic around the area her friends were treading and slowly, so slowly, beckoned the ocean to bring them toward her. It was working. She pulled faster, like they were tied to a fishing line and she was reeling them in. When they finally caught up to the side of the boat, Isaac called for her to release her magic, and she did. She ran down to where the small wooden dinghy had been lowered, leaning over the railing as she watched Isaac and a member of his crew help them inside before hoisting them up onto the deck.

"Oh, thank the Gods," she said to the three of them as Gideon used his magic to dry everyone off.

Their glamours were completely gone, but at this point it hardly seemed to matter. If Isaac and his crew wanted to turn them in for the bounty, Delphine would rather their chances of taking on this crowd than the other.

"Pick up the anchors and release the sails!" Isaac ordered. "Let's give her back some speed!" Then he stepped up next to Delphine and said, "I knew you'd be trouble."

"I'm sorry," Delphine said sincerely. "There was an incident. . . ."

"Don't worry, doll. I meant that as a compliment." He winked at her and then turned to the others. "I'm Captain Isaac Worley. Welcome aboard the *Sea Pearl*."

Neither Gideon nor Hannah looked impressed, but Calla caught Delphine's eye with a look that said, *I get it.*

"Where is this ship going?" Gideon asked, much more concerned with the details of getting them out of this predicament than socializing.

"Noctum," Isaac confirmed. "But without an extra stop. I tried to tell Delphine that other ship wouldn't be any fun."

"Falling into the trap of trusting a charming pirate seemed a little too cliché then," Delphine quipped.

"I could say the same thing about inviting a siren aboard." He grinned at her. "But I promise we'll treat you better than all the guards who'd rather turn you in to the Witch Queens."

Gideon and Hannah were both instantly tense, but it was Calla who questioned, "You know? And you don't wish to do the same?"

"'Course I know," Isaac answered. "The courier delivered those posters before dawn, this morning. They wanted me to put them up around the store. But I don't oblige a monarchy's requests. Ever."

"The posters make an excellent target, though!" someone called, and they all turned their heads just in time to see a dart fly and land right in between Calla's eyes on a poster someone had fixed to one of the masts.

Calla wrinkled her nose.

"Y'all are safe from the queens here," Isaac promised. "Hells, as long as you're at sea, you're safe from them forever, right? If you want to join the crew—"

"Thanks, but we'll be departing at Noctum," Gideon cut him off firmly.

"What's in this for you?" Hannah questioned next. "Why are you helping?"

Isaac smiled. "Let's just say I'm bored of my current company. We could use some new faces around here to liven things up."

Delphine could tell he wanted to say something more but held back, and the answer seemed to be just enough to make Gideon's shoulders relax anyway. She knew the prince would be keeping a close eye on things, though, and she had a feeling the moment he could sneak a look at his compass he would be making sure their trajectory did not change.

Delphine cleared her throat. "Please tell me there are extra rooms for us."

Isaac reached up to ruffle his brown curls as he winced. "Well . . . there's *an* extra room. Singular. But don't worry, it has more than one bed."

"That's a first," Calla muttered.

44

Ezra caught up with Sabine a mile from the trading post on the eastern side of the mountain pass. And as he suspected, she was not happy to see him.

"Do you ever fucking listen?" she seethed. "I told you I didn't need you to come with me!"

"Too bad." He brushed past her. "You can't carry everything we'll need by yourself, so you'll have to deal."

Something whirred past his head, and he halted his steps. Slowly facing her, he could feel the flames that were now always simmering in his core begin to burn brighter. He strode toward her as she raised a second blade, but before she could launch it, he had both of her wrists gathered in one of his hands and pinned to her left side.

"You can't just stab anyone anytime they do something you don't like," he told her.

"I can and I will," she snarled back at him, fighting against his hold, but he didn't budge.

"All right, then let me rephrase," he said as he squeezed her wrists tighter. "You can't just stab *me* anytime I do something you don't like. You need to learn how to talk out your feelings instead of acting like a child."

She screeched in frustration when she still couldn't free herself from his grip, but he suspected that if she really wanted to break out of it she could. Instead, she bucked and kicked at him, working herself up into a huffing, whimpering mess. He let her tire herself out until she finally sagged forward against him and began to cry. He sighed as he let her wrists go, the blade that had been in her palm clattering to the ground, and wrapped his arms around her to press her into his chest.

She beat a weak fist against his chest. "*No* . . . I don't need you. . . . Let me go. . . . No . . . no . . . no . . . *no* . . . Gods, why did it have to be *Meli*?"

Ezra ran a hand over her golden hair as she cried over her loss, whispering reassurances in her ear as he waited for her sobs to quiet. Eventually, they did, and only her sniffles were left between them. He pulled her face back and wiped away her tears with the pads of his thumbs, smoothing her hair from her face and tucking it behind her ears.

"I hope you realize that you've seen me cry twice now," Sabine rasped, her green eyes still slightly unfocused as she raised them to his face. "Which means I *have* to kill you."

"Kill me later," he told her as he dipped his face down to press a quick kiss onto her temple. "We have a task to finish."

With that, he turned and began heading for the trade post once again. Despite her belief that crying was a weakness, he was going to take it as a sign that he was getting closer and closer to precisely where he wanted to be. Sabine was quiet for the remainder of the walk, and he didn't try to disturb the solemness cocooning her.

But when they reached the buzzing trading post and he caught a glimpse of a very familiar face plastered across the wooden booths that lined either side of the passage, he couldn't help but break their mutual silence with a very shocked "*Fuck*."

Calla's mismatched gaze was staring at him from the Wanted poster. And if he hadn't thought they were on the precipice of the war before, the Fates were making it very clear—one wrong step and they'd be walking off the ledge and right into the raging fires of battle.

))) • (((

When Caspian made it to the Onyx Realm, Amina and Thorne in tow, he was hit with a sudden sense of nostalgia. The kind you only get when you realize the place you've returned to will never be your home again.

"What's the plan here?" Thorne asked as the three of them crouched behind an enormous boulder on the edges of the Guild camp they'd found.

They'd stumbled upon several other campsites before this one, but all had been readily abandoned—just as Amina had warned. Cass had been well aware of the queen's strategy to pull her soldiers from the borders, but seeing it in action—the towns that once held their covens completely barren—was another thing altogether. He wondered where Lysandra was holding her subjects, the ones that had not been trained to fight but would soon find themselves having to do so against their will.

"The plan," Cass finally answered, "is to grab one of those grunts so we can interrogate them." He pointed to a huddle of young witches roughing one another up as they tried to shoot acorns into a distant wooden bowl.

Before Thorne could offer a suggestion, a shadow washed over him and Caspian. Cass glanced up just in time to see Amina unfurling her wings and launching into the sky.

"Well, that's rather impatient," Thorne quipped.

"*Impatient* is synonymous with *Valkyrie* at this point," Cass muttered in agreement as the two of them watched her soar above.

Amina was like a wraith in the sky, dropping so fast to snatch up one of the unsuspecting grunts that she was little more than a blur of color as the chosen witch shrieked in fear. Caspian and Thorne watched as the rest of the Guild members snapped to attention, unsheathing their weapons and holding their breath as they waited for the next attack.

"Everyone back to your tents," a deep voice commanded in the distance. "Betas—check the perimeters. Be sure to keep your eyes on the tops of the trees."

Caspian recognized the voice immediately. A commander named Fernius who he'd crossed paths with back when he was Kestrel's beta. Fern wasn't the friendliest man, but he was supportive of Caspian's cause, which meant Cass had stumbled across the right sector of Guild members.

"Poor Harold," one of the other grunts whispered as they all began to hurry to their tents, their weapons never lowering.

Cass sighed as he gestured with his chin for Thorne to follow him. The two of them moved silently through the forest, ducking out of the line of sight of Fern's men as they scanned the area for where Amina might have landed.

"They're getting closer," Thorne warned as he flicked his gaze behind them, though there was no haste to his gait. "Want me to create a distraction?"

"If you could make a tree fall somewhere over there"—Caspian waved a hand toward the thick of trees in the distance to their right—"that would be great."

The thunderous crack of bark splitting rang out seconds later, and the sound of snapping branches falling to the ground with a *thud* made the gaining footsteps instantly change direction. Right on cue, someone hissed Caspian's name from overhead, and he tilted his face up to see Amina pinning the Onyx witch against the trunk of a tree nearly ten feet up. The poor grunt's eyes were bulging out of his skull, his voice held hostage by Amina's hand gripped tightly over his mouth. In seconds, the Valkyrie landed the two of them back on the ground.

"A bit ostentatious, don't you think?" Caspian asked her.

"You say ostentatious, I say we didn't have to wait an hour for you to strategize how to get things done in the slowest, most boring way possible," she quipped back.

Caspian gave her a lazy smirk. "*Slow* doesn't always mean 'boring.'"

He swore her cheeks flushed, but before he could linger on that detail, she was shoving the grunt at him and Thorne.

"Get on with your questions. We have things to do," Amina snapped, crossing her arms over her chest with indignation.

She hates when I remind her that she's attracted to me, Caspian noted to himself. *Do it more.*

Caspian turned to the Onyx witch now—Harold, his acquaintances had called him—who upon being released from Amina's hold had unsheathed two knives and was now trying to impale one into Thorne's abdomen. The knife bent.

Thorne grimaced. "Sorry about that. Hope it wasn't sentimental or anything."

Harold gaped at him. "Are you . . . are you a Blood Warrior?"

Thorne gave an awkward smile as he turned his left forearm over to reveal the row of dots embedded in his skin. "The fifth."

"Oh Gods," the boy moaned as he flicked his eyes between all of them. "It's all true, then? This is really happening." His breath became shallow. "I thought Commander was just joking about the first Blood Warrior—"

"The first?" Thorne and Caspian asked in sync.

Harold nodded in confirmation before settling his gaze on Caspian and asking, "Who are *you*? Are you from another Guild unit?"

"Yes," Cass confirmed. "My name is Caspian Ironside."

The boy's eyes grew round with shock. "You're *him*? You're on a hit list, you know? We're supposed to report any sight of you or the Onyx Princes."

Thorne and Amina both stiffened. Thorne with discomfort, Amina with anticipation to strike.

Cass, however, only smiled. "But you won't. Because you don't have to follow her orders, do you?"

Harold shook his head. "There were only three with completed rolls in my unit, thanks to you and Prince Gideon. When she called for extra palace guards, about a week ago, our commander specifically sent the three of them away."

Caspian laughed.

"Why are you here? And with a . . ." Harold flicked his eyes over to Amina with wariness as his words trailed off.

"Careful what you say next, witch," she warned.

". . . Valkyrie," Harold finished.

"There's some developing news with the Fates' War that has led to an alliance of sorts with our prickly feathered friend here," Cass explained. "But before we get into all of that, we're going to need you to tell us about the first Blood Warrior."

When Ezra and Sabine made it back to the cottage, their backs and arms weighed down with an egregious amount of supplies—most of which they probably didn't need, but Ezra wasn't going to deny Sabine anything in the current situation—Lark and Meli were already gone. Four new Valkyries, however, had arrived in their place. Sabine seemed to brace herself as they unloaded their goods in the kitchen, and Ezra threw her an understanding look. Nothing worse than everyone around you trying to smother you with pity when you would rather just forget the weight of reality.

"Sabine," one of the Valkyries greeted, her voice low, gray eyes soft with condolence as she approached. "I'm so sorry about—"

"It's nice to see you, too, Sydni," Sabine said loudly, cutting off the girl's words. "Did Baden come with you?"

Sydni sighed, taking the hint. "Yes. He's here. Kellan and Merida came as well. They're the first of several Reapers who should be arriving in the next few hours. And, hopefully, more will come in the next couple of days. Ignia has enacted a curfew while she works on finding a way to stop anyone from leaving."

"I guess all the queens are pulling out the stops," Ezra muttered as he fished out from his pocket the Wanted poster he and Sabine had come across.

Lyra strode into the kitchen just in time to see Ezra unfold Calla's face. They let out a low whistle.

"I suppose it's safe to say we're doing something right," Lyra commented.

"How so?" Ezra lifted a brow.

Lyra tapped the poster with the back of their hand in demonstration. "If they're going through the effort of putting these up all the way out here, it means they know your Blood Warrior has a viable chance of starting this war. The fact that they haven't been able to nail any of you down . . . they're scrambling."

"Good," a gruff masculine voice said behind Lyra. "They can all rot in the fucking Hells."

The Valkyrie was tall enough that his head nearly reached the ceiling and he had to duck almost two feet to kiss Sydni on the cheek. Ezra assumed this was Baden.

The man looked Ezra up and down, though not with disdain or anything charged with malice. "You the witch prince?"

"One of them," Ezra confirmed.

Baden nodded, then asked, "Your mother as much of a royal bitch as our queen?"

"More," Ezra said dryly.

Baden huffed a laugh and gave Ezra a nod in approval before turning to Sydni and Lyra and saying, "Sydni and I got the regular crew together, and they're spreading the word as much as possible among the other Reapers. Some refused to join the cause—they're trying to get their families out instead. Some double downed in support for Ignia. They think we owe her for getting us out of the Fates' War."

Sabine sneered. "Got us out of the Fates' War but at what *cost*?"

Baden nodded. "I'm with you. I'd rather have taken my chances against the queens and lose my magic than reap the souls of every person I know, but hey, at least we got to have wings, right?"

Ezra snorted. "Wings are a nuisance anyway."

Lyra clapped their hands together, demanding everyone's attention. "All right, we need to start getting places to sleep set up for the others. Baden, you and I can talk about flight plans while we wait for them to signal us."

"How long until you think that will happen?" Sydni wondered.

Lyra gave them all a grave look. "We need to be prepared to move at any second from here on out."

45

To say Hannah was not thrilled by the current arrangements was an understatement.

Her first issue: Isaac gave them a room hardly bigger than a broom closet. There was exactly enough space for two sets of bunk beds and a small sliver of floor to walk between them. Gideon and Calla had seemingly resigned to their fates with little objection, immediately settling in and getting to work as they went through everything in their backpacks to clean out whatever had been ruined by ocean water. Delphine, on the other hand, had barely glanced at the room before meandering off to another part of the ship with Isaac.

Which was Hannah's second issue. She needed to talk to Delphine, and that damned pirate was making a mess of everything.

And that's exactly why Hannah found herself roaming the ship, alone, stewing in her thoughts. She hated this version of herself. A version where she criticized the person she loved most for not loving *her*... despite never actually making her feelings clear. But things weren't that easy. When had she had time? When had they gotten a break? And every time she thought she was ready to talk to Delphine, someone else was already swooping in. The price of loving someone everyone else did as well.

But she couldn't do this forever. The waiting. The wanting. It was slowly turning her into a monster, and she hated it.

Everyone thought she was so patient. So sweet and timid and selfless. Not many people understood how much darkness it took to become that way. To see such evil that you were determined to be the complete opposite of it despite the fact that traces of it still brewed within.

She needed to talk to Delphine before she lost the last of that resolve.

I should just go steal her away from him right now, Hannah thought. *We have three days trapped on this ship together. Three days of finally being in one place. There's no better time.*

As if those thoughts had suddenly woken her up, she looked around herself and realized she had no idea how she'd gotten to wherever she was. The corridor looked similar to the others except instead of rooms lining both sides of the hallway there was a section of doors on the left and a giant open space with crates and barrels of supplies on the right.

The cargo hold.

Hannah spun for the stairs that had led her down here, wanting to leave the drafty space as soon as possible—she had only just gotten warm again—but before she could take a single step, she heard the distinct sound of crying. She bit her lip, waffling back and forth on her next decision, but when another sob echoed from the right, she gave in.

Tiptoeing, she followed the sound of sniffling, careful not to make too much noise across the creaky floor. When she reached the start of the rooms, she found that one side was actually just four empty holding cells. A brig. The other side, however, did seem to be rooms, though now she doubted they were bedrooms; they were most likely offices or other similar spaces. The first few doors she crept past were closed, but the very last one was ever so slightly ajar. She carefully peeked through the open crack, squinting to see in the dim lighting, and instantly regretted her curiosity.

A girl who looked not much older than herself was standing against the far wall, tears streaming down her face. A strange man was standing in front of her, saying nothing, just staring with his arms crossed and tapping a foot as if he were disappointed. Hannah couldn't see his face, only the back of his head. The most discernable feature she could make out was the collection of seashells he had woven into the blond tendrils.

"I warned you the transformation would be painful," his deep voice suddenly rang out through the small space, making Hannah and the girl startle in sync. "If you keep screaming, you're going to start upsetting people."

"Good!" the girl shouted. "I hope I do upset someone! I hope—"

A creak reverberated through the hall around Hannah. She sucked in a breath as she glanced down at her feet, noticing that she'd leaned too much of her weight on a loose board. The girl's eyes snapped to the doorway, and Hannah swore they looked right into her own, but the moment the man tensed, Hannah was already fleeing. She raced back down the hall as fast as she could, turning the corner so quickly that she nearly crashed into the staircase. She heard heavy footsteps pounding behind her as she took the steps two at a time.

One flight. Turn. Second flight. Turn. Third flight. Turn—smack into another person.

"Whoa there, shortcake," Isaac said as he steadied Hannah from bouncing off his chest. "Where's the danger?"

In the cargo hold, she wanted to scream.

Instead, she said, a bit breathless, "Sorry. I was just, um, I was . . ."

"Looking for Delphine?" he supplied.

"Yes," Hannah answered truthfully.

"She's in the captain's quarters waiting for dinner to start. I was just coming to invite the rest of you, if you'd like to get your other friends—"

"Would you mind?" Hannah asked, not willing to go back alone. "I really need to, um, get some fresh air. Being down there made me a bit seasick."

He narrowed his unsettling scarlet eyes but didn't call her out on her lie. "Sure."

She waited for him to disappear and then took off across the upper deck, only pausing to ask someone where the captain's quarters were. They pointed her toward the bow. When she reached it, she found an open trapdoor with a set of private stairs. Slipping down below, she emerged into a roomy den with a set of double doors on each side. One of the sets was closed, but the doors in the other were pushed wide open to reveal the large dining room beyond.

"Hannah," Delphine called from where she was lounging at the table.

Hannah hurried over to the seat in front of Delphine, gripping the back of the chair to steady herself. "Delph, we need to talk."

Delphine set down the glass of wine in her hand as she took in Hannah's panicked appearance with concern. "What's wrong?"

"I was down in the cargo hold, and I saw something—"

"The cargo hold?" Delphine interrupted. "What were you doing in the cargo hold?"

Hannah shook her head in frustration. "It doesn't matter! What matters is that I need to talk to you."

"I know," Delphine said more seriously now. "About earlier. Me too, but we should wait until after dinner."

"No, not about earlier— Well, yes, I want to talk about that, too, but this is something else—"

"And this is where I sleep," Isaac announced as he led Calla, Gideon, and three unfamiliar faces down the stairs.

Hannah clamped her mouth shut, and Delphine's silver gaze watched her with a lot more alarm now.

"Choose whichever seat you'd like," Isaac said as he strutted to the head of the table between Delphine and Hannah.

Calla made her way along Delphine's side while Gideon took the chair across—next to Hannah. Isaac's companions each introduced themselves as they took up the remaining chairs at the table, but Hannah forgot the names of the first two, and how to breathe, the second she saw the third man. A man with blond hair threaded with seashells.

"Hullo," the man greeted her with a tight smile. "You can call me Lachlan."

)·)·)·●·(·(·(

Hannah didn't eat a single bite the entire meal and only pretended to sip the wine that was placed in front of her. She needed to do something with her hands to distract herself from the sight of Lachlan watching her like a hawk.

Delphine was busy lingering on every word Isaac said as he regaled everyone with the stories he'd promised of dangerous escapades all over Aetherius and strange encounters with sea creatures. And not at all unnoticed was the man next to Calla—Wesley—clinging to every word *she* was saying. Gideon's eyes had gone obsidian the entire time he watched Wesley refill Calla's glass or laugh a little too hard at something she said. It was starting to become obvious to Hannah that her friends had perhaps had too much wine, but she knew neither she nor Gideon would ever suggest such a thing in front of the others no matter how much they drank.

By the time Isaac was proposing a toast, Hannah was dying to bolt back to their room.

"To new friendships," Isaac said as he raised his glass, and they followed suit.

Hannah sat her glass down and announced, "I think it's time for bed."

Gideon was already pushing back his chair. "I couldn't agree more."

Isaac laughed off their brevity. "Fair enough, you've all had quite the eventful day. Tomorrow, though, there will be a party on the upper deck you can't miss."

Lachlan and the other of Isaac's friends—whom she hadn't bothered to learn the names of—headed back up to the deck first. Wesley, however, had tucked Calla's hand into the crook of his elbow and escorted her out himself, followed by the most hostile version of Gideon Black Hannah had ever seen. She got up from her place and slowly trailed after them, lingering as nonchalantly as she could for Delphine to tell Isaac good night.

When that never happened, Hannah cleared her throat and prompted, "Delph?"

"Hmm?" Delph hummed as she looked up from her conversation.

"Ready to go?" Hannah said.

Isaac gave Hannah a languid smile. "Don't worry, shortcake, I'll escort her back myself later."

Hannah dug her heels in. "No. We're leaving now."

Isaac cut his eyes to Delphine in silent question.

"It's really all right, Hannah," Delphine assured. "I won't be long."

Hannah braced herself for what she was about to do.

"Delphine DeLune, if you value our friendship at all"—Hannah enunciated every word clear and firm—"you will leave with me *right now.*"

Delphine's brows shot up in shock, and Isaac shifted uncomfortably in his seat. A long moment of silence hung in the air until Delphine finally scraped her chair back from the table and stood.

"Good night, Isaac," she said before stalking off for the exit.

"Good night, doll. We'll talk more tomorrow."

Delphine didn't look at Hannah once as she made her way back to the deck, and when Hannah began to turn to hurry after her, Isaac called out quietly.

"Piece of advice, shortcake?" he drawled. "Women don't like it when you act like you own them."

Hannah bit her tongue until the metallic taste of blood filled her mouth, but she left without another word.

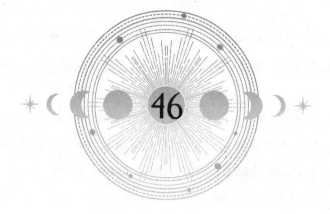

46

Amina was not pleased with her current company. The grunt she'd plucked out of the clearing, Harold—a name that she could not take seriously—had convinced her companions they should take an audience with his commander. And despite her many protests, she was now surrounded by Onyx witches. Most of whom looked as if they wanted to maim her. Which was probably fair, but that wouldn't stop her from slicing her claws through every single one of them if they made one wrong move.

Caspian threw her a look that seemed to demand, *Relax*, but he clearly didn't understand that not every witch was as . . . agreeable . . . as he was when it came to Valkyries.

"Caspian Ironside, it's an honor," the commander declared, his eyes immediately assessing their group and lingering on Amina's scowl a little too long.

She bared her teeth, the mask of the Valkyrie slipping back into its familiar place. Not for the first time this trip, she wished it had been

Lyra dealing with this task. She'd forgotten how much she hated the bravado she had to put on around witches that weren't Caspian and his friends. She'd gotten too comfortable thinking they could all just move around one another without disturbance or acknowledgment. Not that Cass ever let her not acknowledge *his* presence. Especially right now, as he was being showered with inflated compliments and appreciation. He took up more space in her mind than ever.

"Commander Fernius"—Cass dipped his chin in a respectful greeting—"it's been a long time."

"Unfortunately, you're not catching my unit at their best time," the commander said, words gruff. "We just got an influx of untrained whelps from Lysandra"—a flicked gaze in Harold's direction—"and trying to whip them into shape while strategizing how to move in this war when we all reveal our tricks has been a task to say the least."

"I'm surprised she's not sending you new soldiers with their rolls already completed," Caspian admitted.

"She's trying, but the chaos at the palace has allowed for some of the other commanders to help glamour the new recruits and ship them out to our units before she can get to them," the commander confirmed.

"And what's her plan?" Cass asked. "Where are all the witches she's made abandon their homes?"

"She's moved them to the woods around her palace for the foreseeable future. Lysandra knows she's at the heart of the Realms. That the war will most likely fall on her doorstep. So she's built a barrier of obedient bodies to lie in wait. We all knew that's where this was headed."

Cass nodded solemnly, and something pulled taut in Amina's chest. All of their queens had failed them so disastrously. And the Fates... well, they had created the monsters in the first place.

"Any word from the other queens?" Thorne wondered.

"Myrea has moved the Rouge witches closer to our border as well. The Guild is the first line of defense, but after that, the Rouge witches are supposed to move in. As for Althea..."

Althea, Amina recognized, was the Queen of the Terra witches. The more subtle of the three witch queens. But subtle didn't mean not ruthless.

"We haven't received word on her moves yet," the commander finished. "There's a lot of unpredictable factors coming our way. We don't know where all the Blood Warriors are or when things will start. We certainly don't know who's going to organize those who haven't completed their rolls or where to send the children."

"We're working on getting the Blood Warriors," Thorne assured him. "Three of us have already found one another."

"And my friends and I are planning an attack from above," Amina chimed.

The commander shifted his gaze to her. "That so? And just how many Valkyries are really going to come to help? Two? Ten?"

"And you should be grateful for even that," Amina retorted. "Do you have any idea the lengths we're having to go to help you out? To convince our people to risk their lives in a Gods' war?"

"Don't talk to me as if I don't understand that sacrifice, soul stealer," the commander snapped.

"You're not allowed to talk to her like that, Commander."

Amina looked at Caspian with shock. She'd never heard the witch's voice filled with so much darkness before. But one look at his expression and she knew every word had been laced with a threat.

"We're all dealing with things as best we can, and the Valkyries' help is *invaluable*," Caspian continued.

The commander looked as if he wanted to argue that point, especially when he saw Amina's lips curling into a smug grin, but Thorne was already moving on.

"The boy mentioned something about the first Blood Warrior earlier?" Thorne prompted. "Have you had contact with Dex recently?"

The commander raised a brow. "A few weeks ago, in fact. A mutual friend put us in contact after Dex told them he'd heard the final Blood Warrior had been found and that it was . . . Prince Gideon." The commander paused to gauge their reactions, and when none of them denied it, his brows shot up to his hairline. "It's true? He's the sixth? I heard a rumor that there was some girl, a Siphon—"

"There is," Thorne said matter-of-factly. "They're soul-bonded. The Fates got two for the price of one."

The commander rocked back on his heels. "Dear Gods. No wonder Lysandra has been a raging terror lately. Her favorite son is her number one enemy."

"Do you know where Dex might have gone after you spoke to him? Did he say anything else?" Thorne pressed on.

The commander shrugged. "He said he wanted to speak to someone in the Guild to get a gauge on when he needed to be prepared to fight. Figured with the news that Gideon was a Blood Warrior we'd be a good temperature check to see who knew what sort of information. I offered to let him stay in our camp, but he refused, saying it wasn't safe for him to be out and about in the Realms but that he wouldn't be too far."

Thorne nodded. "I know where he is."

Amina nearly sighed in relief as she shifted on her feet impatiently. "Great. Let's go."

Thorne gave her an understanding smile as he meandered away with her while Cass wrapped up a few last details with the commander. The two of them lingered back in the tree line as they waited for Cass to return, and it took everything in her not to yell for him to hurry up. She wanted to get back to Lyra and Sabine.

"I get it," Thorne murmured, seemingly responding to her unspoken thoughts. "Being away from those you love while having to interact with those who are afraid of you. Who see you as a threat. It's tiring."

There was a beat of silence as they watched Cass finally turn away from his conversation and return to them.

"Exhausting," she agreed.

"It will be over soon," Thorne said absentmindedly, his green eyes glazing slightly as he spoke. "And maybe then we'll wish it wasn't. When we look around and see who's left standing."

Amina stayed silent this time.

47

Calla felt amazing. She loved wine. She loved pirates. She especially loved not having to worry about waking up and jumping back into danger the next morning.

"You ever been out of Illustros?" Wesley asked as they made their way over to the deck railing. The ocean spread out before them like an infinite expanse of glass, stars mirrored on its shiny surface like a million little diamonds.

"No," Calla answered, her tone airy. "And I can't say I'm excited Noctum is the first continent I'm going to see, but I am excited that at least I won't have lived and died only seeing one place."

"That's why I love sailing." Wesley nodded. "I know plenty of people who have roots planted in the same exact place they were born, and they love it, but I don't want roots—I want wings. And a boat's sails are the closest I'll ever get in this lifetime."

Calla's eyes widened as she looked back at him. "That's beautiful."

He smiled, the dimples in his cheeks creasing. "You know what I think is beautiful?"

"Hmm?" she hummed as she leaned into him.

He smelled of spice and wine, and though Calla knew that wasn't right, that it very much was not the aroma she was hoping for, her mind didn't seem to care. His boyishly handsome face, hazel eyes, and golden-brown hair were not something she'd usually go for, but something about him just . . . clicked.

"I think your eyes are beautiful," he whispered. "Has anyone ever told you that before?"

"Yes," a deep voice answered.

Calla jumped back from Wesley at the sound of *that* voice. Her heart began pounding as she looked up at Gideon's furious expression, but his eyes weren't on her at all.

"Gideon," she breathed, cheeks suddenly heating in shame.

"Calliope." Gideon's eyes shifted to her face. "Can I have a word?"

Calla began to nod, but Wesley's hand was suddenly on her arm, making her pause.

"We were actually in the middle of a conversation," Wesley said.

Gideon's answering look could have set the man aflame on the spot. "If you don't remove your hand from her, I'll rip it off and throw it to the sharks."

To Wesley's credit, he didn't cower, but he did snatch his hand back.

Gideon jerked his chin to the side, directing Calla to follow him, and she did. He was terrifyingly silent as he led her belowdecks and back to their room. She only glanced over her shoulder once to look at Wesley, but the man had already disappeared.

As soon as they stepped inside the small bunker, Gideon kicked the door shut and locked it. Then he faced Calla, and she braced herself for whatever he was about to say about her behavior.

He crossed his arms over his chest, his voice gruff as he asked, "Are you all right?"

She furrowed her brow. "What do you mean?"

"Calliope, something is very wrong. Your side of the bond feels like *ice*."

Calla swallowed. She didn't understand what he meant. She felt just fine, *warm* even, and his side of the bond . . . She sucked in a sharp breath. She reached for him, for his essence, that familiar feeling of his magic, his presence, through their connection and . . . nothing.

"Whoa, hey, it's okay," he said as he reached to gently tilt her face up to his by her chin. "It could just be the alcohol in your system. Here."

Calla hadn't even realized she'd begun to panic, but the room was spinning now as her breathing became too quick. Gideon turned to grab a canteen of water from their supplies and twisted open the cap before bringing it up between them in offering. She drank until there was nothing left.

"What's happening?" she asked. "I've had wine before. It's never made me feel like this. Act like this."

"I don't know," he answered. "But I should find Hannah and Delphine and make sure we all stay alert. Something about our host and his friends seems off."

"Oh my Gods," she whispered, a sinking feeling settling in her stomach as her mind began to grow clearer and clearer as they spoke. "What did I do? At dinner—"

"*You* didn't do anything," he assured her. "I might genuinely rip off that pirate's arm and throw it into the ocean, though."

"Hand," she choked. "You threatened to rip off his hand before," she clarified, the realization hitting her.

"He's lucky that's all I threatened," said Gideon.

Calla shook her head. "No, I mean, I can remember that detail but can't remember a single other second of you being at dinner. Or anyone else for that matter. It's like now that he's out of my sight I can think . . . but until you interrupted our conversation, there's not a single detail in my mind of you that sticks."

Gideon's expression went from puzzled to terrified in the span of a second. "There was something in your wine."

"But you drank the wine, too—"

"No. I didn't," Gideon revealed. "I only pretended to. As did Hannah. I wasn't going to risk even a sip of inebriation among a bunch of strangers. And now that I think about it, every time I acted as if I was drinking, that woman sitting next to me, whatever her name was, tried to get my attention."

"What's going on?" Calla whispered, fear suddenly spearing through her. "Do you think they're taking us to the queens after all? Trying to drug us so we can't fight?"

Gideon shook his head. "I've been watching the compass and our trajectory all night. And even if I wasn't—the location of the stars doesn't lie. We're absolutely on our way to Noctum. Something else is going on. And until we figure it out, we need to lie low."

"Hannah and Delphine." Calla gasped. "We need to get them—"

"You're staying here," he ordered. "Lock the door behind me and don't answer it unless you hear six knocks and me saying the word"—he looked around the room for something to inspire a code word, his eyes landing on something atop her bed—"Heart Reaver. Okay?"

Calla bit her lip, wanting to insist she go with him, but he was probably right. He'd be much stealthier without her in her inebriated state. So she watched him leave and immediately locked the door behind him.

As soon as Hannah stepped onto the deck, Delphine's furious face appeared right before hers.

"Hannah Carmine," Delphine seethed, "if you value our friendship at all, you will start explaining yourself, *right now.*"

Hannah glanced around, noticing a few late-night stragglers still meandering around them. Worse, she spotted the trio that had accompanied them at tonight's dinner a few yards away, huddled together and throwing glances in Hannah and Delphine's direction.

"Can we please go talk in the room?" Hannah asked.

"No." Delphine shook her head, crossing her arms. "If you felt the need to call me out in the open back there, then you can talk to me out in the open right here."

Hannah knew she deserved that, but she couldn't explain to Delphine what she saw in the cargo hold earlier out in the open like this, nor could she quite explain why she was feeling sick about the entire dinner in general.

So— instead, she blurted out, "I was jealous."

Delphine's anger deflated at that. "Jealous? Of what?"

"That ridiculous pirate," Hannah said. "Thorne. Allex. Anyone who has ever once held your attention for more than a second."

Delphine only stared at Hannah, silver eyes flickering through a million different emotions, but she didn't speak.

Hannah took a shaky breath. "I'm in love with you, Delphine."

Delphine's jaw slackened with disbelief. "You're . . . in love with me?"

"Of course I'm in love with you," Hannah whispered. "Gods, who isn't?"

As if it wasn't a rhetorical question, Delphine muttered, "Ezra Black."

Hannah pushed on as if Delphine hadn't spoken. "I've been in love with you since the moment I laid eyes on you—and I know that applies to nearly every other person in the universe as well, but, Gods, I'm praying that maybe I'll be the one it makes a difference for."

"Hannah," Delphine choked. "Hannah. You're . . . you're my everything. The entire time I was in the Siren's Sea, *you* are who I thought of.

When I desperately wished for home, it was you I wished for. Your voice I heard in the moments I wanted to flip the switch of my morality off."

Hannah heard the word coming before Delphine even spoke it.

"But . . ." Delphine's whisper trailed off.

Hannah always assumed when Delphine finally rejected her, she'd fall into a deep pit of despair she would never be able to claw her way out of. But that wasn't the case at all. No. Hannah was furious.

"Why?" Hannah demanded. "Why do you always go for people who only like you for what's on the surface? Instead of someone who *knows* you, and *gets* you, and *sees* you?"

"It's safer," Delphine answered instantly. "I've done the falling-in-love-with-your-best-friend thing, Hannah. And it was ruinous. I would never risk that with you."

Hannah wanted to sob. "Because I'm not worth the risk? Because I've turned into this monster? I know I look hideous now—"

Delphine looked horrified. "You do *not* look hideous. You are not a monster. And it isn't that *you* aren't worth the risk, but rather *losing* you isn't worth the risk. I cannot be the version of myself you've built up in your head all these years, Hannah. I can never be that person." Delphine closed her eyes. "Maybe it's just the nature of this sort of thing for sirens. We lure people in with the promise of beauty and grandiosity. People want us because they like shiny things and trophies. But you cannot base your entire self off me or my validation. And you immediately asking if it's because you're some sort of monster, or if you're not pretty enough, is all I need to see this case is no different."

Hannah flinched and took a step back.

Delphine reached out for her. "Hannah, please—"

"No." Hannah shook her head. "You're wrong. You say you can't be the version of yourself I've built up in my head? How would you even know what version of you that is? I know you've been burned before. I know the Siren's Sea and all those people from your past made you jaded. But they aren't *me*, Delphine! And I'm not demanding that you have to reciprocate my feelings—I'd *never* do such a thing and never really believed you would anyway, honestly. But do not act as if your rejection is because you're worried I do not see you clearly. You want to know the version of you that's in my head? It's the one that takes men into alleyways and rips off their fingers for trying to put something in your drink. The girl who I spent years touring Estrella with, staying up until dawn talking on the couch, who has an unparalleled taste for extravagant clothes and jewels but the worst possible taste in perfume. The girl who would, and has, killed for her friends, who has an unhealthy obsession with sticky buns, and who is unapologetically selfish when she has to be. Whose laugh I could recognize *anywhere*. Even in the deepest pits of despair and darkness."

They stood there for a long moment, staring at each other, Hannah's chest heaving from her words. Delphine looked torn, but Hannah didn't mean to make her feel that way. She wasn't trying to convince Delphine that they should be together; she was trying to convince Delphine that she knew *exactly* what she wanted. What she was asking for. That she didn't see Delphine as a shiny, elusive entity to collect as a trophy. She wanted Delphine because she knew her. And that mattered.

"Delphine?" a deep voice suddenly said a few feet away.

Both Hannah and Delph snapped their heads to the side and noticed Isaac was standing there, looking between them in concern. Delphine's eyes immediately seemed to glaze over, and despair bloomed in Hannah's core.

"I was just going to ask if you were done here?" he offered.

Delphine swallowed and nodded, not bothering to glance back at Hannah. "Yes."

As Delphine turned to follow Isaac down the stairs, Hannah let her go.

And then she really let her go.

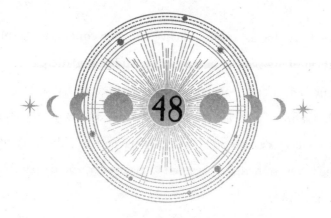

48

When Thorne said he knew where Dex was, Amina had not expected him to lead them only a few miles inland to a place Caspian recognized as Silver Lake. The lake was something out of a fairy tale. The water was mercurial, like a silvered star had fallen from the sky and dissolved into metallic glitter. A pair of black swans glided across its surface; lavender and blue flowers dripped down from around its banks and kissed the water. A bridge of silver and obsidian had been built across the body of water for travelers to pass, but not a single other being was around. It was just them and the lovely woodland creatures.

"Um . . . Thorne?" Cass prompted. "Why are we here?"

Thorne pointed to the peaceful surface of the water. "Dex is in there."

Caspian laughed. But when Thorne's expression remained even, Caspian's drifted between confused and skeptical.

"Why would he be *in* Silver Lake?" Cass questioned.

"Because it's closer to where we all assume the battlefield will be than Oracle's Bay, back in the Terra Realm," Thorne said, and when the confusion still didn't leave their faces, he added, "Dex is a Terra witch. Well, sort of."

"How do you know him?" Caspian asked at the same time that Amina said, "What the Hells do you mean *sort of*?"

"Dex completed his Rolls of Fate when I was just a boy," Thorne explained as he waved them over toward the bank of the lake, toeing the edge and sending a ripple through its silvery surface. "The first Blood Warrior being chosen was a massive deal, as I'm sure you both can assume. And if you were around, I'm also sure you heard the rumors. Which meant the queens had to make an example out of him. That's when the hunts began. Anyone with too many of the same numbers ended up slaughtered—or worse. And Althea is by far the most creative of the three queens. She had Dex placed in a glass box outside of her palace, where everyone would be able to see his suffering. As Blood Warriors, we're indestructible, but we can still feel pain. He had no oxygen, no food, and no strength to break himself out. For nearly seven years, he sat in that box. And we all just moved past it like he wasn't there. Wasn't once one of us. It always haunted me a bit."

Thorne knelt down. Digging his hands into the damp earth as they watched in rapt silence.

"Then, one day, the box was empty. No one knew how he did it. Althea had raged. She offered a small fortune to anyone who might know how he escaped. The glass box hadn't been shattered. He had seemingly just... disappeared. It was about two decades later that I accidentally stumbled upon how."

Amina felt a strange wave of magic pierce the air around them as the earth beneath her feet seemed to warm. Thorne tilted his face up from where his hands were pulsing magic into the ground and looked out toward the lake instead. His green eyes were narrow with concentration, but when Amina squinted into the distance, she didn't see a thing. Not until a few minutes later when a smile broke across Thorne's face and something began to rise from the water. No, not something. Someone.

Amina watched in disgust as a man emerged from the mercurial water, his form covered in glittering silver sludge. So much silt in his hair that at first she thought it was a shade of ash, but as he stomped out of the lake and onto dry land, it became clear that his shoulder-length tresses were a deep, mossy green. His eyes were nearly the same color, perhaps a shade or two darker, and his skin was so pale it was obvious he'd been out of the sun's reach for a while. His body was built like a warrior's, though, and Amina could tell the effort he'd put into his physique was intentional.

"Thorne," the man breathed in disbelief, rivulets of waters running down his face.

Thorne gave the man a bright smile. "Dex. It's been a while."

The two of them embraced each other in a way that was intimate enough to make both Amina and Cass glance away.

When they finally pulled apart, Dex asked, "Has it begun?"

"The war hasn't started," Thorne reassured him. "But we were hoping you might come with us to prepare for it."

At the mention of *us*, Dex finally turned to size up Caspian and

Amina. His eyes had an edge of darkness in them that almost made Amina shiver, but it wasn't the sort of darkness that was malicious. Rather, it seemed hollow.

Dex turned back to Thorne. "The last I heard about you, you were rotting in Lysandra's dungeon. How much did you regret leaving me while you stewed down there?"

"Much," Thorne confirmed before jutting his chin toward Cass. "Luckily, my dear friend Caspian here sprung me out."

Dex tilted his head. "And what is it that you all are up to?"

"We're trying to get the Blood Warriors together. We'll need to be at the front lines doing as much damage to the Witch Queens as possible before the dice is rolled for the final time and we lose our invincibility," Thorne appealed.

"Blood Warriors," Dex emphasized. "The rumors are true, then."

"Aren't they always?" Thorne grinned.

"Who else have you found?" Dex wondered.

"You and Thorne." Caspian began ticking off the names on his fingers. "And then Calla and Gideon. Which means there's still three others."

"You wouldn't happen to know where Piper and Eurydice are?" Thorne questioned.

"I lost track of Piper ages ago," Dex said. "But Eurydice... Has anyone been to the Miroir Mountains lately?"

Caspian shifted his eyes to Amina's, a grin on his face. "As a matter of fact..."

49

T he sea breeze whipping through the air smelled like salt and ruin as Gideon strutted across the upper deck with purpose. His mind was so heavily focused on the fact that he couldn't feel Calliope through their bond that he didn't notice Hannah among the shadows until he was running smack into her.

"*Oof,*" Hannah said as he steadied her from ricocheting off his chest.

He cursed. "Sorry, Han. Where's Delphine?"

Hannah pointed toward the bow, eyes unfocused and hollow as she said, "Captain's quarters."

Gideon cursed, then told her in a low voice, "Get to our room and stay there with Calla."

She blinked up at him, a bit of color returning to her cheeks. "What's going on?"

"Something here is very off," Gideon said as he flicked his eyes around the deck to make sure no one was paying attention to them. All he found was the same huddle of crew members playing cards on the far left of the boat, too wrapped up in their own conversation to notice his and Hannah's.

"Yes, it *is* off here," she agreed, her voice dropping to little more than a whisper. "Gideon, I need to tell you about something that I found earlier."

He nodded as he started toward the bow of the ship, waving her after him. "We just have to make sure Delphine is safe first."

"Safe?" Hannah asked, alarmed.

Gideon felt the anger rush back to him, making his fists clench at his sides as he revealed to her, "They drugged the wine at dinner."

Hannah's breath hitched. *"No."*

She stayed right on his heels as he led them back toward the hidden room. He crouched down to pry the trapdoor open but found it locked.

"I swear to the Gods," he snarled when it wouldn't budge. "I guess we're doing this the hard way."

He stood and summoned his wind, coaxing it into a small tornado that hovered over the wooden slats before punching it straight down and splintering the boards open. The crew was on their feet in an instant at the commotion, but Gideon was already reaching his hand through the hole he'd created to unlatch the door and throw the busted panel out of the way. He let Hannah climb down first before dropping after her, landing nimbly on his feet in the dark corridor between the dining room and the bedroom.

A loud creak came from their left as Isaac threw the door open to see what was going on.

"What in the Hells?" Isaac growled.

Gideon had him pinned against the wall before either of them could blink, his forearm pressed against the pirate's throat as he bared his teeth. "What the fuck did you put in that wine?"

There was a hard glint of something Gideon couldn't name in Isaac's crimson eyes, but all the man choked out was "I don't know what you're talking about."

"What the Hells is going on?" Delphine demanded as she came out of the bedroom, silver eyes ablaze with annoyance.

That's when the other crew members dropped in as well.

"You okay, boss?" the one named Lachlan demanded.

Isaac shoved Gideon away from him, straightening his shirt as he flicked his eyes over to his friend. "I'm fine. Our guest here seems to be having a misunderstanding."

"There's no misunderstanding. Something was in that wine that's messing with Calliope's magic," Gideon accused. "Not to mention whatever nefarious plan you had for Delphine, who's *intoxicated*—"

"Gideon, we were only talking," Delphine interrupted, her words a bit clunky but not slurred, at least. "Goodness, you and your father are scary alike."

Gideon froze at the mention of his father, and out of the corner of his eye he saw a flash of guilt flicker on Delphine's face.

"I didn't mean that in a bad way," she clarified. "It's just—I'm fine. I'm not a damsel. I don't need saving."

"Maybe I'd be willing to hear you out on that if there wasn't still the matter of Calliope's magic acting up since the first sip she took at dinner," he gritted out.

"Gideon—" Delphine began again, but Isaac raised a hand, cutting her off.

"No, he's right. Faery wine can have strange effects on different kinds of beings," Isaac explained. "I thought you all would know that. I deeply apologize for any surprises it may have caused."

Gideon curled his lip. "You gave us *faery wine*? Why in the Hells wouldn't you tell us that?"

"You're right, I wasn't thinking," Isaac obliged, lifting his hands in defense despite the unapologetic look on his face.

Gideon wanted nothing more than to slam a fist into the man's smug expression, but he knew the risk that would entail. Isaac had an entire crew, after all, not to mention the stakes he and his friends were up against being wanted fugitives. It would be foolish to give the pirates a reason to turn the ship around—toward the Witch Realms.

So, instead, he gave the captain a tight smile and said, "If you don't mind excusing us, then, I think I should take the girls back to our room to sober up."

Delphine crossed her arms over her chest. "I'm just fine, right—"

"It's not up for discussion," Gideon inserted, his eyes snapping to her face, daring her to challenge him.

Delphine pressed her lips together, a tense beat of silence lingering between them as she decided if she would press his buttons any further, but she finally sighed in defeat and stomped past them for the stairs. Hannah started after her friend, pausing when she realized Gideon wasn't moving.

"Coming?" she whispered.

"Wait for me on the deck," he told Hannah, his eyes never leaving Isaac's as he spoke.

She hesitated for a second, her eyes flicking between him and the pirate, before nodding and doing as he said.

When she was out of earshot, Gideon stepped toward Isaac once more, making the men at his back unsheathe various weapons, ready to attack if their captain gave the signal. Gideon huffed a dark laugh.

"I want to be very clear about one thing," Gideon said loud enough for his entire audience. "I was raised by the most brutal of the Witch Queens, trained by her most ruthless commander. I have stood before Gods and walked away. I have enough power in my right index finger to wipe out every single man on your crew and shred them into tiny unrecognizable shreds. And if you even *think* about harming one of my girls, I will not hesitate to do that very thing."

Isaac's jaw clenched.

Gideon leaned forward now, bringing his lips to the man's ear to warn, "You might want to tell your friend Wesley that if he even so much as looks in Calliope's direction in front of me again, I will rip his throat out with my teeth. Understood?"

Isaac gave him a tight smile. "More than."

Gideon nodded and spun for the exit, not bothering to glance at any of the others as he made his way up to where Hannah and a very impatient Delphine waited for him.

"Let's go," he muttered to them both.

Nothing was said as they made their way back to the room. When they reached the door, Gideon knocked six times and whispered the secret code before Calliope unlocked the door and let them all pile inside.

"What happened?" she asked.

"They gave you all faery wine," Gideon said. "Or so they claim. I've never been one for faery wine, but I cannot imagine it would have such an effect on a bond as powerful as ours."

Calliope rubbed at her temples. "Well, whether it was the faery wine or just that I drank too much, I definitely don't feel right. I want to sleep."

"All of you should get some sleep," he said.

"Actually, I'm going to go for a swim," Delphine said as she looked around at them. "I think this is much too small of a space for us all."

Gideon and Hannah both went to protest, but Delphine shook her head.

"Save it. Nothing's going to harm me in the water anyway," she said, and before they could say anything more, she slipped from the room and disappeared.

"Is something going on with her?" Gideon wondered.

Hannah winced. "That's my fault. We got into a little . . . spat."

"About?" Calliope asked despite the exhaustion on her face.

Hannah shook her head. "That's a conversation for later. I have something much more pressing right now—I was down in the cargo hold earlier, and Lachlan had a girl down there and she was *sobbing*. He said something about how she knew the transformation was painful, but I don't know what that means. I tried to tell this to Delphine, but I didn't have time before Isaac coaxed her away."

Gideon cursed. This information was not helping his self-control. He wanted to get them off this ship *now*, but they were little more than sitting ducks at this point. He'd known something was wrong at dinner, when Calliope's attention seemed to be eclipsed by that other man so entirely, but he'd just told himself he was being possessive. The same way Kestrel used to be. A quality he refused to feed. So he'd watched as the two of them flirted, as Wesley escorted her from the dining room and told her she was beautiful. Until he hadn't been able to stomach it anymore.

"Whatever is going on, we need to just keep to ourselves," Gideon told them. "Get some rest and wait this out. Don't talk to anyone. Hopefully, Delphine won't be gone too long."

"I'm going to get ready for bed," Hannah said. "If I'm not back in ten..."

Gideon nodded. "I'll go searching."

Once he and Calliope were left alone, she asked, "What do you think is going on here? I'm not entirely sure what I expected of pirates, but a crying girl hidden in the cargo hold doesn't seem to bode well...."

"No, it doesn't," he said. "C'mon, you look dead on your feet."

He guided her toward the right bottom bunk, waiting as she settled herself back against the wall before pulling the thin linen covers all the way up to her chin and tucking them in around her.

"Can you stay here until I fall asleep?" she asked, her eyelids fighting to stay open.

He didn't say a word as he laid himself back on the sliver of mattress next to her, his legs too long for the length of the bed. However, there wasn't a single complaint on his tongue as she wiggled herself closer to rest her head on his chest, the feeling of being so close to her making him instantly more comfortable with the lifelessness of their bond.

"Gideon?" she murmured.

"Yes?" he hummed as he began to pet slow, soothing circles into her hair.

"I..."

And then she was asleep. He let his own eyes close as he listened to the soft sounds of her breathing and hoped to the Gods that the current numbness from her side of the bond was not a terrible omen.

50

It was barely more than a whisper at first. Only her name, echoing across her dreams, in a voice she did not recognize.

Calliope. Calliope. Calliope.

Her eyes blinked open.

Calla sat up in bed and looked around in the dark. Hannah was sound asleep on the top of the bunk across from her. Delphine was still nowhere to be seen despite the room smelling even more of sea salt than it had earlier and the pile of the Delph's damp clothes discarded in the corner.

Calla stood slowly from the bed, trying to keep her steps as quiet as possible on the creaky floor. She stood on her tiptoes to peek up at Gideon's bunk but found that his bed was empty, the linens still neatly made. She wondered if he'd gone to check on their friend.

Was it him calling my name? she wondered.

She slipped from the room, padding toward the stairs that led up to the deck to see if perhaps Gideon had decided to get some fresh air after he determined all of them were safe and sound asleep. As she began to ascend the steps, however, she heard the whispers once more.

Calliope. Come find me.

Her eyes snapped to her right. A warm vibration began to crawl over her skin, and all thoughts except for finding *him* emptied from her head. She slowly climbed back down the stairs, heading toward the direction of the whispers.

That's right, lovely. Come find me.

Calla found herself stopping before an unknown room all the way down the hall. She slowly reached for the door's handle, twisted it, and pushed the door open to reveal a bunker very much like the one she and the others had been staying in. Only this one had a single bed and looked much more lived in.

"Ah, good, you heard me."

Calla felt her cheeks pull into a wide, nearly painful smile when her eyes landed on his.

☽ ☽ ☽ ● ☾ ☾ ☾

Delphine knew she oughtn't be out so late, standing at the front bow of the ship with Isaac, after all the fuss Gideon and Hannah had made earlier. She also knew she didn't really care. The swim had cleared her head—there was nothing like an ocean under the stars—and she'd had the intention of apologizing to Hannah over her reaction to the revelation that Hannah was *in love* with her. A confession Delphine was still reeling from, that was on constant loop in her mind, making it impossible for her to sleep no matter how hard she'd tried to tire herself out with her swim.

Somewhere between tossing and turning in the uncomfortable bunk bed and the stroke of midnight, however, she'd forgotten all about her and Hannah's fight and had become insatiable for something she couldn't name. That is, until she wandered back up onto the deck and saw *him*. It was like an instant relief, seeing his crimson eyes and crooked smile. He'd beckoned her over, apologized for how everything had happened, and asked if she'd stay up and talk with him since he couldn't sleep either.

"Can I ask you something?" he murmured to her now as they gazed out at the dark blue horizon.

"Hmm?" She sighed dreamily, her head resting on his shoulder.

"Have you ever been in love?"

She lifted her head to look at him, that delicious warmth buzzing through her body once more as their eyes met.

"A very long time ago," she admitted.

"What's kept you from finding it again since?"

The answer sparked instantly in her mind, but for some reason when she went to say it aloud, it died on the tip of her tongue. Instead, she shrugged. "Haven't found the right person, I suppose."

He looked at her, thoughtful. "You know, my mother used to say a single kiss was all you needed to know whether or not you could fall in love with someone. She said there was some sort of magic in first kisses."

Delphine smirked. "Surely there's a less cliché way to ask me to kiss you?"

His gaze sparked with a wicked gleam. "Perhaps, but it's still going to work, isn't it?"

It was. She began to lean forward, dying to feel his lips against hers, that insatiable need roaring back to life in full force—

—Isaac was ripped away from her, an inhuman growl sounding from his throat as Gideon held him nearly a foot above the deck by the back of his collar. Delphine was on her feet in a second, fists balling at her sides as she got ready to lay into the prince, but before she could get a single word out of her mouth, she spotted the scene behind the two men.

Standing with their wrists bound by swirling ropes of wind were two of Isaac's guests from dinner—the one named Lachlan and the woman whose name Delphine couldn't remember—as well as an unfamiliar girl who was slumped, half conscious on the ground.

Gideon's fury was palpable as he brought Isaac over the side of the deck and dangled him above the black ocean.

"I'm not sure if you thought I was bluffing earlier," Gideon snarled, "but you're about to find yourself swimming at the bottom of the ocean if you don't explain what's going on here right now."

"How do you still have your magic?" Isaac choked, his expression a mixture of both shock and fury.

Delphine stepped up beside Gideon then, utterly confused. "What are you talking about?"

"The wine at dinner was supposed to seal away your magic for at least four days," Isaac revealed.

Delphine furrowed her brow as she strutted toward the side of the ship and leaned over the railing, reaching her hand out to try and coax a stream of water out of the choppy waves. But there was nothing. No response in the well of magic within her core. Not even a single drop from the sea responding to her call. She had no idea how she hadn't noticed before this moment.

Her shoulders began to heave with anger at the realization of the trap the pirate had so easily set, but when she swung her gaze back over to his face, every single bit of wrath she wanted to unleash on the man completely melted away.

What is wrong with me?

"What the Hells did I tell the two of you about getting this one perfect?" Isaac seethed over Gideon's shoulder.

Lachlan and the woman—Delphine really felt like a traitor to women everywhere that she couldn't remember this girl's name—immediately went on the defensive.

"We enchanted the wine exactly the way you taught us," Lachlan swore.

"Don't be too cross with them," Gideon told Isaac. "Enchanted wine only really works if one actually consumes it."

"But I saw you take several sips from your glass," the woman insisted.

Lachlan turned to her now. "Godsdammit, Lottie. You are a fucking amateur. You must check if the glass is actually *empty*."

Gideon ignored them both as he calmly explained to Isaac, "This is undoubtedly going to end with me snapping at least one person's neck, most likely yours, but before I do, why don't you go ahead and tell me what the fuck you were trying to take our magic for? To turn around and trade us to the Witch Queens, after all?"

Isaac opened his mouth to answer, but before he could, someone said, "What's going on?"

They all snapped their heads toward Hannah.

Hannah's depthless black eyes were sleepy as she came toward them, barefoot. She stopped about a foot away from the half-lucid girl still slumped on the ground, her mouth dropping into a surprised O shape.

"You're the girl I saw in the cargo hold . . ." Hannah whispered before flicking her eyes over to Gideon and Delphine in question.

Lachlan curled a lip at Hannah in disdain. "I knew you were down there, you fucking little spy."

Hannah shifted on her feet as she threw the man an indignant glare. "Maybe you shouldn't leave doors open when you're trying to hide something."

Isaac began to claw at Gideon's hold on his throat then, gasping for breath and thrashing his legs wildly. Gideon pulled the pirate back over the side of the boat and placed him onto his feet.

"I'll give you until the count of three to start fucking talking. One."

Isaac said nothing as he straightened himself out and swallowed a few gulps of air, his glare never leaving Gideon's face.

"Two."

Lottie shifted on her feet.

"All right." Gideon shrugged before spinning toward Lachlan and lunging forward, wrapping the man's windpipe in his grip and snapping his head to the side in a single blink. "Three."

Lottie and the other girl let out twin shrieks as Lachlan dropped to the ground with a heavy *thud*. It seemed to jerk the second girl enough out of her trance for her to crawl to Lachlan's side, hovering over him as her chest heaved with panic and tears streamed down her face.

"What have you *done*?" she sobbed. "I endured torture for him! *What have you done?*"

"Do you understand how long it takes for us to heal from such severe wounds?" Lottie hissed. "We aren't like you natural-born immortals!"

"Then I suppose someone should've answered me," Gideon snarled back, and Delphine could tell that his patience was wearing thinner and thinner the more confusing the details became. "So which one of you wants to be next?"

"Stop!" Lottie pleaded, stepping before Lachlan and the girl protectively. "We're—"

"Shut *up*," Isaac snapped. "Or I'll break your neck myself."

Gideon sighed and waved a hand in Isaac's direction, cutting off his oxygen supply. Isaac choked and gurgled as he clutched his neck, rage filling his eyes as he struggled to breathe.

"Continue speaking," Gideon barked at Lottie. "What do you mean you aren't natural-born immortals? What sort of immortals are you?"

Lottie gulped. "We're called albatrosses. We weren't born immortal—we were made."

Albatrosses. Delphine sucked in a breath as the word triggered a memory in her mind.

Hope that my payback for you will hurt far less than yours did for Ramor.

"You all are working for Jack," Delphine accused.

Gideon's brow furrowed as he glanced at Delphine.

"Let him talk," Delphine ordered Gideon.

Gideon obliged, and despite trying to catch his breath, Isaac grinned and rasped, "Jack says hello."

"What in the Hells is an albatross?" Hannah questioned.

"Abhorrent creatures that will trap you at sea for six years if they manage to steal a kiss from you," Delphine recited, though even as she spoke the truth aloud it didn't curb her appetite for wanting to let Isaac do just that. Her fists balled as she stepped toward him. "What have you done to me?"

Isaac gave her a lazy smile. "Part of the wine's effects. A little gift from Jack himself. Usually we would just find desperate humans who wished to be immortal and offer them a spot in our crew. One kiss and they're transformed into an immortal for at least six years—longer if they continued to renew their tenure. But Jack knew even if you all were desperate enough for an alternate escape route at the port, you'd need a little more . . . coercion to give any of us a kiss. And even as I'm telling you this, you can't help but want to give into that desire, right, lovely?"

Delphine swallowed. He was, in fact, correct. It was like she had been hypnotized, entirely aware of her surroundings yet compelled to give in to the ill-advised desire the moment she looked into his eyes. As if they were the magic word.

"We all had our assignments," Lottie explained. "Wesley with the Siphon, me with you, and Lachlan with her." She gestured at Hannah with her chin before looking back to Gideon. "But you wouldn't look away from the Siphon's face for a second, so even if you had drunk the wine, I would not have been able to properly entice you. Wesley only captured her attention because she's polite and made enough eye contact while they were talking." Lottie's eyes shifted to Hannah then. "Lachlan had the same problem as I did with you. You wouldn't look away from the siren. Jack didn't really warn us about how deeply involved your group dynamics would be."

"I knew there was more to this than faery wine." Gideon glowered. "Calliope nearly let that bastard kiss her. She never even lets strangers touch her—"

"Calla," Hannah suddenly choked out. "Where is Calla?"

Gideon's entire body went tense as he demanded, "What do you *mean* where is she? Did you not leave her in the room?"

Hannah shook her head voraciously. "It's why I came out here! I woke up and no one was there—"

Gideon took off before Hannah even finished speaking.

51

Of all the shocking things Amina had ever experienced, watching a Terra witch create a portal right in front of her had to be at the very top of the list. Dex and Thorne were acting as if it was the most normal occurrence in the world.

The two men stepped through first, heads bent together as they reminisced and caught up on the events of the past few decades. Meanwhile, Caspian looked at Amina with just as much wild disbelief as she was sure was on her own face.

"Guess we know how he got out the glass box," Amina finally said, though she made no moves to step through the floating window that seemingly opened right into a pass of the Miroir Mountains.

Caspian leaned forward to poke at the magical rift in the air, awe in his steely gaze. "How in the world do you think he . . . ?"

Amina shrugged. "If I had to venture a guess, it involves him being some sort of magical anomaly like Calla. The Fates had to choose witches for their Blood Warriors, but clearly they were going to make sure their choices were stacked with the rarest—and most powerful—beings possible."

Caspian glanced back at her, offering a hand. "Ready?"

Amina accepted it, a rare bit of nerves washing over her at the thought of going through the portal alone. Who knew what sort of magic they were about to walk through. If she somehow got flung to the other side of Aetherius, she'd rather not be stranded by herself.

Cass gave her a tight squeeze, as if he was thinking the same thing, and her stomach flipped a bit. A bright light erupted across her vision as they stepped through, but it wasn't enough to keep her from seeing the small smirk on his face.

She scowled.

When they stepped out of the rift, they found Thorne and Dex patiently waiting on the other side.

"Not so bad, hmm?" Dex hummed before waving them all to follow after him.

Amina was relieved to see that they were, in fact, back in the Miroir Mountains, though this pass wasn't familiar and the air was much crisper. She had a feeling they were somewhere much higher up than the cottage.

"Eurydice's lair isn't for the faint of heart," Dex warned the group. "Especially if you don't like small spaces."

He walked over to the mountain's reflective facade on their left, placing both of his palms against the side and making the crystal-like exterior crack open until it revealed a narrow passage. Amina was instantly ready to decline, but Caspian knocked his shoulder against hers in challenge.

"Scared, Valkyrie?" he taunted.

She glared at him, lifting her chin with indignation. "Not in the slightest, witch."

It was Caspian's challenge and that familiar spark of competition that spurred her on, despite the natural apprehension of traveling somewhere where she would not be able to use her wings. With a deep breath, she followed Dex and Thorne into the crevice, trying to ignore the feeling of the cool, sharp walls of the corridor brushing against the exposed skin of her arms and making it pebble. The passage was indeed tight, forcing them all to turn slightly sideways to maneuver through, careful to avoid the edges that jutted out from the jagged walls. She felt Cass following closely at her back, his presence a somewhat reassuring shadow behind her that she would not be left behind.

The path twisted down and down into the mountain, like a corkscrew. Each step forward, however, seemed to echo louder, like they were approaching something hollow in the distance. She glanced back at Cass.

"It sounds like we're almost there," he whispered.

Sure enough, a few moments later the passage widened, and Amina could see where the mouth opened up into a spacious cavern a few yards ahead.

Just before they could reach it, however, Dex called out, "Move to the walls!"

Amina barely had time to react before Caspian was yanking her to the right, his body pressing hers flush against the crystalline wall as they watched spikes suddenly spear down from the ceiling above them. The daggerlike points barely missed Caspian's back, but the ones that crashed down onto Thorne and Dex shattered into a million pieces and crumbled to the ground.

"What the Hells?" Amina hissed as she shoved Caspian away from her and stomped over to jab a finger in Dex's chest. "You couldn't have warned us there were death traps in here?"

"I told you it wasn't for the faint of heart," he said defensively. "I did forget about that one, to be fair, though."

"What else should we expect?" she gritted out.

Dex glanced over his shoulder to the vast chamber ahead of them. "Once we step onto that platform, it's going to begin to rise until we're—well, not me or Thorne, but *you*—are crushed against the ceiling above. Eurydice likes her theatrics, and she's made sure that if any of the queens ever found her location, they'd lose as many soldiers as possible trying to retrieve her."

"I'm leaving," she spat, spinning on her heels to head back down the corridor they entered through—only to find it entirely blocked by the spikes dripping down from the ceiling like stalactites.

Amina cursed.

I hate witches.

Cass had the distinct feeling that Amina was on the verge of slaughtering them all. Otherwise, he would have never risked what he was about to do.

He reached for her hand, yanking her attention back to him. He could see the slight bit of fear in her eyes she wasn't quick enough to mask, the way her breathing was being deliberately slowed, how her hands twitched as her claws itched to swipe out at them.

"I'll make sure you get home, Valkyrie," he vowed. Then, to the others he said, "Go ahead. We'll follow."

Thorne took the hint immediately, beckoning Dex forward without a backward glance.

Cass turned back to Amina and murmured, "You okay?"

She ripped her hand from his grasp as she snarled, "Of course I am. I'm not a fan of being ambushed or backed into a corner, though, and I swear to the Gods if—"

"Anyone ever told you that you're cute when you're pissed?" Caspian smirked.

She sputtered in shock for a second. Whether from being called cute—perhaps a first for someone so regal—or from his lack of reaction to her anger, he didn't know. But he couldn't help it; he laughed.

"I am the Valkyrie whisperer," he complimented himself as he pushed past her and headed off to find the others.

"You are a pain in the ass," she countered as she strode after him. "I swear, once this war is over, I'm going to make it a point to never have to see one of you witches again."

Cass rolled his eyes. "Sure, sure, Valkyrie. Whatever you need to tell yourself to sleep peacefully. But you want to know what I think?"

"Not even a little bit."

"I think," he continued as if she hadn't spoken, "you're secretly enjoying the chaos. I see it, you know? The excitement in your eyes whenever something new or dangerous happens. Like you forgot what being alive was like for a while and you're relieved to feel it again."

Amina stopped walking. He paused as well, angling his body back just enough to gauge her reaction. They stood there for a long moment, regarding each other warily in silence. When she finally opened her mouth to say something, Thorne shouted for them to hurry. Amina's mouth snapped closed once more, and she moved past him as fast as she could. He knew he'd read her correctly. And that she wasn't happy about it.

When they finally caught up to the others at the mouth of the corridor, they saw that the floor was, in fact, lifting, triggered by Thorne's and Dex's weight. Amina hopped up onto the platform easily, Caspian in tow.

"What's the plan now?" Cass asked as they walked toward the center to meet the others.

"There's going to be an opening on the right in just a minute," Dex called out over the loud noise of the platform scraping against the side walls of the cavern. "We won't have much time for all of us to get through, so you and the Valkyrie need to go first."

Caspian nodded and let Dex lead them to where the exit was supposed to appear. He braced himself to go ahead of Amina, shifting between the balls of his feet as he prepared to jump. When the opening began to appear, he didn't hesitate to wedge himself in the slowly growing gap, pushing himself through the narrow channel like a slide. As he inched himself down the tight space, he was suddenly very grateful he didn't mind enclosed spaces.

The farther down he slid, the more momentum he gained, and by the time he reached the exiting end of the tunnel, he was sliding much too fast to stop himself from shooting out like a loosed arrow. He hit the ground rolling with a heavy *thud* as he righted himself back up to his feet in a move that probably wasn't his most graceful. Amina, on the other hand, drifted down to the floor with poise, her wings appearing for the briefest moment to pillow her fall.

She gave him a haughty look.

Thorne and Dex dropped down next, respectively, and when they were all reunited, Caspian finally took in the space around them. The small empty chamber was little more than a mirrored box. The facets of the reflective walls around them warped their reflections.

"What's next?" Amina demanded.

Dex walked over to the far wall and placed his palm against it just as he had earlier, to open the entrance into the mountain. The room around them began to shake with the effort of Dex's magic, and Amina seemed to unwittingly shuffle closer to Caspian, much to his delight.

The wall slowly began to split apart, and Cass watched with intense anticipation as a vertical crystal crypt was revealed behind it. Cushioned inside was a sleeping woman. The deep brown locks of her hair were perfectly plaited, her warm brown skin shining with health. There was not a single wrinkle in her deep plum dress. Her arms were neatly crossed over her chest, and Cass could just make out the six numbers that made up her Rolls of Fate on her left forearm. All threes.

"How do you know so much about this place?" Amina suddenly wondered as they all took in the witch.

"I helped build it for her," Dex revealed.

Amina's brows shot up. "And you couldn't manage to remember the *spikes of death*?"

Dex shrugged. "It was a long time ago."

"How is she still asleep with all this ruckus is what I want to know," Thorne quipped.

"She's a Rouge witch," Dex explained. "She stopped her own heart to preserve herself in here until it was time."

"And how do we wake her up?" Amina demanded.

Dex stepped toward the woman and placed a careful hand on the bare skin of her shoulder as he said, "Eurydice."

For a moment, nothing happened. Dex didn't remove his hand from her skin, however, and Cass watched as warmth slowly came back to her cheeks and her eyes seemed to flutter beneath her eyelids.

And then they burst wide open.

Once she was completely thawed, it became very clear that Eurydice was not happy about being woken up. Her dull lavender eyes regarded Dex, in particular, with disappointment.

"You," she rasped at the Terra witch, her voice dry from the lack of use.

"Expecting someone else?" Dex crossed his arms over his broad chest.

"Hoping," she corrected as she slowly peeled herself from her crypt and stretched her limbs. "All right. Catch me up. How far into it are we? The Fates grace the earth with their presences yet?"

Dex shook his head. "War hasn't begun, but all the Blood Warriors have been chosen. Which means it's time to get into our places."

Eurydice sighed deeply. "And I was having such a peaceful nap."

52

Calla realized something was wrong the moment Wesley touched her skin. It was like being doused with cold water as he reached a hand up to cup her face. Her inner Siphon flared to life, but without its recent desire to latch on to the pirate's blood. In fact, it didn't seem her Siphon knew what it wanted to drain at all. It was the most unsettling feeling she'd ever felt. Almost as empty as the time she'd touched the Witch Eater.

"Wait," she whispered as Wesley tilted his face down at hers. "I don't feel right."

"You feel fine to me," Wesley murmured as he pressed his body more fully against hers.

Calla made a face at his forwardness. It wasn't the sort of thing she thought she was attracted to, yet for some reason she wasn't rushing to move from between him and the wall. "It's just . . . I feel like there's something missing," she insisted. "Like I'm forgetting about something . . ."

Or someone.

His smile went taut. "I don't know what that would be. Now, if you would only let me kiss you . . ." He dipped his head down again, but at the last moment she turned her cheek. He sighed in frustration. "What is it now?" he demanded, impatient.

"What time is it?" she wondered. "Why . . . why am I here? Shouldn't I be sleeping . . . ?"

"You came to me," he told her.

That was true. But she was sure there had been a reason. She racked her brain until she remembered the whispers that woke her.

"Because you called me." She remembered. "I came because I heard you whispering my name. You woke me up."

"I'm not sure I know what you mean," he huffed. "But what does it matter anyway? You're here now and you want to kiss me."

That was also very true. She nodded, inviting him to try once again. He seemed to sigh in relief and swooped in once more—

"*Calliope!*" A muffled shout rang out from the hallway, followed by a series of echoing bangs.

Her heart began to thud rapidly in her chest. She knew that voice.

In front of her, Wesley went rigid as he demanded, "Kiss me. *Now.*"

Her entire body screamed for her to listen to that demand, but something in the back of her mind begged her not to.

"I need some air," she told him as she fought against the war happening within her. "Let me just—"

"No," he snarled as he blocked her from stepping away. "*Kiss me.*"

And it was like the fury in his words, the disdain in his eyes, broke whatever spell she was under. She didn't hesitate as she brought her knee up to his groin before diving away as he grunted and hunched forward. She made to break for the door, but he recovered too quickly, snapping his hand out to grab her by the hair and making her cry out in pain.

"Sorry," Wesley told her, "but I've got quite the offer riding on this kiss. And I'm not going to let you and your pretentious fucking prince screw it—"

Crack.

Calla shoved the heel of her hand into his nose, sending a splatter of blood through the air as he screamed and clutched his face. She turned for the exit once more, and this time she didn't have to worry about being stopped, because a moment later there was Gideon, busting down the door.

Gideon's obsidian eyes roamed over Calla from head to toe, assessing her for any injuries, before shifting over to Wesley and taking in all the blood.

"He tried to force me to kiss him," Calla told Gideon as she glared back at Wesley.

"I know," Gideon stated, tone clipped with barely concealed fury as he stepped up next to her. "And that's why I'm about to fucking kill him."

Wesley's face paled with terror at Gideon's words. He rocked back a step as he began to stammer excuse after excuse, but nothing he said stopped Gideon's stride. And then the others showed up.

"Please tell me you didn't kiss him," Hannah huffed as she seemed to shepherd Delphine into the room.

"No, but what is going on?" Calla asked as they all turned to watch Gideon corner the pirate.

"We'll explain later," Delphine muttered.

"You don't understand," Wesley pleaded to Gideon now. "I didn't have a choice. I owed Jack a favor. He called it in—"

"I don't care if you owed the Godsdamned Fates themselves a favor," Gideon growled. "The moment you touched her without her permission is the moment you signed your own death warrant."

"She came here to *me*. Do you really think I'd ever touch a *Siphon*—"

It was the wrong thing to say for so many reasons.

Gideon's arm was so swift that Wesley didn't have time to blink before he found Gideon's hand wrapped around his throat. Wesley instantly began to choke out an old prayer to the Gods as Gideon squeezed his neck like a vise, but Calla didn't think anything short of a miracle would be able to save him now.

"*Stop*," someone thundered from the doorway, and everyone except Gideon turned their gazes to Isaac as he barreled into the room.

Calla was shocked to see how the pirate had seemed to transform since the last time she'd seen him. No longer a handsome, carefree pirate, he was now a wild crimson-eyed creature.

"If you kill him, I'll set this entire ship on fire and we can all go down with it," Isaac threatened. "You and the blond are the only ones who didn't drink my enchantment, and we have at least a couple more days left until we reach Noctum. You'll have to get tired sometime."

Gideon looked back at the girls. "How many people do you think it takes to navigate a ship?"

Calla shrugged. "I bet we can figure it out on our own. I support you throwing them all overboard."

"I'll help," Hannah agreed.

Isaac blanched a bit at that. "You clearly don't know nothin' about a boat. You need at least six people just to—"

"Perfect," Gideon interrupted. "Now that we have a number, why don't you tell us which five other crew members you'd like to keep, and I'll try and take it into consideration when I'm tossing everyone else over?"

Calla could see the panic begin to bleed into Isaac's eyes at Gideon's threat, and she could see now that he was just a pathetic, smarmy man with a nice face who was in terribly over his head. She didn't know exactly what was going on behind the scenes here, but her friends seemed to have figured out the weak spot in his game.

"Listen, I have to have a crew," he implored. "I have routes to keep up with, oceans to cross, and I can't do it alone. This is Jack's vendetta—not mine. We didn't mean any harm."

"You tried to drug us all so we'd kiss you and you trap us in the water for *years*, and you didn't mean any harm?" Delphine scoffed.

Calla startled. *What in the Hells?*

Isaac's tone turned a bit wild as he insisted, "Desperate times, desperate measures, right? You're all trying to start that war. Do you know what that's going to do to our trading systems? Jack is always one step ahead of everything. Hells, sometimes I think he might even be ahead of the Gods. There's a reason he called in this favor—"

"Oh, please," Delphine scoffed. "He called in this favor because I killed one of his companions. This was his attempt at a sick and twisted punishment and nothing else."

"And if you think we don't understand the gravity of this war, you're sorely mistaken," Calla inserted. "I've spent the entirety of my life thinking about how the outcome might affect our world. Which is precisely why we'll be taking up our own grievances with the Gods and the queens themselves no matter how many of you try to stop us. It is those with power who have the responsibility to wield it correctly. And it is everyone else's responsibility to hold them accountable for not doing so."

Isaac clenched his jaw, but he said nothing more. Whether it was the finality of Calla's words or the fact that he had no further argument, she didn't know, and it didn't really matter. A second later, Gideon spun and shoved a gasping and sputtering Wesley at Isaac's feet.

"You're going to get us to Noctum faster than any other ship you've ever run before," Gideon ordered. "The moment you step out of my carefully drawn lines, people start swimming. Do we understand each other?"

Isaac's fists balled at his side. "Understood."

53

After all the excitement on the *Sea Pearl*, finally arriving in Noctum was underwhelming, in Calla's opinion. Gideon had all but taken the ship hostage, and Calla and Hannah had been busy trying to break Delphine out of Isaac's hypnotic spell. Not to mention the fact that Calla had barely been able to sleep since losing her magic. She was sure her constant pacing had worn a path in the floorboards as she waited for the sparks of her power to return. The irony that she'd spent nineteen years wishing for such a thing to happen, only to become a restless monster when it finally did, was not lost on her. But after three grueling days of enduring the lifeless power in her core and babysitting Delphine while Gideon stayed up around the clock, Noctum finally appeared over the horizon.

The dawning sun was still hanging low when they approached the continent, casting long misty shadows over the choppy waters as Noctum's rocky landscape emerged behind the shroud of the haze. There were dark tempestuous clouds looming above the entire continent, a foreboding omen as the waves beneath the ship grew more and more rageful. A couple miles out, the waters had grown so rough the motion of the boat beneath Calla was making her sick.

That's when Isaac and his crew determined they'd have to drop their anchor and wait until the storm was over to dock.

Gideon wasn't having it. As the crew ran around at Isaac's barking orders, Calla and her girls were following Gideon's. They packed everything they could in their bags and made their way back up to the deck, where Gideon was already lowering the dinghy. He waved for them to load themselves on, and they threw their backpacks over the side before clambering in one after the other. Someone above yelled an expletive when they realized what the four of them were doing, but Gideon was already jumping down from the deck and cutting the ropes that attached the dinghy to the ship before anyone on board could do anything about it.

The tiny wooden boat dropped to the water, and all of them groaned as they shifted into one another with the rough descent. The moment they were in the water, waves folded inside the boat, and with Delphine's magic still inaccessible, there was nothing she could do about it.

Gideon, however, was unperturbed. He continued on as if the ocean wasn't threatening to capsize them at any moment and drag them to a watery grave. When the laughter from above began, Delphine sent up a couple crude gestures with her hands just before Gideon let out a blast of wind directly into the sea and propelled the boat forward.

"All right, I'm going to push this thing to shore, but you'll have to steer!" he yelled over the waves, pointing at the two oars stored on either side of the boat.

Calla and Delphine snapped into position, signaling to Gideon their readiness before he sent another round of wind into the sea, and they skipped forward once more. When they made it past the ship's nose and out into open water, Delphine and Calla placed the tips of their oars into the water and began to curve the dinghy to the left—toward the mainland. The ride was choppy, and Hannah found herself bending over the side to lose the contents of her stomach on more than one occasion, but eventually they made it.

By the time all four of them had climbed out of the little boat and onto the rocky shore, every single one of them agreed they'd rather go back to the Valkyrie Queen's castle before they got back on a ship again.

"That was awful," Hannah moaned as she heaved against the black sands of the beach around them.

Calla went to Gideon's side and lightly brushed the sea-soaked strands of his cobalt hair from his forehead. She gently cupped both of her hands against his face as he worked to catch his breath, and though her Rouge magic still felt cold and unreachable inside of her, she watched as her touch still managed to return the color in his cheeks. Their bond had started to come back to life slowly but surely over the last few days; whatever effects Jack's wine had was unable to grasp on as tightly to the fated magic between them. Which was more than fortunate considering being able to recharge each other was likely the only thing that got them through the past few days.

Watching Gideon have to manhandle an entire crew of reluctant pirates had been quite the show, but he'd done it with the same calm grace he did everything else, and if she hadn't been disgustingly in love with him before, she certainly was now. When she'd told him how impressed she was that he was managing a bunch of wicked imbeciles, he'd just shrugged and said something about having to direct his mother's recruitments in the Guild. But Calla had to silently give credit where credit was almost certainly due—Kestrel had trained him undeniably well to work under such pressure.

"All right," Delphine rallied. "We need to figure out where the Hells we are and what we do next. We're here to find one of the Fates' Dice, yes? None of us know this place or the terrain, and some of us still have no magic."

"Where the Hells do we start?" Calla whispered.

"First, give me the communication thing." Delphine stretched out a hand toward Calla. "I'll let Lyra know we made it here, at least."

Calla dug into her pocket and passed the little gold artifact to Delphine as they all got to their feet. As they took in their surroundings, Calla realized they had missed the loading docks by about three miles and were now standing on a desolate stretch of a gloomy black-sand beach. Nothing about the terrain around them was welcoming. Especially not the impossibly thick wall of gray fog up ahead, blocking anything aside from the shore from view. The jagged rocks that littered the ground at their feet grew thicker and thicker the farther they climbed up the beach until they became less rocklike and more boulderlike.

As they took in their surroundings, a low rumble reverberated through the ground beneath them. The sky darkened even further, and the clouds seemed to gather menacingly overhead. Suddenly, the air grew heavy with a palpable sense of dread. Calla's heart pounded in her chest as a chill ran down her spine. She glanced toward her friends, noticing the fear etched on their faces mirrored her own. But before anyone could speak, the strange gray mist began to move before them, writhing closer and closer until they were enveloped within completely.

Panicked, Calla stumbled backward, trying to disentangle herself from the eerie fog, but when she found herself back on the beach, utterly alone, somehow that was worse.

"Gideon?" she called.

He didn't answer. She tried to search for him through their bond, but she found she couldn't feel any life at the end of it. Her stomach plummeted with fear. So she dove back into the mist, headfirst.

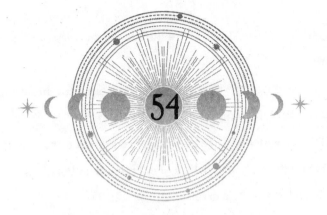

54

The ropes around Calla's wrists were bound so tight that every time she moved, pieces of her skin peeled away. Before her, Myrea was laughing as a fleet of Rouge guards finished building the pyre at Calla's feet.

"Perfect," the Rouge Queen purred as the guards stepped back so Her Majesty could admire their work. "If there's not enough kindling, she'll just have to burn slowly."

Calla swallowed as she glanced around the battlefield, seeing the fallen that had fought with her so fiercely being carried away in defeat. She had failed. The queens had won, and now the Fates were going to let her be punished.

"Before I strike the match, there's one more person I think should be here to see this," Myrea revealed with a vicious smile.

No, Calla thought before she even saw him.

But there he was, being dragged forward by ten of Myrea's guards, his veins bulging with strain as the Rouge witches flexed their hold on his blood.

"I'm so delighted we were able to sever your little bond after all," Myrea said. "It's much more satisfying this way."

Calla's eyes widened at that. She glanced down to her left forearm, and sure enough, the constellation of dots that denoted her Rolls of Fate were no longer the telltale crimson of the soul-bond.

"Now that we have our audience, the show can begin," the queen announced.

The hiss of a match striking ricocheted through the air around them, and Calla watched as the stick dropped to the ground, a wave of flames erupting beneath her. She tried to scream, but Myrea tightened her jaw shut, not even allowing her that one relief.

Myrea made sure that Gideon screamed, however. Made sure to let her guards give the Onyx Prince just enough slack that his rage could be heard across the entire world. He fought their hold on his blood as hard as he could, and Calla could only watch in silence as the fire licked its way up her body. Blisters welled on her skin, and pain unlike she'd ever felt before seared into her bones, but the agony on Gideon's face was worse. It was the sort of pain she knew he would never get over, never survive when she was gone.

As if Myrea heard her thoughts, the woman laughed. "I'll make sure he lives for as long as possible. Until the world around him becomes dust but his memories of this day remain."

Gideon kept fighting, and she couldn't take it anymore. She couldn't scar him so deeply like this all because he loved her. So she did the only thing she could think of. She gathered the very last kernel of power she had left in her core, and she reached out for him. The moment her magic touched him, she knew. It was the way his eyes flashed silver for a single second of relief. And then she burst every single blood vessel in his head and watched him slump to the ground, unconscious.

As Myrea screamed in fury, Calla smiled and continued to burn.

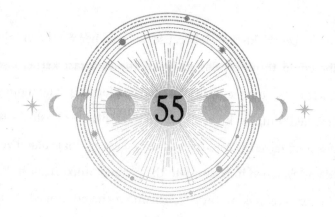

55

Calla was abruptly stumbling out of a cloud of thinning fog to find herself standing before a . . . small village?

There were buildings lining a sandy black cobblestone road as far as her eyes could see. People were bustling about with parasols stretched above them as a light drizzle sprinkled down. The clip-clop of horses pulling carriages echoed around her, and the strong smell of fish and salt wafted over her face, making her nose wrinkle in distaste. When she did a double take to her right, she saw a small crowd of people watching her curiously.

She was about to approach them for help, to see if they knew who she was and where she was, when a familiar voice rang out before her.

"*Calla!*"

With the sound of her name, everything came rushing back to her. The *Sea Pearl*. Crashing onto Noctum's shore. Walking into the mist.

Delphine was suddenly there, wrapping her in a tight hug.

"Oh, finally!" Delphine exclaimed. "We were about to send a search crew in there for you."

"What happened?" Calla gasped as she rocked back on her heels. "What *was* that?"

"That was Noctum's first line of defense," Delphine explained as she wove her fingers through Calla's and pulled her down the road, past the curious crowd. "Apparently, the continent is surrounded by it. A mist that drops you into the middle of your worst nightmare. You have to defeat it in order to leave. You've been in there for *hours*. We had to threaten to sedate Gideon just to get him to the inn to get some rest. I took up his post waiting for you."

A shiver ran over Calla's spine as the slightest impression of the memory of what it felt like to burn echoed through her body. A place of nightmares was right.

Delphine stopped before a quaint redbrick building and pushed open the door, yanking Calla inside after her. Calla quickly recognized the setup as a lobby for an inn—once you've seen one inn, you've seen them all. A giant desk sat to their right with a wall of cubbies built into the wall behind it, each with a number carved below. A girl with long, glossy raven hair and a ghostly complexion stood behind the desk, doodling in the margins of a notebook. When she looked up, Calla stopped cold in utter shock at the sight of her eyes. The left one was a deep midnight blue. The right a shade of amber Calla knew very well.

Siphon.

Delphine grinned as she waved a hand toward the girl and introduced, "Calla, this is Tempest. She's a *Shadow Siphon*."

Tempest gave Calla a bright smile. "I'd shake your hand, but touching others with the Siphon curse is, uh, *complicated*, to say the least."

Calla wouldn't know. It didn't matter anyway, she was too speechless to move as she continued to stare at the girl in awe.

Tempest didn't miss a beat. "Delphine told me you hadn't ever met another Siphon, so I'm sure this is disorienting. Especially after you just left the mist. Are you all right, by the way? Your partner was in quite the state when your friends dragged him in here."

Her words were a bit too fast for Calla at the moment, but one thing she did latch on to was the mention of Gideon being in *quite the state*.

"Where is he?" Calla asked, alarmed now. "Why is it that everyone got out of that damn fog so much quicker than me?"

"Gideon's getting some very much needed sleep upstairs," Delphine informed her. "He looked like he was going to faint by the time he made it out of the mist. He wouldn't tell us what he saw, though." Then she tilted her head and asked, "What did *you* see?"

"Nothing I want to recall right now," Calla mumbled. "Let's just say it involved Myrea and a pyre."

Delphine's mouth formed an O shape at Calla's revelation.

"I want to see him," Calla whispered.

Delphine nodded. "Of course. You both need to rest before our meeting tonight anyway."

"Meeting?" Calla questioned.

"There's a man staying here," Tempest chimed. "He's called the Wayfarer. He's probably the most well-traveled man on this earth, and if there's anything you need to find, he's the one to talk to. You don't even know how serendipitous the timing is that you've come at the same time he's around. He's not an easy one to catch."

Calla's brows lifted with curiosity.

Tempest leaned forward conspiratorially. "He's cursed. They call it the Midnight curse. He can never visit the same place twice—everywhere he goes, the curse's magic gives him a perimeter that he's unable to leave, and after a certain period of time, it transports him to somewhere new."

"But if he can never visit anywhere twice . . ." Calla trailed off as she realized the implications.

Tempest nodded. "He'll travel until there's nowhere left—and then it'll kill him."

"And why is he our key to success?" Calla asked.

"Like I said, if there's anything you need to find, that's something he's apparently very good at. According to my boss anyway. She's the one you should thank for the recommendation—and the meeting." Tempest shrugged. "I've only met him once, when I was checking him in, and he was not in a pleasant mood."

"Then *I* asked Lyra if they'd ever heard of him," Delphine inserted, "and they confirmed the rumors and said he was someone we could trust. They also told me to mention their name when we speak to him, so I guess we'll find out what that's all about soon."

Calla sighed as she rubbed her temples. "All right. I need a nap. Where's our room?"

"Your and Gideon's room, you mean," Delphine said in a singsong voice as she guided Calla toward a wooden staircase across the lobby.

Tempest smiled and waved as they went, and Calla dipped her chin at the girl in acknowledgment. The Shadow Siphon. She'd have to come back to that later.

As they walked up the stairs, Calla flicked her gaze over to Delphine. "What did you and Hannah see in the mist?"

"Well, I've already lived through my worst nightmare," Delphine huffed. "I was back in Reniel's bed . . . with my Siren's oath. At first, I thought I had dreamed my escape and finding you all again. It was such an exhausting idea that I didn't even waste time ripping his throat out, and the moment I did—the illusion disappeared. And I was here."

Calla swallowed. "And Hannah?"

Delphine winced before whispering, "I think she recently lived her own worst nightmare, too. She wouldn't talk to me about it any more than Gideon would his. But I'm sure *you* could ask her."

Calla reached down and squeezed Delphine's hand in comfort, but neither of them said another word the rest of the flight up.

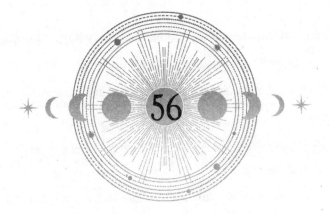

56

Calla slipped into the bedroom, not bothering to knock. The room was pitch-black, the curtains on the windows drawn tightly together. It looked like every other inn they had stayed in together, a huge upgrade from the dreadful bunks of the *Sea Pearl*, but not nearly as cozy as the Valkyries' house in the Miroir Mountains. Still, it was warm and clean, with a bed that looked incredibly inviting sitting in the center. A bed currently being occupied by a very exhausted prince.

Calla crept across the floor to the right side of the bed, wondering if she should wake him or let him keep sleeping. He clearly needed the rest. But the moment she came within a foot of him, he shot up in the bed.

"Hey," she whispered as his eyes sought hers in the dark, the usual silver in them nowhere to be found. "It's me."

He was off the bed in seconds, wrapping his arms around her so tightly that she could barely inhale. She didn't care.

"I'm sorry if I made you worry," she said as he buried his face in the crook of her neck. "I'm sorry I was gone so long."

"Gods, I thought I was going to lose my mind," he finally spoke, his voice gruff.

She pulled back slightly so she could see his face when she asked, "What did it show you?"

"The queens, severing our bond before locking me behind a glass wall and torturing you." His voice was thick with sadness, and it made her chest tighten. "What did it show you?"

"Something very similar," Calla whispered. "Your nightmare is watching me get tortured, and my nightmare is watching you have to see that happen to me."

As his arms tightened around her, Calla fought the desperate need to admit her feelings for him. The mist had made their nightmares feel too real. If those things had actually happened, she'd never have the chance to tell him. How many times would she let such an opportunity pass by before it ended up being her *last* opportunity? Perhaps it was a selfish thing to be thinking at such a time. After he'd just spent days protecting her and their friends from insidious pirates, but—

"I love you, Calliope."

Calla went rigid in his arms. Gideon must have thought she was upset, because he took a step back so he could search her face.

"I'm sorry if it's terribly unromantic timing," he whispered. "But I've been dying to tell you how I've felt about you since the moment we met. When I was in the mist, watching you get tortured behind that glass wall, all I could think about was how I hadn't gotten my chance and how it would haunt me as long as the sight of your pain would."

He held his breath, watching her carefully as he waited for her reaction, and she almost laughed because a few days ago, on their way through the Miroir Mountains, he had been the one to tell her she was overthinking things.

"Gods, Gideon, you have no idea how much I love you," she told him, her mouth curling up at the corners when he let out a breath of relief. "I wanted to tell you when we were driving the carriage to the port, but you had just had that conversation with Ezra about your fathers. And when I tried, you told me not to and assumed that maybe it was because you didn't . . ."

His brows lifted in shock. "I didn't realize *that's* what you had been wanting to tell me. I was worried you were about to offer me pity, and that's one thing I couldn't take. I'll take your apathy, your anger, and your concern, but never your pity."

Calla understood what he meant. There was something about pity that cut deeper than hatred. Luckily, neither one of those things was something she felt for him.

"But Gods, your *love*?" he continued, his words turning reverent. "I won't just take that, I'll earn it. I'll worship it. I will go to the ends of this Godsdamned earth and back to keep it. And though I'm reluctant to thank the Gods for anything, I'll thank them every fucking day I wake up next to you for the rest of my eternity if I must."

Her heart began to thunder in her chest at his words. He stepped closer once more, pressing his forehead down to hers in contentment.

"I'm sorry if I made you feel as if you needed to wait to tell me about your own feelings, though." A slow smirk began to curl up at the corners of his mouth. "I think it's only fair I got to tell you first, considering I loved you first."

Calla scoffed. "That is *not* how it works—"

But before she could finish her sentence, he was tilting her face up into a kiss. One so consuming that she knew, without a doubt, that whatever they had, whatever this was between them, it would not be able to be taken from them. The Fates could try with all their might, could rip out both of their hearts, but it would not matter. They would always find a way to come back together.

When he finally broke their kiss, she let out an embarrassing whimper of protest and felt his chest shake with silent laughter.

"As much as I hate to be the one to interrupt us this time, I would like to shower before our meeting tonight," he murmured, tone regretful.

She sighed. "That's just as well. I need a nap anyway. This meeting, though, what do you think we should expect?"

Gideon stepped past her to dig through his backpack as he answered. "No idea. We don't have any other leads, though, so I suppose we have to hope this one gives us *something*."

Calla nodded in agreement before sitting on the edge of the bed to unlace and kick off her boots. As she tucked herself in for her nap, Gideon promised he wouldn't be long and then quietly shut the door behind him.

A few hours later, Calla and the others were waiting down in the lobby for the mysterious stranger. Tempest was chatting with Delphine animatedly from behind her desk while Hannah solemnly watched from afar. Calla wasn't exactly sure what had happened on the *Sea Pearl* between her two friends, but the moment Gideon revealed the two of them weren't sharing a room here, she knew *something* had occurred there.

"Jack's wine really did a number on everyone," Gideon said to her in a voice too low for the others to hear. "Not everyone handles jealousy well."

"That reminds me"—she narrowed her eyes at him in mock outrage—"you didn't seem upset enough with me for everything that happened with Wesley."

Gideon lifted his pierced brow. "Did you want me to be upset with you?"

"No, but I can think of a relatively similar scenario that happened with us and . . ."

She didn't need to say his name. They both knew she meant the incident with the nymphs making her and Gideon kiss in front of Ezra.

"In the spirit of not giving my brother too hard of a time or making this conversation too sticky," Gideon said wryly, "I'll just say that jealousy only exists where insecurity does. Not to mention, you were under the influence of an enchantment, Calliope. I know, without a doubt, you weren't feeling anything for that ridiculous pirate that wasn't completely fabricated."

Something about being with someone so secure was incredibly attractive to her, and by the way his gaze heated, she knew the bond was letting him know that, too. When the buzz of Delphine and Tempest's conversation suddenly hushed around them, Calla looked up from Gideon to see the cause.

Their guest of honor had finally arrived. A man as tall as Gideon, with black hair that faded to silver at the ends. His eyes were impossibly blue as they flickered over the group, and Calla noticed the way they seemed to linger on Tempest a little longer than the others. The most interesting thing about his appearance, however, was the moving maps inked across every inch of visible skin below his neck.

Calla thought he might be one of the prettiest beings she'd ever laid her eyes on.

"All right, maybe I'll have to rethink the jealousy thing," Gideon teased Calla as she worked to peel her gaze away from the stranger.

"Hello," he greeted, his voice a lot softer than Calla expected. "I'm the Wayfarer."

"Well, that's a mouthful," Delphine commented.

The Wayfarer pretended she hadn't spoken, saying, "I was told you were all looking for something."

"Something was taken from us that we need back," Gideon confirmed. "I have an enchanted compass that led us here."

The Wayfarer looked bored as his eyes slid over to Gideon. "What was taken?"

"Fates' Dice," Gideon revealed. "Two to be exact. The Witch Queens said they were going to hide them from us, and we were hoping the compass might be leading us to Noctum because they hid one of them here."

Intrigue sparked in the Wayfarer's eyes at this revelation. "Well, I have bad news."

Everyone straightened up a bit as Calla said, "Fantastic. What's the bad news?"

The Wayfarer's gaze locked with hers. "You're not going to like where it is."

Delphine narrowed her eyes. "Does that mean—"

"If the queens risked sending something valuable to Noctum, there's only one place I can think of where your sadistic rulers would've hidden it."

"The Trench of Lost Things," Tempest whispered in realization.

The Wayfarer nodded in confirmation, and Calla did not like where this was going.

He shrugged. "If it's not there, I'm afraid I wouldn't have much more insight."

"Can you show us where this place is?" Gideon requested.

"Unfortunately, it's out of my travel perimeters," the Wayfarer told them.

"How far is it, then?" Gideon questioned.

"A four days' trip," Tempest chimed.

They all groaned.

"Well, now that my work here is done..." the Wayfarer stated as he tried to extract himself from the conversation.

Delphine made a tsking noise of disappointment at him. "And Lyra said you'd be helpful," she said flippantly.

The Wayfarer froze. "Lyra?"

Delphine nodded as she lied. "Lyra is a good friend of ours. They're the one who told us to find you."

When the Wayfarer scowled, Calla knew Delphine had said the right thing.

"This is what I get for accepting a favor from Valkyries," he muttered before sighing and reluctantly continuing. "Fine. I have something that can help you all get to the Trench, but in order for me to give it to you, I need some sort of blood-binding guarantee that it will be returned to me by midnight tonight."

They looked around at one another. An oath. He wanted one of them to make a blood oath with him. To Calla's absolute disbelief, Delphine was the one who stepped forward to volunteer.

"Let's get this over with," she said.

"Delphine, you don't have to do this," Calla insisted. "We would never ask you to make another Siren's oath."

Delphine waved off Calla's concern. "Don't worry—things are much different this time."

Calla didn't know what that was supposed to mean but didn't offer any more protest as Delphine swore her oath to the Wayfarer, and they all watched as a brand-new mark appeared on the back of her neck. Delphine reached up to brush her fingertips over the silver ink but didn't seem too disturbed. Perhaps because this oath had a very clear expiration date.

As soon as the oath was locked in place, the Wayfarer disappeared back up the stairs and returned a minute later with a palm-sized talisman.

"A Transvectio Talisman," he told them. "In the blink of an eye, it will take you anywhere you can name, provided the place is within the same continent. Lyra is the one who gave it to me—which is the only reason I'm doing you this favor."

Calla could not even conceive the value of such an item as the Wayfarer gently handed it over to Delphine's waiting palm.

"Thank you," Gideon told him sincerely. Then he turned to the girls and said, "Ready?"

They all huddled around Delphine, each reaching out to place a fingertip on the talisman. Tempest gave them a nod of encouragement as the Wayfarer watched stoically from where he stood.

Delphine took a deep breath and then declared, "The Trench of Lost Things."

A beat. Then the darkness swept in. A billion little black spots crept over Calla's vision as a weightless feeling of floating came over her body. Before she could get used to the feeling, however, the world snapped back into place around her. It took a second for all of them to reorient themselves, but when they did, their jaws dropped.

☽·☽·☽·●·☾·☾·☾

The Trench of Lost Things was the only name that Calla could fathom for the place before her.

The four of them stood, shoulder to shoulder, at the mouth of the trench before them. Anything and everything you could possibly imagine that anyone had ever lost was sitting in a landfill of memories that stretched for miles and miles without end. The one solace was that there was an artificial footpath cutting right down the middle. As the four of them strode forward, eyes darting over the clutter, hopelessness filled Calla.

"No offense, Gideon," Delphine muttered as they all realized the impossibility of this task, "but I fucking hate your mother."

"Join the club," he shot back.

Tears suddenly pricked the corners of Calla's eyes, and Gideon instantly pivoted toward her when he felt the sensation himself.

"We're going to figure it out," he told her.

"How?" A bitter laugh. "They were right, Gideon—they're always going to be a thousand steps ahead of us. *Look* at this place!" Calla waved her hand in the air. "Not even knowing how to scry would help us here! Short of having something that could take us directly to it—"

Calla stopped her sentence short.

"Cal?" Hannah prompted.

"I've got it," Calla said, a wild giggle escaping her lips at the sudden idea that just popped into her head. "I've *got* it."

"Calla, love, you're scaring us," Delphine commented.

She looked at Gideon. "I need you to go back to the inn and get Heart Reaver."

Gideon's brows furrowed for a moment in confusion as he registered her request before his expression turned into one of absolute awe. "You are brilliant."

He took the talisman from Delphine and disappeared.

"Are you going to tell us what you're planning?" Hannah wondered.

There was no time to explain, however, when Gideon returned a moment later, Heart Reaver in hand. Calla took it from him, the feeling of its hilt heavy in her palm, its hilt warming at her touch.

"Please work," she muttered before taking a deep breath. Picturing in her mind the target she needed the dagger to hit true, she reared her arm back as far as she could before snapping it forward and sending the dagger through the air.

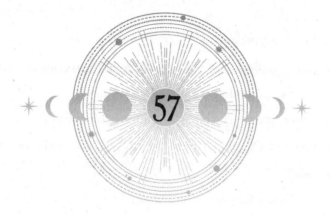

57

Ezra's sole bit of peace in the chaos that had quickly flooded the cottage was that he got to keep a bedroom instead of having to squeeze onto the floor with the new Valkyrie recruits downstairs. Even better was the fact that he was sharing said bedroom with Sabine. Considering she'd all but threatened to gut him if he didn't make space for her after Lyra began dealing out the other rooms to "actual couples." And despite being rather adamant about keeping a barrier of pillows between them every night—because, in her words, they weren't an "actual couple"—she still somehow managed to weasel herself to his side of the bed during the night until he was nearly falling off the edge.

He didn't care what she labeled them, though. Not as long as she let him kiss her until they both couldn't breathe every night and it was time to wedge the pillows between their bodies.

Their routine had become comforting. Wake up, make breakfast for everyone, work on his flying until it was dinnertime, shower, sleep. He'd gotten so used to it that when Caspian, Amina, and Thorne returned with two other Blood Warriors in tow, he was perturbed it would cut into his and Sabine's sparring time.

Caspian let out a low whistle when he saw the current state of the cottage's living room.

"I guess we ought to be thankful so many of them are showing up," he commented to Ezra and Thorne as the three of them left the others to speak to Lyra about logistics.

"Lyra said the same thing," Ezra grunted as he toed a pile of dirty laundry. Then, "What's the update on the Blood Warriors? How many have you found?"

"Two," Thorne stated. "Still missing Piper—the second—as well as the fourth. No one seems to know who the latter might be, though."

"What happens if the war starts before we find them?" Ezra asked.

Thorne shrugged. "I imagine the Fates have something up their sleeves for that. All I know is they originally planned for six of us to lead everyone into this battle, and we have at least five before it's even begun. Not bad if you ask me."

"And they're ready to fight?" Ezra pressed on.

"Dex definitely is," Caspian chimed. "I think if we'd told him it was time to march into battle the second we found him, he'd have been ready."

Thorne nodded. "Spite is a great motivator for anything."

The rest of the afternoon involved Ezra showing the two of them the ropes. Filling them in on the latest news from Sydni and Baden, who had a whisper trail all the way back to Valor so they could try and get ahead of whatever the Valkyrie Queen was planning. Lark, Lyra's twin, had shown back up a few days ago after taking care of things with Meli to give them intel on how some of the other Reapers were going to try and infiltrate those joining Ignia's ranks against the witches.

By the time Caspian and Thorne had finished carving out a place to sleep on the floor of Ezra's bedroom—an inevitable turn of events with the space inside the house growing more and more scarce—a rowdy game of cards had broken out downstairs, and Cass and Thorne didn't hesitate to bound off and jump in. Ezra, however, stayed upstairs, lying back on the bed as he listened to the hum of voices muffled through the walls, feeling suddenly adrift.

"You're missing the party."

He turned his head to see her leaning in the doorway, arms crossed as Sabine watched him. Her golden hair was neatly plaited into two braids that framed her face. The style made her look so innocent despite the fact that he knew better.

"I like your hair," he said.

Sabine smiled as she padded over to him. "Amina helped. I'm still getting the hang of how to deal with it being so long."

Ezra sat up as she approached, letting her wedge herself forward between his knees and drape her arms over his shoulders. He wrapped his own arms around her waist and pulled her in closer.

"What's wrong?" she murmured.

"I'm not sure," he admitted.

Except, he *was* sure. Ezra was sure that what was wrong was exactly this. How much he enjoyed being near her. Their time together. How much he hated that Cass and Thorne would be crashing the nightly routine he'd grown so fond of.

Most of all he was sure that just weeks ago he had felt so at peace with the fact that he might die again soon. That he'd done it once and he had no qualms about sacrificing himself again for the cause. And now the idea of leaving *her* filled him with dread. Especially after what she'd sacrificed to bring him back.

"I don't believe you," Sabine told him, cutting through his thoughts.

Instead of answering, he only pulled her in closer, until he could press a lingering kiss against her lips. Mourning everything he was about to lose that he never thought he'd have again.

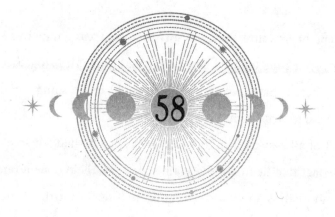

58

Heart Reaver soared through the air with purpose.

Calla and the others took off after the dagger as if their heels were on fire, tearing through the middle of the trench as they kept their eyes trained above them. Gideon and Delphine had the longest strides by far, and they pulled ahead as they tried to keep up with the enchanted blade lest they lose it in this mess as well.

When Calla's lungs began to burn—she was *not* built for running—and Heart Reaver began to leave even Gideon and Delphine behind, Calla started to worry this was the end of the road. That the Fates did not want their war to begin after all. That Calla's hold on her own destiny was just as out of reach as it had ever been.

And then Heart Reaver began to drift down in a perfect arc to the left.

Gideon's pace picked up and Calla's entire body buzzed with anticipation as he, and the dagger, finally came to a sudden halt. A minute later, the rest of them caught up, Delphine and Hannah making room for Calla to break through the piles of clutter around them to meet Gideon. Calla's chest heaved with effort as she tried to recover from her sprint, searching Gideon's face for any sort of confirmation that it had worked. That Heart Reaver found the Fates' Die.

He gave her a beaming smile as he unfurled his hand to reveal the black-and-red cube sitting in the middle of his left palm, Heart Reaver clutched in his right. "You did it."

Calla wanted to weep as she launched herself into his arms. He caught her easily, spinning her around in triumph as a shot of pride speared through her from his side of the bond.

Once he set her back down on her feet, she said, "We should roll it now. Before it can get away from us again."

Gideon nodded in agreement, holding it out between them in his flattened palm. "You do the honors."

Calla plucked the die from his hand and clenched her fist around it. As she shook it in her hand, its strange pulsing magic grew heavier. She glanced back to where Hannah and Delphine were watching in anticipation, the memory of the last time she'd rolled a die slamming back into her. That night had been the start to all of this.

Calla looked back to Gideon. "Together?"

"Together," he vowed.

She released the die.

It bounced along the ground between the piles of books, and jewels, and forgotten heirlooms. Bouncing next to stray spoons, and shoes, and handwritten letters. And when it landed, a beacon of gold-and-crimson light shooting into the sky, toward the Gods, Calla didn't need to be able to see it to know what number it had landed on.

Six.

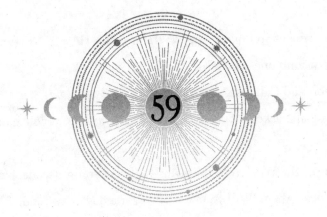

59

When they all returned to the inn, Tempest was gone for the night, a sign that said CLOSED UNTIL MORNING sitting atop the front desk. Hannah left to get some sleep while Calla and Gideon waited downstairs with Delphine to return the talisman to the Wayfarer. It was midnight on the dot when the man finally appeared.

"Thank you," Calla told him sincerely. "Truly, if there's any way we could repay you—"

"Unless you know how to break a curse," the Wayfarer muttered, "it's unnecessary. Besides, I'm not very fond of your queens anyway. They always made things difficult for me when I ended up in their Realms."

"Shocking," Gideon commented, tone dripping in sarcasm.

The Wayfarer smirked. "Must be Hells to be one of their sons *and* a Blood Warrior."

"An understatement," Gideon said dryly.

"I met one of you once," the Wayfarer said. "Here in Noctum actually. The second one, I believe."

Gideon and Calla exchanged a look.

Then Calla asked, "You wouldn't happen to know their name? Or where they are?"

"Hmm," the Wayfarer hummed. "It's been over a decade, but I can try and locate them. Will you be around for a day or two more?"

"If there's a Blood Warrior here, we'll be staying," Gideon confirmed.

"All right." The Wayfarer sighed. "I'll let you know what I find by tomorrow evening."

With that, the Wayfarer left. Calla and Gideon bid Delphine good night before they all returned to their own rooms as well. Once Gideon shut the door behind them, Calla felt a sudden overwhelming wave of nervousness hit her. She decided to make a quick excuse to wash up for the night, grabbing her toothbrush and dashing to their attached bathroom. When she looked at herself in the mirror, she saw how flushed her cheeks were, and she tried to keep her emotions in check so Gideon would not sense them.

As she brushed her teeth and her hair, she glanced down at the newest addition to her Rolls of Fate. Only one more roll to go.

But that's not what she wanted to think about right now. Right now all she wanted to think about was how she and Gideon were sharing a room, alone, for the first time since they had admitted they were in love with each other. And the fact that, for the first time, there was not any immediate danger or an ounce of tiredness in her body. Not even from the sprint through the trench. No, Calla was suddenly very, very awake.

When she walked back into the bedroom, nerves going haywire, her heart almost stopped as she spotted Gideon taking a drink of water, shirtless. Her eyes traced down his body, from his face to the harpy eagle tattooed across his chest to his rippling abs, as he swallowed another gulp of water. Gods, he was beautiful. In a way that ought to have been a sin.

Once again, the knowledge of her lack of experience compared to his hit her like a ton of bricks. And when he screwed the lid back on to the canteen and set it aside, his eyes flashing pure silver as he did his own scan over her figure, Calla desperately wished she could freeze time and run to Delphine for advice.

"Hey," he said as he stepped closer, tilting her chin up with the knuckle of his index finger until she was looking right into his eyes. "It's only you and me. Whatever worries are going on in your head—let them go. Nothing has to happen tonight, or any other night, if you aren't ready."

It was just like him to know exactly what to say to give her every ounce of reassurance she needed. Because he was right. It was only them. Whoever else he'd ever had in his bed before her did not matter. What mattered was that she was here now, and she trusted him implicitly. And that she *was* ready. More than that. She was eager.

As if he saw every one of her thoughts written on her face, he whispered, "Are you sure?"

She nodded. "Are *you*—"

"You have no idea," he interrupted, "how sure I am. I've never wanted anything as badly as I've wanted you."

"I don't know what I'm doing," she admitted, letting out a shaky breath. "The only experience I have is through Delphine's stories, and I'm not sure they're the most realistic examples to follow."

Gideon huffed a laugh.

"You'll have to show me . . ." Calla trailed off.

His answering smirk made her stomach clench in pure anticipation. Gideon brought her lips to his then, his hands running down the sides of her arms, down to her wrists, before she pressed her own hands to the planes of his stomach. He deepened the kiss as she lightly trailed her fingers over his abdomen, and he made a sound of encouragement in the back of his throat as she continued to explore. He was showing her, just as she'd asked.

Gideon slowly walked her toward the bed, stopping when they reached the edge and breaking their kiss. She took in a shaky breath as he reached between them and slowly lifted the hem of her shirt.

"Any time you need me to stop," he told her, tone deadly serious, "you tell me to stop. Okay?"

Calla nodded, whispering, "Same for you."

He pressed a light kiss beneath her jaw before tugging her shirt off the rest of the way. Next, he unbuttoned her pants and then his own, kicking the clothing away until they were both standing in only their undergarments. As he captured her mouth with his own once more, he bent down to pick her up, lifting her by the underside of her thighs and letting her wrap her legs securely around his waist before gently climbing atop the bed and laying her all the way back.

Her heartbeat was thrumming erratically—or maybe that was his. It was hard to tell in a moment where they were so consumed by each other and the soul-bond made them feel like they were one and the same, inextricably melded together. She let her hands twist into his hair as he kissed her until she became dizzy from need. When he pulled away to begin kissing other parts of her—her neck, her clavicles, her navel—a small whimper of want fell from her mouth before she could stop it. She felt him smile against her feverish skin at the sound, and before she could even be embarrassed about it, he was kissing places that made all thoughts in her head empty.

"I love your curves," he murmured as he left a trail of kisses over the soft, plump part of her belly.

"I can tell." She giggled softly, his kisses tickling her skin as they continued up and up, dusting over her sternum and stopping at the pulse of her throat.

"Mmm," he hummed against her lips, his left hand sliding down to the dip in her waist.

Soon enough every scrap of clothing between them was ripped away, and her frantic hands were exploring him with equal fervor, trying to memorize the lines of his body, the way he moved against her. She always thought she'd be shy, being so bare in front of someone else like this, but there was nothing to be shy about with Gideon. He knew her soul already, and her body felt inconsequential in comparison.

"This might be uncomfortable at first," he told her quietly, lifting his head to look her in the eyes. "Tell me if it's too much and I can stop."

"Please never stop," she whispered back.

He rested his forehead down on hers, his eyes flooding silver with affection as he lined their bodies up.

"Take a deep breath," he told her.

There was a quick, sharp pain, but he made sure to overcompensate for it with a world-tilting kiss, and a moment later she felt nothing but pure bliss. It was more intense than she could have ever imagined, emphasized by their soul-bond and the way it amplified each other's ecstasy.

"*Calla,*" he whispered over and over and over again. Too gone to say her full name.

She held on to him tighter, burying her face into the crook of his neck so she could feel the vibrations of her name from his throat against her lips as he spoke.

"No curse will ever be able to take my heart," he vowed. "Because you took it a very long time ago and I have no desire for you to return it. You will have me until they take my soul—and even then, wherever souls go, ours will go there together."

They moved together in perfect sync, over and over again, until a bright crimson light erupted around them. Their Rolls of Fate glowed as Calla and Gideon swelled well over the threshold of pleasure Calla thought she was capable of, and the light remained until their heartbeats slowed and they crashed back down to earth. Together.

S taying in her own room was torture, Delphine decided. If it had been up to her when they arrived at the inn, she'd have absolutely made Hannah share a room with her and forced them to speak to each other. But Hannah had beat her to the punch, requesting a room alone, and now here they were—*not* speaking. Though Hannah's words echoed plenty in her mind.

I'm in love with you, Delphine. . . . Why do you always go for people who only like you for what's on the surface?

And then Delphine proved her point tenfold when she'd fallen under Isaac's spell.

Calla had seemed to snap out of her trance on her own just fine, but Delphine had taken days for the damn enchantment to wear off. No matter that her mind had logically known she was supposed to hate that damned pirate, her body had been unwilling to accept the reality of the fabrication, and she could tell that it'd been a ruthless act for Hannah to watch.

Which was precisely how she knew she hadn't lied when she said it was safer for them to never cross the line between friendship and something more. She'd fallen in love with Celeste, and that had ended in utter disaster. Such disaster that she knew, without a doubt, she'd never see Celeste again. A price Delphine could more than bear. But *Hannah*? She would rather go back to the Siren's Sea for the rest of eternity than lose Hannah.

Hannah, who risked unleashing the darkness of her magic trying to save Delphine from being dragged back to the Siren's Sea. Whose gentle voice was the only thing that made Delphine keep her sanity under Reniel's hold. Whose face Delphine knew better than her own.

Hannah, whom Delphine had thought about every waking moment during Reniel's torture to remind herself of what she needed to fight for—to go home to. Because Hannah was the only version of home that had ever stayed consistent when that concept had been taken from her time and time again.

"Oh my Gods . . ." she whispered aloud as she sat straight up in bed.

I'm in love with Hannah.

She felt something slide down her cheek. Of course she was in love with Hannah. Hannah, whom she'd burn the world down for. Who vowed to tear the world apart for Delphine if that's what it took for them to be reunited.

What had she done? What had she stolen from herself out of fear? Stolen from *them*. She was a coward. And Hannah deserved better. She knew that. She knew she should let Hannah heal from her rejection, from the way she'd left her standing there to follow after a man who had been less of a man and more of an omen of how the rest of Delphine's life was going to look. And she knew she should stay away, should let the wound she'd clawed into her friend's heart scab until it became just another faint scar of something that once happened in the past. But Delphine never claimed to not be selfish.

The idea of ending this war with only regrets of what they could've been had her climbing out of bed and heading down the hall until she stopped in front of Hannah's door. She knocked. Once. Twice.

When Hannah's face finally appeared before her, Delphine was silent.

"What do you want, Delphine?" Hannah asked quietly.

Delphine took a deep breath. "I want you."

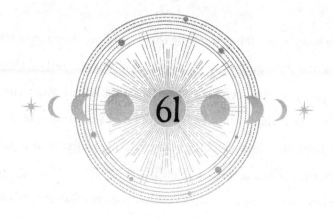

61

I want to stay here forever.

Calla was lying on Gideon's bare chest beneath the tangled sheets as he drew lazy circles down her spine over the material of the oversized shirt she'd borrowed to sleep in. She knew they ought to sleep, but she had never been more electrified in her entire life, a million thoughts running through her head.

Calla looked up at him through her lashes. "Was that all right?"

The corners of his lips curled down as he admonished, "It should be a crime that you just asked me that question. *All right* is not even close to what that was. Try *world-shattering.*"

She wrinkled her nose as she moved to lie flat on her stomach, folding her arms over his chest so she could prop her chin up on them as she spoke. "No need to flatter me."

He sighed in exasperation. "Calliope."

She rolled her eyes. "Gideon. I am not so fragile that I would unravel if I am not the best you've ever had right from the jump."

"You *are* the best I've ever had," he said softly, "because I've never had anything with anyone I've ever loved. It's a different thing."

The way he was looking at her, like he would steal all the stars in the sky and name them after her, she was inclined to believe him.

"I love you, too," she whispered.

He smiled and gently rolled her over until she was pressed back against the bed once more, making sure to lean all his weight onto his forearms as he bent down to kiss her.

When he broke the kiss, he whispered, "Say it again."

She hummed. "I love you, Gideon Black."

He kissed the top of her head. "I'll never get tired of hearing— Calliope?"

Calla furrowed her brows at the sudden look of alarm on his face. She reached up to cup his cheek and let out a strangled gasp when she saw that her hand was *disappearing*.

Her vision slowly began to fade, her hearing, too, and a hollow feeling consumed her as she slowly began to vanish into thin air. The roar of her name on Gideon's lips was the last thing she knew.

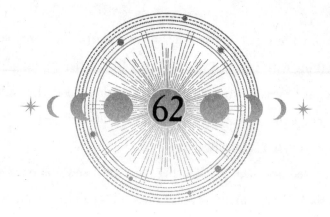

62

Hannah stood in the doorway, staring at Delphine, with those three little words echoing over and over in her mind.

I want you. I want you. I want you.

She never thought she'd hear those words from Delphine's mouth. Not directed at her, at least. Especially after everything that happened on the boat...

"Nothing has changed," Hannah finally said, the words nearly getting stuck in her throat.

"My mind has," said Delphine, as if she were afraid her time was running out and if she didn't say the words now, Hannah would close the door on her forever.

Truthfully, Hannah was thinking about it. Being rejected in front of an audience was one thing. Being given false hope was another.

"You said it was too risky," Hannah reminded her. "You said it would be *ruinous*."

"No, I said it had been ruinous for me in the past," Delphine corrected. "But that was the past. With someone else. Not with you. That was never fair of me to say."

"And what if it ends the same way?" Hannah asked, emotion sending a flush of heat over her face. "You were right. I'd rather not risk our friendship. I've built myself around you too intrinsically over these last few years. We met when all my wounds were still open, and you were like a balm to all the pain I had endured. And now the scar tissue has formed too tightly around us together and it might hurt, but I have to separate myself from you now."

"No." Delphine stepped closer, until their chests were nearly flush. "*No.* I didn't realize before because I just . . . I put you in a box. I stashed you away in my mind as a friend because I couldn't imagine ever deserving the love of someone like you. I didn't imagine you'd ever want me like that. You've seen so much of me . . . things that most people have looked away from or tried to pretend didn't exist. My mother always told me I'm nothing if I am not pretty, clever, powerful. And it's hard for me to remember that isn't true sometimes. But I've never worried about being any of those things—including the ugliest sides of them—around you. I'm sorry it's taken me so much time to realize that."

Hope began to swell in Hannah's heart. She knew if she didn't crush it now that it would destroy her.

"You can't do this to me if you aren't sure," Hannah choked out. "You have to walk away if you aren't sure. I can't—"

A deep roaring sound suddenly erupted from down the hall, cutting off the rest of her sentence as both of them startled.

"That came from Calla and Gideon's room," Delphine said, alarmed.

Hannah peeked her head out of the doorway in the direction of the disturbing noise, and sure enough, the door to the other room flew open, nearly ripping off its hinges. And out stepped Gideon, shirtless, with a look of complete and utter terror on his face.

He dropped to his knees. *"She's gone."*

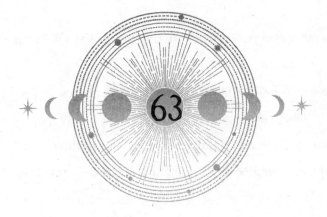

Calla didn't know where she was. The room was dark and hot, *too* hot, despite the fact that she was only wearing Gideon's shirt and it barely reached her mid-thigh. Beneath her bare feet was plush carpet, and there was the distinct smell of sweat and tobacco in the air. There was no natural light coming from anywhere, which meant it was egregiously dark, and her eyes were not being quick to adjust.

"Did I interrupt you at an inconvenient time?" a voice asked from somewhere in front of her.

A small flame blazed to life for a quick moment before dimming to a smaller spark, the faint crackling sound of paper burning with it. A cigarette.

A moment later and a small gas lamp was also ignited, the soft warm light illuminating the person in front of her.

Jack.

His amber eyes were alight with mischief as he took in her compromising appearance.

"Disheveled hair, swollen lips, a man's shirt," Jack rattled off. "You finally put that prince out of his misery?"

"What the fuck am I doing here, Jack?" she seethed.

"Don't be impolite or I'll make his torture so much worse than I'm already planning to," Jack told her before taking a drag of his cigarette.

She glowered at the man. "Isn't the whole smoking-in-the dark-as-you-wait-for-your-latest-victim bit a tad cliché even for you? Don't you ever get tired of playing at being a villain?"

"I'm not playing at anything, sweetheart," he told her. "I am a villain to plenty. I'm also a savior to plenty. Just depends on my mood."

"And what mood are you in today?"

He grazed his eyes over her practically naked figure and gave her a lazy smile. She stumbled back from him, a look of disgust on her face. Before she could hurl an insult, however, he laughed and said, "Oh, don't get your panties in a twist—if you're even wearing any—I don't want the prince's seconds."

"You're an utter fiend. And one day," she said slowly, delivering a threat in every word, "you're going to wear out my patience and I'm going to splatter you into a million pieces."

"What's stopping you from doing that now?" he taunted, his smile knowing.

The fact that I don't know where I am or how I would get back to

Gideon. Oh, and because my magic has still not fully returned from the drugged wine you had that bastard pirate give me.

"I must say, when Isaac alerted me of their failed task, I was rather proud of you and your little crew," Jack told her. "I'm going to have to sink the *Sea Pearl* now, of course, but I admire your crew's tenacity."

"Why did you try and get us trapped at sea?" she demanded.

"One of the Witch Queens offered me a bargain too good to pass up if I was able to postpone you starting the war. Plus, it really would hinder my empire if you devastated the Witch Realms. Ah, well, I am nothing if not adaptable."

Nothing about his answer was particularly shocking. "How in the Hells did you get me here? And where *is* here?"

"The latter is none of your business," he told her. "As for the former, I figured you might need a little help jogging your memory, so let me remind you—I gave you and your prince a spell and a token to help you find the Valley of Souls in exchange for a favor from each of you. I'm collecting yours."

Calla's brows furrowed in confusion. "No. No, we paid you that favor. We found notes from ourselves—"

"And what did those notes say?" he cut in. "The exact terms that I just stated to you, or that you already paid them?"

Calla's stomach sank like a stone. "You . . . you tricked us. You made it seem like we paid you back already. You took away our memories."

"And you burned down one of my favorite investment properties in Estrella," Jack smiled. "I'd say I let you off rather easy for long enough."

"Is *that* why you're torturing me?" she growled. "Because our old apartment burned down?"

He shrugged. "Maybe I just think you're fun to torture. You're certainly the most profitable. Have you not seen the posters the Witch Queens have been putting up? You're worth a small fortune. I could cash in right now."

She narrowed her eyes. The way he said he *could* suggested he had other plans. Hopefully, less insidious ones.

"What favor are you calling in?" she demanded.

He stood from the couch he'd been lounging on, flicking his cigarette's ashes onto the floor as he did.

"If I'm honest, I wasn't planning to call yours in so soon. But then some intel came to me, and I knew I had to move fast," he explained. "Besides, I'll still have your prince's favor in my back pocket to decide what to do with after the Fates' War, and that seems just as good given the two of you are officially involved." A leering grin.

Calla rolled her eyes and tapped her foot impatiently. She didn't have time for whatever tangent he was about to go off on. Gideon was probably worried sick.

"Your siren, Delphine, paid me a visit not too long ago. Killed Ramor. Revealed to me that she knows a few things that I am very unhappy with her knowing. I'm sure she's told you?"

Calla didn't miss a beat, her poker face carefully sliding into place as she lifted her chin and lied, "We keep nothing from each other."

By the slight flicker of fury in his amber eyes, Calla had a feeling he bought it.

"Well, when you see her again, you can tell her she cost seventeen people their lives," he revealed darkly. "I traced her trail all the way back to the Siren's Sea, and I heard something interesting. About an artifact she possesses."

Calla had no idea what he was talking about, but she couldn't give that away now. So she said, "And you want me to get her to give it to you as my favor?"

"Ah, every time we meet, you're a little more clever than before," he praised, his tone dripping with condescension.

"And how am I supposed to get the artifact to you?" she asked.

He leaned over to the small side table that the gas lamp was sitting on next to the couch and picked up a small mirrored box she hadn't noticed before. He opened the box and showed it to her. It was empty.

"You're going to put it in here and seal it," he explained. "Then you're going to read the inscription on the lid. It will get to me."

"And then my debt will be paid?" she confirmed with him, practically grinding her teeth down to her gums with the anger she felt for being foolish enough to get trapped in this situation.

"One hundred percent," he vowed.

"Fine." She ripped the box from his grasp. "Now send me back *exactly* where you summoned me from."

Before she blinked again, he moved, pushing her back into a wall and pressing the tip of the knife he was now palming into the skin of her throat.

"Of course," he crooned. "But first, I'd like to have a little fun for your prince's benefit. Consider *this* my payback for burning down my apartments."

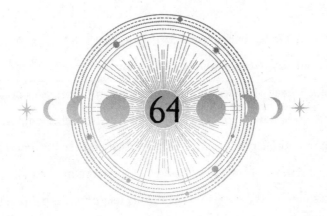

64

It took Hannah, Delphine, the Wayfarer, *and* Tempest to get Gideon under control when the cuts began—long, shallow wounds slicing through his neck, over his forearms, dripping blood down his bare torso.

From what they could piece together, Calla had somehow *vanished* into thin air. Gideon would have torn the place down if it hadn't been for Tempest's ability to call and manipulate shadows into bands of rope that tied his hands together behind his back. The Wayfarer had offered to knock him unconscious, but Hannah and Delphine had protested greatly, not wanting to put Calla in an even worse predicament wherever she was.

Hannah felt terrible for Gideon. His eyes were staring at nothing, haunted, as they all crowded around him and tried to figure out what to do. The cuts, at least, had stopped.

"Where the Hells do we even start?" Delphine whispered to Hannah. "And why is that always the question we're asking?"

As if the Gods themselves heard Delphine's words, a small voice suddenly called down the hallway, "Gideon?"

Gideon's head snapped up. He fought against Tempest's hold, wriggling in the shadowy bindings to try and free himself. Tempest looked to Hannah and Delphine in question, and when they both nodded, the girl snapped her fingers and released Gideon from his prison.

He was out of the door in seconds, his feet pounding down the hall as he ran for her. When they all spilled out of the room where they'd been babysitting him, they saw him and Calla just as they crashed together. Like two magnets.

Gideon gathered Calla up into him before slowly kneeling, lowering them both to the ground. One of his hands came up to gently cup the back of her head as she buried her face into his neck. The connection the two of them had to each other was so apparent that Hannah almost had to look away.

She and Delphine gave the two of them a brief moment before tiptoeing closer.

"What happened?" Delphine asked Calla as Gideon loosened his hold just enough for Calla to look up at them.

"Jack," Calla offered in explanation, her voice surprisingly clear. "He summoned me using my blood. Gideon and I owe him favors—"

"The fuck we do," Gideon growled. "We already paid those off. We have written proof."

Calla shook her head, her eyes mournful. "The proof we have only states what we promised him—not that we paid. Unfortunately, he was within his rights to collect."

The string of expletives that came out of Gideon's mouth was so creative that it made Hannah blush.

"And the cuts?" Delphine demanded when it was clear that Gideon's rage wasn't going to allow him to speak in coherent sentences.

Calla cupped Gideon's face in her hands. "He was only trying to torture you. He's pissed we burned his apartment building down all those months ago." Her eyes flicked over to Delphine. "They were just shallow little cuts. I'm fine, I promise. But we all need to talk." Her glance slid past them, toward where Tempest and the Wayfarer lingered in the hall. "Privately."

"Well, you better make that talk quick," the Wayfarer announced. "Because the reason I'm even awake at this hour is that I've got some news for you all. I found the second Blood Warrior."

)·)·)·●·(·(·(

Calla shut the door to her and Gideon's room after she insisted on getting a second of privacy to process what just happened. Not to mention she needed *clothes*.

"You swear you're all right?" Gideon asked as she set the box that Jack had given her down on the dresser and began searching the floor for her discarded garments.

"I'm not afraid of Jack," she told him quietly. "I won't give him the satisfaction after everything he's done to us. The whole thing just caught me off guard." She looked up at him as she pulled on her pants, hopping a bit to get them over her thighs and hips. "Are you okay?"

"Not even a little bit," he answered truthfully. "But we can talk about that another time."

Calla nodded and finished getting dressed while he packed up their things. A knock at the door sounded, and Calla let Delphine and Hannah in.

"All right, Mr. Cursed out there said we have five minutes or he's going back to bed, so start spilling," Delphine ordered as she plopped herself on the end of the bed.

As Calla bent down to tie the laces of her boots, she addressed Delphine. "Jack said you had some sort of information on him?"

Delphine's brows raised. "Yes. Well, *information* may be generous. I strung together some whispers I heard while I was searching for him so I could find all of you. I may have overexaggerated my certainty in the truth of them to his face and bluffed that I'd told others just in case he tried to kill me."

"Well, he killed, like, seventeen other people over your exaggeration," Calla informed Delph, though it wasn't accusatory. The Gods knew they all had blood on their hands—or would very soon.

Delphine shrugged, not disturbed by the information. "They were all Jack's seedy accomplices anyway."

"So what's the secret?" Hannah wondered, tone holding an impatient curiosity.

Delphine licked her lips in anticipation, leaning forward as she dished, "Rumor has it, there's a girl. And a curse."

"Isn't there always," Gideon murmured, making Delphine smirk.

"The girl is apparently the only person who can love him. From the insight I overheard, it seems to me that anyone who falls in love with him meets a terrible demise. Except for her," Delphine gushed.

"And where is this girl?" Calla asked, enthralled by such a revelation. Jack? Caring for someone besides himself? Not just someone—the *only* one, apparently.

"That's the burning question." Delphine shrugged. "No one knows. Not even Jack. But Jack said it's why he has so many eyes and ears and connections—he's waiting for someone to eventually find her. Built an entire empire in order to entice her back. Or use against her—who knows with him. The people who are close enough to him to know even the broadest of details about the situation didn't even have any real, tangible, clue as to her identity, whereabouts, or why she disappeared. And now I suppose most of those I talked to are dead."

"Well, that explains why he looked into your disappearance from the Siren's Sea," Calla said. "He's livid with you."

Delphine rolled her eyes as she picked at one of her nails. "He can kiss my ass."

"He said you had some sort of rare artifact," Calla pressed on.

"That's the favor he wanted from me—to get the artifact from you and hand it over to him."

Now Delphine stood from the bed. "No. No. *No.* Is that bastard *kidding* me? How does he know *everything*?!"

"What artifact?" Hannah prompted as Delphine began to pace.

Delphine was quiet for a long moment, but she finally paused and dug into the top of her dress before pulling out a small black iron key.

"It's called the Obsidian Key. Reniel wore it for as long as I can remember," Delphine explained to them. "It can lock or unlock *anything*. It's how I unbound myself from my Siren's oath. Bellator told me not to tell anyone I had it. There's only two in existence, and the uses are limited. This one only has six turns left."

"May I see?" Gideon asked.

Delphine gently placed it in his waiting palm, watching carefully as he brought it closer to his face to inspect it.

"So someone found out Reniel lost the key, deduced that you took it, and then informed Jack?" Hannah guessed.

"What if Gideon's fath—I mean *Bellator*—told Jack himself?" Calla asked.

Gideon's eyes cut to Delphine to gauge her answer, but Delphine shook her head with confidence. "Bellator didn't seem the type to gossip or work for someone like that. He helped me leave and, like I mentioned, told me not to tell anyone about the Obsidian Key."

"Well, however Jack found out, now he wants it," Calla said.

"There's no way we can just hand over something this valuable," Delphine reasoned. "I won't."

Calla bit her lip. "I don't know what will happen if I don't bring it to him."

Delphine looked like she wanted to argue, but one look at the worry in Calla's face, and she caved. "I *hate* that man. I should've killed him when I saw him. *You* should've killed him when you saw him."

"I thought about it," Calla admitted. "But then I figured I needed him to get back to all of you, so my hands were a bit tied there as well."

"Did he give you any sort of deadline?" Hannah asked.

"No," Calla realized.

Delphine perked up. "If he didn't give you a deadline, we're holding on to it for as long as we can."

Calla looked at Gideon for his thoughts on the matter.

He shrugged. "Fair enough to me."

A fist pounded on the door then.

When Delphine threw it open, they found the Wayfarer, arms crossed, waiting on the other side.

"Are you all done chitchatting?" he asked.

"Usually I would find someone so brooding very attractive," Delphine quipped at him, "but you desperately need to relax."

Tempest, who was standing just a few feet behind the Wayfarer, covered her mouth to hide her snicker. The Wayfarer turned—glaring at them both in turn—before stomping away and down the stairs. The rest of them followed, Calla lingering in the hall as she waited for Gideon to do one last routine check of the room before they caught up with the others.

"All right," the Wayfarer announced. "The second Blood Warrior resides on the west side of the continent in some remote coastal town. My sources said they live in the town's lighthouse."

At the mention of *west*, Gideon pulled out his compass. They all waited for the arrow to stop spinning, and when it did, in fact, stop on west, the Wayfarer looked impressed.

"I guess that settles it," Calla said.

"Pest here will take you all there and then return to me with the talisman," the Wayfarer continued. "Which means this is goodbye. Hopefully forever. I'm rather bored of Illustros and its problems."

"Pest?" Delphine questioned.

Tempest stepped forward, shooting the Wayfarer an indignant look. "He says I talk too much."

"You do," he shot back at her.

Calla stepped in before this continued any longer. If Ezra and Delphine's spats were any indication, they could be here forever. "Thank you both for your generosity. If we ever *do* happen to meet again, consider us friends. We owe you."

"I'll remember that, fated one. "The Wayfarer smirked at Calla but inclined his head in acknowledgment of her thanks. "Good luck with the war."

He hesitated, only for a moment, as he handed over the Transvectio Talisman to Tempest, who stepped forward and offered it up for all of them to latch on to. Calla was careful not to touch the girl's skin, recalling the earlier warning about Siphons coming into contact with each other. Tempest spoke the name of their destination, and a second later they arrived.

65

We definitely aren't in Illustros anymore, Hannah thought when Tempest dropped them off with a final farewell before disappearing.

Remote and *coastal* were accurate descriptors, but unlike the pink sands and vibrant colors Hannah had experienced with Delphine and Calla in Illustros, everything here was very *gray*. The town was nestled between rugged onyx cliffs and the thick charcoal mist that separated it from the sea. The town itself was a collection of weather-beaten structures, their facades worn by the salty winds that the ocean's relentless waves sent their way. The buildings, constructed from slate and stone, seemed to blend seamlessly into the rocky terrain, a hundred different shades of black and gray, almost as if they were carved from the very cliffs they rested upon. Narrow winding streets snaked their way through the town, flanked by ancient gas lampposts that cast a pathetic glow against the rolling mist.

And up ahead, like a beacon calling out to them, was the lighthouse.

"Of course we have to walk up a hill," Calla muttered.

Hannah nearly slipped on the slick cobblestones as they began their ascent through the town. Delphine was there in a split second, wrapping an arm around Hannah's waist to steady her.

"Thanks," Hannah whispered, trying to keep her heartbeat calm despite the proximity of their faces as she straightened herself up.

Delphine nodded, her eyes flicking down to Hannah's mouth so quickly before she stepped away that Hannah thought maybe she'd imagined it.

When they finally reached the lighthouse, a grueling forty-five minutes later, none of them were in any mood to make a good first impression on someone new, but they didn't have much of a choice. The exterior of the lighthouse was weathered and worn and not at all welcoming. Its paint was faded and peeling, its windows like unblinking eyes that peered out into the endless expanse of the ocean, watching, waiting. The mournful cries of seagulls echoed through the night, their eerie calls adding to the sense of foreboding that hung heavy in the air.

Gideon knocked on the worn wooden door, and they all waited. No one answered. He tried the handle next, to check if the door might be unlocked, but no such luck.

"They might be asleep," Calla offered. "We probably should've just waited until morning."

"Time is of the essence, unfortunately," Gideon said.

"We got a message from Caspian while you were gone with Jack," Delphine informed her.

Calla started. "Why didn't you tell me?"

"We got a little distracted," Delphine said defensively. "With Gideon losing his mind and all."

"Well, what did Caspian say?" Calla prompted.

"Thorne found the original Blood Warrior, and they're working on hunting down the other two as we speak." Delphine looked back to the door. "Which means I don't really care if they're sleeping. They're about to wake up."

Delphine began beating both her fists on the door. "Hello!"

Gideon and Calla watched, exasperated at Delph's tactic, while Hannah found herself trying not to laugh.

"Could I see the messenger, Delphine?" Gideon asked. "I'd like to send Caspian some information as well."

Delphine dug into her pocket and handed over the gold artifact to Gideon before turning back to her task.

"I'll stay here all night," she threatened in a singsong voice.

"Looking for me?" a lilting voice called from above.

Their heads all snapped up in sync to find a woman with long aubergine hair leaning out one of the windows. Hannah could hardly make out the details of her features from so far below, but her lips were painted an unmistakable plum color, and her eyes were the color of ice.

An Onyx witch.

"I'm not much up for company," she crooned down to them. "Perhaps another time."

"Listen, lady," Delphine scowled. "You might as well come open the door because we're coming in regardless. I am tired, my outfit is dirty, I haven't had decent food in *weeks—*"

The woman slammed the window shut.

"Well, this isn't off to the best start," Calla said.

"Why do all Onyx witches have a particular talent for enraging me?" Delphine griped. Then, to Gideon, "No offense. I'll make an exception for you, considering you and Calla apparently finally fu—"

"*Delphine!*" Calla screeched.

"What?" Delphine asked innocently. "Is now not the time to bring up that I'm pissed you have yet to share all the details with your best friends? The walls at that inn were *not* thick."

"*This is not the time,*" Calla said as she covered her face with her hands, mortified. Gideon, for his part, didn't look too fazed.

Delphine didn't get the chance to rebut because the door in front of them ripped open, revealing the Onyx witch in all her glory. She would have been stunning, Hannah thought, if not for the intensity of her eyes. They were quite unnerving, though perhaps she herself had no room to talk.

"I was wondering when this day would come," the woman declared as she took the four of them in. "I was hoping moving all the way out here would mean no one would bother to show up on my doorstep, however."

"May we come in?" Gideon asked. "We need to talk."

The woman glanced over to Delphine, who gave her a wicked smile.

"It doesn't seem I have a choice, does it?" the woman asked.

"Correct answer," Delphine said as she shouldered past them all and pushed her way inside.

Calla and Hannah both threw apologetic looks in the woman's direction as they followed suit. The woman shut the door and crossed her arms expectantly.

Gideon cleared his throat. "I'm Gideon Black, Prince—

"Of the Onyx Realm," the woman finished with a nod. "I know. I must admit I'm astonished to see you on this side of things."

"Yes, well, Gideon is one of us," Calla inserted.

The woman lifted a brow. "One of us?"

"A Blood Warrior," Calla explained. "I'm Calliope Rosewood. These are my friends Hannah and Delphine."

The woman eyed them each in turn before finally offering, "I'm Piper."

"It's nice to meet you, Piper," Calla said at the same time that Delphine asked, "Which number are you?"

"The second," Piper answered. "How close is it?"

There was no need to clarify what she was speaking off. Calla rolled up the sleeve of her shirt and displayed her Rolls of Fate for the woman to see.

The woman gave a low whistle.

"We're trying to gather all of the Blood Warriors to start the war on our own terms," Calla explained. "We were hoping you'd come with us."

Piper was already shaking her head. "There's a reason I left Illustros, darling. I paid in blood, sweat, and tears to make it off that damn continent, and I am not going back."

Gideon's expression darkened. "We've paid as much—if not more. None of us wants to be in this position, but the Fates haven't given us a choice. Don't you want this to end? Instead of hiding for the rest of eternity?"

Piper laughed. "I don't mind the hiding. I enjoy living here, alone, just fine. I haven't left this lighthouse in nearly two decades."

Hannah wrinkled her nose and shot a look at Delphine, who was frowning in equal measure. That sounded miserable.

"Aren't you afraid the Fates will find a much more insidious way to get you on the battlefield?" Calla questioned.

Piper narrowed her eyes. "What do you mean?"

"I mean that we're here, politely asking you to come with us," Calla said. "But who knows what will happen the moment I roll that last Fates' Die? The Fates may plop us all right onto the battlefield. Wouldn't you rather be prepared? Know who your allies are?"

Piper sucked in a sharp breath. "Fates' Die?"

Calla winced a bit. "Yes. That's our next task. The queens took them from us and hid them. One was here, in Noctum, and now we're going to have to begin looking for the other."

"You have no idea how tired we are of traveling," Delphine grumbled.

Piper sighed. "I may have something that can help with that."

They all looked at her in surprise.

"Follow me." She waved a beckoning hand at them.

As Piper began to lead them toward the base of the spiraling staircase, Gideon and Calla were quick on her heels. Delphine, however, put a gentle hand on Hannah's shoulder, silently asking her to stay back.

Hannah raised her brows in question.

"I don't trust her," Delphine whispered to Hannah.

Hannah tilted her head, waiting for further explanation. It wasn't unusual for Delphine to be skeptical of new people. Unless they were attractive pirates.

I probably need to let that go, she chided herself. *None of that was her fault.*

"She says she hasn't left this lighthouse in two decades, but she absolutely *reeks* of witch hazel," Delphine said.

Hannah hadn't even noticed that little detail.

"Maybe she has a perfume with witch hazel in it?" Hannah suggested. "She is still an Onyx witch."

"A perfume that doesn't run out for two decades?" Delphine said skeptically.

"Delph, Han," Calla called down to them, "are you coming?"

"Yes!" Hannah answered before pulling Delphine with her toward the stairs.

"I don't like this," Delphine muttered, but when they reached the top landing with the others, she didn't say anything else. Just kept her shrewd starlight eyes on Piper's face, as if she were waiting for the woman's expression to reveal some sort of deception at any second.

"All right, what I'm about to show you is not something you can ever speak about to anyone else," Piper told them before taking a step toward the only other thing occupying the stark white space around them.

It was something large and oval, covered by a gray sheet. Piper grabbed a corner of the sheet and ripped it down to reveal a giant gilded oculus beneath.

Calla made a startled gasp. "I've seen this before. In a dream..."

"Whatever you need, this will take you directly to it," Piper told them.

"Where did you get this?" Calla asked.

"It was a gift," Piper said. "When I made it clear I was dedicated to never seeing the outside world again, the one who owned this before me said I should keep it. So I have a window into the universe whenever I begin to feel trapped. Go ahead. Ask for it to show you your Fates' Die."

They all watched as Calla and Gideon exchanged a wordless conversation in that way they did, before Gideon waved a hand for Calla to go ahead. Calla stepped forward, lifting her chin as she scrutinized her reflection in the mirror.

Then she requested, "Show me the Fates' Die."

The oculus's glass surface began to ripple, Calla's reflection fading away as it morphed into something else. A vision of a dim room, its back wall lined with bookshelves and maps. A glossy black table sitting in front of it. The only thing on its surface? The Fates' Die.

"Wait," Gideon whispered as he took a step forward, his eyes darting across the image.

Calla reached out to brush her fingertips against the oculus's surface, her hand sinking right into the glass.

Gideon sucked in a breath. "Calliope, *no*, that's—"

But it was too late. A gust of wind suddenly kicked up around them, and Hannah spun to see Piper blasting her magic as hard as she could to make Calla and Gideon tumble forward through the mirror and out of sight. As soon as they were gone, the mirror's surface returned to normal once more. Delphine let out a grunt of rage as she dove forward, tackling Piper to the ground, her sharpened claws ripping through the woman's clothes. When Delphine's claws met the witch's skin, however, an earsplitting shriek rang out around them, as if Delphine were scratching steel.

Piper laughed. "You cannot hurt me, siren. I'm a Blood Warrior. I am *invincible*."

She bucked Delphine off her, and they both jumped back up to their feet, scowling at each other with rage.

"*Why?*" Delphine snarled. "We were only asking you for help! We weren't going to force you to come back with us!"

"Sure you weren't," Piper spat. "That's all anyone ever wants from me. Return to Illustros, prepare for war, bend to the will of the Fates. I've had enough. I will die in this place, alone, if I have to. But I will not step foot onto that battlefield. Besides, I did them a favor, didn't I? They were transported exactly to what they were looking for."

Hannah stepped up to Delphine's side as she said, "You better hope

Calla wasn't correct. That the Fates don't drop you right into the middle of the fight without a single clue of who your allies are."

Piper's expression faltered, but Hannah didn't give her a chance to repent. She only hooked her arm through Delphine's and tugged her toward the oculus.

"Show me Caspian Ironside," Hannah said.

The moment the mirror showed her a glimpse of Caspian's warm, smiling face, Hannah didn't waste a moment pulling Delphine through with her.

66

The moment Gideon crashed into the study of the Onyx Palace with Calliope, he knew they were absolutely screwed. He'd recognized the trap too late.

As the two of them got back on their feet, he spun, glancing around the familiar space for the Fates' Die, only to find—

—his mother.

Lysandra's smugness was so palpable around them that Gideon could've cut it with his blade. She was leaning against the very mahogany table the oculus had shown them, and when he glanced past her to its center, sure enough, there it sat. The final Fates' Die.

Calliope stepped up next to him, shoulder to shoulder, lifting her chin as they both recognized the predicament beginning to unfurl around them.

"Welcome home, my prince," Lysandra purred. "I'm so very glad to see that my little bargain with Piper was worth giving up the Oculus of

Obscura for. I suppose it's poetic to trade one of my prized possessions for another."

"I am not your possession," Gideon snarled at her.

"Doesn't seem that way to me at the moment." Lysandra laughed as she reached across the table and plucked the die from its surface. "You both really know how to make a scene wherever you go, don't you? I had so many people reporting from the Miroir Mountains of your little escape that I had time to deliver the oculus to Piper *days* before you arrived. You should be quite embarrassed."

"Funny," Gideon snapped. "I was going to say the same thing about you hiding one of the die in a place called the Trench of Lost Things."

She shrugged. "I knew if you managed to use that damn compass of yours to find the first Fates' Die, it'd need to be hidden somewhere that would make it easy for you to reach Piper next—and then she would lead you right back to me. I will say that I thought the Trench of Lost Things would be a bit more of a challenge, but it's become clear that where there's desperation, there's a way with the two of you."

Gideon's loathing for her reached a new all-time high. Before he could help himself, he was seething. "Is that the same mindset you had when you decided to conceive Ezra to take on my curse?"

His mother's face twisted with shock. *"Who told you that?"*

Gideon smirked. "I believe the Valkyrie Queen sends her lowest regards."

A snarl ripped from Lysandra's throat at the mention of the Valkyrie Queen. "That insipid *bitch*. You cannot believe—"

"Did you or did you not risk letting your own son *die* just to give his curse to another son you only birthed for that purpose?" Calliope accused with rage.

"And if it had worked, you'd be thanking me, girl," his mother addressed. "Because you would not have to be worrying about your heartless fate right now, would you?"

"Did Bellator know you let me die?" Gideon asked, shifting the queen's attention back to him, away from Calliope. "Is that why he left you?"

Lysandra moved so quick that Gideon didn't even see the slap coming. Calliope stumbled back as his mother continued to slam him into the shelves lining the wall behind him.

"Do not *ever* speak that name here, do you understand me?" she growled. "I will rip out your heart *myself*."

"Then do it," Gideon murmured, locking his eyes with hers.

Lysandra's breathing was labored, her expression full of fury, but he saw the brief flicker of pain that flashed in her gaze before she could conceal it, and he knew right then that it didn't matter what he did, what he said, what name he invoked or how much he hated her—he was the one thing she would never let go of. Whether that was because she wished to torture him or because, deep down, there was some sort of maternal love she couldn't rid herself of, he didn't know.

"There will be more Blood Moons, you know," his mother rasped.

"I can wait the two of you out. Bide my time until the next opportunity comes along that grants me enough power to sever your soul-bond and then make sure to rip out her heart so that you will *never* see her again."

"Is that because you want me to be just as miserable as you? So that I might find solidarity in your company?" Gideon taunted.

Calliope snorted. "Except Bellator is still alive. He *chose* to leave, isn't that right?"

Lysandra spun on Calliope, but before the queen took a step, Calliope lifted her hands and seized Gideon's mother's limbs. He felt it then, the return of Calla's magic. A bright spot of heat blooming in his core at the same time as it did in hers. He watched as her cheeks flushed pink from the effort—her beauty never ceasing to stun him—but as quickly as the spark of her power had returned, it flickered out once more.

"*Guards!*" Lysandra howled as Calliope's grip faded away.

An entire unit of guards flooded into the study around them, four of the bastards immediately seizing Calliope. Gideon sent a blast of his magic into his mother as he tried to lunge for Calliope, but a pile of guards was on top of him in a matter of seconds.

His mother recovered easily, smoothing a hand over her hair as she fixed a smile on her face. "Take her to the dungeons. Then show my son to his old bedroom. I wouldn't want him to be uncomfortable."

Gideon fought against the guards' holds, but it was no use. He watched them drag Calla away, fighting as hard as she could herself, but he knew her magic still hadn't recovered fully from whatever enchantment that bastard pirate had put on her. He promised himself then and there that when this war was over, when they were safe and the world was less complicated, he would hunt Jack down and kill him for his little trick with the wine. Slowly.

"Gideon," Calliope choked out. "I'll be fine."

His mother wouldn't have to rip his heart out to make her point. This was just as painful.

"I'll always love you," he vowed to her before they took her from the room.

He thought he'd lost his mind when she'd disappeared at the inn. Right after the best moments of his entire life. But now? He was going to finally break.

He wasn't even sure what happened the moment she was out of his sight. All he knew was that the room around him turned to rubble. That within his chest there was a raging heart. And he'd be damned before he'd let anyone have it but *her*.

"*Knock him out, you imbeciles,*" his mother's voice ordered.

Then everything went dark.

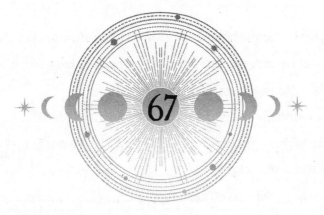

67

Hannah and Delphine crashed out through the oculus and onto the floor at Caspian's feet. Hannah squeaked in pain as her head conked into Delphine's, a migraine instantly rippling through her temples.

"What in the Hells?" Caspian exclaimed as he jumped to help them both back to their feet.

"Where did the two of you come from?" another familiar voice asked. Ezra.

Hannah glanced around to see that the four of them were standing in the clearing just out front of the cottage in the Miroir Mountains. Cass and Ezra both looked tired, and slightly damp, and she wondered if they had been doing some sort of sparring in the snow when she and Delphine dropped in.

"Noctum," Hannah remembered to answer as she rubbed the throbbing bump on her forehead. "We found the second Blood Warrior."

Caspian's face lit up. "Are they on their way?"

Delphine let out a bitter laugh. "*No.* That *asshole* tricked Calla and Gideon right into Lysandra's arms and refuses to have anything to do with helping us or the war."

"She essentially said she'd rather die," Hannah added.

"Then why not just die on the battlefield like the rest of us?" another familiar voice snorted.

Hannah turned to see Thorne approaching from the cottage's doorway, having been alerted to all the commotion she and Delphine must have made. Hannah gave him a sheepish wave with her fingers. He smiled back warmly.

"Glad to see the two of you are all right, at least," Thorne noted.

Cass nodded in agreement as he stepped forward to squeeze Hannah into a hug. Delphine stepped back to give them some room to embrace.

"Missed you, little witch." He hummed ruefully.

Hannah gave him a squeeze. "I missed you, too, Cass."

He set her back on her feet as Delphine propped a hand on her hip and speared Ezra with an expectant look.

"What about you, Prince? Did you miss us?" she taunted.

"Just like Cass, I certainly missed *Hannah*," he quipped back before reaching out to give Hannah's head an affectionate pat.

Delphine stuck her tongue out at him.

"What's been going on here?" Hannah prompted before they got too sidetracked. "Did any of you track down the other Blood Warriors?"

"Two of 'em," Thorne confirmed.

"And the Valkyries?" Delphine wondered.

"We've got a lot of introductions to make," Cass informed. "But before we get to that—elaborate on Calla and Gideon being with *Lysandra*?"

Hannah and Delphine flinched in tandem.

Delphine explained, "There was this whole thing with an oculus. . . . Lysandra basically paid Piper off to trick Calla and Gideon into her clutches. There's nothing we can do now except . . . go get them."

"Wait," Ezra inserted. "You mean you think we should move in *now*?"

Hannah and Delphine exchanged a loaded look before Hannah finally nodded and said, "The sooner we can move, the better. Calla and Gideon found one of the Fates' Dice and made their fifth rolls already. And I have a feeling the last Fates' Die is closer than any of us might think. If they find it and roll it and we aren't ready . . ."

Caspian nodded. "You're right. It's time to get all our ducks in a row. The queens claimed they hid both those dice, but I don't believe for a second that they risked having both of them out of their sight."

Ezra huffed a laugh of agreement. "I'd bet money my mother has it on her person as we speak."

For a moment, they all just stared at one another as the reality of what Ezra suggested slowly sunk in. Then, all at once, they were rushing toward the cottage.

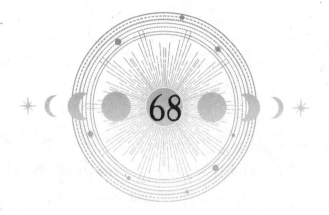

68

Gideon was sealed in his old bedroom for nearly three days before he felt it happen. Three days where he refused to eat a single bite, or drink, unless someone told him what was happening to Calliope. It was on the third night that he woke up, cold as ice, unable to feel her. He ripped the covers away, yanking up the left arm of his shirt—

—to see that his numbers were scarlet.

He nearly vomited in relief. But something was still wrong. His mother had done something. And he'd had enough.

He went to his bedroom door and ripped it open. The guards that were standing outside in the hallway, ten of them every shift, startled to attention.

"Where is she?" he snarled at them.

"Back in your room, Prince," the one in charge ordered. A muscular man with platinum hair and a well-groomed beard.

Gideon didn't bother with any more words. He sent a gust of his magic right into the man's abdomen, making the guard fly back into the wall with a grotesque *crack*. The other guards began to move instantly, and so the dance begun. Gideon knew he could hold his own long enough to get away; the problem was if he exerted all his magic now, there would be none left to help Calliope out of the dungeon. Still, when he slammed his fist into one of the other grunt's faces, splitting open the skin of his knuckles as he broke the witch's jaw, the sharp pain felt intensely satisfying.

"Prince Gideon," another guard barked as he approached from down the hall. "Your tantrum has wonderful timing. Your mother has summoned you to meet her in the throne room."

The bearded guard he'd been addressing before looked relieved as he stepped aside for Gideon to be able to adhere to his mother's summons.

"Godsdamned royals," he heard the man mutter to someone else as he strode after the messenger with purpose.

Gideon swept past his escort to bust through the double-door entrance into the all-too-familiar throne room, a dark sense that he'd seen this exact scene before washing over him as he stalked forward.

"Gideon, darling," Queen Lysandra crooned.

He bared his teeth. "Mother."

"Come now, Gideon, why the hostility? Haven't you missed me?" she asked from where she was perched on her throne in the middle of the white marble room.

He had definitely experienced this before, but he didn't have time to focus on that.

"Where is she?" he demanded.

Lysandra leaned her chin down to rest on her hand as a wicked smile unfurled on her face. "Who?"

Gideon practically snarled as he asked again, *"Where is she?"*

"Oh, does it truly matter, Gideon? You can't save her. You can't even save yourself. We both know how this story ends."

"No. You don't get to decide how this ends," he said. "You started this in the first place. This is your fault."

Lysandra laughed darkly. "My dearest boy, you've gotten yourself into this mess. It was never supposed to be you. I had *him* to spare you from this. I tried to ensure your fate. You're the one who undid all of my careful planning. For her."

"Where. Is. She?"

"I'll tell you what, Gideon." She sat up straight. "I'll make you a trade."

The realization suddenly hit him. The demon's oak vision. Gideon *knew* this was a trap. Knew exactly what her request was going to be.

Still, he played along. "What do you want?"

She smiled. "Quite a loaded question, darling. I want a lot of things. But this conversation isn't about what we want, is it? It's about what we need."

He waited for the request to come. For her to ask for his brother's heart.

"Bring me Ezra's heart, and I'll give you the girl. Let's see where your loyalties truly lie."

What she didn't know but he did, of course, was that he *could* bring her Ezra's heart. All he had to do was go back to Valkyrie Queen's palace.

"Tell me where she is first," he demanded.

"Sealed behind a magic barrier that will not release her without Ezra's beating heart," her mother told him. "The location doesn't really matter without that piece of the puzzle, does it, my dear? And surely you wouldn't choose a girl over your brother, would you?"

"Is that your grand plan?" he asked. "To lock her away so she is unable to start the war? Do you think Ezra isn't noble enough to give up his heart for such a cause?"

Her lips curled back. "Even if Ezra were, you still won't have the die. So go ahead, Gideon. Get rid of your brother and finish the job I started years ago."

"You *never* fucking deserved him," Gideon told her.

She shrugged. "I never tried to."

He spun on his heels and strutted out of the room.

"Let him go," his mother boomed at the guards as he moved through the palace he once called home like a wraith escaping out of the Hells.

He understood now that this place had never been a home.

As he made his way outside and headed right for the stables, he fished the messenger he'd taken from Delphine out of his pocket and wrote out a pleading request to whoever was on the other end. He pocketed the artifact once more as he pushed through the stable door with a little too much force, startling the stable hands working inside. He paid them no mind.

His favorite horse, a blue rose stallion named Equinox, whinnied the moment he entered.

"Hello, old friend," he greeted the beast before making quick work of saddling him, ignoring the staff as they protested his thievery.

He mounted Equinox in one swift motion and dug his heels into the beast's flanks, sending them both shooting into the night.

☽ ·☽ ·☽ ·● ·☾ ·☾ ·☾

"We need Ezra's heart," Caspian announced to the group as he read Gideon's message, once, twice, three times before it disappeared.

"Sorry, but I'm out of the heart-donation business," Ezra responded from where he and Sabine were thumb wrestling at the dining room table.

"Lysandra's trapped Calla somewhere. She can't be rescued unless we use Ezra's heart to unlock it," Caspian explained as he looked to each of his friends around the room in turn. Amina, Lyra, and Delphine were chatting across the table from Ezra and Sabine, each gaping at his news in disbelief.

"Gods, how do things always find a way to get *worse*?" Delphine gritted out in frustration.

Ezra, on the other hand, looked devastated as he dropped his hand from Sabine's grip. And though the Valkyrie's movement was subtle, Caspian noticed how she pressed closer to Ezra to comfort him.

"Why would she make the key your heart?" Amina wondered, tilting her head at what she probably perceived as Ezra's odd reaction.

Ezra gave a bitter laugh. "To punish both Gideon and me in different ways. She doesn't believe Gideon would rip out my heart to save

Calla—and that would mean our mother wins. But if Gideon did have the stomach to do such a thing, I'd be dead. And she wins that way, too."

Sabine's eyes darkened as she inserted, "Well, it's a good fucking thing your heart is already out of your chest, isn't it?"

Amina snorted. "Yes, but it's back at the—" Her words cut off as she spotted the mirrored looks on Sabine's and Caspian's faces. Then, "No. Absolutely Godsdamned *not*."

Lyra sighed as they stood from the table, their chair scraping against the floor with the movement. "C'mon, Amina. We didn't do all this work to let it fall apart because of one pathetic attempt at sabotage."

Amina let out a string of curses but didn't protest further as Lyra turned to Cass and said, "You good with coming along? We could use that nifty ability of yours that stops people from breathing."

"It's my heart. Shouldn't I go?" Ezra suggested.

Lyra shook their head. "Your flying has progressed greatly, but this needs to be an in-and-out situation. Stay here with Sabine and keep everyone in line."

Ezra looked like he wanted to protest further, but Cass shook his head. "They're right. We got this, Ez."

Ezra muttered a begrudging "Fine" before excusing himself from the table and bolting from the room. Cass sighed deeply, but there was no time to console the prince. Ezra would have to lick his wounds and get over it, because not even ten minutes later, Caspian, Amina, and Lyra launched themselves into the night.

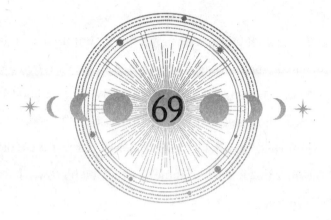

69

The only thing keeping Calla warm was her fury.

The bond had gone frigid the moment Lysandra's guards had sealed her inside. Ironically, sometime during the lonely night, her magic had finally fully come back to her. In a way, it had been a gift not having it these last few days. It made her realize just how much being a Blood Siphon was intrinsic to her sense of self.

Despite what her current predicament might suggest, she was powerful and a force to be reckoned with. And if it was the last thing she ever did, she'd prove that to the Witch Queens. To the world.

He'll come for me, she thought. And there wasn't a single bone in her body that doubted that. *He'll rescue me, and that doesn't mean I'm weak. It doesn't mean I'm useless. It just means the person I've chosen to tie my fate to . . . is worthy of it.*

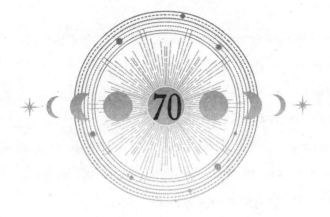

70

As Amina and Lyra touched down on the roof of the Valkyrie Queen's palace, Lyra setting Caspian on his feet since he refused to let Amina carry him herself, the three of them finalized their plan.

Lyra and Cass wished Amina luck as she began to descend toward the palace's front terrace, an act she was becoming rather bored of at this point. How many times would she have to return to this place? To face Ignia without giving in to her desire to rip her to shreds? She only had so much patience.

Fortunately, the moment she touched down on the ground, she was seized by Ignia's guards. She didn't bother struggling against their holds. This was precisely what she was hoping for. Quick. In and out. Make her deal with Ignia and go.

When they brought her inside, however, it was clear that they were not taking her to the queen; the word *dungeon* was being thrown around a little too much for her liking. Now she did drag her feet a bit.

"Aren't you going to take me to Ignia?" she demanded as they began to pull her toward the wrong wing of the palace.

One of the guards laughed. "You're being held for treason. You'll be lucky if you aren't dead before dawn."

Alarm began to ring in her head. "No. No, I need an audience with her *now*. She owes me this! Tell her if she doesn't let me see her, I'll make sure Rovin's soul is torn to pieces and—"

"Stop," a powerful voice rang out through the corridor.

Amina smiled in victory. And relief.

The guards turned in the direction of Ignia's demand, but their grips on Amina's arms didn't loosen.

"Your Highness?" one of them prodded for their next order.

"Deliver her to me," Ignia allowed, and the guards didn't hesitate this time. They marched Amina back down the hall and deposited her right before Ignia's expectant silhouette.

"Leave us," Ignia said. They obeyed.

Amina and the queen faced each other down for what felt like the millionth time. One thing different about this time, however, was that now they both knew not to underestimate the other. Finally, the queen jerked her chin in a command for Amina to follow her, and moments later, they were back in that same fateful study.

I loathe this room.

"I suggest you explain within the next thirty seconds why you think you have the right to speak Rovin's name in my home, before I rip you to shreds with my own hands this time," the queen said evenly.

Despite the threat, Amina now noticed the heavy circles beneath the woman's eyes, the disheveled ensemble that looked to have been worn for the last two days straight. Her Highness had been losing sleep. Excellent.

"Well," Amina began, "I do own his soul. I figured I was allowed to say his name whenever I pleased."

Despite the damning evidence of her exhaustion, fire ignited in the queen's eyes.

"*Where is it?*" she snarled.

"My Esprit," Amina admitted.

Predictably, the queen moved in a flurry of anger, pinning Amina back against the wall aggressively, but Amina barely felt the hit. Not when she was so amused at the way Ignia was clambering for the amulet around her neck. When the queen ripped it away, however, she found the amber stone dormant, the telltale glow of a trapped soul nowhere to be found.

Ignia bared her teeth.

"That is not my Esprit." Amina laughed. "My dear friend Lyra has been holding on to mine for quite some time now. Since right before you banished me, in fact."

An enraged mewling sound choked out of the queen's throat.

Amina laughed again. "Rovin's soul has been roaming around your kingdom on Lyra's neck this whole time. And if you want it back, I suggest you make me a deal."

It was the queen's turn to laugh. "After everything you've done, what in your right mind makes you think I'd ever make a deal with you?"

Amina sighed. "The war will go on either way. The Witch Realms will be left in shambles, and thanks to your own foolish deal with the Fates, half of your kingdom is still going to turn on you. But at least you'll still have the possibility of your lover returning from the dead if we all don't slaughter you on that battlefield, right?"

"I will end you one day," Ignia vowed, pure hatred in her eyes. "Whether it's in the Fates' War or after, I will not forget your traitorous plight."

"The feeling is mutual." Amina smirked.

The queen smiled viciously. "Then I have a counteroffer."

71

By the time Gideon arrived at the cave, he'd pushed Equinox so hard that the stallion's heart was at risk of puttering out entirely. He swung himself out of the saddle as the beast slowly folded to the ground, chest heaving with effort. Gideon knelt on the ground and patted the horse's snout with affection.

"You did well, friend," he soothed as he removed the bridle from the stallion's head. He undid the saddle next, tossing it all to the side. "You're free."

He left the horse and trekked the rest of the way on foot. His memory of the only time he'd been to the cave he knew she was in was fuzzy. The cave his mother had once taken him to, telling him it was the only place she could come when she wished to be entirely alone with her thoughts, out of the reach of the rest of her kingdom. Luckily, he didn't have to rely on just his memory.

He flicked open his compass and looked down at it, waiting for the arrow to let him know what he wanted most in the world. When it finally stopped, he smiled.

Calla felt him before she heard his voice. Her magic buzzing with an electric feeling as it recognized his nearby.

She pushed herself to her feet and rushed to the mouth of the cave, only stopping when the painful static that enclosed her zapped her skin.

When he finally came into view and spotted her waiting for him, he picked up his pace. His face, bathed in moonlight, looked both devastated and relieved to see her at the same time.

Before he could cross the threshold to her, however, she yelled, *"Don't."*

He froze, his breathing heavy as he watched her from just beyond the barrier that separated them. "Calliope."

"Hi," she whispered back.

"We're going to get you out," he promised. "Caspian is already working on getting Ezra's heart back from the Valkyrie Queen—"

She sucked in a breath. "Is that the key?"

Gideon nodded, solemn. "They're at the palace as we speak." He made a sound of frustration at himself as he shoved a hand through his hair. "I shouldn't have let us leave there the first time without it. I *knew* that's what she was going to ask for, and it slipped my mind—"

"You knew?" Calla chimed in, puzzled.

Gideon swallowed. "Remember when I told you my demon's oak vision showed me my mother had captured you?"

Calla stiffened with surprise. She did remember.

It doesn't have to happen like that, he'd told her then. Swore to her it wouldn't. But here they were.

His face twisted with devastation, as if he knew exactly what she was thinking.

"I know," he said, voice gruff. "I know I failed. I promised she'd never take you, and I let it happen anyway. If I could trade places with you, I would." He lowered himself to his knees, like a sinner begging the Gods for their forgiveness. "If you want me to repent for the rest of eternity, I will. I owe both you and Ezra that much."

But Calla was not one of the Gods and she certainly didn't need him to *repent*. If she'd learned anything since that promise he made her, about not letting his vision come true, it was that you could not stop fate, no matter how much you wanted to. She knew what he'd seen, and she still chose to follow him. And she'd do it all again.

She lowered herself to the ground in front of him.

"Gideon. I think it's time to admit to ourselves that the Witch Eater was right," she whispered. "About the fact that we get to make our own decisions but it still may not change the destination. I've been resisting that notion for so long, but . . . look at us. You think you've failed, yet I'm starting to think you accomplished exactly what you were meant to: getting us here, together."

His laugh was cynical. "Let's not act like dragging you here wasn't a selfish endeavor. I could've left you out of this entirely, back in Estrella. I could've gone to the Witch Eater by myself and made sure it worked before I offered to take you to them."

"But then I might not have you in the way I do now," she insisted. "I certainly wouldn't be this version of myself. And I . . . I love this version of myself. The one that doesn't loathe my power. The one that actually believes I deserve someone like you to love me."

"No," he admonished. "You never had to do anything to deserve *me*, Calliope. You deserve to be happy, to be respected, to have a chance at a peaceful eternity regardless of my presence."

"Yes," she agreed. "But I'm choosing to have all of those things *with* you. Because I also deserve a choice. And if I can't have all of that with you, I really don't want any of it."

His eyes flashed silver at her words, his hands twitching at his sides as if it were taking all his strength not to reach for her right then.

"Is being trapped in a cave waiting for someone to deliver your brother's heart ideal?" she continued, and he snorted. "No, it isn't, but you told me what you saw back in the Neverending Forest and I still followed you all the way here, didn't I? And if I had been told back then exactly how much of a certainty your vision actually was, I can't say I would have still followed you. But that was when I didn't know what it felt like to be loved by you."

His eyes closed. "I don't deserve you."

"You never had to do anything to deserve me, Gideon," she recited his own words back to him. "You deserve to be happy, to be respected, to have a chance at a peaceful eternity regardless of my presence . . . but I think it'd be nice if you chose all of that with me, too."

He blinked his eyes back open. "I've spent all my nights dreaming of a version of my life with you in it since the first time I heard my brother speak your name. A version that I knew I might never be able to have but at least I had never known and lost. Now I do have it, and I've never been so terrified."

Her entire body flushed with emotion.

"Every wish I've ever had has been granted in you, Calliope Rosewood."

His words jolted something inside of her, the filmy ghost of a memory somewhere in the back of her mind, but before she could grasp it, it slipped away. Whatever that feeling was, it told her all she needed to know. She was *exactly* where she was meant to be.

"I'll accept Rovin's soul in exchange for the Onyx Prince's heart," Ignia told Amina. "But I want something else as well."

Amina's nerves were instantly on edge. What else could—

"I want the Onyx witch," Ignia revealed. "The one with the smile that could launch a thousand ships. And I believe, fortunately for you, you brought him with you, yes?"

The sharp shrill of a bell later, the door to the study busted wide open, two guards dragging Cass inside. Cass, who was still managing to smile like a fiend. He winked at Amina. She resisted the urge to chastise him on the spot.

"And Lyra?" Ignia asked the guards.

The two men looked at each other guiltily before one of them stated, "Killed three soldiers before escaping."

Ignia rolled her eyes in utter exasperation. "Useless."

Caspian leaned toward Amina conspiratorially and whispered, "Lyra is a *master* at escaping."

Amina waved a hand in dismissal at him. She knew that already.

Turning back to Ignia, she said, "All right, you've got the witch. Now, the trade?"

Caspian startled a bit, eyes flicking over to Amina's face for a semblance of explanation, but he didn't utter a word.

"Don't you want to know why I wish to keep him?" Ignia wondered.

Amina shrugged as nonchalantly as possible. "As long as I get what I came for, I don't really care."

"Well, *I* would love to know," Caspian inserted, voice a bit strained.

Ignia smirked at Cass. "Because you are going to deliver a little message to your queen for me. Right before I lead my Valkyries onto the battlefield to reap as many unsuspecting witch souls as they can to finish paying off my debt to the Fates."

"And I kill you here and now instead?" Caspian asked cheerily.

The Valkyrie Queen rolled her eyes. "If I perish before my debt is fulfilled, Amina and the rest of my subjects will lose their magic much like your own people if they are on the losing side of the Fates' War. Our land will become barren once more. Nothing will ever thrive here again. It's why your little soul-bonded friends didn't kill me either. No one wants that burden when it comes down to it, right? To make such a detrimental decision on behalf of others?"

Amina could hardly breathe at this new piece of information, but even beneath her shock, a newfound respect for Calla and Gideon emerged. They could have easily damned every Valkyrie in existence to rid themselves of an opponent, and they hadn't.

"So? Do we have a deal?" Ignia pressed.

Before Amina could agree to it, Caspian said, "Yes. Now make the bargain with Amina and give her the heart."

Ignia nodded as she plunged her hand into the skirts of her gown and revealed Ezra's still-beating heart.

Two slices of a blade, six drops of blood, and a magically binding agreement later, Ezra's heart was clutched in Amina's hand.

"Lyra will deliver Rovin's soul to your door as soon as I am safely in the air and out of your reach," Amina informed the queen. "I suggest keeping better track of it than you have in the past."

"What makes you think I'll ever let it out of my sight again?" Ignia snapped as if she couldn't resist.

Amina shrugged as she backed out of the room. "Wouldn't matter anyway. Villains always think keeping their weaknesses in plain sight means their enemies won't find them."

With one last lingering glance at Caspian, she escaped the Valkyrie Queen's palace for what was hopefully the very last time.

73

Hannah was sitting outside in the cold, watching the stars, when she heard the footsteps approaching.

"Hi."

Hannah turned to see Delphine looking more rested than she had in a while, her blue cheeks flushed with color, though her silver eyes were cautious. As if Hannah were an animal she might spook if she moved too close too quickly.

"Hi," Hannah said softly.

Delphine paused a few feet away. "Is now a good time to talk?"

Hannah had, truthfully, been dreading this. "Probably better now than when we're on a battlefield."

Delphine tried to smile at the joke, but it didn't quite reach her eyes. Delph looked down at her hands, and it struck Hannah that this might have been the first time she'd ever seen Delphine *nervous*.

"I'm going to say something selfish," Delphine admitted.

"A first," Hannah joked with a small smile.

Delphine shot her a look that seemed to say *Be serious*.

"Thorne and the others are packing up with the plan to head out in the morning," Delphine revealed.

"And?" Hannah prompted.

Delphine took a deep breath. "I know you told me that I should walk away from you if I'm not completely sure. And I think that was more than fair."

Hannah gave a cautious nod. She *knew* it was more than fair. She'd spent her entire childhood trying to earn a mother's love that she never could. A mother who, Hannah now understood, had no love to give her in the first place. And for as deeply as she felt for Delphine, she knew now that she had to stop trying to convince others she deserved to receive the same depth of feelings she had for them. It was fair to no one.

"But," Delphine continued, "I don't think it was fair to make me decide so quickly."

Hannah's brows raised, a slight flash of annoyance shooting through her as she countered, "We're about to go to war, Delphine. I don't think there's any more time to let you weigh the pros and cons of returning my feelings when I've waited *years* to—"

Delphine jabbed a finger toward Hannah as she cut in with "There. You've had *years* to decide that you were sure about me. I've only just found out about your feelings."

"Then you should have paid more attention!" Hannah exploded, lurching up to her feet to face Delphine head-on. "I was always right there. *Always.*"

"I know," Delphine whispered. "This is where I'm going to be selfish."

Hannah furrowed her brow in confusion. "You mean there's more?"

Delphine nodded and took a deep breath. "I think you should have to believe me when I tell you, right now, that . . . I'm sure."

Hannah gaped at her. She felt her mouth opening and closing like a fish out of water, but she couldn't help it.

Delphine stepped closer, sliding her hands around Hannah's waist, pulling her close. She lowered her forehead to Hannah's, her starlit eyes shining bright with vulnerability as she repeated, "I'm sure."

Hannah wanted to argue. Wanted to say that it *was* the most selfish thing Delphine had ever said. That she couldn't expect for them to bypass all the insecurity and years of false hope with two single words from Delphine's lips.

Maybe it was the looming war. Or that Hannah just wanted Delphine that much. Or maybe she just *trusted* Delphine that much.

Hannah didn't waste a second longer.

She rocked up onto the balls of her feet and crushed her lips to Delphine's. Her hands sliding up to tangle in the silver strands of her hair as she waited for the moment Delphine would push her away and break her heart for the final time.

But that moment never came, and Delphine twisted her hands into Hannah's hair and deepened the kiss. Showing Hannah exactly how sure she was.

When Hannah awoke at dawn, something about the day felt very different. A charge was in the air. A heaviness. Something was beginning. Or ending. It was hard to tell.

But Hannah couldn't be bothered to worry about a war or the intensifying weight of death growing in her core as she stretched and turned over in bed to snuggle into—nobody.

She sat up, groggy, looking at the empty spot where Delphine was supposed to be.

"Hey, gorgeous, it's about time you woke up."

Hannah sat up fully to see Delphine brushing her hair at the foot of their bed. This was it. Her wildest dream had finally come true. She stared at Delphine in utter disbelief.

Delphine lifted a single silver brow at Hannah's expression. "Why does it look like you've seen a ghost?"

Because this scene has haunted my every waking moment since the Neverending Forest, Hannah thought, but she didn't want to say that aloud. She wanted to be calm, collected.

Delphine placed the gilded hairbrush she had been using onto the wooden dresser behind her and lifted one blue knee onto the bed. She had an almost-wicked smirk on her face as she lifted her other leg up and crawled onto the mattress at Hannah's feet.

Hannah waited in anticipation as Delphine slinked up the bed and over her body, gently pushing her shoulders to lay her back down.

Delphine bent and gave Hannah a gentle kiss on her collarbone, causing a shiver to run down her spine and goose bumps to prick up on her skin. She could feel Delphine's heartbeat as their chests pressed together, making Hannah's head swim.

"Promise me something," Delphine whispered.

"Anything," Hannah breathed.

"Promise me we will have plenty of time for everything after all of this is over. After we finally get Calla back. After this war."

"Everything?" Hannah asked.

"Everything." Delphine nodded. "I want to know what it's like to experience the world by your side as more than just your friend."

Hannah smiled as she nudged the top of her nose against Delph's and said, "I promise."

A knock suddenly rapped against the bedroom door, and both of their heads turned.

"Ladies?" Thorne's voice called from the other side. "It's time."

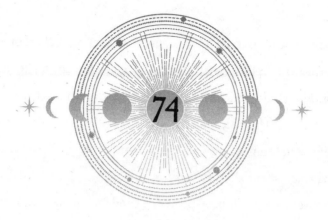

Calla awoke to the light of a breaking dawn and the sound of fluttering wings.

"If I had a wish for every time this damned heart was the key to breaking a magical barrier," Amina joked nonchalantly as she and Lyra landed in front of the cave.

Gideon was on his feet in seconds, rubbing the sleep from his eyes as the Valkyries approached—Ezra's heart in hand. Calla stood slowly, stretching her limbs, before Amina tossed over Ezra's heart unceremoniously. Calla caught it easily out of the air, wrinkling her nose at the grotesque squelch it made when it hit her palm. The pulse of its heartbeat in her hands was unnerving.

She took a deep breath. The moment of truth.

Calla stepped forward, waiting for the painful zap of the magic seal to burn against her skin, but it never came. Instead, the barrier's power began to crackle and absorb right into Ezra's heart. Calla watched in horror as the organ swelled, until it burst into grotesque bloody smithereens.

"*Yuck*," Amina hissed as she lunged out of the splash zone.

Calla could only blink in disbelief.

"That is *not* what happened when my exile was lifted," Amina griped.

"Probably because for you it was just a key to get out," Gideon murmured as he wiped a few of the heart's splattered bits from his face. "For my mother, this was a way to destroy something she knew we cared about."

"Hope he didn't want it back," Lyra deadpanned.

Calla turned to Gideon, ready to say how sorry she was, but the relief on his face when he wrapped her up in his arms told her the heart didn't matter. It wasn't Ezra's anymore anyway. Ezra had a new life, a new heart, a new future. A rebirth that his mother had never touched. Never scarred.

"Surprised you didn't lock yourself up in there with her, Prince," Amina said as she tapped her foot impatiently at their display. "Wouldn't that have been the romantic thing to do?"

"Then who would've gotten me dinner last night?" Calla responded in Gideon's defense as she stepped back from his embrace and turned to face the Valkyrie. "All right, give us an update. Where are we at with . . . everything?"

"You mean the impending war?" Amina asked. "On the precipice. I imagine this is one of the last moments everyone you know will still be alive, so enjoy it while you can."

Despite the slight drip of sarcasm, the truth of her words settled deep into Calla's bones. Everything was about to change.

"My brother just informed me they're on the move," Lyra confirmed, tone grave. "It's beginning."

"Who is *they*?" Gideon asked. "Are all our friends safe? What about the other Blood Warriors?"

"Thorne and Caspian managed to find the first and third Blood Warriors—and obviously we all know now what happened with the second, who you found. No one knows any information about the fourth, though," Lyra explained.

Calla bit her lip. "Can we even start this war without the others?"

"The war starts the second you both roll that last die, doesn't it?" Amina pointed out. "We can't continue to wait for people we can't find or who refuse to show up for people in need because it might inconvenience them. They're cowards anyway. None of the queens are waiting any longer. Ignia knows that Lysandra and the others have already gathered the entirety of their Realms' subjects and they're all lying in wait. She plans to send her own forces onto the witches whether the war has actually begun or not—to reap souls for her tithe. They'll probably go straight for the Onyx Realm, but we've got plenty of Valkyries heading for the Rouge Realm to try and stave the Rouge witches as long as they can. No one has heard a single thing from the Terra Realm, though."

Calla blanched. "The Valkyrie Queen is starting her own war? *Now?*"

Lyra nodded. "Correct. Which is why we need to move. No more waiting for other players. We're what you've got. The Fates can take it or leave it."

Calla looked at Gideon. "Ready?"

"No," he murmured.

"We'll give you two a minute," Lyra allowed. Amina began to protest, but Lyra was already tugging her away, leaving Gideon and Calla to have one last moment of privacy, of peace, before they headed for the battlefield.

"I love you," Gideon told her, his hand coming up to hold her face, the pad of his thumb brushing over her cheekbone. "Whatever happens..."

"Whatever happens, it happens to us together," she reminded him.

He nodded. "Together."

She reached up on the tips of her toes to kiss him, perhaps for the last time. This kiss felt different from all the others. It wasn't a hazy kiss born from the influence of a nymph, or one born of desperation and weak resolve. It had none of the sweetness of the kisses they'd stolen in secret, when they still didn't know what they meant to each other, or the passionate need of the kisses they'd shared that night in the inn.

No, this kiss was one that branded her *soul*.

And she knew, in this moment, that he had always been her destiny.

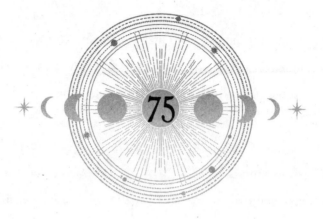

The scent of petrichor and rain clung to the tension in the air like a treacherous omen when word of war reached the Terra Witch Queen's doorstep. Her witches were already six feet underground. Not in their graves yet, but in their pursuit of the battlefield. Moving like worms beneath the earth, waiting for the signal of blood soaking into the soil.

The queen had always known her realm would be the last whisper on the wind. That by the time the sixth Blood Warrior had been found and fate began to shift, her witches would already be late. However, late to war was last to die—a fact that she'd been planning on for centuries. Unlike the others, hope had long perished in her land, in her bones. Many were sure she would not even show up to death's invitation, had thought her Realm to be too quiet for all the rumors that been snaking their way through the continent over the past few weeks.

But anyone who thought such a thing was very wrong.

After all, she'd helped create this land. And she would watch it burn.

A RAGING HEART

Caspian strode through the Onyx Palace with the confidence of a man who already knew when and how he was going to die. The palace was surprisingly empty—or maybe it wasn't surprising. After all, he knew very well where everyone was. Hiding in the shadows of the Onyx Realm, waiting for a war to begin.

When he reached Lysandra's throne room, the queen sat straight up as if she had been waiting for his very arrival.

"Caspian Ironside," she purred. "I haven't seen your handsome face in ages. Tell me, what was it like putting a knife so deep into my back?"

Caspian gave Lysandra a lazy smile. "The time of my life."

She scowled. "When your peers begin falling around you because of your treasonous little project with my Guild, the blood will be staining *your* hands."

Caspian's smile didn't wane a bit, but he did say, "I'm not sure I know what you mean."

"Did you think I really wouldn't figure out your game? One slipup from a grunt and a couple days of torture and I realized just how much treachery you and my son have plagued me with over the years. Not to worry, though, the units have already begun making a dent in finding every witch with uncompleted rolls and making them finish. And you're about to join them."

Caspian felt his grin grow as he raised his chin and said, "Well, you better get on with it. Because I have a message for you—from your sister Ignia."

Lysandra slowly rose from her throne, her coal eyes becoming glassy, unseeing, as she realized exactly what had brought him to the lion's den. He didn't even need to speak the words himself.

"Ignia is on her way. Here."

Caspian gave her a confirming salute. "I hope your sisterly reunion goes well."

The cold snap that went through the room around him was quick. Lysandra's wind wrapped around his neck and wrists like vises, dragging him across the marble floor toward her as she dug something out of the bodice of her dress. A Witch's Die.

She pressed the die into his hand, leaning forward until their chests were nearly flush and she was able to bring her mouth right next to his ear. "I look forward to seeing you on the front lines, shoving a knife through your friends' hearts."

If she was looking for him to flinch or cower, he didn't. In fact, he pressed himself closer as he growled, "I look forward to watching Calla end you all."

He and the Onyx Queen watched each other carefully as he finally pulled away, his fists tightening at his sides, the corners of his lips fighting to stay neutral.

Before either of them could utter another taunt, two Onyx Guards came rushing into the room. Their footsteps continued to echo in the hollow palace as one of them announced, "Your Highness, something is arriving."

Lysandra let go of her hold over Caspian, pushing past him as she strutted after her men. Only turning back to say, "I'll let you finish your final roll in peace. The last bit of peace you're going to have before I sink my power into you on that battlefield."

Caspian waited for her and the guards to disappear from the room before lifting his left fist and unfurling his fingers to reveal the Fates' Die. The Witch's Die was still burning in his other hand, but it was the least of his concerns. It could melt through his flesh and bone all it wanted, pleading for him to roll it, but he was going to be in the earth long before he ever allowed himself to complete his Rolls of Fate.

He lifted the Fates' Die closer to his face, inspecting the pulsing black-and-red cube with resignation.

"Villains always think keeping their weaknesses in plain sight means their enemies won't find them," he echoed Amina's words from earlier. Triumphant.

Caspian smiled as he felt the ground beneath his feet begin to rumble. It was time to find Calla.

76

As Ezra flew Sabine through the sky, with every mile they grew closer to the Onyx Realm, he had to fight the urge to turn around and bring her right back to the cottage. He wanted to lock them inside and pretend the outside world didn't exist, that his brother and his friends were alive and happy, that his mother was ten feet in the ground, and that the Fates had grown too bored to keep playing their games with any of them.

Sabine held him a little tighter as their friends and newest allies soared through the clouds around them. A few of them were showing off, spinning and dipping through the air, and Ezra wondered if they all thought this might be the last time they felt the thrill of flying.

Half of them were heading to the border of the Rouge Realm, in hopes of intercepting Myrea's men before they came too close to the heart of the battle. Ezra still wasn't confident they had enough fighters on their side, but it was too little too late now.

"Ezra?" Sabine whispered.

He glanced down at her face, her green eyes shining with an emotion she'd never shown him before. "Yes?"

She swallowed. "Don't . . . don't die again, okay?"

Ezra gave her a grim smile. "Okay."

When the Realms finally came into view, he could see the spires of his mother's onyx castle just over the horizon line. Worse, he could see the lines and lines of Onyx witches marching toward an enormous clearing littered with gold-and-red witch hazel, pouring in from the margins of the woods that surrounded their land.

The fleet around him paused, hovering as they watched their opponents head toward the soon-to-be graveyard below. Someone shouted something up ahead, and Sabine made a strangled noise as she shifted in his arms.

"Oh shit," she cursed as she pointed to something just past the borders of the Onyx Realm.

Another army, this one made of Rouge witches, encroaching the borders of the Onyx Realm.

"This is it, harpy," he murmured to her.

"What about the Terra witches?" she asked. "We have no one protecting us from the north."

He shook his head. "Not sure. The Terra Queen has always been the most aloof. I don't know if she's even visited our realm since I was born. She'll be a wild card."

"Maybe they didn't get the message—" Sabine began, but her words cut off as her face went ashen.

"What's wrong?" he demanded as he followed the direction of her stare.

In the distance, coming right toward them, were hundreds and hundreds of flying brown specks. If they hadn't been in the sky, Ezra might have thought it looked like an infantry of ants barreling toward them.

The Valkyries. The ones that wouldn't join their cause—or at least didn't know about it.

Some sort of projectile went flying past Ezra's head, the whistle of it snapping against his eardrums.

"We need to land!" Sabine shouted, twisting in his arms to call out to the others. "To the ground!"

And just like that, their allies began falling out of the sky like stars.

77

Em watched as her master unraveled the last bit of crimson yarn and circled it around the Onyx Realm on the map tacked to the wall. The only thing left in the deserted cottage.

The Witch Eater couldn't really experience nostalgia in the way other beings did. They were too ancient, too immortal. Even Em's distant, buried emotions were more tangible than the Witch Eater's. But if her boss *were* able to be nostalgic, she thought that perhaps that was what was happening now.

"She's coming," the Witch Eater rasped, dipping their chin in a nod of approval.

The Witch Eater turned to Em then, bowing their head in what felt like reverence.

"You've served me well, child. May your soul find peace in the fires of salvation."

Em bowed their head back, a flood of power washing over her as the remnants of her contract to the Witch Eater were finally, blessedly paid and her master finally released her soul into the ether.

When Amina and Lyra placed Calla and Gideon into the center of the clearing, Calla heard her name being whispered on the wind.

Calliope Rosewood. Calliope Rosewood. Calliope Rosewood.

She looked to Gideon to see if he might have heard it, too, and by the taut expression on his face, she knew that he had. Everything around them was too still, too quiet, and for a moment, it was hard for her to imagine that she was standing amid a future graveyard. She wondered if they had arrived too soon. If Caspian hadn't yet given Ignia's message to the Onyx Queen. If the Valkyries weren't encroaching imminently and this was all one terrible misunderstanding.

But then a battle cry rang over their heads in the distance and Gideon glanced up.

"Look," he told them, his tone clear and sharp.

A gust of wind whipped through the clearing as Lyra and Amina immediately unfurled their wings and took to the air, shooting like arrows toward the expanse of sky pocked with approaching Valkyries. Calla looked out toward the trees that circled the solemn field around them.

"They're watching us," she whispered. "I can feel their eyes."

"They're waiting for a signal," Gideon said, his voice steady, his silver eyes shrewd.

Then she heard her name again. And this time it wasn't a whisper. It was a harking.

"Calliope!"

Calla spun toward the sound of Caspian's voice, but before she could take a single step, a single breath, witches began to pour out of the woods. Hundreds. Thousands. Hundreds of thousands.

"A signal," she whispered, as she felt her inner Siphon flare to life with anticipation.

It was time to face her fate. The part of her that was so exhausted waiting for her life to really begin was ready for it. The looming omen of the Fates' War constantly hanging above her like a dark cloud, ready to drench her with pain and sorrow the moment she actually began to enjoy her life. The other part of her, the part that was sinking like a heavy stone in her stomach as she watched her fellow witches ascend onto the battlefield with twisted faces of agony, realized that she had never really understood what war meant. How it devastated. How, for the luckier ones, it tore their beings into pieces and left them bleeding corpses of unfulfilled potential at the feet of those who would be unlucky enough to survive and carry the harrowing burden of its memories.

It didn't take long for the battlefield to turn into a frenzied symphony of clashing weapons and swirling magic. To ruin lives and futures. Each person who fell, a scar on Calla's heart that she'd have to carry inside of her forever.

Somewhere in between bracing themselves for impact and the first wave of magic, she and Gideon were ripped apart. She could feel every hit and scratch he took through their bond, of course. Every rush of adrenaline as he slammed another dagger into a familiar face. The air around them grew thin as the Onyx witches fought for control of it, and she swore she could even hear Gideon's siren-like commands from somewhere to her left as she grasped her opponents' shoulders with her Rouge magic and tossed them away from her.

Calla knew when she felt her energy began to burn up too quickly that she needed to get to Gideon again. These witches were not even the Guild. They were just Lysandra's poor indebted subjects forced onto the front lines of this battle, and Calla was trying to take as much care as she possibly could incapacitating them without ever killing, but the effort was already emptying her reservoir of power. When she looked for Gideon, she could see her prince was taking the same meticulous care. Knocking out the untrained witches with ease and slipping through the frenzy before he accidentally made a move that was fatal.

Calliope dropped another witch to her feet, stepping over the body as she tried to gain her bearings. Where were their allies from the Guild? Their help?

Don't worry, Great Muse, that melodic voice whispered again. *Here they come.*

Calla felt a heavy force of magic at her back, and when she turned to face the south woods, what she saw left her in disbelief. Witches of every kind flooding toward the melee with determination. Several stallions stomped with them, making the ground beneath her feet rumble, a single rider at the helm of the brigade.

Something touched Calla's shoulder then, and she instantly whipped around, latching her Siphon onto the person. Then she noticed his Rolls of Fate. All ones. She instantly let go.

"It's going to be a pleasure fighting with you, Calliope Rosewood," Dex announced as the recognition hit her. "Eurydice and Thorne are heading out to search for where the queens are hunkering down, giving their orders. I wanted to warn you about the Terra witches before I joined them."

"Terra witches?" Calla asked as she glanced around. The only witches she could see were Onyx.

"They're in the—"

His words cut off as something sprang from the ground between them. A Terra witch, hands bloody, nails ripped to shreds, their yellowish gaze wild as it locked onto Calla and Dex. Their face was smeared with dirt, the odor clinging to them the pungent scent of petrichor and sweat. The witch lunged for Dex first. But Dex was immovable. Every hit the Terra witch made bounced off of him as if he were made of rubber. In two flicks of his wrist, the witch was lying at their feet. Dead.

"You don't have to kill them," Calla hissed.

Dex gave her an exasperated look. "This is war, sweetheart." He flicked his gaze behind her as the earth beneath them began to vibrate even more. "Son of a bitch."

Terra witches began to spring up in every direction. One after the other they joined the fray of fighting witches, and Calla and Dex found themselves circling back-to-back as they took hit after hit. She'd never experienced a Terra witch's magic before. They had the ability to shift the ground beneath her feet, making her stumble and dodge the crumbling planes of earth as she clutched the blood vessels in their minds and popped them in turn until there was a circle of bodies surrounding them.

"Incoming!" a deep, unfamiliar voice shouted somewhere behind her just as she took a rock to the temple and dropped another body.

Calla swiped at the dripping blood flowing down the side of her face as she twisted to see a fast-approaching rider leading a new legion of witches into battle, a smile on his sharp face as he paused beside them and dropped down from his horse, landing heavy on his feet. He was an Onyx witch, his coal eyes shrewd as he traced them over Calla and Dex, head to toe. His dark hair was twisted into natural locs that reached past the tops of his shoulders, his deep brown skin covered in vibrant tattoos. There was a golden hoop pierced through his septum and a gilded sword strapped across his broad chest.

The clang of metal and grunts of effort intensified around them with his arrival, and before he said who he was, Calla somehow knew.

He dipped his chin at the two of them. "The name is Apollo. I'm the fourth."

Dex gave the man a brutal smile. "It's about Godsdamned time you appeared, eh?"

Apollo smiled back as he nodded over to the witches he'd ushered in, the ones now launching themselves at their indebted brethren. "I brought some help. Hope you don't mind."

Dex looked to Calla. "You're worried about people dying? You need to find the last die. Make your final roll."

With that, the other two Blood Warriors sprang into action, Dex making a beeline out of the fray and Apollo remounting his horse to cut through the throngs of fighting witches like a steel blade. They were right. She needed to find Caspian. She needed to make that roll and summon the Fates to the havoc of their making.

Unfortunately, when Calla finally managed to clear a path before her, the familiar face that she finally spotted did not belong to Gideon or Caspian or anyone else she would have hoped to see.

No, standing before her, weapon pointed directly toward her heart, was Kestrel Whitehollow.

"Hello, Calliope Rosewood."

Kestrel's long white hair had been chopped in a way that she knew he did not approve. The edges jagged as if he had done it himself without looking. Which was precisely what had happened. This had been a punishment. A show of authority from his queen before he was made to march onto this battlefield.

"I'm sorry this is how our final paths cross," he told her.

And then his blade came down. Calla reached her arms out and grasped every ounce of blood in his body. Stopping the arch of his sword mid-swing. Her breathing grew labored as she held him there, and she could see the surprising amount of pain in his eyes as she pushed and pushed and pushed against her hold.

"You have to move," he gritted out between clenched teeth. "In three . . . two . . . one . . ."

Just as his countdown ended, she felt him snap her hold in half, and she dove to the side. She tumbled across the ground and wasn't able to right herself in time before he lifted his arms again.

I have to Siphon, she told herself. *I have to kill him. He's too skilled for me to fight hand to hand.*

But how could she do such a thing? What would that do to Gideon? It wasn't fair. None of this was fair. This is not whose blood she wanted on her hands. Not these innocent people's. Not even Kestrel's.

"Calliope, *move*," Kestrel hissed at her.

She rolled away as his blade came down again. She managed to climb back to her feet, but this time when he swung, she saw that it was going to hit. She braced herself for the impact of it, throwing her hands out to grasp hold of his blood once more, but it was unnecessary. Because just before his sword made impact, someone else's clashed against it.

Gideon's.

Gideon sent a sweeping blast of magic directly into Kestrel's core, making the man fly back. Then he turned to her.

"Replenish our energy!" he told her as he stretched his hand toward her in offering.

She clasped it and sent a burst of power through both of them, watching as the crimson light of their soul-bond flooded the battlefield.

"Get to Caspian!" Gideon demanded. "Run for him and don't stop for anything!"

Calla nodded at him as she twisted around to search for Caspian. Her eyes sliding over the chaos around her as she tried to block out the sounds of agony.

There, a whisper told her.

She whipped her head to the left, and sure enough, there was Caspian diving into the fray. She took off and didn't look back.

When Amina and Lyra finally rejoined their allies, they found most of them fallen on the ground, digging arrows out of their wings. Thankfully, Ezra had managed to get Sabine down safely, and Lyra wasted no time giving them both their orders.

"Ezra, stay at Sabine's back. For all intents and purposes, you're her wings now," Lyra ordered.

Ezra readily nodded.

Amina looked to the rest of the mending Valkyries—Sydni, Baden, and the other sixty or so brave souls in their half of the treasonous brigade who dared to defy Ignia. "We have a duty to protect our people just as the witches have a duty to protect theirs. Our goal here is to stop any more reapings. When our brethren attack, we counterattack. We will *not* pay Ignia's debt for her. We will be the undoing of the pain the tithe has caused us all these centuries."

The others nodded in reverence at her words, saluting to her plight. Lyra dipped their chin in a nod of shared respect.

Amina smirked at Lyra and Sabine in turn. "Ready, Slayers?"

Sabine let out a cry of excitement as she unsheathed her daggers and waited for Amina's next orders. Amina could see Ignia's Valkyries begin to dip and dive toward the chaos in the center of the battlefield, some rising with glowing blue spirits already clutched in their taloned hands. This was it.

Amina made to follow her allies as they summoned their wings and took off.

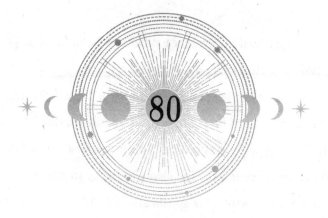

CASPIN

Caspian was running, his heart pounding so hard he thought his chest might crack open.

This is it.

He looked around him. The large wide-open field had yellow-and-red witch hazel littering the horizon line he was racing toward just as he remembered so vividly from his demon's oak vision.

"Cass!" someone yelled.

Caspian skidded to a stop. He looked around wildly for the owner of the voice.

"Caspian! Here!"

Then he saw her. Calla was running straight for him, her long, dark hair whipping behind her.

"Caspian, hurry! Throw me the die!"

"Stop them!" another voice screeched. One of Lysandra's guards.

But he knew they wouldn't be able to stop him. Knew exactly what was coming next.

He easily dodged two faceless figures and kept moving, focusing on Calla getting closer and closer. Just as he was about to reach her, a figure stepped in front of him, making him halt so suddenly he almost barreled to the ground. And without a second thought, Caspian lifted his left arm and flung the die over the shoulder of the man that was blocking him. Calla lurched forward and snatched the die out of the air as someone else screeched his name behind him.

And he finally knew who that voice belonged to: Amina.

His eyes searched for her frantically, and when they finally found her, he gave her one last wink.

Then a sword went right through his heart.

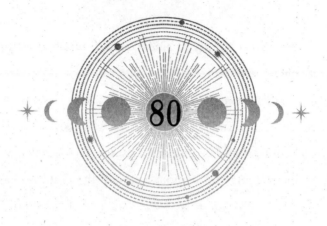

AMINA

Amina started forward. And then she heard his name.

"Cass!" someone yelled.

Amina halted her stride as she searched for the origin of that cry behind her. It was the Siphon's voice.

"Caspian! Here!" Calla yelled again.

There.

Amina spotted Calla as she barreled straight for Caspian.

"Caspian, hurry! Throw me the die!"

"Stop them!" another voice screeched. An Onyx guard. One that was moving in too close to Cass, undetected.

Lyra called out her name, but Amina's feet were already moving. No. No. She was not done with him yet.

As she moved closer, he moved farther away. Getting closer and closer to Calla. Just as he was about to reach her, the undetected guard slid into his path, and Amina pushed herself as fast as she could to reach him. She yelled his name as he lifted his arm and flung something over to Calla, the sound of her wild voice almost unrecognizable to her own ears.

She watched as he searched for her, and when he finally found her, the Godsdamned witch *winked*.

Then a sword went right through his heart.

Calla didn't think twice as she lunged for the guard responsible for that killing blow. Her talons reaching out to shred his throat to pieces, snatching Caspian out of the way of the bastard's falling body before he could flatten either of them to the ground. Cass tried to speak as Amina worked to yank the sword from his chest, but with the blade came his impaled heart.

"Fuck," she cried as she realized what she'd done. "Fuck. Fuck. Fuck."

Cass laughed. He *laughed*.

"That's all right, Valkyrie." He smiled softly as his eyes began to flutter shut. "I always knew this was how it was going to end. Tell my friends I—"

"No, you annoying bastard," she snarled at him. "Don't you *dare* . . ."

But it was too late. She could see the glowing edges of his soul already begin to rise from his body. To free itself of this linear plane.

"No," she whispered as she reached out before she even realized what she was doing. Her nails glowed the same haunting blue of his life force now, snatching the wispy essence of his being out of the air before it could escape her clutches and bringing it to the amulet around her neck. When the warmth of his soul settled into her Esprit, his body went fully limp and cold on the ground before her.

She leaned forward and pressed her lips to his forehead as a single tear ran down her cheek.

"I'll make sure you get home, witch," she vowed.

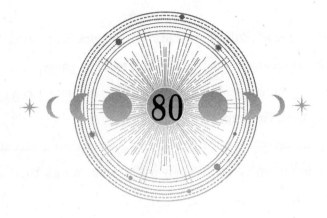

GIDEON

As many times as Gideon had imagined coming to blows with Kestrel these last few months, this was not how he wanted it to go down. They were a match made in heaven—at fighting. Every blow Kestrel would deliver, Gideon was ready to block. And vice versa. He was the commander's protégé after all. They'd have been locked in a death match for hours if it weren't for the fact that Gideon could grow tired but Kestrel couldn't.

"It's Myrea's orders," Kestrel gritted out as he swung his sword down once again, making Gideon spin out of the way just in the nick of time.

Gideon had to make sure he didn't get himself injured and put Calliope in any additional danger. One poorly timed move and it could be a domino effect of tragedy.

"We aren't allowed to stop going until our bones grind themselves to dust from the effort," Kestrel continued as he released another bone-shaking blow.

Gideon, however, didn't have that sort of magical motivation. Which meant his muscles were screaming at him to take a pause.

"Gideon, you have to kill me," Kestrel choked out. "I can't stop. I won't stop. Until I'm dead."

"No," Gideon spat as he rallied his energy once more and sent a shot of wind into Kestrel's core. It barely made the man rock back a single step. "I will not kill you."

Kestrel's mouth twisted into a grim smile. "Why not? It isn't like you haven't wanted to before."

"This is different," Gideon argued, striking back in full force.

On and on, dancing around each other, careful not to upset the delicate balance of the game between them. Just like they had in their previous relationship.

And then, finally, Gideon made a mistake. It was a small one, an anticipated block to the left instead of matching Kestrel's feign to the right. In seconds the commander utilized that mistake to sweep Gideon's feet from beneath him and pin him to the ground. Blade hovering above his former lover's heart.

"Kill me," Kestrel demanded with a sneer as the tip of his blade began to sink into Gideon's chest.

"No," Gideon snarled back, trying to dislodge Kestrel's body off his.

"*Kill me, you fucking fool,*" Kestrel growled. "If you die, she dies. It needs to be me."

At the mention of Calliope, Gideon's heart raged with the pain of the situation the Fates had put him in. But Kestrel was right. If it came down to it, he would never let Calliope die.

"Ah." Kestrel finally seemed to sigh with relief. "There's your sense. If you won't do it for me, you know you'd always do it for her."

For the first time, Kestrel spoke those words without bitterness.

"I love you, Gideon Black," Kestrel murmured. "I hope the two of you never have to part. I hope the rest of your eternity together is filled with light and happiness. So much happiness."

Gideon watched as Kestrel accepted his fate. Watched as his hand lifted up his blade toward the commander's heart. And then he watched as someone *else* ripped the organ from Kestrel's chest.

Kestrel and Gideon looked over with disbelief as they found Delphine—*Delphine*—standing there with the beating organ clutched in her hand.

"A promise is a promise." She nodded at Kestrel.

The only way to describe the commander's face as he looked at the siren was one of deep gratitude. With that, Delphine disappeared as quickly as she'd come, leaving Gideon to bid a final farewell to his former partner alone.

"I love you, too," Gideon whispered as the shine of Kestrel's eyes began to fade. And with that single admission, Gideon felt Kestrel's spirit finally find peace.

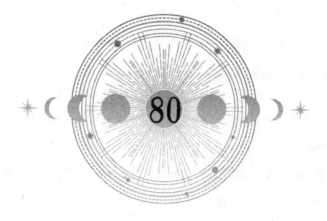

DELPHINE

Delphine was still not convinced they ought to have let Hannah near the battlefield, but her girlfriend—something she still had not gotten tired of saying—had threatened to never forgive her if she didn't let her onto the battlefield. The problem was that the moment Hannah stepped foot into the fray, Myrea's magic took ahold of her.

Delphine saw it right away, the abnormal way Hannah's body went taut, the way her face became strained as she tried to fight the hold. But it was no use. Her feet would not cooperate, would only carry her deeper and deeper into the fight, her depthless black eyes becoming glassy each time she spotted an opponent and poised to attack.

Delphine became Hannah's shadow. No one got within three feet of her witch lest they wanted to feel what it was like for her to claw them to shreds. She tried to use her siren's song as much as she could, keeping those around them at bay as Hannah continued to fight Myrea's hold.

All the while fending herself from Hannah's attacks. Because as she kept the others back, she became the closest enemy.

Somewhere in the distance, Delphine heard the shout of a familiar name, the scream of a familiar voice. But her eyes didn't leave Hannah for a moment.

"C'mon, baby," Delphine encouraged, her magical influence leaking into her voice as she spoke. "Fight it for me. You're more powerful than her. You can do things that bitch queen would never be able to imagine."

For a moment, Hannah's actions faltered, but before hope could take root in Delphine's heart, Hannah sent a blast of power in her direction again.

Delphine was about to try singing one more time when a flurry of movement caught the corner of her eye. Kestrel and Gideon were locked in a death grip, and Kestrel had a knife perched directly over Gideon's heart.

Godsdammit.

"Don't move," Delphine ordered the circle of witches surrounding her and Hannah with as much magic as she could manage to muster. They all froze.

In a blink, Delphine slinked from the circle of frozen bodies and made her way toward Kestrel's back. Without a second thought, she reached through the commander's flesh and grasped the beating organ within his chest. The deed was done in seconds.

Kestrel met her eyes with relief.

"A promise is a promise." She nodded at him.

She didn't waste a second as she returned to Hannah, but when she found her girlfriend, it was not in the same state that she'd left her. Seconds. She'd been gone for seconds.

And in that time Hannah had already transformed.

The witch she knew was gone. Replaced with a being exploding with dark power. Dark magic. Black veins spiderwebbing over every inch of her skin as inky black magic leaked into the air around them.

It was the return of the necromancer.

CALLIOPE

Calla was running so fast her heartbeats barely had enough time to catch up with her pace.

This is it.

"Cass!" she yelled as she made her way toward the witch.

Caspian skidded to a stop, searching for her in the crowd.

"Caspian! Here!" she called again.

Then he saw her.

"Caspian, hurry! Throw me the die!"

"Stop them!" someone yelled up ahead.

She ignored it all and kept running, Gideon's voice in her mind telling her to stop for nothing.

She watched as Caspian dodged past two witches to get to her, not missing a step as he pushed himself faster and faster. They were so close. Just as he was about to reach her, someone stepped in front of him, blocking her view. But that didn't stop Cass. She watched as he flung the die over the other witch's shoulder. Calla dove forward, her breath caught in her throat as she reached out—

—and snagged the die out of the air.

The moment the Fates' Die hit her palm, everything around her quieted.

The entire world stilled.

Power pulsed from the tiny magic cube in her hand, beckoning her to complete her final roll.

It's time to make your move, Calliope Rosewood.

Calla took a deep breath and tossed the die to the ground.

It rolled, once, twice, three times.

Then it settled.

Six red dots smiled up at her as a burst of gold-and-scarlet light emanated through the battlefield. Time stopped, and for a single blissful moment, there was nothing.

And then, a chorus of laughter.

It's time for the real fun to begin.

The Fates were here.

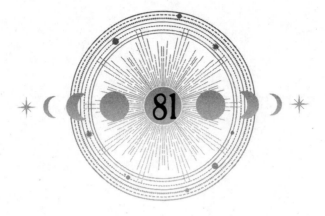

The threads of Fate are such fragile little things when they become so tangled. And so incredibly formidable when you forge them yourself.

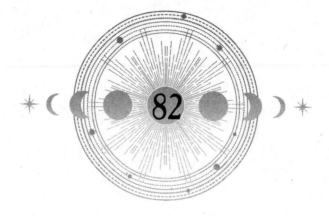

82

Gideon needed to get to her.

Everyone around him was still shedding blood, despite whatever sort of magic had just been unleashed around them. The magic hold the queens had over them would not allow them to stop. Would make them continue on and on until they met the same end as Kestrel.

None of it mattered to him at this moment, though. All he cared about was her. He could feel her heart thundering through their bond, the burn of the last six etching itself into his arm now that she'd made their final roll.

He couldn't see anything past the tumultuous crowd except a flood of golden light, and he knew that's where he'd find her. The Fates had arrived.

Gideon pushed himself faster and faster. Someone called his name, and for a split second, he shifted his eyes in their direction. Thorne.

"What's happening?" Thorne called to him as he stood, casually, among the combat.

Alarms went off in Gideon's head immediately, and he skidded to a halt.

"Thorne," he warned. "The final roll was made! You aren't—"

Just before Gideon could get his final words out, Thorne's mouth formed a little O shape as someone's blade severed through the tendons in his neck. Gideon's stomach churned at the sight, deep sorrow sinking into his core as he stumbled another step toward the man. He could barely keep from heaving as Thorne's headless corpse dropped to the ground, the macabre sight a spear through his emotional armor.

Gideon scrambled closer, digging his hands into the dirt as if he could easily make a grave in such a situation. He gritted his teeth together as a roar of rage ripped from his throat and the blood-soaked soil wedged itself beneath his fingernails.

They hadn't known each other long, but Thorne had been kind and helpful and *good*. He deserved a proper burial.

Someone tackled him from his right, pinning him to the ground with a grunt. Gideon didn't hesitate as he wildly clawed at his assailant, wrapping a rope of wind around their neck and strangling them until they turned blue. When the witch's body went limp, Gideon shoved it aside shakily and got back to his feet as someone else let out a battle cry and lunged toward him.

This is why you can't linger, he told himself. *You have to keep going.*

Gideon disposed of two more bodies before turning back to Thorne's lifeless corpse and whispering an ode of respect in a language long dead.

May your soul find peace, Thorne.

Hannah felt death in every inch of the air around her. Her heart was pumping magic out in double time as it awakened in her with its full force. She felt death in every breath, in every fiber of her being.

She was becoming death herself.

When the transformation was complete, she felt the hold of the Rouge Queen's power *snap*, crumbling away until there was nothing left. And as soon as she was released, she unleashed herself onto the battlefield. Her magic plunged into the earth around her, calling to the fallen that littered the ground at her feet. Rows and rows of undead beings clambered forward, a taste for more death swelling in their tongues. A single flick of her wrist and they lunged, shredding anybody that did not move out of the way quick enough. She nimbly wove the threads of darkness in her grip until she had a tapestry of death, and then she unleashed the Hellish fate across the battlefield.

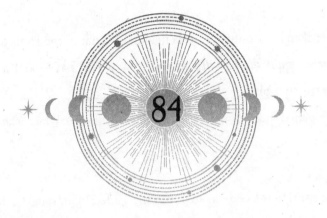

When Calla stepped into the gilded light, she felt like a God herself.

Hello, Calliope Rosewood, the Fates greeted her. Or, at least, three of them did. The golden figures were standing side by side, awaiting her audience patiently. The creepy masks adorning their faces just as they had on the statues of their likeness in the afterlife.

It's so nice to finally see you in person.

"Aren't there supposed to be four of you?" she asked as her heart thundered in her chest. "Did your cohort have some sort of prior engagement or something else that made them too busy to see to the war you've been waiting centuries for?"

A chime of laughter. Then, *Something like that.*

Calla felt the corners of her lips tilt down. She didn't like that answer. When they didn't say anything else, however, she became restless.

"Well? What now?" she demanded.

You tell us, Great Muse. How would you like this to end?

She rocked back onto her heels in shock. What in the Hells did they mean, *how would she like this to end*? She would have liked it to not begin in the first place.

She opened her mouth to say something else when she heard *his* voice.

"Calliope."

Calla spun to see Gideon step into the gilded light, relief on his face as he strutted forward to sweep her into his arms.

"Thank the Gods," he whispered into her hair.

You're welcome, Prince.

Gideon's eyes flicked to the Fates in disbelief before shifting back to Calla in question.

She shook her head in frustration. "I don't know what we're supposed to do. All of the dice have been rolled. All of our cards have been played."

"And yet a war still rages behind us," Gideon finished for her before turning to the Fates and ordering, "When does it end for you? When every person on the queens' sides are wasted? Are you going to make sure we claim every death before you call the end?"

She began the war. She can stop it.

Calla nearly choked. They were trying to put this burden on *her*? Flames of rage erupted in her belly at the notion. Gideon remained steady at her side.

"Whatever you choose to do, I'm right behind you," he reminded her.

She tilted her chin up. "This ends now."

She turned on her heels, plunging out of the filtered golden light and into—

—complete and utter darkness.

"What the Hells?" she rasped in shock.

And then she smelled it. The charred smell of dark magic. She and Gideon exchanged a loaded look.

"Hannah," Calla breathed.

Before she could make her way farther into the inky mist, however, someone ripped her sideways by the tendrils of her hair. Gideon snarled as he reached out for her, but it was too late.

"I wouldn't make any sudden moves, Prince. Not unless you're both ready to part with your hearts right now."

Myrea held Calla at arm's length as she stared Gideon down.

"Let. Her. Go," Gideon demanded, using the full effect of his siren's voice.

Myrea laughed. "I see you've discovered a little something about your lineage. Unfortunately for you, such a trick will not work on me twice. Your little stunt back at my palace made me realize I needed to take extra precautions when dealing with the two of you and your insolence."

"I'm surprised those precautions don't extend to staying off this battlefield," Calla retorted. "I thought that's what all your defenseless subjects were for, to keep your hands from getting dirty."

"Yes, well, if you want something done right, you have to do it yourself," Myrea sneered back. "Lysandra was too sentimental with her whelp, and it cost me having your heart on a spike when I wanted it. But she isn't here now and it's my turn to call all of the shots."

As the Rouge Queen spoke, something in the air began to shift. The darkness had slowly begun to grow more . . . palpable. And even Calla's magic could feel something shift inside of her.

Hannah's darkness had been fully unleashed—that much was obvious—but something about it prodded a memory out of the depths of her mind. Something about why Myrea was so afraid of necromancy.

Calla flicked her eyes over to Gideon. "They said I could stop this, right?"

Gideon's face was strained as he watched her, the stress in his body refusing to dissipate as long as she was in Myrea's grasp. But he answered, "Yes."

"They chose me to end this. So I will."

Myrea yanked Calla's hair until her back was completely flush with the queen's chest, the woman's hand reaching up to wrap around her throat like a vise. Everything around them was shrouded in shadow, the details of the ongoing war blurred as the darkness grew thicker and thicker.

"You are not the chosen one, Calliope Rosewood," Myrea hissed in her ear. "You are the cursed one."

Calla tried to gulp a breath of air, and the hand around her throat tightened.

"Calla," Gideon said desperately. Her eyes went right to him. "You have the power here. You know what you can do."

She felt Myrea shake with laughter.

"Please," the queen cackled cruelly. "She's a pathetic—"

Before the woman could finish her sentence, Calla decided how she wanted this to end. She felt her Rouge magic lock onto every drop of blood in Myrea's veins, and a second later, her inner Siphon pulled with all its might. Then all she saw was red.

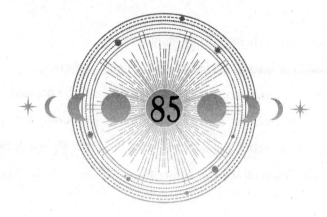

H annah felt the girl's sorrow. Heard her desperate cries as she begged for Hannah to stop. But it was too late.

Hannah's army of undead ravaged everything around them. Her power so thick that it was severing the connections of others' magic. She watched the scene before her through the ice of her emotions. Watched how witches that were relentlessly spilling blood moments before suddenly began to wake up as if they had been sleepwalking this entire time. Dropping their weapons as her darkness snaked through the air around them, slowly sucking the life out of each of their bodies, their magic. Turning everything so very numb.

Witches were crawling through the dirt, missing limbs and eyes, half dead as they tried to resist the call for more bloodshed. But their queen's magic had a relentless hold. Their pleas did not matter. Their will was not enough. The six little numbers embedded into their arms were the only thing they could obey.

But not Hannah. She obeyed nothing but the darkness inside of her now. And it was finally calling her home. Demanding to reclaim her blood and bones.

The burning started in her fingertips first, before the fire spread all the way down her limbs and into her core, and she knew then that the darkness was slowly consuming its host.

Enough, a small, quiet voice said from somewhere within. *That's enough. You've done enough. It's time to stop now.*

Hannah felt as the hands began to reach up from the earth and slide along her skin. Start to drag her down.

Down.

Down.

Her love's desperate cries caressing her until she was pulled deep beneath the earth. And then there was finally, blessedly, nothing.

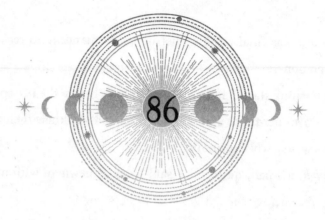

86

There was only one thing that could make Ezra leave Sabine's side in this calamity. And that was his shot at the killing blow.

From above the battlefield, he could see a strange fog slowly fold itself among the fighting. Witches on both sides began to pause, unaware of where the dark magic might have been coming from. But Ezra knew precisely what was happening.

This time no one had been able to stop Hannah.

"The dead," Sabine whispered as she peered down with him, leaning forward in his arms. "They're . . . rising."

"Necromancy," Ezra said solemnly.

"Is the battle . . . stopping?" she wondered in disbelief.

Ezra was shocked to see she was right. Something about Hannah's magic was extinguishing the fight. Even for the Valkyries who had been reaping, Hannah's magic was making it hard to see the glow of the souls.

Ezra was about to say they should find Calla and his brother, but before he could, he spotted something. Someone. All the way across the clearing, hiding like a coward among the shadows of the trees.

His breathing faltered.

"What's wrong?" Sabine demanded when she noticed the change in his demeanor.

He swallowed and then nodded toward the tree line. "My mother."

"What are you—"

But before she could finish her question, he was diving for the ground. Specifically, for where he spotted Lyra standing in wait as they assessed the odd turn of events unfolding around them.

Ezra placed Sabine on her feet next to the other Valkyrie and said, "I'll be right back."

Sabine let out a shrill protest as he took off once more, but he ignored it. He didn't need her to see the person he was about to turn into.

When he reached the edge of the forest, he landed heavily on his feet. It was quiet. Nothing but the ruffling of leaves and the sound of his heart pounding in his ears as he scanned the shadows for her.

He felt her before he saw her.

"My, how you've changed, Ezra Black," her saccharine voice purred as she stepped into his view.

She looked as she always had to him. Cold. Unyielding.

"Mother," he greeted, his voice taut with the deception of that title being applied to her.

"I don't believe I've given you enough credit," she said.

"You never have," he retorted. "But what for, specifically, this time?"

"I thought I had built you up to crumble," she admitted to him. "But it seems you've gone and rebuilt yourself. Tell me, what kind of heart is beating in your chest now?"

"One that's been untouched by you," he said.

She huffed a laugh but didn't deign to respond.

When he had enough of her silence, he finally let out the anger he'd been harboring since the day Gideon had told him why Ezra had been born.

"Why?" he demanded to know.

She didn't seem to need any elaboration. "Everything I did was for him. He's my son."

"I was your son, too," Ezra spat.

Lysandra shrugged. "Not in the same way. By birth, sure. But the moment I had him, I made a vow to do anything and everything to keep him safe. Even if that meant having a second child to fulfill such a promise. You're not a parent. You wouldn't understand."

Ezra laughed darkly. "That's bullshit, and you know it. *Such bullshit.* This isn't about some sick, twisted vow you made to keep Gideon safe—you tried to kill him, too, remember? This is about your sadistic need to be in control of everything and everyone around you. Your inability to love things properly because you don't value such a thing. You value power. You're a shell of a person and nothing Gideon, or I, could have ever done would have pleased you."

Lysandra smirked. "Is that all you've got? I gave up caring what the world thought of me ages ago, darling. I have no interest in being loved.

Such a concept bores me. It's so very . . . mortal. Everything fades with time. Everything. What one day seems like a passionate, life-altering affair soon becomes a stale, drill routine. The only things we are left with when we die are our names and our legacies. Gideon was to be my legacy. So I put all my effort into him. And look. After today, everyone will remember his name. When no one had even seemed to know that you *died*."

Ezra wanted to vomit at her words. At the ice in them. The . . . truth in them.

"That's right, my darling," she purred. "Even when I do not win—I win. The war will be over before either of us know it, and even if I am stripped of my power and kingdom, my legacy will remain. I will never die."

Ezra was upon her in a blink, raising his forearm against her throat and slamming her back against a nearby tree. Her face twisted into a scowl now.

"I will make sure your name is never spoken by a single soul ever again. You and your sisters will be indistinguishable from one another. Nothing more than the boring, tired villains of a child's tale. Centuries from now, the only thing people will remember about this war are those who gave their lives to save innocent people."

When she tried to speak, he pressed his arm farther into her windpipe.

"And you're wrong about how things fade. About love," he told her. "Time might change all things—but change is not always bad.

Sometimes we change into things that are much better than what we started with. And it's never too late for that. I imagine you wouldn't understand how love can change from passion into companionship because none of your partners have ever found you tolerable enough to find out. Is that why Gideon's father left you?"

A blast of power shot through his core and sent him sprawling to the ground. He didn't stay down long, however. Rolling back to his feet, he watched her carefully as she began to circle him, teeth bared.

"Don't speak of Gideon's father," she seethed.

"Sore spot?" Ezra laughed. "I have a friend—well, *friend* is a loose term—who met him recently, you know. Spent time with him. Mentioned how much he *loathed* you."

He might have been exaggerating the details he'd heard from Delphine, but the satisfaction he felt when his mother's pallid complexion turned bright red made him grateful for his extraordinary poker face.

"I'll kill you, boy," she seethed. "You don't think I will?"

"Try," he taunted, spreading his arms wide in invitation.

She lunged.

And he unleashed the beast crawling beneath his skin.

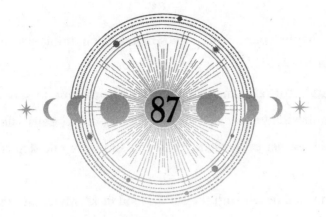

87

Myrea's blood filled the air like mist, and her hold on Calla instantly slackened. Calla spun toward her.

"What the Hells?" Myrea gasped as she fell to her knees, her legs giving out beneath her as Calla continued to siphon her energy. "You shouldn't be able to take directly from me when the others are still standing...."

"I am no longer the simple nightmare you once had," Calla told her. "The daughter of your past lover, a symbol of everything you could never have. No, I am so much worse than that now. I am my mothers' revenge." Calla leaned down until her eyes were level with the queen's. "I am the curse the Fates themselves chose for you—a girl with a raging heart. And your inevitable demise."

Myrea gritted her teeth as she looked up at Calla with disdain. "You won't kill me."

Calla felt a giggle bubble up in her throat. "What makes you say that?"

"It's not in your nature. Your morals. You think you're better than that."

"I think if it takes me doing one villainous thing to save anyone else from having to bear the burden, then I'll do it," Calla said as she smoothed out her expression. "I kill you and we're one step closer to this war being over."

"And you'll be left with the Fates. Good luck," Myrea sneered. "My sisters and I gave you all *everything*."

"Evil people are capable of good things. Good people are capable of evil things. What I'm realizing now is that maybe being left with the Fates isn't such a bad ending. Fate is the architect of an infinite number of futures. But we possess the tools to build those futures ourselves. And I think, had I been in your position all that time ago, I would have built a much different one than this."

Myrea's breathing grew heavy as her lavender eyes began to plead.

Calla smiled. "I think such a momentous turn in history deserves an audience, though, don't you?"

Calla turned to the battlefield, noting that Hannah's magic had seemed to slowly dissipate, blowing away on the wind like smokey will-o'-the-wisps. Calla raised her hands and reached out with her magic. Every ounce of it that she had left in her body.

She grabbed on to every being she could feel before her. Every ounce of life she was able to hold. And she made everything stop. She turned their bodies until they were standing at attention.

Then she latched on to Myrea. She wrapped her Siphon around the queen's poisonous blood. Contracting her hold and making it pulse beneath the woman's skin. They both watched as the veins spiderwebbing beneath Myrea's pale ivory skin pulsed painfully.

Then Calla began to pull, and Myrea began to scream.

"*I surrender!*" Myrea choked out as Calla began to rip her insides to shreds.

But Calla didn't stop. She clawed and clawed and clawed until the queen's skin tore itself apart, until her blood swirled in the air as thick as the dark magic had before. Until there was nothing left except the woman's black heart.

You started this, Calla told herself. *And now you're ending it.*

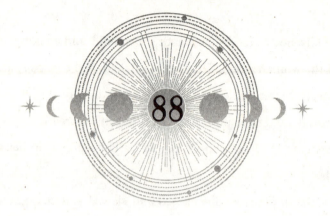

Ezra hadn't thought transforming into a dragon would be so... colorful. But with these new eyes, everything around him was almost so vibrant it was painful. He watched Lysandra through his new gaze, smelled the fear that soiled her scent as she stared back at him in utter shock.

He chuffed at her, smoke swirling up from his monstrous snout as he poised himself above her with the promise of pain. A roar bellowed from deep inside of him as she cowered. Before he struck, he gave her one final chance to speak her last words.

"You have never been my son," she whispered to him.

At those words, all the fury inside him deflated. He blinked at her, once, twice. He stretched his maw open, demonstrating exactly how easy it would be to crush her inside his sharp jaws. One snap of his teeth and it would be over. Forever.

Instead, he folded. Transforming back into his human form was a lot more painful.

"I've never been your son," he repeated. Then he laughed. "I have never been more grateful for anything you've ever said to me in my entire life."

He shook a hand through his hair as she watched him, stoic.

"I'm not going to kill you," he decided. "I don't ever want to think about you again. And killing you would mean that you'd always be the one and only life I've ever taken, and you don't deserve to take up that sort of space in my mind."

With that, Ezra nodded, pleased with his decision, and made to turn away.

"Luckily, I don't have the same qualms as our dear Ezra," a bright voice suddenly rang out.

Ezra whipped back around to find Sabine slinking out of the dark like a phantom and launching her talons right into Lysandra's chest. Lysandra shrieked in shock as she watched Sabine reap her very soul from her body. When the glowing bluish essence of the Onyx Queen had completely torn away from the lifeless corpse, Sabine fished out one of the amber necklaces he saw many of the Valkyries wearing today.

"*There,*" Sabine said proudly as she showed Ezra the now-glowing amulet. "This way we can wait for your conscience to ease up and decide how to torture her later."

Ezra stared at Sabine in awe.

Sabine squirmed a bit. "What?"

In two strides, Ezra had her wrapped in his arms and was pulling her face to his to give her a passionate, life-altering kiss.

When he finally pulled back for air, he stated, "We're together. You and I."

She scoffed at him. "What makes you think that?"

"I love you," he told her. "I think you might be the greatest gift I've ever received."

Her cheeks flushed with his admission, her swollen mouth falling open in disbelief. But before she could say anything insulting, or crude, or pull out a dagger, he kissed her again. Thankful every second that he had died all that time ago in order to feel this alive right now.

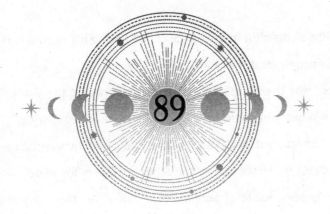

89

The moment Calla let go of Myrea's essence, the Fates decided to emerge from their shroud of light to face the wreckage. Their audience did not bow or cheer or even riot. Everyone simply stood, as wonderstruck by Calla's carnage as they were by the faces of the Gods.

And when the Gods themselves turned to Calla, their eyes were filled with respect.

The war is over, they declared. *All of the queens have fallen or surrendered. Your Blood Warriors have claimed their victories.*

Calla suddenly felt an intense vibrating warmth prick the hairs on the back of her neck and glanced over her shoulder to find Gideon approaching.

When he reached her, he took her face in his hands, his silver gaze filled with pride as he admired her. "You truly went all in."

"I said I would," she whispered.

He dipped his chin in deference before letting her go and turning to face their people, and the Gods, by her side.

"What was the point of this?" someone cried at the Gods. "All of this loss? When you could have had the queens to begin with!"

The Fates turned to Calla now, as if she could answer the question. But she didn't understand it either. So many fallen, for what?

Your queens made a bargain that relied on them proving they deserved their power, the Fates answered. *It is clear now that they did not. If they had, they might have decided to give up their own instead of allowing their people to do so for them.*

"Are the other queens dead as well?" Calla demanded.

"Althea has been captured by the Guild," someone at the front answered her question. Someone decorated like a commander of the very army he spoke of. "When the units revealed they were not under Lysandra's influence, she was given the option of surrendering or being torn to pieces. No one has seen Lysandra, however."

"We have," a familiar voice quipped.

Calla spun to see Sabine approaching looking awfully . . . cheery. Ezra was right on the Valkyrie's heels.

"I got the Onyx Queen's soul right here, in fact." Sabine held up an Esprit.

Calla tensed as she waited for Gideon's reaction, but the prince only nodded in Ezra's direction. A signal of abject approval. Ezra smiled.

As part of the queens' bargains, it is now time for all witches with completed Rolls of Fate to be stripped of their magic. The rest of you, however... congratulations. Your curses have been lifted.

No one cheered. Okay, a few people cheered, but for the most part everyone was utterly silent.

"It's not fair," Calla seethed at the Gods, stepping forward. "None of us made this bargain with you. We were all born into something we didn't ask for. It's not fair to punish our people like this while the queens get to escape in death."

Fairness is not what the three of us tend to do, the Fates told her. *You'll want our fourth kin for that.*

"That would require them to be here—" Gideon began before a familiar grating voice cut him off.

"And so we meet again, fated ones."

The rasped words came from across the clearing. Everyone turned to face the ancient one in tandem, those closest to the monstrous being cringing away in terror as they parted the massive crowd.

The Witch Eater.

"Of course," Gideon muttered.

"You're the fourth Fate?" Calla carped, hands balling at her sides.

"For now, at least," the Witch Eater confirmed.

"What the Hells does *for now* mean?" Gideon demanded.

"I was not born a God," the Witch Eater revealed. "Rather I was made into one. By the last Fate who was in my place. And so on. I chose my title, the Witch Eater, when it was decided that I would be the one to consume the witches' magic after this war. Once my job is complete, it will be time to pass the responsibility to the next being who will assume my role."

Gideon came to the conclusion before Calla did. "You mean you hope that Calliope will..."

Calla balked. "Never. I will never be one of you—you *monsters*."

"Monsters? For offering bargains to those in need? For keeping true to our end of the stipulations?"

"People *died* today," Calla spat. "And now you want to take their magic, too! Yes. You are monsters."

"Well, I suppose, perhaps, we can offer you a loophole of sorts," the Witch Eater said as they looked to their cohorts, who nodded agreeably. "I must have a certain amount of power in order to release you all from this bargain. The sort of power that you possess yourself, Great Muse."

"You want me... to sacrifice my magic?" she whispered.

Gideon sucked in a breath, like he could feel the turmoil that bled through her at such a thought. Not after all she'd been through to finally accept it. Not just accept it, love it. Love herself. She couldn't. She...

She looked out into the faces of her people staring back at her. Faces that at one point might have sneered at her mismatched eyes and her touch. To find... hope.

Calla swallowed. "I..." Her words trailed off.

After a pregnant beat, the Witch Eater prompted, "Yes?"

Calla took a deep breath and squared her shoulders. "No, you cannot have my magic. Well, not only my magic."

"Go on," the Witch Eater urged, and Calla could swear the ancient one was smiling.

"Instead of taking all of the magic from those who completed their Rolls before the war... could you take only a bit of magic from... each of us?"

A murmur broke out across the field, and Calla looked back at Gideon. He dipped his head in encouragement, the silver in his eyes swirling with pride as he waited for her next move.

Calla turned back to witch eater, lifting her chin and declaring, "I know what the queens have done to us over all these centuries—prepared to turn us against one another, taken away those we love because of things we couldn't control. But we can control *this*. We can decide the Fates of our people for ourselves."

The Witch Eater waited expectantly for the reactions of the others, but no one said anything. They barely even blinked.

The Witch Eater laughed. "People are fickle, Great Muse. Why don't I offer you one last boon?"

Calla felt defeated as everyone continued to watch the ordeal in silence. How could they not be blazing with motivation? How could they not be as ready to jump into a new reality as she was?

"Take my place with the Fates, and I'll give you all a single-month deferral on your decision before I claim your magic."

Calla sucked in a breath.

"Calla, don't." Ezra shook his head as he stepped toward her. "If these assholes don't want to take the good grace of what you're already offering, you certainly don't need to give up any more of yourself to the Fates."

Calla bit her lip and swung her gaze to Gideon next.

He shrugged. "Wherever you go, I follow. It's your choice. Always."

Ezra scowled at his brother. "If they take her to the afterlife—"

"She will not be confined to the afterlife. She will only be confined to her responsibilities as the Fates' keeper. As long as she continues her plight—whatever she might choose—and agrees to choose her successor when the time comes, she will have as normal of an eternity as any of us are really promised," the Witch Eater explained.

"What else?" Calla demanded now.

The Witch Eater tilted their head in question.

"What else would I be sacrificing? Would my appearance turn into yours? Would I be unable to see my friends, my partner, live by the parameters I choose? What *else*?"

The Witch Eater shook their head. "My appearance had nothing to do with my position—but that's another story for another time. You would be able to see your friends, your prince, as much as you pleased. More, in fact, given the added abilities you will gain."

"Added abilities?" Gideon questioned.

"She'll be as close to a God as anyone who isn't born one could be," the Witch Eater confirmed. "Naturally, that comes with a few perks, Prince."

Ezra, who had looked rather put out by this entire conversation until now, suddenly looked thoughtful. Sabine laughed next to him.

Calla looked at Gideon one last time. "Anywhere?"

"Everywhere," he replied. No hesitation.

Calla looked back to the Witch Eater and said, "All right."

Make me a God.

The Fates laughed in delight as they swarmed her, and before she knew it, she was being transported away.

When Calla opened her eyes, she found herself back at the foot of the stone steps in the afterlife, the ones she and Gideon had refused to climb in favor of finding Ezra in the Valley of Souls. Now, instead of Gideon at her side, there was the Witch Eater. The rest of the Fates, however, were nowhere to be seen.

"We will climb all one thousand steps together, girl," the Witch Eater told her. "Now is the time you decide on your plight. What you might want to bring to your new world."

Calla took a deep breath as they stepped onto the first of the marble steps. She noticed this time that there were no gilded threads draped around her.

"You do not have the same sort of life force when you become a God," the Witch Eater explained. "Though you were immortal before, that was only in health and lifespan. Now you will be immortal in all the ways that are invulnerable. Nigh, unperishable."

She was quiet for a moment as they continued their way up the stairs, considering what she might want to ask next. "What was your plight? Besides taking away all of our magic?"

The Witch Eater's clear, glassy eyes seemed almost thoughtful. "I wanted to keep power only where it was deserved. Change is the way of the young—it is important to believe in things so strongly when you are forming your sense of self, but as you age, see the true nature of people for what it is, you realize that you cannot control things the way you desperately wish to. So you transform yourself first, become the example you wish to see, and hope you inspire others to follow. I was born a fae, you know."

No, Calla didn't know, though this news somehow didn't shock her. The Witch Eater had always seemed to speak in riddles to her.

"I ended up courtless because someone with too much power did not wield it responsibly. I thought the Fates hated me, too. More so, maybe. And I wanted change. Desperately. When destiny came knocking on my door, I took advantage of it. The Fates let me know what their next bargains were, their next game. And I became the Witch Eater. The being who would consume the power of the newly made witches if their power grew to corrupt them. And, as you know, it did."

"Do you regret your decision?" she wondered as the top of the stairs slowly came into view.

"Regret is not something one as old as I can feel," they said. "A better question would be do I think I did everything I could with the position I was given?"

"And?" she prompted.

They turned to look at her. "I picked you out myself. When Gideon's mother allowed him to die, for that single split second that I had to pick another soul to become the final Blood Warrior, I chose you. I was speaking true when I said the two of you were never supposed to cross paths. But you've always derailed Fate, haven't you, Calliope Rosewood? And, oh, the pair the two of you have made."

Calla gaped at the ancient one, stunned. "Does that mean . . . *Gideon* was the true—"

"Sixth Blood Warrior, yes," the Witch Eater finished in confirmation. "And despite his shifted fate, he still managed to find his way back to that very title. Because we always find our true destinies even when we are determined to avoid them, don't we?"

Calla was silent the rest of their walk to the top of the stairs. What was it that she believed in more than anything else? That she'd want to spend an entire eternity devoting herself to?

When they reached the other Fates, the Witch Eater went to stand by their side.

"Calliope Lillian Rosewood," the Witch Eater stated. "What is the title you will choose for yourself?"

Calla thought about everything she'd been through since starting this journey. Her friends. Gideon. Her mothers. Her magic.

She looked down at her hands, and out of the corner of her eye she spotted the heart-shaped jewel shining in the hilt of her dagger, and smiled.

When she looked up, she declared, "Heart Mender."

Gideon was suffering. The moment Calliope and the Fates disappeared, he was left with a battlefield of fallen soldiers and friends and an entire congregation looking at him for guidance. But he didn't have any. Not when his light was missing.

"Prepare the bodies of every fallen friend to be honored and buried," he ordered the expectant witches. "We will not leave them here like this."

People began to move. Maybe because he was the only technical heir they had ever known, or maybe because his siren voice demanded obedience, but whatever it was he was grateful just to be useful.

"Sabine said the Valkyries are going to want an audience with Calla when she's, you know, a God and all," Ezra told him.

Gideon cursed. This had the potential to quickly turn into another nightmare.

"Where's the Valkyrie Queen?" he asked Ezra.

"Sydni and Baden managed to capture her before Baden's . . . death. Over on the second battlefield in the Rouge Realm. I think there's a third uprising happening in the Land of the Valkyries as well, but I figured we had our own fish to fry before I tried to get involved in *that*," Ezra explained.

Gideon nodded. Then, "About Mother—"

Before Gideon could say anything more, however, Amina and Sabine were suddenly approaching with a very familiar body. Caspian.

"*No*," Gideon choked out as he lunged toward his friend, knees hitting the ground as the gently laid Caspian's lifeless form on the ground.

"Don't get too upset," Amina assured softly. "I've got his soul. We just need a heart."

"I suppose some things never change," Ezra whispered.

Gideon glanced up. "What about the others? Hannah? Delphine?"

He already knew Thorne had been one of the fallen. And Kestrel.

Ezra, Sabine, and Amina shared a loaded look.

"Hannah . . ." Ezra croaked, "is gone."

Gideon scrambled to his feet. "What the Hells does that mean?"

"Something about the darkness taking her after her necromancy magic raised that army," Amina answered.

"Where's Delphine?" Gideon demanded.

Before he could take off looking for her, however, a searing pain began to rip through his chest and everything went black.

☽ ☽ ☽ ● ☾ ☾ ☾

"You didn't say anything about my heart," Calla growled as she ripped the Witch Eater's hand from her chest.

"We are heartless fates," the Witch Eater told her. "That's what so many call us, anyway. How do you think that title came about?"

"But if you take my heart—"

"We will take the prince's, too, yes," the Witch Eater confirmed.

A RAGING HEART

"And then I suppose you'll have to put some of that new power to use, hmm?"

"What power? How would I know how to use it?" she protested.

So dramatic. The Fates laughed.

"It's your time, girl," the Witch Eater said seriously now. "To be a Fate is to be heartless. But that does not always mean uncaring, or unfeeling. It means to live with your heart outside of your body. To give it away to those who need it most. And doesn't that sound fitting for you, Heart Mender?"

Calla gulped. This was all a little too much a little too soon. What was she thinking, becoming a God? It was a ridiculous notion.

And yet . . . she had always been so desperate to be destined for *more*.

Her decision must have been written all over her face because the Witch Eater didn't waste another moment before plunging their hand into her chest.

Gideon should have always known how this was going to end, but his missing heart wasn't what killed him. It was the bond burning away, his numbers slowly disappearing one by one, turning back to fresh, unmarred skin. She was becoming something he could no longer reach. Too high above him.

He heard someone say to grab his heart, to shove it back into his body. But no matter how much they pushed, it wouldn't go.

He choked out, "Give it to Caspian." A pained inhale. Then, with his last bit of breath, he whispered, "Tell her that even if my heart is not hers, my soul always will be."

And then everything faded out once again.

92

If feeling like a God meant not feeling *him*, Calla didn't want it.

For a moment, everything around her was dim, and aching, and so excruciatingly painful. Her left arm burned as the bond was torn away from her. The hollow cavity of her chest felt like it was slowly filling up with molten hot lava, the magic in her veins turning to lightning.

And all she could think about was him, him, him.

What was he feeling? Did he think she'd chosen to get rid of it intentionally? That she didn't want it anymore? What would he think of her now? He had told her to choose her fate for herself, but what if he didn't like this version of her? Resented what she was becoming?

When it was over, everything was so crisp. Clear. She knew her senses had been heightened, but she couldn't tell in what way. They just . . . were. As if she had always been this version of herself, unable to remember anything different.

When she opened her eyes, the first thing she saw was the other Fates bending over her with their creepy masks.

Congratulations, Heart Mender. You have been Made.

She looked around, but the Witch Eater was nowhere in sight. She asked where they were.

The have passed their Godly gifts to you, and now they are gone.

"Gone? Where?"

Wherever they please.

"And can I go? Wherever I please?"

For now.

Calla didn't hesitate to climb back to her feet, ready to return to Gideon and her friends as soon as possible. To help with the aftermath of the Fates' War. Except...

"How do I go places?"

You're a God now, Heart Mender. Simply think of where you wish to be, and you will be there.

And so Calla closed her eyes and pictured him.

When she opened her eyes, she was suddenly back on the battlefield in the middle of the Onyx Realm.

I could get used to this, she thought.

"Calla!" someone called.

Ezra.

And at his feet? Gideon.

Calla crashed to the ground by his side, a sob racking through her when she saw the open shell of his chest.

"Where's his heart?" she demanded.

"It wouldn't go back in," Ezra explained mournfully. "He said—he said to give it to Caspian."

Calla blanched. "Caspian is *dead*?"

"Not anymore," Sabine inserted, unhelpful.

Calla brushed a strand of cobalt hair from Gideon's face. She couldn't believe this was happening to her again. Another person she loved losing their heart because of her.

It's a good thing you are what you are now, hmm? a voice whispered inside her mind.

The Fates?

It didn't matter. What mattered was that the voice was right.

She swallowed as she placed her hands over Gideon's chest.

"I am the Heart Mender," she whispered to him. "And I demand that your heart come back to me right now. Understand?"

They all waited with bated breaths, but when nothing happened, Sabine cleared her throat awkwardly.

Calla tried again. Reaching deep inside herself, pulling at the well of magic she'd always had inside of her. This time, however, she found that the well was depthless. Unending reams of power waited beneath the surface. She could do anything. She could build entire worlds if she so wished. All she had to do first was get him back.

"I am the Heart Mender," she whispered again as she pulled at the threads of gilded power inside of her. Her hands began to glow, and above her, her friends gaped in disbelief.

Come back to me, she whispered to him in his mind. *Come back, come back, come back. Let me fix your heart. Let me make it so there are no cracks or scars. Just like you did for me.*

A second later, Gideon's chest rose as it filled with air.

Then, a heartbeat.

Calla didn't leave Delphine's side throughout the entire funeral or any moment after.

It'd been three days since the world had changed. Three days of dealing with the Valkyries before ultimately deciding to strip Ignia of her power and absolving the rest of the Valkyries of their tithe. Three days since she'd retied her life force to Gideon's.

And three days since they'd lost Hannah.

Now Calla and Delphine were sitting in the very spot where Hannah had sunk into the earth, letting their tears water the newly budding chrysanthemums that had begun to pop up there.

"I'm never going to get over this," Delphine whispered.

Calla laid her head on the other girl's shoulder. "Me either."

Delphine pressed her palms to the earth and cried, "Come back to me. Please. *Please. Please. Please. Please. Please. Please.*"

They sat there until the day turned to night. Until Delphine's pleas became ragged and her cheeks were permanently stained with tears. And then they sat there for two days more.

Eventually, Gideon and the others made them leave, but Delphine vowed to Hannah she would be back to visit every dawn for the rest of her immortal life.

I t took nearly four months for any semblance of normalcy to return to their lives, if you could call it normalcy.

Calla's new duty to the Fates meant keeping an egregiously detailed record of every little deal people made with the gilded Gods, and it had consumed nearly every waking moment she had until she got the hang of it. She tried to curb their maliciousness where she could, to bring levity to the misfortunate contracts naive beings forged with them. But she was still learning how to play the game. And she had to admit, if even just to herself, it was nice to be playing the game instead of being used by the game for once.

Amina and the Valkyries had been dealing with their own turmoil in their lands, situating themselves in the same way the witches were trying to—how to move on without a monarchy. Ezra, had gone with them, not willing to be separated from Sabine, and Calla had no room to criticize him for it. Caspian, thankfully, had stayed behind with Gideon and Calla to help the Witch Realms, despite whatever spark had been budding between him and Amina. Cass was an invaluable piece to their puzzle, and Calla had honestly considered begging him to stay if he hadn't readily agreed. Plus, he was the only one who could seem to get Delphine out and about on a daily basis.

And then there was Gideon.

If Calla thought being a God would save her from the all-consuming wave of hormones and butterflies she got every time she saw his face, she was wrong. In fact, somehow it was *worse*.

When she'd managed to bring a heart back to his chest, she thought that was the happiest she would ever be able to be. And then that very night he'd asked her to bind herself to him again.

They had been lying outside, beneath the stars. Trying to decide how to move on from everything that had just happened. If they ever could.

He'd turned to her and asked, "Would you want to live with me?"

She shifted onto her side to face him. "Live with you *where*?"

"Anywhere you want," he said as he leaned over to brush a strand of her hair away from her face. "Anywhere but the Neverending Forest, at least."

"You mean you don't want to make that our annual vacation spot?" she snorted.

He huffed a laugh but then quickly sobered.

"What?" she wondered.

"I wanted to ask you something."

"Yes?"

"I wanted to know if there was a way to get the soul-bond back," he told her, voice soft.

Calla's brows raised as she sat up. "You would *want* it back?"

He followed suit, sitting up as he locked their gazes, his eyes pure silver as he implored, "Desperately."

"You just want to have direct access to a God," she quipped.

"That's a perk," he admitted with a crooked grin. Then, more serious, he said, "More so is the fact that I miss your soul being so intertwined with my own. I miss your heartbeat inside my chest. And, most of all, I don't want to risk breathing a second of air longer than you on this earth. Wherever you go, I'll follow."

"Wherever I go, we go together," she murmured as he tilted her chin up to place a kiss on the underside of her jaw.

"Together," he agreed.

And this time when he kissed her, long into the night, she thought maybe her fate hadn't been so ruinous after all. That all the reckless roads they'd followed had led them here. To a place with so much love, and grief, but—most of all—potential.

It would be hard to forge a new world from scratch. To reconcile that who she was in this moment was nowhere near who she had been nearly a year ago when they had met. That she had lost so many people she'd loved along the way.

But, Gods, how she loved who she was right here, right now.

Epilogue

Time was a curious thing.

Seasons passed, one after the other, in a never-ending loop of life and death. All the blood spilled in war had soaked deep into the earth's soil, washed away by both rain and tears. Tears from the girl made of ocean and starlight, who would show up every day at dawn to offer her grief to a lost love that even so much time had not succeeded in washing from her heart. Tears that would sink deep beneath the surface, trickling down until they reached the familiar bones buried deep beneath the earth's surface.

For years, the delicate bones had been collecting those splashes of salt and sorrow, bathing in the devotion of their devastating love as they stored away their strength and began to mend. The starlit girl didn't see it yet, the light that would illuminate the darkness, but if she looked closely enough, there were always signs—the lavender that sprouted out of the ground in the shape of a small familiar figure, flowers untouched by storms, or snow, or fire, or death. Signs in the way the air seemed to shift with awakening magic, stronger and stronger with each dawn that the girl paid her visits.

Most of all, it was the way the wind seemed to whisper *that* name, a symphony of hope. Try as she might, the starlit girl could not ignore the unmistakable name of her lost love.

Hannah. Hannah. Hannah.

A searching hand broke through the surface. Reaching for the girl that had brought it back to life.

And another heart began to mend.

Acknowledgments

I am currently sitting in my new office, in a new state, staring at this acknowledgment page with a bit of disbelief. I started the first version of what would eventually become *A Ruinous Fate* when I was just sixteen years old. Passing out pages of it to friends in high school, dreaming of being an author one day.

And here I am, at this conclusion to my first series. An ending that I once worried I wouldn't be able to reach because right after I finished *A Reckless Oath*, I got very sick. And yet all I could think about was how devastated I'd be if I could not finish this story.

I don't think I would truly be the person I am today if I had not written *A Ruinous Fate* and taken a chance on querying it. Because of *A Ruinous Fate*, I was able to lay the first brick in building my career. I am now a full-time writer, a best-selling author, and a believer that dreaming for big, seemingly impossible, things is not silly or frivolous. Because of this series I got to go to festivals and thank the very authors who came before me and built me into a reader and made me want to do what they did. And though I am sad to be leaving this world, I have also never been so grateful for having gotten to spend this time in it with these characters.

I'd like to thank my wonderful agent, Emily Forney, always, for taking a chance on me when I was just an eager, bright-eyed, writer who had absolutely no idea what I was doing. I feel so fortunate to have gotten to build my career with you from the very beginning and am so thankful for everything we've created together over the years. We've worked on so many stories together at this point, and it's hard to wrap my head around all we've accomplished in these last few years, but I will always be the most touched that you chose *A Ruinous Fate* to champion first. I cannot wait to see what we do next!

To my husband, Iz, and my best friends, Darci and Em, who quite literally have read about a thousand different versions of this series and probably love it more than anyone else. In 2020 when I was lost and miserable that I had yet to accomplish this life-long dream, all three of you pushed me Every. Single. Day. To get up and write that first book. You read those drafts over and over and over again and never once doubted that I would be able to sell it. You've been with me through every step of my career, showed up to every single book signing and festival, cheered me on in the wings, and still get excited even when I have the most miniscule book updates to share. I genuinely do not know what I would do without the three of you in so many ways.

And to Dee, Gabi, and Raye, who were also there from day one of this book. I'm so grateful for all the enthusiasm and love over the years.

And I really hope you all know that if you ever need me, I'm there.

To my editors Kelsey Sullivan, Rebecca Kuss, and Candice Snow, for getting *A Raging Heart* to the finish line! To Cassidy Leyendecker—thank you for giving me that first opportunity to become a published author.

To everyone at Hyperion who worked on this series over the years as well as all of my audiobook narrators, cover artists and designers!

To every friend and fellow author I've met along the way since those very early days, who have always supported me—you know who you are, and I am so grateful for you. I know over the years we might not talk as much as we once did when we were all in quarantine, glued to our phones, but I truly hope that each of you are flourishing and are so so happy, and that one day soon we'll get to see each other.

To the librarians and booksellers who have changed my life by recommending my books and literally placing them in the hands of readers, thank you from the bottom of my heart for everything you do. I will never stop thanking all of you for as long as I live.

And to you dearest reader.

If you made it this far in this series I know the dedication that takes. Years of waiting for books, of putting your time into reading them. I know what it's like to finish a series you like and see that the author went on to write things that are very different (not in a bad way—just different! You know?). Because I totally understand that's what I did. That the Heartless Fates series is sort of its own special little piece of my heart that is much different than the other things I am creating at the moment. And I don't know if you'll continue to follow me to my other series as you grow up, because maybe your taste will change or maybe I've changed too much. But I want you to know that I am honored that you went on this journey with me. That you stayed to the end of Calla's story, no matter how you felt about it at times (sorry to everyone whose heart I crushed during this series), and that you picked up any of my books in the first place. All of you have given me the gift of being able to share my stories and that's something that has changed me forever.

All my love. Anywhere. Everywhere.